D0269170

DICK FRANCIS

DICK FRANCIS

FOR KICKS

FLYING FINISH

For Kicks first published in Great Britain in 1965
by Michael Joseph Ltd
Flying Finish first published in Great Britain in 1966
by Michael Joseph Ltd

This volume first published in Great Britain in 1986
jointly by

William Heinemann Limited   Martin Secker & Warburg Limited

and

Octopus Books Limited
Michelin House
81 Fulham Road
London SW3 6RB

This edition produced exclusively for W. H. Smith

Reprinted 1988

ISBN 0 7064 2764 5

For Kicks © 1965 by Dick Francis
Flying Finish © 1966 by Dick Francis

Printed at The Bath Press, Avon

CONTENTS

For Kicks   9

Flying Finish   179

FOR KICKS

Chapter One

The Earl of October drove into my life in a pale blue Holden which had seen better days, and danger and death tagged along for the ride.

I noticed the car turn in through the gateposts as I walked across the little paddock towards the house, and I watched its progress up our short private road with a jaundiced eye. Salesmen, I thought, I can do without. The blue car rolled to a gentle halt between me and my own front door.

The man who climbed out looked about forty-five and was of medium height and solid build, with a large well-shaped head and smoothly brushed brown hair. He wore grey trousers, a fine wool shirt, and a dark, discreet tie, and he carried the inevitable brief case. I sighed, bent through the paddock rails, and went over to send him packing.

'Where can I find Mr. Daniel Roke?' he asked. An English voice, which even to my untuned ear evoked expensive public schools; and he had a subtle air of authority inconsistent with the opening patter of representatives. I looked at him more attentively, and decided after all not to say I was out. He might even, in spite of the car, be a prospective customer.

'I,' I said, without too much joy in the announcement, 'am Daniel Roke.'

His eyelids flickered in surprise.

'Oh,' he said blankly.

I was used to this reaction. I was no one's idea of the owner of a prosperous stud-farm. I looked, for a start, too young, though I didn't feel it; and my sister Belinda says you don't often meet a business man you can mistake for an Italian peasant. Sweet girl, my sister. It is only that my skin is sallow and tans easily, and I have black hair and brown eyes. Also I was that day wearing the oldest, most tattered pair of jeans I possessed, with unpolished jodhpur boots, and nothing else.

I had been helping a mare who always had difficulty in foaling: a messy job, and I had dressed for it. The result of my – and the mare's – labours was a weedy filly with a contracted tendon in the near fore and a suspicion of one in the off fore too, which meant an operation, and more expense than she was likely to be worth.

My visitor stood for a while looking about him at the neat white-railed paddocks, the L-shaped stable-yard away ahead, and the row of cedar-shingled foaling boxes off to the right, where my poor little newcomer lay in the straw. The whole spread looked substantial and well maintained, which it was; I worked very hard to keep it that way, so that I could reasonably ask good prices for my horses.

The visitor turned to gaze at the big blue-green lagoon to the left, with the snow-capped mountains rising steeply in rocky beauty along the far side of it. Puffs of cloud like plumes crowned the peaks. Grand and glorious scenery it was, to his fresh eyes.

But to me, walls.

'Breathtaking,' he said appreciatively. Then turning to me briskly, but with some hesitation in his speech, he said, 'I . . . er . . . I heard in Perlooma that you have . . . er . . . an English stable hand who . . . er . . . wants to go back home . . .' He broke off, and started again. 'I suppose it may sound surprising, but in certain circumstances, and if he is suitable, I am willing to pay his fare and give him a job at the other end . . .' He tailed off again.

There couldn't, I thought, be such an acute shortage of stable boys in England that they needed to be recruited from Australia.

'Will you come into the house?' I said. 'And explain?'

I led the way into the living-room, and heard his exclamation as he stepped behind me. All our visitors were impressed by the room. Across the far end a great expanse of window framed the most spectacular part of the lagoon and mountains, making them seem even closer and, to me, more overwhelming than ever. I sat down in an old bentwood rocker with my back to them, and gestured him into a comfortable arm-chair facing the view.

'Now, Mr. . . . er?' I began.

'October,' he said easily. 'Not Mister. Earl.'

'October . . . as the month?' It was October at the time.

'As the month,' he assented.

I looked at him curiously. He was not my idea of an earl. He looked like a hard-headed company chairman on holiday. Then it occurred to me that there was no bar to an earl being a company chairman as well, and that quite probably some of them needed to be.

'I have acted on impulse, coming here,' he said more coherently. 'And I am not sure that it is ever a good thing to do.' He paused, took out a machine-turned gold cigarette case, and gained time for thought while he flicked his lighter. I waited.

He smiled briefly. 'Perhaps I had better start by saying that I am in Australia on business – I have interests in Sydney – but that I came down here to the Snowies as the last part of a private tour I have been making of your main racing and breeding centres. I am a member of the body which governs National Hunt racing – that is to say, steeplechasing, jump racing – in England, and naturally your horses interest me enormously . . . Well, I was lunching in Perlooma' he went on, referring to our nearest township, fifteen miles away, 'and I got talking to a man who remarked on my English accent and said that the only other pommie he knew was a stable-hand here who was fool enough to want to go back home.'

'Yes,' I agreed. 'Simmons.'

'Arthur Simmons,' he said, nodding. 'What sort of man is he?'

'Very good with horses,' I said. 'But he only wants to go back to England when he's drunk. And he only gets drunk in Perlooma. Never here.'

'Oh,' he said. 'Then wouldn't he go, if he were given the chance?'

'I don't know. It depends what you want him for.'

He drew on his cigarette, and tapped the ash off, and looked out of the window.

'A year or two ago we had a great deal of trouble with the doping of racehorses,' he said abruptly. 'A very great deal of trouble. There were trials and prison sentences, and stringent all-round tightening of stable security, and a stepping-up of regular saliva and urine tests. We began to test the first four horses in many races, to stop doping-to-win, and we tested every suspiciously beaten favourite for doping-to-lose. Nearly all the results since the new regulations came into force have been negative.'

'How satisfactory,' I said, not desperately interested.

'No. It isn't. Someone has discovered a drug which our analysts cannot identify.'

'That doesn't sound possible,' I said politely. The afternoon was slipping away unprofitably, I felt, and I still had a lot to do.

He sensed my lack of enthusiasm. 'There have been ten cases, all winners. Ten that we are sure of. The horses apparently look conspicuously stimulated – I haven't myself actually seen one – but nothing shows up in the tests.' He paused. 'Doping is nearly always an inside job,' he said, transferring his gaze back to me. 'That is to say, stable lads are nearly always involved somehow, even if it is only to point out to someone else which horse is in which box.' I nodded. Australia had had her troubles, too.

'We, that is to say, the other two Stewards of the National Hunt Committee, and myself, have once or twice discussed trying to find out about the doping from the inside, so to speak . . .'

'By getting a stable lad to spy for you?' I said.

He winced slightly. 'You Australians are so direct,' he murmured. 'But that was the general idea, yes. We didn't do anything more than talk about it, though, because there are many difficulties to such a plan and frankly we didn't see how we could positively guarantee that any lad we approached was not already working for . . . er . . . the other side.'

I grinned. 'And Arthur Simmons has that guarantee?'

'Yes. And as he's English, he would fade indistinguishably into the racing scene. It occurred to me as I was paying my bill after lunch. So I asked the way here and drove straight up, to see what he was like.'

'You can talk to him, certainly,' I said, standing up. 'But I don't think it will be any good.'

'He would be paid far in excess of the normal rate,' he said, misunderstanding me.

'I didn't mean that he couldn't be tempted to go,' I said, 'but he just hasn't the brain for anything like that.'

He followed me back out into the spring sunshine. The air at that altitude was still chilly and I saw him shiver as he left the warmth of the house. He glanced appraisingly at my still bare chest.

'If you'll wait a moment, I'll fetch him,' I said, and, walking round the corner of the house, whistled shrilly with my fingers in my teeth towards the small bunk-house across the yard. A head poked enquiringly out of a window, and I shouted 'I want Arthur.'

The head nodded, withdrew, and presently Arthur Simmons, elderly, small, bow-legged and of an endearing simplicity of mind, made his crab-like way towards me. I left him and Lord October together, and went over to see if the new filly had taken a firm hold on life. She had, though her efforts to stand on her poor misshapen foreleg were pathetic to see.

I left her with her mother, and went back towards Lord October, watching him from a distance taking a note from his wallet and offering it to Arthur. Arthur wouldn't accept it, even though he was English. He's been here so long, I thought, that he's as Australian as anyone. He'd hate to go back to Britain, whatever he says when he's drunk.

'You were right,' October said. 'He's a splendid chap, but no good for what I want. I didn't even suggest it.'

'Isn't it expecting a great deal of any stable lad, however bright, to uncover something which has got men like you up a gum-tree?'

He grimaced. 'Yes. That is one of the difficulties I mentioned. We're scraping the bottom of the barrel, though. Any idea is worth trying. Any. You can't realise how serious the situation is.'

We walked over to his car, and he opened the door.

'Well, thank you for your patience, Mr. Roke. As I said, it was an impulse, coming here. I hope I haven't wasted too much of your afternoon?' He smiled, still looking slightly hesitant and disconcerted.

I shook my head and smiled back and he started the car, turned it, and drove off down the road. He was out of my thoughts before he was through the gate-posts.

Out of my thoughts; but not by a long way out of my life.

He came back again the next day at sundown. I found him sitting patiently smoking in the small blue car, having no doubt discovered that there was no one in the house. I walked back towards him from the stable block where I had been doing my share of the evening's chores, and reflected idly that he had again caught me at my dirtiest.

He got out of the car when he saw me coming, and stamped on his cigarette.

'Mr. Roke.' He held out his hand, and I shook it.

This time he made no attempt to rush into speech. This time he had not come on impulse. There was absolutely no hesitation in his manner: instead, his natural air of authority was much more pronounced, and it struck me that it was with this power that he set out to persuade a boardroom full of hard directors to agree to an unpopular proposal.

I knew instantly, then, why he had come back.

I looked at him warily for a moment: then gestured towards the house, and led him again into the living-room.

'A drink?' I asked. 'Whisky?'

'Thank you.' He took the glass.

'If you don't mind,' I said, 'I will go and change.' And think, I added privately.

Alone in my room I showered and put on some decent trousers, socks and house-shoes, and a white poplin shirt with a navy blue silk tie. I brushed back my damp hair carefully in front of the mirror, and made sure my nails were clean. There was no point in entering an argument at a social disadvantage. Particularly with an earl as determined as this.

He stood up when I went back, and took in my changed appearance with one smooth glance.

I smiled fleetingly, and poured myself a drink, and another for him.

'I think,' he said, 'that you may have guessed why I am here.'

'Perhaps.'

'To persuade you to take the job I had in mind for Simmons,' he said without preamble, and without haste.

'Yes,' I said. I sipped my drink. 'And I can't do it.'

We stood there eyeing each other. I knew that what he was seeing was a good deal different from the Daniel Roke he had met before. More substantial. More the sort of person he would have expected to find, perhaps. Clothes maketh man, I thought wryly.

The day was fading, and I switched on the lights. The mountains outside the window retreated into darkness; just as well, as I judged I would need all my resolution, and they were both literally and figuratively ranged behind October. The trouble was, of course, that with more than half my mind I wanted to take a crack at his fantastic job. And I knew it was madness. I couldn't afford it, for one thing.

'I've learned a good deal about you now,' he said slowly. 'On my way from here yesterday it crossed my mind that it was a pity you were not Arthur Simmons; you would have been perfect. You did, if you will forgive me saying so, look the part.' He sounded apologetic.

'But not now?'

'You know you don't. You changed so that you wouldn't, I imagine. But you could again. Oh, I've no doubt that if I'd met you yesterday inside this house looking as civilised as you do at this moment, the thought would never have occurred to me. But when I saw you first, walking across the paddock very tattered and half bare and looking like a gypsy, I did in fact take you for the hired help . . . I'm sorry.'

I grinned faintly. 'It happens often, and I don't mind.'

'And there's your voice,' he said. 'That Australian accent of yours . . . I know it's not as strong as many I've heard, but it's as near to cockney as dammit, and I expect you could broaden it a bit. You see,' he went on firmly, as he saw I was about to interrupt, 'if you put an educated Englishman into a stable as a lad, the chances are the others would know at once by his voice that he wasn't genuine. But they couldn't tell, with you. You look right, and you sound right. You seem to me the perfect answer to all our problems. A better answer than I could have dreamt of finding.'

'Physically,' I commented dryly.

He drank, and looked at me thoughtfully.

'In every way. You forget, I told you I know a good deal about you now. By the time I reached Perlooma yesterday afternoon I had decided to . . . er . . . investigate you, one might say, to find out what sort of man you really were . . . to see if there were the slightest chance of your being attracted by such a . . . a job.' He drank again, and paused, waiting.

'I can't take on anything like that,' I said. 'I have enough to do here.'
The understatement of the month, I thought.

'Could you take on twenty thousand pounds?' He said it casually,
conversationally.

The short answer to that was 'Yes'; but instead, after a moment's
stillness, I said 'Australian, or English?'

His mouth curled down at the corners and his eyes narrowed. He was
amused.

'English. Of course,' he said ironically.

I said nothing. I simply looked at him. As if reading my thoughts he
sat down in an arm-chair, crossed his legs comfortably, and said 'I'll tell
you what you would do with it, if you like. You would pay the fees of
the medical school your sister Belinda has set her heart on. You would
send your younger sister Helen to art school, as she wants. You would
put enough aside for your thirteen-year-old brother Philip to become a
lawyer, if he is still of the same mind when he grows up. You could
employ more labour here, instead of working yourself into an early grave
feeding, clothing, and paying school fees for your family.'

I suppose I should have been prepared for him to be thorough, but I
felt a surge of anger that he should have pried so very intimately into my
affairs. However, since the time when an angry retort had cost me the
sale of a yearling who broke his leg the following week, I had learned
to keep my tongue still whatever the provocation.

'I also have had two girls and a boy to educate,' he said. 'I know what
it is costing you. My elder daughter is at university, and the twin boy
and girl have recently left school.'

When I again said nothing, he continued, 'You were born in England,
and were brought to Australia when you were a child. Your father,
Howard Roke, was a barrister, a good one. He and your mother were
drowned together in a sailing accident when you were eighteen. Since
then you have supported yourself and your sisters and brother by horse
dealing and breeding. I understand that you had intended to follow your
father into the law, but instead used the money he left to set up business
here, in what had been your holiday house. You have done well at it.
The horses you sell have a reputation for being well broken in and
beautifully mannered. You are thorough, and you are respected.'

He looked up at me, smiling. I stood stiffly. I could see there was still
more to come.

He said 'Your headmaster at Geelong says you had a brain and are
wasting it. Your bank manager says you spend little on yourself. Your
doctor says you haven't had a holiday since you settled here nine years
ago except for a month you spent in hospital once with a broken leg.
Your pastor says you never go to church, and he takes a poor view of it.'
He drank slowly.

Many doors, it seemed, were open to determined earls.

'And finally,' he added, with a lop-sided smile, 'the bar keeper of the
Golden Platypus in Perlooma says he'd trust you with his sister, in spite
of your good looks.'

'And what were your conclusions, after all that?' I asked, my resentment a little better under control.

'That you are a dull, laborious prig,' he said pleasantly.

I relaxed at that, and laughed, and sat down.

'Quite right,' I agreed.

'On the other hand, everyone says you do keep on with something once you start it, and you are used to hard physical work. You know so much about horses that you could do a stable lad's job with your eyes shut standing on your head.'

'The whole idea is screwy,' I said, sighing, 'It wouldn't work, not with me, or Arthur Simmons, or anybody. It just isn't feasible. There are hundreds of training stables in Britain, aren't there? You could live in them for months and hear nothing, while the dopers got strenuously to work all around you.'

He shook his head. 'I don't think so. There are surprisingly few dishonest lads, far fewer than you or most people would imagine. A lad known to be corruptible would attract all sorts of crooks like an unguarded gold-mine. All our man would have to do would be to make sure that the word was well spread that he was open to offers. He'd get them, no doubt of it.'

'But would he get the ones you want? I very much doubt it.'

'To me it seems a good enough chance to be worth taking. Frankly, any chance is worth taking, the way things are. We have tried everything else. And we have failed. We have failed in spite of exhaustive questioning of everyone connected with the affected horses. The police say they cannot help us. As we cannot analyse the drug being used, we can give them nothing to work on. We employed a firm of private investigators. They got nowhere at all. Direct action has achieved absolutely nothing. Indirect action cannot achieve less. I am willing to gamble twenty thousand pounds that with you it can achieve more. Will you do it?'

'I don't know,' I said, and cursed my weakness. I should have said, 'No, certainly not.'

He pounced on it, leaning forward and talking more rapidly, every word full of passionate conviction. 'Can I make you understand how concerned my colleagues and I are over these undetectable cases of doping? I own several racehorses – mostly steeplechasers – and my family for generations have been lovers and supporters of racing . . . The health of the sport means more to me, and people like me, than I can possibly say . . . and for the second time in three years it is being seriously threatened. During the last big wave of doping there were satirical jokes in the papers and on television, and we simply cannot afford to have it happen again. So far we have been able to stifle comment because the cases are still fairly widely spaced – it is well over a year since the first – and if anyone enquires we merely report that the tests were negative. But we *must* identify this new dope before there is a widespread increase in its use. Otherwise it will become a worse menace to racing than anything which has happened before. If dozens of undetectably doped winners start turning up, public faith will be destroyed altogether, and steeplechasing will suffer damage which it will take years to recover from, if it ever does. There is much more at stake than a pleasant pastime. Racing is an industry employing thousands of people . . . and not the least of them are stud owners like you. The collapse of public support would mean a great deal of hardship.

'You may think that I have offered you an extraordinarily large sum of money to come over and see if you can help us, but I am a rich man, and, believe me, the continuance of racing is worth a great deal more than that to me. My horses won nearly that amount in prize money last season, and if it can buy a chance of wiping out this threat I will spend it gladly.'

'You are much more vehement today,' I said slowly, 'than you were yesterday.'

He sat back. 'Yesterday I didn't need to convince you. But I felt just the same.'

'There must be someone in England who can dig out the information you want,' I protested. 'People who know the ins and outs of your racing. I know nothing at all. I left your country when I was nine. I'd be useless. It's impossible.'

That's better, I approved myself. That's much firmer.

He looked down at his glass, and spoke as if with reluctance. 'Well . . . we did approach someone in England . . . A racing journalist, actually. Very good nose for news: very discreet, too; we thought he was just the chap. Unfortunately he dug away without success for some weeks. And then he was killed in a car crash, poor fellow.'

'Why not try someone else?' I persisted.

'It was only in June that he died, during steeplechasing's summer recess. The new season started in August and it was not until after that that we thought of the stable lad idea, with all its difficulties.'

'Try a farmer's son,' I suggested. 'Country accent, knowledge of horses . . . the lot.'

He shook his head. 'England is too small. Send a farmer's son to walk a horse round the parade ring at the races, and what he was doing would soon be no secret. Too many people would recognise him, and ask questions.'

'A farm worker's son, then, with a high I.Q.'

'Do we hold an exam?' he said sourly.

There was a pause, and he looked up from his glass. His face was solemn, almost severe.

'Well?' he said.

I meant to say 'No,' firmly. What I actually said was again 'I don't know.'

'What can I say to persuade you?'

'Nothing,' I said. 'I'll think about it. I'll let you know tomorrow.'

'Very well.' He stood up, declined my offer of a meal, and went away as he had come, the strength of his personality flowing out of him like heat. The house felt empty when I went back from seeing him off.

The full moon blazed in the black sky, and through a gap in the hills behind me Mount Kosciusko distantly stretched its blunt snow-capped summit into the light. I sat on a rock high up on the mountain, looking down on my home.

There lay the lagoon, the big pasture paddocks stretching away to the bush, the tidy white-railed small paddocks near the house, the silvery roof of the foaling boxes, the solid bulk of the stable block, the bunkhouse, the long low graceful shape of the dwelling house with a glitter of moonlight in the big window at the end.

There lay my prison.

It hadn't been bad at first. There were no relations to take care of us, and I had found it satisfying to disappoint the people who said I couldn't earn enough to keep three small children, Belinda and Helen and Philip, with me. I liked horses, I always had, and from the beginning the business went fairly well. We all ate, anyway, and I even convinced myself that the law was not really my vocation after all.

My parents had planned to send Belinda and Helen to Frensham, and when the time came, they went. I dare say I could have found a cheaper school, but I had to try to give them what I had had . . . and that was why Philip was away at Geelong. The business had grown progressively, but so had the school fees and the men's wages and the maintenance costs. I was caught in a sort of upward spiral, and too much depended on my being able to keep on going. The leg I had broken in a steeplechase when I was twenty-two had caused the worst financial crisis of the whole nine years: and I had had no choice but to give up doing anything so risky.

I didn't grudge the unending labour. I was very fond of my sisters and brother. I had no regrets at all that I had done what I had. But the feeling that I had built a prosperous trap for myself had slowly eaten away the earlier contentment I had found in providing for them.

In another eight or ten years they would all be grown, educated and married, and my job would be done. In another ten years I would be thirty-seven. Perhaps I too would be married by then, and have some children of my own, and send them to Frensham and Geelong . . . For more than four years I had done my best to stifle a longing to escape. It was easier when they were at home in the holidays, with the house ringing with their noise and Philip's carpentry all over the place and the girls' frillies hanging to dry in the bathroom. In the summer we rode or swam in the lagoon (the lake, as my English parents called it) and in the winter we ski-ed on the mountains. They were very good company and never took anything they had for granted. Nor, now that they were growing up, did they seem to be suffering from any form of teenage rebellions. They were, in fact, thoroughly rewarding.

It usually hit me about a week after they had gone back to school, this fierce aching desperation to be free. Free for a good long while: to go further than the round of horse sales, further than the occasional quick trip to Sidney or Melbourne or Cooma.

To have something else to remember but the procession of profitable days, something else to see besides the beauty with which I was surrounded. I had been so busy stuffing worms down my fellow nestlings' throats that I had never stretched my wings.

Telling myself that these thoughts were useless, that they were self-pity, that my unhappiness was unreasonable, did no good at all. I continued at night to sink into head-holding miseries of depression, and kept these moods out of my days – and my balance sheets – only by working to my limit.

When Lord October came the children had been back at school for eleven days, and I was sleeping badly. That may be why I was sitting on a mountain side at four o'clock in the morning trying to decide whether or not to take a peculiar job as a stable lad on the other side of the world. The door of the cage had been opened for me, all right. But the tit-bit that had been dangled to tempt me out seemed suspiciously large.

Twenty thousand English pounds . . . A great deal of money. But then he couldn't know of my restless state of mind, and he might think that a smaller sum would make no impression. (What, I wondered, had he been prepared to pay Arthur?)

On the other hand, there was the racing journalist who had died in a car crash . . . If October or his colleagues had the slightest doubt it was an accident, that too would explain the size of his offer, as conscience money. Throughout my youth, owing to my father's profession, I had learned a good deal about crime and criminals, and I knew too much to dismiss the idea of an organised accident as fantastic nonsense.

I had inherited my father's bent for orderliness and truth and had grown up appreciating the logic of his mind, though I had often thought him too ruthless with innocent witnesses in court. My own view had always been that justice should be done and that my father did the world no good by getting the guilty acquitted, I would never make a barrister, he said, if I thought like that. I'd better be a policeman, instead.

England, I thought. Twenty thousand pounds. Detection. To be honest, the urgency with which October viewed the situation had not infected me. English racing was on the other side of the world. I knew no one engaged in it. I cared frankly little whether it had a good or a bad reputation. If I went it would be no altruistic crusade: I would be going only because the adventure appealed to me, because it looked amusing and a challenge, because it beckoned me like a siren to fling responsibility to the wind and cut the self-imposed shackles off my wilting spirit.

Common sense said that the whole idea was crazy, that the Earl of October was an irresponsible nut, that I hadn't any right to leave my family to fend for themselves while I went gallivanting round the world, and that the only possible course open to me was to stay where I was, and learn to be content.

Common sense lost.

Chapter Two

Nine days later I flew to England in a Boeing 707.

I slept soundly for most of the thirty-six hours from Sydney to Darwin, from Darwin to Singapore, Rangoon and Calcutta, from Calcutta to Karachi and Damascus, and from Damascus to Dusseldorf and London Airport.

Behind me I left a crowded week into which I had packed months of paper-work and a host of practical arrangements. Part of the difficulty was that I didn't know how long I would be away, but I reckoned that if I hadn't done the job in six months I wouldn't be able to do it at all, and made that a basis for my plans.

The head stud-groom was to have full charge of the training and sale of the horses already on the place, but not to buy or breed any more. A firm of contractors agreed to see to the general maintenance of the land and buildings. The woman currently cooking for the lads who lived in the bunk-house assured me that she would look after the family when they came back for the long Christmas summer holiday from December to February.

I arranged with the bank manager that I should send post-dated cheques for the next term's school fees and for the fodder and tack for the horses, and I wrote a pile for the head groom to cash one at a time for the men's food and wages. October assured me that 'my fee' would be transferred to my account without delay.

'If I don't succeed, you shall have your money back, less what it has cost me to be away,' I told him.

He shook his head, but I insisted; and in the end we compromised. I was to have ten thousand outright, and the other half if my mission were successful.

I took October to my solicitors and had the rather unusual appointment shaped into a dryly-worded legal contract, to which, with a wry smile, he put his signature alongside mine.

His amusement, however, disappeared abruptly when, as we left, I asked him to insure my life.

'I don't think I can,' he said, frowning.

'Because I would be . . . uninsurable?' I asked.

He didn't answer.

'I have signed a contract,' I pointed out. 'Do you think I did it with my eyes shut?'

'It was your idea.' He looked troubled. 'I won't hold you to it.'

'What really happened to the journalist?' I asked.

He shook his head and didn't meet my eyes. 'I don't know. It looked like an accident. It almost certainly *was* an accident. He went off the road at night on a bend on the Yorkshire moors. The car caught fire as it rolled down into the valley. He hadn't a hope. He was a nice chap . . .'

'It won't deter me if you have any reason for thinking it was not an accident,' I said seriously, 'but you must be frank. If it was not an accident, he must have made a lot of progress . . . he must have found out something pretty vital . . . it would be important to me to know where he had gone and what he had been doing during the days before he died.'

'Did you think about all this before you agreed to accept my proposition?'

'Yes, of course.'

He smiled as if a load had been lifted from him. 'By God, Mr. Roke, the more I see of you the more thankful I am I stopped for lunch in Perlooma and went to look for Arthur Simmons. Well . . . Tommy Stapleton – the journalist – was a good driver, but I suppose accidents can happen to anyone. It was a Sunday early in June. Monday, really. He died about two o'clock at night. A local man said the road was normal in appearance at one-thirty, and at two-thirty a couple going home from a party saw the broken railings on the bend and stopped to look. The car was still smouldering: they could see the red glow of it in the valley, and they drove on into the nearest town to report it.

'The police think Stapleton went to sleep at the wheel. Easy enough to do. But they couldn't find out where he had been between leaving the house of some friends at five o'clock, and arriving on the Yorkshire moors. The journey would have taken him only about an hour, which left nine hours unaccounted for. No one ever came forward to say he'd spent the evening with them, though the story was in most of the papers. I believe it was suggested he could have been with another man's wife . . . someone who had a good reason for keeping quiet. Anyway, the whole thing was treated as a straightforward accident.

'As to where he had been during the days before . . . we did find out, discreetly. He'd done nothing and been nowhere that he didn't normally do in the course of his job. He'd come up from the London offices of his newspaper on the Thursday, gone to Bogside races on the Friday and Saturday, stayed with friends near Hexham, Northumberland, over the week-end, and, as I said, left them at five on Sunday, to drive back to London. They said he had been his normal charming self the whole time.

'We, that is, the other two Stewards and I – asked the Yorkshire police to let us see anything they salvaged from the car, but there was nothing of any interest to us. His leather briefcase was found undamaged half-way down the hillside, near one of the rear doors which had been wrenched off during the somersaulting, but there was nothing in it besides the usual form books and racing papers. We looked carefully. He lived with his mother and sister – he was unmarried – and they let us search their house for anything he might have written down for us. There was nothing. We also contacted the sports editor of his paper and asked to see any possessions he had left in his office. There were only a few personal oddments and an envelope containing some press cuttings about doping.

We kept that. You can see them when you get to England. But I'm afraid they will be no use to you. They were very fragmentary.'

'I see,' I said. We walked along the street to where our two cars were parked, his hired blue Holden, and my white utility. Standing beside the two dusty vehicles I remarked. 'You want to believe it was an accident ... I think you want to believe it very much.'

He nodded soberly. 'It is appallingly disturbing to think anything else. If it weren't for those nine missing hours one would have no doubt at all.'

I shrugged. 'He could have spent them in dozens of harmless ways. In a bar. Having dinner. In a cinema. Picking up a girl.'

'Yes, he could,' he said. But the doubt remained, both in his mind and mine.

He was to drive the hired Holden back to Sydney the following day and fly to England. He shook hands with me in the street and gave me his address in London, where I was to meet him again. With the door open and with one foot in the car he said, 'I suppose it would be part of your ... er ... procedure ... to appear as a slightly, shall we say, unreliable type of stable lad, so that the crooked element would take to you?'

'Definitely,' I grinned.

'Then, if I might suggest it, it would be a good idea for you to grow a couple of sideburns. It's surprising what a lot of distrust can be caused by an inch of extra hair in front of the ears!'

I laughed. 'A good idea.'

'And don't bring many clothes,' he added. 'I'll fix you up with British stuff suitable for your new character.'

'All right.'

He slid down behind the wheel.

'Au revoir, then, Mr. Roke.'

'Au revoir, Lord October,' I said.

After he had gone, and without his persuasive force at my elbow, what I was planning to do seemed less sensible than ever. But then I was tired to death of being sensible. I went on working from dawn to midnight to clear the decks, and found myself waking each morning with impatience to be on my way.

Two days before I was due to leave I flew down to Geelong to say goodbye to Philip and explain to his headmaster that I was going to Europe for a while; I didn't know exactly how long, I came back via Frensham to see my sisters, both of whom exclaimed at once over the dark patches of stubble which were already giving my face the required 'unreliable' appearance.

'For heaven's sake shave them off,' said Belinda. 'They're far too sexy. Most of the seniors are crazy about you already and if they see you like that you'll be mobbed.'

'That sounds delicious,' I said, grinning at them affectionately.

Helen, nearly sixteen, was fair and gentle and as graceful as the flowers she liked to draw. She was the most dependent of the three, and had suffered worst from not having a mother.

'Do you mean,' she said anxiously, 'that you will be away the whole summer?' She looked as if Mount Kosciusko had crumbled.

'You'll be all right. You're nearly grown up now,' I teased her.

'But the holidays will be so dull.'

'Ask some friends to stay, then.'

'Oh!' Her face cleared. 'Can we? Yes. That would be fun.'

She kissed me more happily goodbye, and went back to her lessons.

My eldest sister and I understood each other very well, and to her alone, knowing I owed it to her, I told the real purpose of my 'holiday'. She was upset, which I had not expected.

'Dearest Dan,' she said, twining her arm in mine and sniffing to stop herself crying, 'I know that bringing us up has been a grind for you, and if for once you want to do something for your own sake, we ought to be glad, only please do be careful. We do . . . we do want you back.'

'I'll come back,' I promised helplessly, lending her my handkerchief. 'I'll come back.'

The taxi from the air terminal brought me through a tree-filled square to the Earl of October's London house in a grey drizzle which in no way matched my spirits. Light-hearted, that was me. Springs in my heels.

In answer to my ring the elegant black door was opened by a friendly-faced manservant who took my grip from my hand and said that as his lordship was expecting me he would take me up at once. 'Up' turned out to be a crimson-walled drawing-room on the first floor where round an electric heater in an Adam fireplace three men stood with glasses in their hands. Three men standing easily, their heads turned towards the opening door. Three men radiating as one the authority I had been aware of in October. They were the ruling triumvirate of National Hunt racing. Big guns. Established and entrenched behind a hundred years of traditional power. They weren't taking the affair as effervescently as I was.

'Mr. Roke, my lord,' said the manservant, showing me in.

October came across the room to me and shook hands.

'Good trip?'

'Yes, thank you.'

He turned towards the other men. 'My two co-Stewards arranged to be here to welcome you.'

'My name is Macclesfield,' said the taller of them, an elderly stooping man with riotous white hair. He leaned forward and held out a sinewy hand. 'I am most interested to meet you, Mr. Roke.' He had a hawk-eyed piercing stare.

'And this is Colonel Beckett.' He gestured to the third man, a slender ill-looking person who shook hands also, but with a weak limp grasp. All three of them paused and looked at me as if I had come from outer space.

'I am at your disposal,' I said politely.

'Yes . . . well, we may as well get straight down to business,' said October, directing me to a hide-covered armchair. 'But a drink first?'

'Thank you.'

He gave me a glass of the smoothest whisky I'd ever tasted, and they all sat down.

'My horses,' October began, speaking easily, conversationally, 'are trained in the stable block adjoining my house in Yorkshire. I do not train them myself, because I am away too often on business. A man named Inskip holds the licence – a public licence – and apart from my own horses he trains several for my friends. At present there are about thirty-five horses in the yard, of which eleven are my own. We think it would be best if you started work as a lad in my stable, and then you can move on somewhere else when you think it is necessary. Clear so far?'

I nodded.

He went on, 'Inskip is an honest man, but unfortunately he's also a bit of a talker, and we consider it essential for your success that he should not have any reason to chatter about the way you joined the stable. The hiring of lads is always left to him, so it will have to be he, not I, who hires you.

'In order to make certain that we are short-handed – so that your application for work will be immediately accepted – Colonel Beckett and Sir Stuart Macclesfield are each sending three young horses to the stables two days from now. The horses are no good, I may say, but they're the best we could do in the time.'

They all smiled. And well they might. I began to admire their staff work.

'In four days, when everyone is beginning to feel over-worked, you will arrive in the yard and offer your services. All right?'

'Yes.'

'Here is a reference.' He handed me an envelope. 'It is from a woman cousin of mine in Cornwall who keeps a couple of hunters. I have arranged that if Inskip checks with her she will give you a clean bill. You can't appear too doubtful in character to begin with, you see, or Inskip will not employ you.'

'I understand,' I said.

'Inskip will ask you for your insurance card and an income tax form which you would normally have brought on from your last job. Here they are.' He gave them to me. 'The insurance card is stamped up to date and is no problem as it will not be queried in any way until next May, by which time we hope there will be no more need for it. The income tax situation is more difficult, but we have constructed the form so that the address on the part which Inskip has to send off to the Inland Revenue people when he engages you is illegible. Any amount of natural-looking confusion should arise from that; and the fact that you were not working in Cornwall should be safely concealed.'

'I see,' I said. And I was impressed as well.

Sir Stuart Macclesfield cleared his throat and Colonel Beckett pinched the bridge of his nose between the thumb and forefinger.

'About this dope,' I said, 'you told me your analysts couldn't identify it, but you didn't give me any details. What is it that makes you positive it is being used?'

October glanced at Macclesfield, who said in his slow rasping elderly

voice. 'When a horse comes in from a race frothing at the mouth with
his eyes popping out and his body drenched in sweat, one naturally
suspects that he has been given a stimulant of some kind. Dopers usually
run into trouble with stimulants, since it is difficult to judge the dosage
needed to get a horse to win without arousing suspicion. If you had seen
any of these particular horses we have tested, you would have sworn that
they had been given a big overdose. But the test results were always
negative.'

'What do your pharmacists say?' I asked.

Beckett said sardonically, 'Word for word? It's blasphemous.'

I grinned. 'The gist.'

Beckett said, 'They simply say there isn't a dope they can't identify.'

'How about adrenalin?' I asked.

The Stewards exchanged glances, and Beckett said, 'Most of the horses
concerned did have a fairly high adrenalin count, but you can't tell from
one analysis whether that is normal for that particular horse or not.
Horses vary tremendously in the amount of adrenalin they produce
naturally, and you would have to test them before and after several races
to establish their normal output, and also at various stages of their
training. Only when you know their normal levels could you say whether
any extra had been pumped into them. From the practical point of view
. . . adrenalin can't be given by mouth, as I expect you know. It has to
be injected, and it works instantaneously. These horses were all calm and
cool when they went to the starting gate. Horses which have been
stimulated with adrenalin are pepped up at that point. In addition to
that, a horse often shows at once that he has had a subcutaneous adrenalin
injection because the hairs for some way round the site of the puncture
stand up on end and give the game away. Only an injection straight into
the jugular vein is really foolproof; but it is a very tricky process, and we
are quite certain that it was not done in these cases.'

'The lab chaps,' said October, 'told us to look out for something
mechanical. All sorts of things have been tried in the past, you see.
Electric shocks, for instance. Jockeys used to have saddles or whips made
with batteries concealed in them so that they could run bursts of current
into the horses they were riding and galvanize them into winning. The
horses' own sweat acted as a splendid conductor. We went into all that
sort of thing very thoroughly indeed, and we are firmly of the opinion
that none of the jockeys involved carried anything out of the ordinary in
any of their equipment.'

'We have collected all our notes, all the lab notes, dozens of press
cuttings, and anything else we thought could be of the slightest help,'
said Macclesfield, pointing to three boxes of files which lay in a pile on
a table by my elbow.

'And you have four days to read them and think about them,' added
October, smiling faintly. 'There is a room ready for you here, and my
man will look after you. I am sorry I cannot be with you, but I have to
return to Yorkshire tonight.'

Beckett looked at his watch and rose slowly. 'I must be going, Edward.'
To me, with a glance as alive and shrewd as his physique was failing,

he said, 'You'll do. And make it fairly snappy, will you? Time's against us.'

I thought October looked relieved. I was sure of it when Macclesfield shook my hand again and rasped. 'Now that you're actually here the whole scheme suddenly seems more possible ... Mr. Roke, I sincerely wish you every success.'

October went down to the street door with them, and came back and looked at me across the crimson room.

'They are sold on you, Mr. Roke, I am glad to say.'

Upstairs in the luxurious deep-green carpeted, brass bedsteaded guest room where I slept for the next four nights I found the manservant had unpacked the few clothes I had brought with me and put them tidily on the shelves of a heavy Edwardian wardrobe. On the floor beside my own canvas and leather grip stood a cheap fibre suitcase with rust-marked locks. Amused, I explored its contents. On top there was a thick sealed envelope with my name on it. I slit it open and found it was packed with five-pound notes; forty of them, and an accompanying slip which read 'Bread for throwing on waters.' I laughed aloud.

Under the envelope October had provided everything from under-clothes to washing things, jodhpur boots to rainproof, jeans to pyjamas.

Another note from him was tucked into the neck of a black leather jacket.

'This jacket completes what sideburns begin. Wearing both, you won't have any character to speak of. They are regulation dress for delinquents! Good luck.'

I eyed the jodhpur boots. They were second-hand and needed polishing, but to my surprise, when I slid my feet into them, they were a good fit. I took them off and tried on a violently pointed pair of black walking shoes. Horrible, but they fitted comfortably also, and I kept them on to get my feet (and eyes) used to them.

The three box files, which I had carried up with me after October had left for Yorkshire, were stacked on a low table next to a small arm-chair, and with a feeling that there was no more time to waste I sat down, opened the first of them, and began to read.

Because I went painstakingly slowly through every word, it took me two days to finish all the papers in those boxes. And at the end of it found myself staring at the carpet without a helpful idea in my head. There were accounts, some in typescript, some in longhand, of interviews the Stewards had held with the trainers, jockeys, head travelling-lads, stable lads, blacksmiths and veterinary surgeons connected with the eleven horses suspected of being doped. There was a lengthy report from a firm of private investigators who had interviewed dozens of stable lads in 'places of refreshment', and got nowhere. A memo ten pages long from a bookmaker went into copious details of the market which had been made on the horses concerned: but the last sentence summed it up: 'We can trace no one person or syndicate which has won consistently on these horses, and therefore conclude that if any one person or syndicate is involved, their betting was done on the Tote.' Further down the box I found a letter from Tote Investors Ltd., saying that not one of their credit clients had backed all the horses concerned, but that of course they had no check on cash betting at racecourses.

The second box contained eleven laboratory reports of analyses made on urine and saliva samples. The first report referred to a horse called Charcoal and was dated eighteen months earlier. The last gave details of tests made on a horse called Rudyard as recently as September, when October was in Australia.

The word 'negative' had been written in a neat hand at the end of each report.

The press had had a lot of trouble dodging the laws of libel. The clippings from daily papers in the third box contained such sentences as 'Charcoal displayed a totally uncharacteristic turn of foot,' and 'In the unsaddling enclosure Rudyard appeared to be considerably excited by his success.'

There were fewer references to Charcoal and the following three horses, but at that point someone had employed a news-gathering agency: the last seven cases were documented by clippings from several daily, evening, local and sporting papers.

At the bottom of the clippings I came across a medium sized manilla envelope. On it was written 'Received from Sports Editor, Daily Scope, June 10th'. This, I realised, was the packet of cuttings collected by Stapleton, the unfortunate journalist, and I opened the envelope with much curiosity. But to my great disappointment, because I badly needed some help, all the clippings except three were duplicates of those I had already read.

Of these three, one was a personality piece on the woman owner of Charcoal, one was an account of a horse (not one of the eleven) going berserk and killing a woman on June 3 in the paddock at Cartmel, Lancashire, and the third was a long article from a racing weekly discussing famous cases of doping, how they had been discovered and how dealt with. I read this attentively, with minimum results.

After all this unfruitful concentration I spent the whole of the next day wandering round London, breathing in the city's fumes with a heady feeling of liberation, asking the way frequently and listening carefully to the voices which replied.

In the matter of my accent I thought October had been too hopeful, because two people, before midday, commented on my being Australian. My parents had retained their Englishness until their deaths, but at nine I had found it prudent not to be 'different' at school, and had adopted the speech of my new country from that age. I could no longer shed it, even if I had wanted to, but if it was to sound like cockney English, it would clearly have to be modified.

I drifted eastwards, walking, asking, listening. Gradually I came to the conclusion that if I knocked off the aitches and didn't clip the ends of my words, I might get by. I practised that all afternoon, and finally managed to alter a few vowel sounds as well. No one asked me where I came from, which I took as a sign of success, and when I asked the last man, a barrow-boy, where I could catch a bus back to the West, I could no longer detect much difference between my question and his answer.

I made one purchase, a zip-pocketed money belt made of strong canvas webbing. It buckled flat round my waist under my shirt, and into it I packed the two hundred pounds; wherever I was going I thought I might be glad to have that money readily available.

In the evening, refreshed, I tried to approach the doping problem from another angle, by seeing if the horses had had anything in common.

Apparently they hadn't. All were trained by different trainers. All were owned by different owners: and all had been ridden by different jockeys. The only thing they all had in common was that they had nothing in common.

I sighed, and went to bed.

Terence, the manservant, with whom I had reached a reserved but definite friendship, woke me on the fourth morning by coming into my room with a laden breakfast tray.

'The condemned man ate hearty,' he observed, lifting a silver cover and allowing me a glimpse and a sniff of a plateful of eggs and bacon.'

'What do you mean?' I said, yawning contentedly.

'I don't know what you and his lordship are up to, sir, but wherever you are going it is different from what you are used to. That suit of yours, for instance, didn't come from the same sort of place as this little lot.'

He picked up the fibre suitcase, put it on a stool, and opened the locks. Carefully, as if they had been silk, he laid out on a chair some cotton pants and a checked cotton shirt, followed by a tan coloured ribbed pullover, some drain-pipe charcoal trousers and black socks. With a look of disgust he picked up the black leather jacket and draped it over the chair back, and neatly arranged the pointed shoes.

'His Lordship said I was to make certain that you left behind everything you came with, and took only these things with you,' he said regretfully.

'Did you buy them?' I asked, amused, 'or was it Lord October?'

'His Lordship bought them.' He smiled suddenly as he went over to the door. 'I'd love to have seen him pushing around in that chain store among all those bustling women.'

I finished my breakfast, bathed, shaved, and dressed from head to foot in the new clothes, putting the black jacket on top and zipping up the front. Then I brushed the hair on top of my head forwards instead of back, so that the short black ends curved on to my forehead.

Terence came back for the empty tray and found me standing looking at myself in a full-length mirror. Instead of grinning at him as usual I turned slowly round on my heel and treated him to a hard, narrow-eyed stare.

'Holy hell!' he said explosively.

'Good,' I said cheerfully. 'You wouldn't trust me then?'

'Not as far as I could throw that wardrobe.'

'What other impressions do I make on you? Would you give me a job?'

'You wouldn't get through the front door here, for a start. Basement entrance, if any. I'd check your references carefully before I took you on; and I don't think I'd have you at all if I wasn't desperate. You look shifty ... and a bit ... well ... almost dangerous.'

I unzipped the leather jacket and let it flap open, showing the checked shirt collar and tan pullover underneath. The effect was altogether sloppier.

'How about now?' I asked.

He put his head on one side, considering. 'Yes, I might give you a job now. You look much more ordinary. Not much more honest, but less hard to handle.'

'Thank you, Terence. That's exactly the note, I think. Ordinary but dishonest.' I smiled with pleasure. 'I'd better be on my way.'

'You haven't got anything of your own with you?'

'Only my watch,' I assured him.

'Fine,' he said.

I noticed with interest that for the first time in four days he had failed to punctuate any sentence with an easy, automatic 'sir', and when I picked up the cheap suitcase he made no move to take it from me and carry it himself, as he had done with my grip when I arrived.

We went downstairs to the street door where I shook hands with him and thanked him for looking after me so well, and gave him a five pound note. One of October's. He took it with a smile and stood with it in his hand, looking at me in my new character.

I grinned at him widely.

'Goodbye Terence.'

'Goodbye, and thank you ... sir,' he said; and I walked off leaving him laughing.

The next intimation I had that my change of clothes meant a violent drop in status came from the taxi driver I hailed at the bottom of the square. He refused to take me to King's Cross station until I had shown him that I had enough money to pay his fare. I caught the noon train to Harrogate and intercepted several disapproving glances from a prim middle-aged man with frayed cuffs sitting opposite me. This was all satisfactory, I thought, looking out at the damp autumn countryside flying past; this assures me that I do immediately make a dubious impression. It was rather a lop-sided thing to be pleased about.

From Harrogate I caught a country bus to the small village of Slaw, and having asked the way walked the last two miles to October's place, arriving just before six o'clock, the best time of day for seeking work in a stable.

Sure enough, they were rushed off their feet: I asked for the head lad, and he took me with him to Inskip, who was doing his evening round of inspection.

Inskip looked me over and pursed his lips. He was a stringy, youngish man with spectacles, sparse sandy hair, and a sloppy-looking mouth.

'References?' In contrast, his voice was sharp and authoritative.

I took the letter from October's Cornish cousin out of my pocket and gave it to him. He opened the letter, read it, and put it away in his own pocket.

'You haven't been with racehorses before, then?'

'No.'

'When could you start?'

'Now,' I indicated my suitcase.

He hesitated, but not for long. 'As it happens, we are short-handed. We'll give you a try. Wally, arrange a bed for him with Mrs. Allnut, and he can start in the morning. Usual wages,' he added to me, 'eleven pounds a week, and three pounds of that goes to Mrs. Allnut for your keep. You can give me your cards tomorrow. Right?'

'Yes,' I said: and I was in.

Chapter Three

I edged gently into the life of the yard like a heretic into heaven, trying not to be discovered and flung out before I became part of the scenery. On my first evening I spoke almost entirely in monosyllables, because I didn't trust my new accent, but I slowly found out that the lads talked with such a variety of regional accents themselves that my cockney-Australian passed without comment.

Wally, the head lad, a wiry short man with ill-fitting dentures, said I was to sleep in the cottage where about a dozen unmarried lads lived, beside the gate into the yard. I was shown into a small crowded upstairs room containing six beds, a wardrobe, two chests of drawers, and four bedside chairs; which left roughly two square yards of clear space in the centre. Thin flowered curtains hung at the windows, and there was polished linoleum on the floor.

My bed proved to have developed a deep sag in the centre over the years, but it was comfortable enough, and was made up freshly with white sheets and grey blankets. Mrs. Allnut, who took me in without a second glance, was a round, cheerful little person with hair fastened in a twist on top of her head. She kept the cottage spotless and stood over the lads to make sure they washed. She cooked well, and the food was plain but plentiful. All in all, it was a good billet.

I walked a bit warily to start with, but it was easier to be accepted and to fade into the background than I had imagined.

Once or twice during the first few days I stopped myself just in time from absent-mindedly telling another lad what to do; nine years' habit died hard. And I was surprised, and a bit dismayed, by the subservient attitude every one had to Inskip, at least to his face: my own men treated me at home with far more familiarity. The fact that I paid and they earned gave me no rights over them as men, and this we all clearly understood. But at Inskip's, and throughout all England, I gradually realised, there was far less of the almost aggressive egalitarianism of Australia. The lads, on the whole, seemed to accept that in the eyes of the world they were of secondary importance as human beings to Inskip and October. I thought this extraordinary, undignified, and shameful. And I kept my thoughts to myself.

Wally, scandalised by the casual way I had spoken on my arrival, told me to call Inskip 'Sir' and October 'My lord' – and said that if I was a ruddy communist I could clear off at once: so I quickly exhibited what he called a proper respect for my betters.

On the other hand it was precisely because the relationship between me and my own men was so free and easy that I found no difficulty in becoming a lad amongst lads. I felt no constraint on their part and, once the matter of accents had been settled, no self-consciousness on mine. But I did come to realise that what October had implied was undoubtedly true: had I stayed in England and gone to Eton (instead of its equivalent, Geelong) I could not have fitted so readily into his stable.

Inskip allotted me to three newly arrived horses, which was not very good from my point of view as it meant that I could not expect to be sent to a race meeting with them. They were neither fit nor entered for races, and it would be weeks before they were ready to run, even if they proved to be good enough. I pondered the problem while I carried their hay and water and cleaned their boxes and rode them out at morning exercise with the string.

On my second evening October came round at six with a party of house guests. Inskip, knowing in advance, had had everyone running to be finished in good time and walked round himself first, to make sure that all was in order.

Each lad stood with whichever of his horses was nearest the end from which the inspection was started. October and his friends, accompanied by Inskip and Wally, moved along from box to box, chatting, laughing, discussing each horse as they went.

When they came to me October flicked me a glance, and said, 'You're new, aren't you?'

'Yes, my lord.'

He took no further notice of me then, but when I had bolted the first horse in for the night and waited further down the yard with the second one, he came over to pat my charge and feel his legs; and as he straightened up he gave me a mischievous wink. With difficulty, since I was facing the other men, I kept a dead-pan face. He blew his nose to stop himself laughing. We were neither of us very professional at this cloak and dagger stuff.

When they had gone, and after I had eaten the evening meal with the other lads, I walked down to the Slaw pub with two of them. Half way through the first drinks I left them and went and telephoned to October.

'Who is speaking?' a man's voice inquired.

I was stumped for a second: then I said 'Perlooma,' knowing that that would fetch him.

He came on the line. 'Anything wrong?'

'No,' I said. 'Does anyone at the local exchange listen to your calls?'

'I wouldn't bet on it.' He hesitated. 'Where are you?'

'Slaw, in the phone box at your end of the village.'

'I have guests for dinner; will tomorrow do?'

'Yes.'

He paused for thought. 'Can you tell me what you want?'

'Yes,' I said. 'The form books for the last seven or eight seasons, and every scrap of information you can possibly dig up about the eleven . . . subjects.'

'What are you looking for?'

'I don't know yet,' I said.

'Do you want anything else?'

'Yes, but it needs discussion.'

He thought. 'Behind the stable yard there is a stream which comes down from the moors. Walk up beside it tomorrow, after lunch.'

'Right.'

I hung up, and went back to my interrupted drink in the pub.

'You've been a long time,' said Paddy, one of the lads I had come with. 'We're one ahead of you. What have you been doing – reading the walls in the Gents?'

'There's some remarks on them walls,' mused the other lad, a gawky boy of eighteen, 'that I haven't fathomed yet.'

'Nor you don't want to,' said Paddy approvingly. At forty he acted as unofficial father to many of the younger lads.

They slept one each side of me, Paddy and Grits, in the little dormitory. Paddy, as sharp as Grits was slow, was a tough little Irishman with eyes that never missed a trick. From the first minute I hoisted my suitcase on to the bed and unpacked my night things under his inquisitive gaze I had been glad that October had been so insistent about a complete change of clothes.

'How about another drink?'

'One more, then,' assented Paddy. 'I can just about run to it, I reckon.'

I took the glasses to the bar and bought refills: there was a pause while Paddy and Grits dug into their pockets and repaid me elevenpence each. The beer, which to me, tasted strong and bitter was not, I thought, worth four miles' walk, but many of the lads, it appeared, had bicycles or rickety cars and made the trek on several evenings a week.

'Nothing much doing, tonight,' observed Grits gloomily. He brightened. 'Pay day tomorrow.'

'It'll be full here tomorrow, and that's a fact,' agreed Paddy. 'With Soupy and that lot from Granger's and all.'

'Granger's?' I asked.

'Sure, don't you know nothing?' said Grits with mild contempt. 'Granger's stable, over t'other side of the hill.'

'Where have you been all your life?' said Paddy.

'He's new to racing, mind you,' said Grits, being fair.

'Yes, but all the same!' Paddy drank past the half-way mark, and wiped his mouth on the back of his hand.

Grits finished his beer and sighed. 'That's it, then. Better be getting back, I suppose.'

We walked back to the stables, talking as always about horses.

The following afternoon I wandered casually out of the stables and started up the stream, picking up stones as I went and throwing them in, as if to enjoy the splash. Some of the lads were punting a football about in the paddock behind the yard, but none of them paid any attention to me. A good long way up the hill, where the stream ran through a steep, grass sided gully, I came across October sitting on a boulder smoking a cigarette. He was accompanied by a black retriever, and a gun and a full game bag lay on the ground beside him.

'Doctor Livingstone, I presume,' he said, smiling.

'Quite right, Mr. Stanley. How did you guess?' I perched on a boulder near to him.

He kicked the game bag, 'The form books are in here, and a note book with all that Beckett and I could rake up at such short notice about those eleven horses. But surely the reports in the files you read would be of more use than the odd snippets we can supply?'

'Anything may be useful . . . you never know. There was one clipping in that packet of Stapleton's which was interesting. It was about historic dope cases. It said that certain horses apparently turned harmless food into something that showed a positive dope reaction, just through chemical changes in their body. I suppose it isn't possible that reverse could occur? I mean, could some horses break down any sort of dope into harmless substances, so that no positive reaction showed in the test?'

'I'll find out.'

'There's only one other thing,' I said. 'I have been assigned to three of those useless brutes you filled the yard up with, and that means no trips to racecourses. I was wondering if perhaps you could sell one of them again, and then I'd have a chance of mixing with lads from several stables at the sales. Three other men are doing three horses each here, so I shouldn't find myself redundant, and I might well be given a raceable horse to look after.'

'I will sell one,' he said, 'but if it goes for auction it will take time. The application forms have to go to the auctioneer nearly a month before the sale date.'

I nodded. 'It's utterly frustrating. I wish I could think of a way of getting myself transferred to a horse which is due to race shortly. Preferably one going to a far distant course, because an overnight stop would be ideal.'

'Lads don't change their horses in mid-stream,' he said rubbing his chin.

'So I've been told. It's the luck of the draw. You get them when they come and you're stuck with them until they leave. If they turn out useless, it's just too bad.'

We stood up. The retriever, who had lain quiet all this time with his muzzle resting on his paws, got to his feet also and stretched himself, and wagging his tail slowly from side to side looked up trustingly at his master. October bent down, gave the dog an affectionate slap, and picked up the gun. I picked up the game bag and swung it over my shoulder.

We shook hands, and October said, smiling, 'You may like to know that Inskip thinks you ride extraordinarily well for a stable lad. His exact words were that he didn't really trust men with your sort of looks, but that you'd the hands of an angel. You'd better watch that.'

'Hell,' I said, 'I hadn't given it a thought.'

He grinned and went off up the hill, and I turned downwards along the stream, gradually becoming ruefully aware that however much of a lark I might find it to put on wolf's clothing, it was going to hurt my pride if I had to hash up my riding as well.

The pub in Slaw was crowded that evening and the wage packets took a hiding. About half the strength from October's stable was there – and also a group of Granger's lads, including three lasses, who took a good deal of double-meaning teasing and thoroughly enjoyed it. Most of the talk was friendly bragging that each lad's horses were better than those of anyone else.

'My bugger'll beat yours with his eyes shut on Wednesday.'

'You've got a ruddy hope . . .'

'. . . Yours couldn't run a snail to a close finish.'

'. . . The jockey made a right muck of the start and never got in touch . . .'

'. . . Fat as a pig and bloody obstinate as well.'

The easy chat ebbed and flowed while the air grew thick with cigarette smoke and the warmth of too many lungs breathing the same box of air. A game of darts between some inaccurate players was in progress in one corner, and the balls of bar billiards clicked in another. I lolled on a hard chair with my arm hooked over the back and watched Paddy and one of Granger's lads engage in a needle match of dominoes. Horses, cars, football, boxing, films, the last local dance, and back to horses, always back to horses. I listened to it all and learned nothing except that these lads were mostly content with their lives, mostly good natured, mostly observant and mostly harmless.

'You're new, aren't you?' said a challenging voice in my ear.

I turned my head and looked up at him. 'Yeah,' I said languidly.

These were the only eyes I had seen in Yorkshire which held anything of the sort of guile I was looking for. I gave him back his stare until his lips curled in recognition that I was one of his kind.

'What's your name?'

'Dan,' I said, 'and yours?'

'Thomas Nathaniel Tarleton.' He waited for some reaction, but I didn't know what it ought to be.

'T. N. T.' said Paddy obligingly, looking up from his dominoes. 'Soupy.' His quick gaze flickered over both of us.

'The high explosive kid himself,' I murmured.

Soupy Tarleton smiled a small, carefully dangerous smile: to impress me, I gathered. He was about my own age and build, but much fairer, with the reddish skin which I had noticed so many Englishmen had. His light hazel eyes protruded slightly in their sockets, and he had grown a narrow moustache on the upper lip of his full, moist-looking mouth. On the little finger of his right hand he wore a heavy gold ring, and on his left wrist, an expensive wrist watch. His clothes were of good material, though distinctly sharp in cut, and the enviable fleece-lined quilted jacket he carried over his arm would have cost him three weeks' pay.

He showed no signs of wanting to be friendly. After looking me over as thoroughly as I had him, he merely nodded, said 'See you,' and detached himself to go over and watch the bar billiards.

Grits brought a fresh half pint from the bar and settled himself on the bench next to Paddy.

'You don't want to trust Soupy,' he told me confidentially, his raw boned unintelligent face full of kindness.

Paddy put down a double three, and looking round at us gave me a long, unsmiling scrutiny.

'There's no need to worry about Dan, Grits,' he said. 'He and Soupy, they're alike. They'd go well in double harness. Birds of a feather, that's what they are.'

'But you said I wasn't to trust Soupy,' objected Grits, looking from one to the other of us with troubled eyes.

'That's right,' said Paddy flatly. He put down a three-four and concentrated on his game.

Grits shifted six inches towards Paddy and gave me one puzzled, embarrassed glance. Then he found the inside of his beer mug suddenly intensely interesting and didn't raise his eyes to mine again.

I think it was at that exact moment that the charade began to lose its light-heartedness. I liked Paddy and Grits, and for three days they had accepted me with casual good humour. I was not prepared for Paddy's instant recognition that it was with Soupy that my real interest lay, nor for his immediate rejection of me on that account. It was a shock which I ought to have foreseen, and hadn't: and it should have warned me what to expect in the future, but it didn't.

Colonel Beckett's staff work continued to be of the highest possible kind. Having committed himself to the offensive, he was prepared to back the attack with massive and immediate reinforcements: which is to say that as soon as he had heard from October that I was immobilized in the stable with three useless horses, he set about liberating me.

On Tuesday afternoon, when I had been with the stable for a week, Wally, the head lad, stopped me as I carried two buckets full of water across the yard.

'That horse of yours in number seventeen is going tomorrow,' he said. 'You'll have to look sharp in the morning with your work, because you are to be ready to go with it at twelve-thirty. The horse box will take you to another racing stables, down near Nottingham. You are to leave this horse there and bring a new one back. Right?'

'Right,' I said. Wally's manner was cool with me; but over the week-end I had made myself be reconciled to the knowledge that I had to go on inspiring a faint mistrust all round, even if I no longer much liked it when I succeeded.

Most of Sunday I had spent reading the form books, which the others in the cottage regarded as a perfectly natural activity; and in the evening, when they all went down to the pub, I did some pretty concentrated work with a pencil, making analyses of the eleven horses and their assisted wins. It was true, as I had discovered from the newspaper cuttings in London, that they all had different owners, trainers and jockeys: but it was not true that they had absolutely nothing in common. By the time I had sealed my notes into an envelope and put it with October's notebook into the game bag under some form books, away from the inquiring gaze of the beer-happy returning lads, I was in possession of four unhelpful points of similarity.

First, the horses had all won selling chases – races where the winner was subsequently put up for auction. In the auctions three horses had been bought back by their owners, and the rest had been sold for modest sums.

Second, in all their racing lives all the horses had proved themselves to be capable of making a show in a race, but had either no strength or no guts when it came to a finish.

Third, none of them had won any races except the ones for which they were doped, though they had occasionally been placed on other occasions.

Fourth, none of them had won at odds of less than ten to one.

I learned both from October's notes and from the form books that several of the horses had changed trainers more than once, but they were such moderate, unrewarding animals that this was only to be expected. I was also in possession of the useless information that the horses were all by different sires out of different dams, that they varied in age from five to eleven, and that they were not all of the same colour. Neither had they all won on the same course, though in this case they had not all won on different courses either; and geographically I had a vague idea that the courses concerned were all in the northern half of the country – Kelso, Haydock, Sedgefield, Stafford and Ludlow. I decided to check them on a map, to see if this was right, but there wasn't one to be found chez Mrs. Allnut.

I went to bed in the crowded little dormitory with the other lads' beery breaths gradually overwhelming the usual mixed clean smells of boot polish and hair oil, and lost an argument about having the small sash window open more than four inches at the top. The lads all seemed to take their cue from Paddy, who was undoubtedly the most aware of them, and if Paddy declined to treat me as a friend, so would they: I realized that if I had insisted on having the window tight shut they would probably have opened it wide and given me all the air I wanted. Grinning ruefully in the dark I listened to the squeaking bed springs and their sleepy, gossiping giggles as they thumbed over the evening's talk; and as I shifted to find a comfortable spot on the lumpy mattress I began to wonder what life was really like from the inside for the hands who lived in my own bunk house, back home.

Wednesday morning gave me my first taste of the biting Yorkshire wind, and one of the lads, as we scurried round the yard with shaking hands and running noses, cheerfully assured me that it could blow for six months solid, if it tried. I did my three horses at the double, but by the time the horse box took me and one of them out of the yard at twelve-thirty I had decided that if the gaps in my wardrobe were anything to go by, October's big square house up the drive must have very efficient central heating.

About four miles up the road I pressed the bell which in most horse boxes connects the back compartment to the cab. The driver stopped obediently, and looked enquiringly at me when I walked along and climbed up into the cab beside him.

'The horse is quiet,' I said, 'and it's warmer here.'

He grinned and started off again, shouting over the noise of the engine. 'I didn't have you figured for the conscientious type, and I was damn right. That horse is going to be sold and has got to arrive in good condition . . . the boss would have a fit if he knew you were up in front.'

I had a pretty good idea the boss, meaning Inskip, wouldn't be at all surprised; bosses, judging by myself, weren't as naïve as all that.

'The boss can stuff himself,' I said unpleasantly.

I got a sidelong glance for that, and reflected that it was dead easy to give oneself a bad character if one put one's mind to it. Horse box drivers went to race meetings in droves, and had no duties when they got there. They had time to gossip in the canteen, time all afternoon to wander about and wag their tongues. There was no telling what ears might hear that there was a possible chink in the honesty of the Inskip lads.

We stopped once on the way to eat in a transport café, and again a little further on for me to buy myself a couple of woollen shirts, a black sweater, some thick socks, woollen gloves and a knitted yachting cap like those the other lads had worn that bitter morning. The box driver, coming into the shop with me to buy some socks for himself, eyed my purchases and remarked that I seemed to have plenty of money. I grinned knowingly, and said it was easy to come by if you knew how; and I could see his doubts of me growing.

In mid-afternoon we rolled in to a racing stable in Leicestershire, and it was here that the scope of Beckett's staff work became apparent. The horse I was to take back and subsequently care for was a useful hurdler just about to start his career as a novice 'chaser, and he had been sold to Colonel Beckett complete with all engagements. This meant, I learned from his former lad, who handed him over to me with considerable bitterness, that he could run in all the races for which his ex-owner had already entered him.

'Where is he entered?' I asked.

'Oh, dozens of places, I think – Newbury, Cheltenham, Sandown, and so on, and he was going to start next week at Bristol.' The lad's face twisted with regret as he passed the halter rope into my hand. 'I can't think what on earth persuaded the Old Man to part with him. He's a real daisy, and if I ever see him at the races not looking as good and well cared for as he does now, I'll find you and beat the living daylights out of you, I will straight.'

I had already discovered how deeply attached racing lads became to the horses they looked after, and I understood that he meant what he said.

'What's his name?' I asked.

'Sparking Plug . . . God awful name, he's no plug . . . Hey, Sparks, old boy ... hey, boy ... hey, old fellow ...' He fondled the horse's muzzle affectionately.

We loaded him into the horse box and this time I did stay where I ought to be, in the back, looking after him. If Beckett were prepared to give a fortune for the cause, as I guessed he must have done to get hold of such an ideal horse in so few days, I was going to take good care of it.

Before we started back I took a look at the road map in the cab, and found to my satisfaction that all the race courses in the country had been marked in on it in indian ink. I borrowed it at once, and spent the journey studying it. The courses where Sparking Plug's lad had said he was entered were nearly all in the south. Overnight stops, as requested. I grinned.

The five race courses where the eleven horses had won were not, I found, all as far north as I had imagined. Ludlow and Stafford, in fact, could almost be considered southern, especially as I found I instinctively based my view of the whole country from Harrogate. The five courses seemed to bear no relation to each other on the map: far from presenting a tidy circle from which a centre might be deduced, they were all more or less in a curve from north east to south west, and I could find no significance in their location.

I spent the rest of the journey back as I spent most of my working hours, letting my mind drift over what I knew of the eleven horses, waiting for an idea to swim to the surface like a fish in a pool, waiting for the disconnected facts to sort themselves into a pattern. But I didn't really expect this to happen yet, as I knew I had barely started, and even electronic computers won't produce answers if they are not fed enough information.

On Friday night I went down to the pub in Slaw and beat Soupy at darts. He grunted, gestured to the bar billiards, and took an easy revenge. We then drank a half pint together, eyeing each other. Conversation between us was almost non-existent, nor was it necessary: and shortly I wandered back to watch the dart players. They were no better than the week before.

'You beat Soupy, didn't you Dan?' one of them said.

I nodded, and immediately found a bunch of darts thrust into my hand.

'If you can beat Soupy you must be in the team.'

'What team?' I asked.

'The stable darts team. We play other stables, and have a sort of Yorkshire League. Sometimes we go to Middleham or Wetherby or Richmond or sometimes they come here. Soupy's the best player in Granger's team. Could you beat him again, do you think, or was it a fluke?'

I threw three darts at the board. They all landed in the twenty. For some unknown reason I had always been able to throw straight.

'Cor,' said the lads. 'Go on.'

I threw three more: the twenty section got rather crowded.

'You're in the team, mate, and no nonsense,' they said.

'When's the next match?' I asked.

'We had one here a fortnight ago. Next one's next Sunday at Burndale, after the football. You can't play football as well as darts, I suppose?'

I shook my head. 'Only darts.'

I looked at the one dart still left in my hand. I could hit a scuttling rat with a stone; I had done it often when the men had found one round the corn bins and chased it out. I saw no reason why I couldn't hit a galloping horse with a dart: it was a much bigger target.

'Put that one in the bull,' urged the lad beside me.

I put it in the bull. The lads yelled with glee.

'We'll win the league this season,' they grinned. Grits grinned too. But Paddy didn't.

Chapter Four

October's son and daughters came home for the week-end, the elder girl in a scarlet T.R.4 which I grew to know well by sight as she drove in and out past the stables, and the twins more sedately, with their father. As all three were in the habit of riding out when they were at home Wally told me to saddle up two of my horses to go out with the first string on Saturday, Sparking Plug for me and the other for Lady Patricia Tarren.

Lady Patricia Tarren, as I discovered when I led out the horse in the half light of early dawn and held it for her to mount, was a raving beauty with a pale pink mouth and thick curly eyelashes which she knew very well how to use. She had tied a green head-scarf over her chestnut hair, and she wore a black and white harlequined ski-ing jacket to keep out the cold. She was carrying some bright green woollen gloves.

'You're new,' she observed, looking up at me through the eyelashes. 'What's your name?'

'Dan . . . Miss,' I said. I realized I hadn't the faintest idea what form of address an earl's daughter was accustomed to. Wally's instructions hadn't stretched that far.

'Well . . . give me a leg up, then.'

I stood beside her obediently, but as I leaned forward to help her she ran her bare hand over my head and around my neck, and took the lobe of my right ear between her fingers. She had sharp nails, and she dug them in. Her eyes were wide with challenge. I looked straight back. When I didn't move or say anything she presently giggled and let go and calmly put on her gloves. I gave her a leg up into the saddle and she bent down to gather the reins, and fluttered the fluffy lashes close to my face.

'You're quite a dish, aren't you, Danny boy,' she said, 'with those googoo dark eyes.'

I couldn't think of any answer to her which was at all consistent with my position. She laughed, nudged the horse's flanks, and walked off down the yard. Her sister, mounting a horse held by Grits, looked from twenty yards away in the dim light to be much fairer in colouring and very nearly as beautiful. Heaven help October, I thought, with two like that to keep an eye on.

I turned to go and fetch Sparking Plug and found October's eighteen-year-old son at my elbow. He was very like his father, but not yet as thick in body or as easily powerful in manner.

'I shouldn't pay too much attention to my twin sister,' he said in a cool, bored voice, looking me up and down, 'she is apt to tease.' He nodded and strolled over to where his horse was waiting for him; and I gathered that what I had received was a warning off. If his sister behaved as provocatively with every male she met, he must have been used to delivering them.

Amused, I fetched Sparking Plug, mounted, and followed all the other horses out of the yard, up the lane, and on to the edge of the moor. As usual on a fine morning the air and the view were exhilarating. The sun was no more than a promise on the far distant horizon and there was a beginning-of-the-world quality in the light. I watched the shadowy shapes of the horses ahead of me curving round the hill with white plumes streaming from their nostrils in the frosty air. As the glittering rim of the sun expanded into full light the colours sprang out bright and clear, the browns of the jogging horses topped with the bright stripes of the lads' ear-warming knitted caps and the jolly October's daughters.

October himself, accompanied by his retriever, came up on to the moor in a Land Rover to see the horses work. Saturday morning, I had found, was the busiest training day of the week as far as gallops were concerned, and as he was usually in Yorkshire at the week-end he made a point of coming out to watch.

Inskip had us circling round at the top of the hill while he paired off the horses and told their riders what to do.

To me he said, 'Dan; three-quarter speed gallop. Your horse is running on Wednesday. Don't over-do him but we want to see how he goes.' He directed one of the stable's most distinguished animals to accompany me.

When he had finished giving his orders he cantered off along the broad sweep of green turf which stretched through the moorland scrub, and October drove slowly in his wake. We continued circling until the two men reached the other end of the gallops about a mile and a half away up the gently curved, gently rising track.

'O.K.' said Wally to the first pair. 'Off you go.'

The two horses set off together, fairly steadily at first and then at an increasing pace until they had passed Inskip and October, when they slowed and pulled up.

'Next two,' Wally called.

We were ready, and set off without more ado. I had bred, broken and rebroken uncountable race-horses in Australia, but Sparking Plug was the only good one I had so far ridden in England, and I was interested to see how he compared. Of course he was a hurdler, while I was more used to flat racers, but this made no difference, I found: and he had a bad mouth which I itched to do something about, but there was nothing wrong with his action. Balanced and collected, he sped smoothly up the gallop, keeping pace effortlessly with the star performer beside him, and though, as ordered, we went only three-quarters speed at our fastest, it was quite clear that Sparking Plug was fit and ready for his approaching race.

I was so interested in what I was doing that it was not until I had reined in – not too easy with that mouth – and began to walk back, that I realised I had forgotten all about messing up the way I rode. I groaned inwardly, exasperated with myself: I would never do what I had come to England for if I could so little keep my mind on the job.

I stopped with the horse who had accompanied Sparking Plug in front of October and Inskip, for them to have a look at the horses and see how much they were blowing. Sparking Plug's ribs moved easily: he was scarcely out of breath. The two men nodded, and I and the other lad slid off the horses and began walking them round while they cooled down.

Up from the far end of the gallop came the other horses, pair by pair, and finally a bunch of those who were not due to gallop but only to canter. When everyone had worked, most of the lads remounted and we all began to walk back down the gallop towards the track to the stable. Leading my horse on foot I set off last in the string, with October's eldest daughter riding immediately in front of me and effectively cutting me off from the chat of the lads ahead. She was looking about her at the rolling vistas of moor, and not bothering to keep her animal close on the heels of the one in front, so that by the time we entered the track there was a ten yard gap ahead of her.

As she passed a scrubby gorse bush a bird flew out of it with a squawk and flapping wings, and the girl's horse whipped round and up in alarm. She stayed on with a remarkable effort of balance, pulling herself back up into the saddle from somewhere below the horse's right ear, but under her thrust the stirrup leather broke apart at the bottom, and the stirrup iron itself clanged to the ground.

I stopped and picked up the iron, but it was impossible to put it back on the broken leather.

'Thank you,' she said. 'What a nuisance.'

She slid off her horse. 'I might as well walk the rest of the way.'

I took her rein and began to lead both of the horses, but she stopped me, and took her own back again.

'It's very kind of you,' she said, 'but I can quite well lead him myself.' The track was wide at that point, and she began to walk down the hill beside me.

On closer inspection she was not a bit like her sister Patricia. She had smooth silver blonde hair under a blue head scarf, fair eye lashes, direct grey eyes, a firm friendly mouth, and a composure which gave her an air of graceful reserve. We walked in easy silence for some way.

'Isn't it a gorgeous morning,' she said eventually.

'Gorgeous,' I agreed, 'But cold.' The English always talk about the weather, I thought: and a fine day in November is so rare as to be remarked on. It would be hotting up for summer, at home . . .

'Have you been with the stable long?' she asked, a little further on.

'Only about ten days.'

'And do you like it here?'

'Oh, yes. It's a well run stable . . .'

'Mr. Inskip would be delighted to hear you say so,' she said in a dry voice.

I glanced at her, but she was looking ahead down the track, and smiling.

After another hundred yards she said, 'What horse is that that you were riding? I don't think that I have seen him before, either.'

'He only came on Wednesday . . .' I told her the little I knew about Sparking Plug's history, capabilities and prospects.

She nodded. 'It will be nice for you if he can win some races. Rewarding, after your work for him here.'

'Yes,' I agreed, surprised that she should think like that.

We reached the last stretch to the stable.

'I am so sorry,' she said pleasantly, 'but I don't know your name.'

'Daniel Roke,' I said: and I wondered why to her alone of all the people who had asked me that question in the last ten days it had seemed proper to give a whole answer.

'Thank you,' she paused: then having thought, continued in a calm voice which I realised with wry pleasure was designed to put me at my ease, 'Lord October is my father. I'm Elinor Tarren.'

We had reached the stable gate. I stood back to let her go first, which she acknowledged with a friendly but impersonal smile, and she led her horse away across the yard towards its own box. A thoroughly nice girl, I thought briefly, buckling down to the task of brushing the sweat off Sparking Plug, washing his feet, brushing out his mane and tail, sponging out his eyes and mouth, putting his straw bed straight, fetching his hay and water, and then repeating the whole process with the horse that Patricia had ridden. Patricia, I thought, grinning, was not a nice girl at all.

When I went in to breakfast in the cottage Mrs. Allnut gave me a letter which had just arrived for me. The envelope, postmarked in London the day before, contained a sheet of plain paper with a single sentence typed on it.

'Mr. Stanley will be at Victoria Falls three p.m. Sunday.'

I stuffed the letter into my pocket, laughing into my porridge.

There was a heavy drizzle falling when I walked up beside the stream the following afternoon. I reached the gully before October, and waited for him with the rain drops finding ways to trickle down my neck. He came down the hill with his dog as before, telling me that his car was parked above us on the little used road.

But we'd better talk here, if you can stand the wet,' he finished, 'in case anyone saw us together in the car, and wondered.'

'I can stand the wet,' I assured him, smiling.

'Good . . . well, how have you been getting on?'

I told him how well I thought of Beckett's new horse and the opportunities it would give me.

He nodded, 'Roddy Beckett was famous in the war for the speed and accuracy with which he got supplies moved about. No one ever got the wrong ammunition or all left boots when he was in charge.'

I said 'I've sown a few seeds of doubts about my honesty, here and there, but I'll be able to do more of that this week at Bristol, and also next week-end, at Burndale. I'm going there on Sunday to play in a darts match.'

'They've had several cases of doping in that village in the past,' he said thoughtfully. 'You might get a nibble, there.'

'It would be useful . . .

'Have you found the form books helpful?' he asked, 'have you given those eleven horses any more thought?'

'I've thought of little else,' I said, 'and it seems just possible, perhaps it's only a slight chance, but it does just seem possible that you might be able to make a dope test on the next horse in the sequence *before* he runs in a race. That is to say, always providing that there is going to be another horse in the sequence . . . and I don't see why not, as the people responsible have got away with it for so long.'

He looked at me with some excitement, the rain dripping off the down-turned brim of his hat.

'You've found something?'

'No, not really. It's only a statistical indication. But it's more than even money, I think, that the next horse will win a selling chase at Kelso, Sedgefield, Ludlow, Stafford or Haydock.' I explained my reasons for expecting this, and went on, 'It should be possible to arrange for wholesale saliva samples to be taken before all the selling chases on those particular tracks – it can't be more than one race at each two-day meeting – and they can throw the samples away without going to the expense of testing them if no . . . er . . . joker turns up in the pack.'

'It's a tall order,' he said slowly, 'but I don't see why it shouldn't be done, if it will prove anything.'

'The analysts might find something useful in the results.'

'Yes. And I suppose even if they didn't, it would be a great step forward for us to be able to be on the lookout for a joker, instead of just being mystified when one appeared. Why on earth,' he shook his head in exasperation, 'didn't we think of this months ago? It seems such an obvious way to approach the problem, now that you have done it.'

'I expect it is because I am the first person really to be given all the collected information all at once, and deliberately search for a connecting factor. All the other investigations seemed to have been done from the other end, so to speak, by trying to find out in each case separately who had access to the horse, who fed him, who saddled him, and so on.'

He nodded gloomily.

'There's one other thing,' I said. 'The lab chaps told you that as they couldn't find a dope you should look for something mechanical . . . do you know whether the horses' skins were investigated as closely as the jockeys and their kit? It occurred to me the other evening that I could throw a dart with an absolute certainty of hitting a horse's flank, and any good shot could plant a pellet in the same place. Things like that would sting like a hornet . . . enough to make any horse shift along faster.'

'As far as I know, none of the horses showed any signs of that sort of thing, but I'll make sure. And by the way, I asked the analysts whether horses' bodies could break drugs down into harmless substances, and they said it was impossible.'

'Well, that clears the decks a bit, if nothing else.'

'Yes.' He whistled to his dog, who was quartering the far side of the gully. 'After next week, when you'll be away at Burndale, we had better meet here at this time every Sunday afternoon to discuss progress. You will know if I'm away, because I won't be here for the Saturday gallops. Incidentally, your horsemanship stuck out a mile on Sparking Plug yesterday. And I thought we agreed that you had better not make too good an impression. On top of which,' he added, smiling faintly, 'Inskip says you are a quick and conscientious worker.'

'Heck . . . I'll be getting a good reference if I don't watch out.'

'Too right you will,' he agreed, copying my accent sardonically. 'How do you like being a stable lad?'

'It has its moments . . . Your daughters are very beautiful.'

He grinned, 'Yes: and thank you for helping Elinor. She told me you were most obliging.'

'I did nothing.'

'Patty is a bit of a handful,' he said, reflectively, 'I wish she'd decide what sort of a job she'd like to do. She knows I don't want her to go on as she has during her season, never-ending parties and staying out till dawn . . . well, that's not your worry, Mr. Roke.'

We shook hands as usual, and he trudged off up the hill. It was still drizzling mournfully as I went down.

Sparking Plug duly made the 250 mile journey south to Bristol, and I went with him. The racecourse was some way out of the city, and the horse box driver told me, when we stopped for a meal on the way, that the whole of the stable block had been newly rebuilt there after fire had gutted it.

Certainly the loose boxes were clean and snug, but it was the new sleeping quarters that the lads were in ecstasies about. The hostel was a surprise to me too. It consisted mainly of a creation room and two long dormitories with about thirty beds in each, made up with clean sheets and fluffy blue blankets. There was a wall light over each bed, polyvinyl tiled flooring, under-floor heating, modern showers in the washroom and a hot room for drying wet clothes. The whole place was warm and light, with colour schemes which were clearly the work of a professional.

'Ye gods, we're in the ruddy Hilton,' said one cheerful boy, coming to a halt beside me just through the dormitory door and slinging his canvas grip on to an unoccupied bed.

'You haven't seen the half of it,' said a bony long-wristed boy in a shrunken blue jersey, 'up that end of the passage there's a ruddy great canteen with decent chairs and a telly and a ping pong table and all.'

Other voices joined in.

'It's as good as Newbury.'

'Easily.'

'Better than Ascot, I'd say.'

Heads nodded.

'They have bunk beds at Ascot, not singles, like this.'

The hostels at Newbury and Ascot were, it appeared, the most comfortable in the country.

'Anyone would think the bosses had suddenly cottoned on to the fact that we're human,' said a sharp faced lad, in a belligerent, rabble-raising voice.

'It's a far cry from the bug-ridden doss houses of the old days,' nodded a desiccated, elderly little man with a face like a shrunken apple. 'But a fellow told me the lads have it good like this in America all the time.'

'They know if they don't start treating us decent they soon won't get anyone to do the dirty work,' said the rabble-raiser. 'Things are changing.'

'They treat us decent enough where I come from,' I said, putting my things on an empty bed next to his and nerving myself to be natural, casual, unremarkable. I felt much more self-conscious than I had at Slaw, where at least I knew the job inside out and had been able to feel my way cautiously into a normal relationship with the other lads. But here I had only two nights, and if I were to do any good at all I had got to direct the talk towards what I wanted to hear.

The form books were by now as clear to me as a primer, and for a fortnight I had listened acutely and concentrated on soaking in as much racing jargon as I could, but I was still doubtful whether I would understand everything I heard at Bristol and also afraid that I would make some utterly incongruous impossible mistake in what I said myself.

'And where do you come from?' asked the cheerful boy, giving me a cursory looking over.

'Lord October's,' I said.

'Oh yes, Inskip's, you mean? You're a long way from home . . .'

'Inskip's may be all right,' said the rabble-raiser, as if he regretted it. 'But there are some places where they still treat us like mats to wipe their feet on, and don't reckon that we've got a right to a bit of sun, same as everyone else.'

'Yeah,' said the raw-boned boy seriously. 'I heard that at one place they practically starve the lads and knock them about if they don't work hard enough, and they all have to do about four or five horses each because they can't keep anyone in the yard for more than five minutes!'

I said idly 'Where's that, just so I know where to avoid, if I ever move on from Inskip's?'

'Up your part of the country . . .' he said doubtfully. 'I think.'

'No, further north, in Durham . . .' another boy chimed in, a slender, pretty boy with soft down still growing on his cheeks.

'You know about it too, then?'

He nodded. 'Not that it matters, only a raving nit would take a job there. It's a blooming sweat shop, a hundred years out of date. All they get are riff-raff that no one else will have.'

'It wants exposing,' said the rabble-raiser belligerently. 'Who runs this place?'

'Bloke called Humber,' said the pretty boy, 'he couldn't train ivy up a wall ... and he has about as many winners as tits on a billiard ball ... You see his head travelling lad at the meetings sometimes, trying to pressgang people to go and work there, and getting the brush off, right and proper.'

'Someone ought to do something,' said the rabble-raiser automatically: and I guessed that this was his usual refrain: 'someone ought to do something'; but not, when it came to the point, himself.

There was a general drift into the canteen, where the food proved to be good, unlimited, and free. A proposal to move on to a pub came to nothing when it was discovered both that the nearest was nearly two (busless) miles away and that the bright warm canteen had some crates of beer under its counter.

It was easy enough to get the lads started on the subject of doping, and they seemed prepared to discuss it endlessly. None of the twenty odd there had ever, as far as they would admit, given 'anything' to a horse, but they all knew someone who knew someone who had. I drank my beer and listened and looked interested, which I was.

'. . . nobbled him with a squirt of acid as he walked out of the bleeding paddock . . .'

'. . . gave it such a whacking dollop of stopping powder that it died in its box in the morning . . .'

'Seven rubber bands came out in the droppings . . .'

'. . . Overdosed him so much that he never even tried to jump the first fence: blind, he was, stone blind . . .'

'. . . gave him a bloody great bucket full of water half an hour before the race, and didn't need any dope to stop him with all that sloshing about inside his gut.'

'Poured half a bottle of whisky down his throat.'

'. . . used to tube horses which couldn't breathe properly on the morning of the race until they found it wasn't the extra fresh air that was making the horses win but the cocaine they stuffed them full of for the operation . . .'

'They caught him with a hollow apple packed with sleeping pills . . .'

'. . . dropped a syringe right in front of an effing steward.'

'I wonder if there's anything which hasn't been tried yet?' I said.

'Black magic. Not much else left,' said the pretty boy.

They all laughed.

'Someone might find something so good,' I pointed out casually, 'that it couldn't be detected, so the people who thought of it could go on with it for ever and never be found out.'

'Blimey,' exclaimed the cheerful lad, 'you're a comfort, aren't you? God help racing, if that happened. You'd never know where you were. The bookies would all be climbing the walls.' He grinned hugely.

The elderly little man was not so amused.

'It's been going on for years and years,' he said, nodding solemnly.

'Some trainers have got it to a fine art, you mark my words. Some trainers have been doping their horses regular, for years and years.'

But the other lads didn't agree. The dope tests had done for the dope-minded trainers of the past; they had lost their licences, and gone out of racing. The old rule had been a bit unfair on some, they allowed, when a trainer had been automatically disqualified if one of his horses had been doped. It wasn't always the trainer's fault, especially if the horse had been doped to lose. What trainer, they asked, would nobble a horse he'd spent months training to win? But they thought there was probably *more* doping since that rule was changed, not less.

'Stands to reason, a doper knows now he isn't ruining the trainer for life, just one horse for one race. Makes it sort of easier on his conscience, see? More lads, maybe, would take fifty quid for popping the odd aspirin into the feed if they knew the stable wouldn't be shut down and their jobs gone for a burton very soon afterwards.

They talked on, thoughtful and ribald; but it was clear that they didn't know anything about the eleven horses I was concerned with. None of them, I knew, came from any of the stables involved, and obviously they had not read the speculative reports in the papers, or if they had, had read them separately over a period of eighteen months, and not in one solid, collected, intense bunch, as I had done.

The talk faltered and died into yawns, and we went chatting to bed, I sighing to myself with relief that I had gone through the evening without much notice having been taken of me.

By watching carefully what the other lads did, I survived the next day also without any curious stares. In the early afternoon I took Sparking Plug from the stables into the paddock, walked him round the parade ring, stood holding his head while he was saddled, led him round the parade ring again, held him while the jockey mounted, led him out on to the course, and went up into the little stand by the gate with the other lads to watch the race.

Sparking Plug won. I was delighted. I met him again at the gate and led him into the spacious winner's unsaddling enclosure.

Colonel Beckett was there, waiting, leaning on a stick. He patted the horse, congratulated the jockey, who unbuckled his saddle and departed into the weighing room, and said to me sardonically, 'That's a fraction of his purchase price back, anyway.'

'He's a good horse, and absolutely perfect for his purpose.'

'Good. Do you need anything else?'

'Yes. A lot more details about those eleven horses . . . where they were bred, what they ate, whether they had had any illnesses, what cafés their box drivers used, who made their bridles, whether they had racing plates fitted at the meetings, and by which blacksmiths . . . anything and everything.'

'Are you serious?'

'Yes.'

'But they had nothing in common except that they were doped.'

'As I see it, the question really is what was it that they had in common that made it *possible* for them to be doped.' I smoothed Sparking Plug's nose. He was restive and excited after his victory. Colonel Beckett looked at me with sober eyes.

'Mr. Roke, you shall have your information.'

I grinned at him. 'Thank you; and I'll take good care of Sparking Plug ... he'll win you all the purchase price, before he's finished.'

'Horses away,' called an official: and with a weak-looking gesture of farewell from Colonel Beckett's limp hand, I took Sparking Plug back to the racecourse stables and walked him round until he had cooled off.

There were far more lads in the hostel that evening as it was the middle night of the two-day meeting, and this time, besides getting the talk round again to doping and listening attentively to everything that was said, I also tried to give the impression that I didn't think taking fifty quid to point out a certain horse's box in his home stable to anyone prepared to pay that much for the information was a proposition I could be relied on to turn down. I earned a good few disapproving looks for this, and also one sharply interested glance from a very short lad whose outsize nose sniffed monotonously.

In the washroom in the morning he used the basin next to me, and said out of the side of his mouth, 'Did you mean it, last night, that you'd take fifty quid to point out a box?'

I shrugged. 'I don't see why not.'

He looked round furtively. It made me want to laugh. 'I might be able to put you in touch with someone who'd be interested to hear that – for fifty per cent cut.'

'You've got another think coming,' I said offensively. 'Fifty per cent ... what the hell do you think I am?'

'Well ... a fiver, then,' he sniffed, climbing down.

'I dunno ...'

'I can't say fairer than that,' he muttered.

'It's a wicked thing, to point out a box,' I said virtuously, drying my face on a towel.

He stared at me in astonishment.

'And I couldn't do it for less than sixty, if you are taking a fiver out of it.'

He didn't know whether to laugh or spit. I left him to his indecision, and went off grinning to escort Sparking Plug back to Yorkshire.

Chapter Five

Again on Friday evening I went down to the Slaw pub and exchanged bug-eyed looks with Soupy across the room.

On the Sunday half the lads had the afternoon off to go to Burndale for the football and darts matches, and we won both, which made for a certain amount of back slapping and beer drinking. But beyond remarking that I was new, and a blight on their chances in the darts league, the Burndale lads paid me little attention. There was no one like Soupy among them in spite of what October had said about the cases of doping in the village, and no one, as far as I could see, who cared if I were as crooked as a cork-screw.

During the next week I did my three horses, and read the form books, and thought: and got nowhere. Paddy remained cool and so did Wally, to whom Paddy had obviously reported my affinity with Soupy. Wally showed his disapproval by giving me more than my share of the afternoon jobs, so that every day, instead of relaxing in the usual free time between lunch and evening stables at four o'clock, I found myself bidden to sweep the yard, clean the tack, crush the oats, cut the chaff, wash Inskip's car or clean the windows of the loose boxes. I did it all without comment, reflecting that if I needed an excuse for a quick row and walked out later on I could reasonably, at eleven hours a day, complain of overwork.

However, at Friday midday I set off again with Sparking Plug, this time to Cheltenham, and this time accompanied not only by the box driver but by Grits and his horse, and the head travelling lad as well.

Once in the racecourse stables I learned that this was the night of the dinner given to the previous season's champion jockey, and all the lads who were staying there overnight proposed to celebrate by attending a dance in the town. Grits and I, therefore, having bedded down our horses, eaten our meal, and smartened ourselves up, caught a bus down the hill and paid our entrance money to the hop. It was a big hall and the band was loud and hot, but not many people were yet dancing. The girls were standing about in little groups eyeing larger groups of young men, and I bit back just in time a remark on how odd I found it; Grits would expect me to think it normal. I took him off into the bar where there were already groups of lads from the racecourse mingled with the local inhabitants, and bought him a beer, regretting that he was with me to see what use I intended to make of the evening. Poor Grits, he was torn between loyalty to Paddy and an apparent liking for me, and I was about to disillusion him thoroughly. I wished I could explain. I was tempted to spend the evening harmlessly. But how could I justify passing over an unrepeatable opportunity just to keep temporarily the regard of one slow-witted stable lad, however much I might like him? I was committed to earning ten thousand pounds.

'Grits, go and find a girl to dance with.'

He gave me a slow grin. 'I don't know any.'

'It doesn't matter. Any of them would be glad to dance with a nice chap like you. Go and ask one.'

'No. I'd rather stay with you.'

'All right, then. Have another drink.'

'I haven't finished this.'

I turned round to the bar, which we had been leaning against, and banged my barely touched half pint down on the counter. 'I'm fed up with this pap,' I said violently. 'Hey, you, barman, give me a double whisky.'

'Dan!' Grits was upset at my tone, which was a measure of its success. The barman poured the whisky and took my money.

'Don't go away,' I said to him in a loud voice. 'Give me another while you're at it.'

I felt rather than saw the group of lads further up the bar turn round and take a look, so I picked up the glass and swallowed all the whisky in two gulps and wiped my mouth on the back of my hand. I pushed the empty glass across to the barman and paid for the second drink.

'Dan,' Grits tugged my sleeve, 'do you think you should?'

'Yes,' I said, scowling. 'Go and find a girl to dance with.'

But he didn't go. He watched me drink the second whisky and order a third. His eyes were troubled.

The bunch of lads edged towards us along the bar.

'Hey, fella, you're knocking it back a bit,' observed one, a tallish man of my own age in a flashy bright blue suit.

'Mind your own ruddy business,' I said rudely.

'Aren't you from Inskip's?' he asked.

'Yea . . . Inskip's . . . bloody Inskip's . . .' I picked up the third glass. I had a hard head for whisky, which was going down on top of a deliberately heavy meal. I reckoned I could stay sober a long time after I would be expected to be drunk; but the act had to be put on early, while the audience were still sober enough themselves to remember it clearly afterwards.

'Eleven sodding quid,' I told them savagely, 'that's all you get for sweating your guts out seven days a week.'

It struck a note with some of them, but Blue-suit said, 'Then why spend it on whisky?'

'Why bloody not? It's great stuff – gives you a kick. And, by God, you need something in this job.'

Blue-suit said to Grits, 'Your mate's got an outsized gripe.'

'Well . . .' said Grits, his face anxious, 'I suppose he has had a lot of extra jobs this week, come to think . . .'

'You're looking after horses they pay thousands for and you know damn well that the way you ride and groom them and look after them makes a hell of a lot of difference to whether they win or not, and they grudge you a decent wage . . .' I finished the third whisky, hiccupped and said, 'It's bloody unfair.'

The bar was filling up, and from the sight of them and from what I could catch of their greetings to each other, at least half the customers were in some way connected with racing. Bookmakers' clerks and touts as well as stable lads – the town was stuffed with them, and the dance had been put on to attract them. A large amount of liquor began disappearing down their collective throats, and I had to catch the barman on the wing to serve my fourth double whisky in fifteen minutes.

I stood facing a widening circle with the glass in my hand, and rocked slightly on my feet.

'I want,' I began. What on earth did I want? I searched for the right phrases. 'I want . . . a motor-bike. I want to show a bird a good time. And go abroad for a holiday . . . and stay in a swank hotel and have them running about at my beck and call ... and drink what I like ... and maybe one day put a deposit on a house ... and what chance do I have of any of these? I'll tell you. Not a snowball's hope in hell. You know what I got in my pay packet this morning ... ? Seven pounds and fourpence ...'

I went on and on grousing and complaining, and the evening wore slowly away. The audience drifted and changed, and I kept it up until I was fairly sure that all the racing people there knew there was a lad of Inskip's who yearned for more money, preferably in large amounts. But even Grits, who hovered about with an unhappy air throughout it all and remained cold sober himself, didn't seem to notice that I got progressively drunker in my actions while making each drink last longer than the one before.

Eventually, after I had achieved an artistic lurch and clutch at one of the pillars, Grits said loudly in my ear, 'Dan, I'm going now and you'd better go too, or you'll miss the last bus, and I shouldn't think you could walk back, like you are.'

'Huh?' I squinted at him. Blue-suit had come back and was standing just behind him.

'Want any help getting him out?' he asked Grits.

Grits looked at me disgustedly, and I fell against him, putting my arm round his shoulders: I definitely did not want the sort of help Blue-suit looked as though he might give.

'Grits, me old pal, if you say go, we go.'

We set off for the door, followed by Blue-suit, me staggering so heavily that I pushed Grits sideways. There were by this time a lot of others having difficulty in walking a straight line, and the queue of lads which waited at the bus stop undulated slightly like an ocean swell on a calm day. I grinned in the safe darkness and looked up at the sky, and thought that if the seeds I had sown in all directions bore no fruit there was little doping going on in British racing.

I may not have been drunk, but I woke the next morning with a shattering headache, just the same: all in a good cause, I thought, trying to ignore the blacksmith behind my eyes.

Sparking Plug ran in his race and lost by half a length. I took the opportunity of saying aloud on the lads' stand that there was the rest of my week's pay gone down the bloody drain.

Colonel Beckett patted his horse's neck in the cramped unsaddling enclosure and said casually to me, 'Better luck next time, eh? I've sent you what you wanted, in a parcel.' He turned away and resumed talking to Inskip and his jockey about the race.

We all went back to Yorkshire that night, with Grits and me sleeping most of the way on the benches in the back of the horse box.

He said reproachfully as he lay down, 'I didn't know you hated it at Inskip's ... and I haven't seen you drunk before either.'

'It isn't the work, Grits, it's the pay.' I had to keep it up.

'Still there are some who are married and have kids to keep on what you were bleating about.' He sounded disapproving, and indeed my behaviour must have affected him deeply, because he seldom spoke to me after that night.

There was nothing of interest to report to October the following afternoon, and our meeting in the gully was brief. He told me however that the information then in the post from Beckett had been collected by eleven keen young officer cadets from Aldershot who had been given the task as an initiative exercise, and told they were in competition with each other to see which of them could produce the most comprehensive report of the life of his allotted horse. A certain number of questions – those I had suggested – were outlined for them. The rest had been left to their own imagination and detective ability, and October said Beckett had told him they had used them to the full.

I returned down the hill more impressed than ever with the Colonel's staff work, but not as staggered as when the parcel arrived the following day. Wally again found some wretched job for me to do in the afternoon, so that it was not until after the evening meal, when half the lads had gone down to Slaw, that I had an opportunity of taking the package up to the dormitory and opening it. It contained 237 numbered typewritten pages bound into a cardboard folder, like the manuscript of a book, and its production in the space of one week must have meant a prodigious effort not only from the young men themselves, but from the typists as well. The information was given in note form for the most part, and no space had anywhere been wasted in flowing prose: it was solid detail from cover to cover.

Mrs. Allnut's voice floated up the stairs. 'Dan, come down and fetch me a bucket of coal, will you please?'

I thrust the typescript down inside my bed between the sheets, and went back to the warm, communal kitchen-living-room where we ate and spent most of our spare time. It was impossible to read anything private there, and my life was very much supervised from dawn to bedtime; and the only place I could think of where I could concentrate uninterruptedly on the typescript was the bathroom. Accordingly that night I waited until all the lads were asleep, and then went along the passage and locked myself in, ready to report an upset stomach if anyone should be curious.

It was slow going: after four hours I had read only half. I got up stiffly, stretched, yawned, and went back to bed. Nobody stirred. The following night, as I lay waiting for the others to go to sleep so that I could get back to my task, I listened to them discussing the evening that four of them had spent in Slaw.

'Who's that fellow who was with Soupy?' asked Grits. 'I haven't seen him around before.'

'He was there last night too,' said one of the others 'Queer sort of bloke.'

'What was queer about him?' asked the boy who had stayed behind, he watching the television while I in an arm-chair caught up on some sleep.

'I dunno,' said Grits. 'His eyes didn't stay still, like.'

'Sort as if he was looking for someone,' added another voice.

Paddy said firmly from the wall on my right, 'You just all keep clear of that chap, and Soupy too. I'm telling you. People like them are no good.'

'But that chap, that one with that smashing gold tie, he bought us a round, you know he did. He can't be too bad if he bought us a round . . .'

Paddy sighed with exasperation that anyone could be so simple. 'If you'd have been Eve, you'd have eaten the apple as soon as look at it. You wouldn't have needed a serpent.'

'Oh well,' yawned Grits. 'I don't suppose he'll be there tomorrow. I heard him say something to Soupy about time getting short.'

They muttered and murmured and went to sleep, and I lay awake in the dark thinking that perhaps I had just heard something very interesting indeed. Certainly a trip down to the pub was indicated for the following evening.

With a wrench I stopped my eyes from shutting, got out of my warm bed, repaired again to the bathroom, and read for another four hours until I had finished the typescript. I sat on the bathroom floor with my back against the wall and stared sightlessly at the fixtures and fittings. There was nothing, not one single factor, that occurred in the life histories of all of the eleven microscopically investigated horses. No common denominator at all. There were quite a few things which were common to four or five – but not often the same four or five – like the make of saddle their jockeys used, the horse cube nuts they were fed with, or the auction rings they had been sold in: but the hopes I had had of finding a sizeable clue in those packages had altogether evaporated. Cold, stiff, and depressed, I crept back to bed.

The next evening at eight I walked alone down to Slaw, all the other lads saying they were skint until pay-day and that in any case they wanted to watch Z Cars on television.

'I thought you lost all your cash on Sparks at Cheltenham,' observed Grits.

'I've about two bob left,' I said, producing some pennies. 'Enough for a pint.'

The pub, as often on Wednesdays, was empty. There was no sign of Soupy or his mysterious friend, and having bought some beer I amused myself at the dart board, throwing one-to-twenty sequences, and trying to make a complete ring in the trebles. Eventually I pulled the darts out of the board, looked at my watch, and decided I had wasted the walk; and it was at that moment that a man appeared in the doorway, not from the street, but from the saloon bar next door. He held a glass of gently fizzing amber liquid and a slim cigar in his left hand and pushed open the door with his right. Looking me up and down, he said, 'Are you a stable lad?'

'Yes.'

'Granger's or Inskip's?'

'Inskip's.'

'Hmm.' He came further into the room and let the door swing shut behind him. 'There's ten bob for you if you can get one of your lads down here tomorrow night . . . and as much beer as you can both drink.'

I looked interested. 'Which lad?' I asked. 'Any special one? Lots of them will be down here on Friday.'

'Well, now, it had better be tomorrow, I think. Sooner the better, I always say. And as for which lad . . . er . . . you tell me their names and I'll pick one of them . . . how's that?'

I thought it was damn stupid, and also that he wished to avoid asking too directly, too memorably for . . . well . . . for me?

'O.K. Paddy, Grits, Wally, Steve, Ron . . .' I paused.

'Go on,' he said.

'Reg, Norman, Dave, Jeff, Dan, Mike . . .'

His eyes brightened. 'Dan,' he said. 'That's a sensible sort of name. Bring Dan.'

'I am Dan,' I said.

There was an instant in which his balding scalp contracted and his eyes narrowed in annoyance.

'Stop playing games,' he said sharply.

'It was you,' I pointed out gently, 'who began it.'

He sat down on one of the benches and carefully put his drink down on the table in front of him.

'Why did you come here tonight, alone?' he asked.

'I was thirsty.'

There was a brief silence while he mentally drew up a plan of campaign. He was a short stocky man in a dark suit a size too small, the jacket hanging open to reveal a monogrammed cream shirt and golden silk tie. His fingers were fat and short, and a roll of flesh overhung his coat collar at the back, but there was nothing soft in the way he looked at me.

At length he said, 'I believe there is a horse in your stable called Sparking Plug?'

'Yes.'

'And he runs at Leicester on Monday?'

'As far as I know.'

'What do you think his chances are?' he asked.

'Look, do you want a tip, mister, is that what it is? Well, I do Sparking Plug myself and I'm telling you there isn't an animal in next Monday's race to touch him.'

'So you expect him to win?'

'Yes, I told you.'

'And you'll bet on him I suppose.'

'Of course.'

'With half your pay? Four pounds, perhaps?'

'Maybe.'

'But he'll be favourite. Sure to be. And at best you'll probably only get even money. Another four quid. That doesn't sound much, does it, when I could perhaps put you in the way of winning . . . a hundred?'

'You're barmy,' I said, but with a sideways leer that told him that I wanted to hear more.

He leaned forward with confidence. 'Now you can say no if you want to. You can say no, and I'll go away, and no one will be any the wiser, but if you play your cards right I could do you a good turn.'

'What would I have to do for a hundred quid?' I asked flatly.

He looked round cautiously, and lowered his voice still further. 'Just add a little something to Sparking Plug's feed on Sunday night. Nothing to it, you see? Dead easy.'

'Dead easy,' I repeated: and so it was.

'You're on, then?' he looked eager.

'I don't know your name,' I said.

'Never you mind.' He shook his head with finality.

'Are you a bookmaker?'

'No,' he said. 'I'm not. And that's enough with the questions. Are you on?'

'If you're not a bookmaker,' I said slowly, thinking my way, 'and you are willing to pay a hundred pounds to make sure a certain favourite doesn't win, I'd guess that you didn't want just to make money backing all the other runners, but that you intend to tip off a few bookmakers that the race is fixed, and they'll be so grateful they'll pay you say, fifty quid each, at the very least. There are about eleven thousand bookmakers in Britain. A nice big market. But I expect you go to the same ones over and over again. Sure of your welcome, I should think.'

His face was a study of consternation and disbelief, and I realized I had hit the target, bang on.

'Who told you . . .' he began weakly.

'I wasn't born yesterday,' I said with a nasty grin. 'Relax. No one told me.' I paused. 'I'll give Sparking Plug his extra nosh, but I want more for it. Two hundred.'

'No. The deal's off.' He mopped his forehead.

'All right.' I shrugged.

'A hundred and fifty then,' he said grudgingly.

'A hundred and fifty,' I agreed. 'Before I do it.'

'Half before, half after,' he said automatically. It was by no means the first time he had done this sort of deal.

I agreed to that. He said if I came down to the pub on Saturday evening I would be given a packet for Sparking Plug and seventy-five pounds for myself, and I nodded and went away, leaving him staring moodily into his glass.

On my way back up the hill I crossed Soupy off my list of potentially useful contacts. Certainly he had procured me for a doping job, but I had been asked to stop a favourite in a novice 'chase, not to accelerate a dim long priced selling plater. It was extremely unlikely that both types of fraud were the work of one set of people.

Unwilling to abandon Colonel Beckett's typescript I spent chunks of that night and the following two nights in the bathroom, carefully rereading it. The only noticeable result was that during the day I found the endless stable work irksome because for five nights in a row I had had only three hours' sleep. But I frankly dreaded having to tell October on Sunday that the eleven young men had made their mammoth investigation to no avail, and I had an unreasonable feeling that if I hammered away long enough I could still wring some useful message from those densely packed pages.

On Saturday morning, though it was bleak, bitter and windy, October's daughters rode out with the first string. Elinor only came near enough to exchange polite good mornings, but Patty, who was again riding one of my horses, made my giving her a leg up a moment of eyelash-fluttering intimacy, deliberately and unnecessarily rubbing her body against mine.

'You weren't here last week, Danny boy,' she said, putting her feet in the irons. 'Where were you?'

'At Cheltenham . . . miss.'

'Oh. And next Saturday?'

'I'll be here.'

She said, with intentional insolence, 'Then kindly remember next Saturday to shorten the leathers on the saddle before I mount. These are far too long.'

She made no move to shorten them herself, but gestured for me to do it for her. She watched me steadily, enjoying herself. While I was fastening the second buckle she rubbed her knee forwards over my hands and kicked me none too gently in the ribs.

'I wonder you stand me teasing you, Danny boy,' she said softly, bending down, 'a dishy guy like you should answer back more. Why don't you?'

'I don't want the sack,' I said, with a dead straight face.

'A coward, too,' she said sardonically, and twitched her horse away.

And she'll get into bad trouble one day, if she keeps on like that, I thought. She was too provocative. Stunningly pretty of course, but that was only the beginning; and her hurtful little tricks were merely annoying. It was the latent invitation which disturbed and aroused.

I shrugged her out of my mind, fetched Sparking Plug, sprang up on to his back and moved out of the yard and up to the moor for the routine working gallops.

The weather that day got steadily worse until while we were out with the second string it began to rain heavily in fierce slashing gusts, and we struggled miserably back against it with stinging faces and sodden clothes. Perhaps because it went on raining, or possibly because it was, after all, Saturday, Wally for once refrained from making me work all afternoon, and I spent the three hours sitting with about nine other lads in the kitchen of the cottage, listening to the wind shrieking round the corners outside and watching Chepstow races on television, while our damp jerseys, breeches and socks steamed gently round the fire.

I put the previous season's form book on the kitchen table and sat over it with my head propped on the knuckles of my left hand, idly turning the pages with my right. Depressed by my utter lack of success with the eleven horses' dossiers, by the antipathy I had to arouse in the lads, and also, I think, by the absence of the hot sunshine I usually lived in at that time of the year, I began to feel that the whole masquerade had been from the start a ghastly mistake. And the trouble was that having taken

October's money I couldn't back out; not for months. This thought depressed me further still. I sat slumped in unrelieved gloom, wasting my much needed free time.

I think now that it must have been the sense that I was failing in what I had set out to do, more than mere tiredness, which beset me that afternoon, because although later on I encountered worse things it was only for that short while that I ever truly regretted having listened to October, and unreservedly wished myself back in my comfortable Australian cage.

The lads watching the television were making disparaging remarks about the jockeys and striking private bets against each other on the outcome of the races.

'The uphill finish will sort 'em out as usual,' Paddy was saying. 'It's a long way from the last . . . Aladin's the only one who's got the stamina for the job.'

'No,' contradicted Grits. 'Lobster Cocktail's a flyer . . .'

Morosely I riffled the pages of the form book, aimlessly looking through them for the hundredth time, and came by chance on the map of Chepstow racecourse in the general information section at the beginning of the book. There were diagrammatic maps of all the main courses showing the shape of the tracks and the positioning of fences, stands, starting gates and winning posts, and I had looked before at those for Ludlow, Stafford and Haydock, without results. There was no map of Kelso or Sedgefield. Next to the map section were a few pages of information about the courses, the lengths of their circuits, the names and addresses of the officials, the record times for the races, and so on.

For something to do, I turned to Chepstow's paragraph. Paddy's 'long way from the last', was detailed there: two hundred and fifty yards. I looked up Kelso, Sedgefield, Ludlow, Stafford and Haydock. They had much longer run-ins than Chepstow. I looked up the run-ins of all the courses in the book. The Aintree Grand National run-in was the second longest. The longest of all was Sedgefield, and in third, fourth, fifth, and sixth positions came Ludlow, Haydock, Kelso and Stafford. All had run-ins of over four hundred yards.

Geography had nothing to do with it: those five courses had almost certainly been chosen by the dopers because in each case it was about a quarter of a mile from the last fence to the winning post.

It was an advance, even if a small one, to have made at least some pattern out of the chaos. In a slightly less abysmal frame of mind I shut the form book and at four o'clock followed the other lads out into the unwelcome rain-swept yard to spend an hour with each of my three charges, grooming them thoroughly to give their coats a clean healthy shine, tossing and tidying their straw beds, fetching their water, holding their heads while Inskip walked round, rugging them up comfortably for the night, and finally fetching their evening feed. As usual it was seven before we had all finished, and eight before we had eaten and changed and were bumping down the hill to Slaw, seven of us sardined into a rickety old Austin.

Bar billiards, darts, dominoes, the endless friendly bragging, the ingredients as before. Patiently, I sat and waited. It was nearly ten, the hour when the lads began to empty their glasses and think about having to get up the next morning, when Soupy strolled across the room towards the door, and, seeing my eyes on him, jerked his head for me to follow him. I got up and went out after him, and found him in the lavatories.

'This is for you. The rest on Tuesday,' he said economically; and treating me to a curled lip and stony stare to impress me with his toughness, he handed me a thick brown envelope. I put it in the inside pocket of my black leather jacket, and nodded to him. Still without speaking, without smiling, hard-eyed to match, I turned on my heel and went back into the bar: and after a while, casually, he followed.

So I crammed into the Austin and was driven up the hill, back to bed in the little dormitory, with seventy five pounds and a packet of white powder sitting snugly over my heart.

Chapter Six

October dipped his finger in the powder and tasted it.

'I don't know what it is either,' he said, shaking his head. 'I'll get it analysed.'

I bent down and patted his dog, and fondled its ears.

He said 'You do realise what a risk you'll be running if you take his money and don't give the dope to the horse?'

I grinned up at him.

'It's no laughing matter,' he said seriously. 'They can be pretty free with their boots, these people, and it would be no help to us if you get your ribs kicked in . . .'

'Actually,' I said, straightening up, 'I do think it might be best if Sparking Plug didn't win . . . I could hardly hope to attract custom from the dopers we are really after if they heard I had double-crossed anyone before.'

'You're quite right.' He sounded relieved. 'Sparking Plug must lose; but Inskip . . . how on earth can I tell him that the jockey must pull back?'

'You can't,' I said. 'You don't want them getting into trouble. But it won't matter much if I do. The horse won't win if I keep him thirsty tomorrow morning and give him a bucketful of water just before the race.'

He looked at me with amusement. 'I see you've learned a thing or two.'

'It'd make your hair stand on end, what I've learned.'

He smiled back. 'All right then. I suppose it's the only thing to do. I wonder what the National Hunt Committee would think of a Steward conspiring with one of his own stable lads to stop a favourite?' He laughed. 'I'll tell Roddy Beckett what to expect . . . though it won't be so funny for Inskip, nor for the lads here, if they back the horse, nor for the general public, who'll lose their money.'

'No,' I agreed.

He folded the packet of white powder and tucked it back into the envelope with the money. The seventy-five pounds had foolishly been paid in a bundle of new fivers with consecutive numbers: and we had agreed that October would take them and try to discover to whom they had been issued.

I told him about the long run-ins on all of the courses where the eleven horses had won.

'It almost sounds as if they might have been using vitamins after all,' he said thoughtfully. 'You can't detect them in dope tests because technically they are not dope at all, but food. The whole question of vitamins is very difficult.'

'They increase stamina?' I asked.

'Yes, quite considerably. Horses which "die" in the last half mile – and as you pointed out, all eleven are that type – would be ideal subjects. But vitamins were among the first things we considered, and we had to eliminate them. They can help horses to win, if they are injected in massive doses into the bloodstream, and they are undetectable in analysis because they are used up in the winning, but they are undetectable in other ways too. They don't excite, they don't bring a horse back from a race looking as though benzedrine were coming out of his ears.' He sighed. 'I don't know . . .'

With regret I made my confession that I had learned nothing from Beckett's typescript.

'Neither Beckett nor I expected as much from it as you did,' he said. 'I've been talking to him a lot this week, and we think that although all those extensive inquiries were made at the time, you might find something that was overlooked if you moved to one of the stables where those eleven horses were trained when they were doped. Of course, eight of the horses were sold and have changed stables, which is a pity, but three are still with their original trainers, and it might be best if you could get a job with one of those.'

'Yes,' I said. 'All right. I'll try all three trainers and see if one of them will take me on. But the trail is very cold by now . . . and joker number twelve will turn up in a different stable altogether. There was nothing, I suppose, at Haydock this week?'

'No. Saliva samples were taken from all the runners before the selling chase, but the favourite won, quite normally, and we didn't have the samples analysed. But now that you've spotted that those five courses must have been chosen deliberately for their long finishing straights we will keep stricter watches there than ever. Especially if one of those eleven horses runs there again.'

'You could check with the racing calendar to see if any has been entered,' I agreed. 'But so far none of them has been doped twice, and I can't see why the pattern should change.'

A gust of bitter wind blew down the gully, and he shivered. The little stream, swollen with yesterday's rains, tumbled busily over its rocky bed. October whistled to his dog, who was sniffing along its banks.

'By the way,' he said, shaking hands, 'the vets are of the opinion that the horses were not helped on their way by pellets or darts, or anything shot or thrown. But they can't be a hundred per cent certain. They didn't at the time examine all the horses very closely. But if we get another one I'll see they go over every inch looking for punctures.'

'Fine.' We smiled at each other and turned away. I liked him. He was imaginative and had a sense of humour to leaven the formidable big-business-executive power of his speech and manner. A tough man, I thought appreciatively: tough in mind, muscular in body, unswerving in purpose: a man of the kind to have earned an earldom, if he hadn't inherited it.

Sparking Plug had to do without his bucket of water that night and again the following morning. The box driver set off to Leicester with a pocketful of hard-earned money from the lads and their instructions to back the horse to win; and I felt a traitor.

Inskip's other horse, which had come in the box too, was engaged in the third race, but the novice 'chase was not until the fifth race on the card, which left me free to watch the first two races as well as Sparks' own. I bought a race card and found a space on the parade ring rails, and watched the horses for the first race being led round. Although from the form books I knew the names of a great many trainers they were still unknown to me by sight; and accordingly, when they stood chatting with their jockeys in the ring, I tried, for interest, to identify some of them. There were only seven of them engaged in the first race, Owen, Cundell, Beeby, Cazalet, Humber . . . Humber? What was it that I had heard about Humber? I couldn't remember. Nothing very important, I thought.

Humber's horse looked the least well of the lot, and the lad leading him round wore unpolished shoes, a dirty rain-coat and an air of not caring to improve matters. The jockey's jersey, when he took his coat off, could be seen to be still grubby with mud from a former outing, and the trainer who had failed to provide clean colours or to care about stable smartness, was a large, bad-tempered looking man leaning on a thick, knobbed walking stick.

As it happened, Humber's lad stood beside me on the stand to watch the race.

'Got much chance?' I asked idly.

'Waste of time running him,' he said, his lip curling. 'I'm fed to the back molars with the sod.'

'Oh. Perhaps your other horse is better, though?' I murmured, watching the runners line up for the start.

'My other horse?' He laughed without mirth. 'Three others, would you believe it? I'm fed up with the whole sodding set up. I'm packing it in at the end of the week, pay or no pay.'

I suddenly remembered what I had heard about Humber. The worst stable in the country to work for, the boy in the Bristol hostel had said: they starved the lads and knocked them about and could only get riff-raff to work there.

'How do you mean, pay or no pay?' I asked.

'Humber pays sixteen quid a week, instead of eleven,' he said, 'but it's not bloody worth it. I've had a bellyful of bloody Humber. I'm getting out.'

The race started, and we watched Humber's horse finish last. The lad disappeared, muttering, to lead it away.

I smiled, followed him down the stairs, and forgot him, because waiting near the bottom step was a seedy, black-moustached man whom I instantly recognised as having been in the bar at the Cheltenham dance.

I walked slowly away to lean over the parade ring rail, and he inconspicuously followed. He stopped beside me, and with his eyes on the one horse already in the ring, he said, 'I hear that you are hard up.'

'Not after today, I'm not,' I said, looking him up and down.

He glanced at me briefly. 'Oh. Are you so sure of Sparking Plug?'

'Yeah,' I said with an unpleasant smirk. 'Certain.' Someone, I reflected, had been kind enough to tell him which horse I looked after: which meant he had been checking up on me. I trusted he had learned nothing to my advantage.

'Hmm.'

A whole minute passed. Then he said casually, 'Have you ever thought of changing your job . . . going to another stable?'

'I've thought of it,' I admitted, shrugging. 'Who hasn't?'

'There's always a market for good lads,' he pointed out, 'and I've heard you're a dab hand at the mucking out. With a reference from Inskip you could get in anywhere, if you told them you were prepared to wait for a vacancy.'

'Where?' I asked; but he wasn't to be hurried. After another minute he said, still conversationally, 'It can be very . . . er . . . lucrative . . . working for some stables.'

'Oh?'

'That is,' he coughed discreetly, 'if you are ready to do a bit more than the stable tells you to.'

'Such as?'

'Oh . . . general duties,' he said vaguely. 'It varies. Anything helpful to, er, the person who is prepared to supplement your income.'

'And who's that?'

He smiled thinly. 'Look upon me as his agent. How about it? His terms are a regular fiver a week for information about the results of training gallops and things like that, and a good bonus for occasional special jobs of a more, er, risky nature.'

'It don't sound bad,' I said slowly, sucking in my lower lip. 'Can't I do it at Inskip's?'

'Inskip's is not a betting stable,' he said. 'The horses always run to win. We do not need a permanent employee in that sort of place. There are however at present two betting stables without a man of ours in them, and you would be useful in either.'

He named two leading trainers, neither of whom was one of the three people I had already planned to apply to. I would have to decide whether it would not be more useful to join what was clearly a well-organized spy system, than to work with a once-doped horse who would almost certainly not be doped again.

'I'll think it over,' I said. 'Where can I get in touch with you?'

'Until you're on the pay roll, you can't,' he said simply. 'Sparking Plug's in the fifth, I see. Well, you can give me your answer after that race. I'll be somewhere on your way back to the stables. Just nod if you agree, and shake your head if you don't. But I can't see you passing up a chance like this, not one of your sort.' There was a sly contempt in the smile he gave me that made me unexpectedly wince inwardly.

He turned away and walked a few steps, and then came back.

'Should I have a big bet on Sparking Plug, then?' he asked.

'Oh . . . er . . . well . . . if I were you I'd save your money.'

He looked surprised, and then suspicious, and then knowing. 'So that's how the land lies,' he said. 'Well, well, well.' He laughed, looking at me as if I'd crawled out from under a stone. He was a man who despised his tools. 'I can see you're going to be very useful to us. Very useful indeed.'

I watched him go. It wasn't from kind-heartedness that I had stopped him backing Sparking Plug, but because it was the only way to retain and strengthen his confidence. When he was fifty yards away, I followed him. He made straight for the bookmakers in Tattersalls and strolled along the rows, looking at the odds displayed by each firm; but as far as I could see he was in fact innocently planning to bet on the next race, and not reporting to anyone the outcome of his talk with me. Sighing, I put ten shillings on an outsider and went back to watch the horses go out for the race.

Sparking Plug thirstily drank two full buckets of water, stumbled over the second last fence, and cantered tiredly in behind the other seven runners to the accompaniment of boos from the cheaper enclosures. I watched him with regret. It was a thankless way to treat a great-hearted horse.

The seedy, black-moustached man was waiting when I led the horse away to the stables. I nodded to him, and he sneered knowingly back.

'You'll hear from us,' he said.

There was gloom in the box going home and in the yard the next day over Sparking Plug's unexplainable defeat, and I went alone to Slaw on Tuesday evening, when Soupy duly handed over another seventy-five pounds. I checked it. Another fifteen new fivers, consecutive to the first fifteen.

'Ta,' I said. 'What do you get out of this yourself?'

Soupy's full mouth curled. 'I do all right. You mugs take the risks, I get a cut for setting you up. Fair enough, eh?'

'Fair enough. How often do you do this sort of thing?' I tucked the envelope of money into my pocket.

He shrugged, looking pleased with himself. 'I can spot blokes like you a mile off. Inskip must be slipping, though. First time I've known him pick a bent penny, like. But those darts matches come in very handy . . . I'm good, see. I'm always in the team. And there's a lot of stables in

Yorkshire . . . with a lot of beaten favourites for people to scratch their heads over.'

'You're very clever,' I said.

He smirked. He agreed.

I walked up the hill planning to light a fuse under T.N.T., the high explosive kid.

In view of the black-moustached man's offer I decided to read through Beckett's typescript yet again, to see if the eleven dopings could have been the result of systematic spying. Looking at things from a fresh angle might produce results, I thought, and also might help me make up my mind whether or not to back out of the spying job and go to one of the doped horse's yards as arranged.

Locked in the bathroom I began again at page one. On page sixty-seven, fairly early in the life history of the fifth of the horses, I read 'Bought at Ascot Sales, By D. L. Mentiff, Esq., of York for four hundred and twenty guineas, passed on for five hundred pounds to H. Humber of Posset, County Durham, remained three months, ran twice unplaced in maiden hurdles, subsequently sold again, at Doncaster, being bought for six hundred guineas by N. W. Davies, Esq., of Leeds. Sent by him to L. Peterson's training stables at Mars Edge, Staffs, remained eighteen months, ran in four maiden hurdles, five novice chases, all without being placed. Races listed below.' Three months at Humber's. I smiled. It appeared that horses didn't stay with him any longer than lads. I ploughed on through the details, page after solid page.

On page ninety-four I came across the following: 'Alamo was then offered for public auction at Kelso, and a Mr. John Arbuthnot, living in Berwickshire, paid three hundred guineas for him. He sent him to be trained by H. Humber at Posset, County Durham, but he was not entered for any races, and Mr. Arbuthnot sold him to Humber for the same sum. A few weeks later he was sent for resale at Kelso. This time Alamo was bought for three hundred and seventy-five guineas by a Mr. Clement Smithson, living at Nantwich, Cheshire, who kept him at home for the summer and then sent him to a trainer called Samuel Martin at Malton, Yorkshire, where he ran unplaced in four maiden hurdles before Christmas (see list attached).'

I massaged my stiff neck. Humber again.

I read on.

On page one hundred and eighty, I read, 'Ridgeway was then acquired as a yearling by a farmer, James Green, of Home Farm, Crayford, Surrey, in settlement of a bad debt. Mr. Green put him out to grass for two years, and had him broken in, hoping he would be a good hunter. However, a Mr. Taplow of Pusey, Wilts, said he would like to buy him and put him in training for racing. Ridgeway was trained for flat races by Ronald Streat of Pusey, but was unplaced in all his four races that summer. Mr. Taplow then sold Ridgeway privately to Albert George, farmer, of Bridge Lewes, Shropshire, who tried to train him himself but said he found he didn't have time to do it properly, so he sold him to a man a cousin of his knew near Durham, a trainer called Hedley Humber.

Humber apparently thought the horse was no good, and Ridgeway went up for auction at Newmarket in November, fetching two hundred and ninety guineas and being bought by Mr. P. J. Brewer, of the Manor, Witherby, Lancs . . .'

I ploughed right on to the end of the typescript, threading my way through the welter of names, but Humber was not mentioned anywhere again.

Three of the eleven horses had been in Humber's yard for a brief spell at some distant time in their careers. That was all it amounted to.

I rubbed my eyes, which were gritty from lack of sleep, and an alarm clock rang suddenly, clamorously, in the silent cottage. I looked at my watch in surprise. It was already half past six. Standing up and stretching, I made use of the bathroom facilities, thrust the typescript up under my pyjama jacket and the jersey I wore on top and shuffled back yawning to the dormitory, where the others were already up and struggling puffy-eyed into their clothes.

Down in the yard it was so cold that everything one touched seemed to suck the heat out of one's fingers, leaving them numb and fumbling, and the air was as intense an internal shaft to the chest as iced coffee sliding down the oesophagus. Muck out the boxes, saddle up, ride up to the moor, canter, walk, ride down again, brush the sweat off, make the horse comfortable, give it food and water, and go in to breakfast. Repeat for the second horse, repeat for the third, and go in to lunch.

While we were eating Wally came in and told two others and me to go and clean the tack, and when we had finished our tinned plums and custard we went along to the tack room and started on the saddles and bridles. It was warm there from the stove, and I put my head back on a saddle and went solidly asleep.

One of the others jogged my legs and said, 'Wake up Dan, there's a lot to do,' and I drifted to the surface again. But before I opened my eyes the other lad said, 'Oh leave him, he does his share,' and with blessings on his head I sank back into blackness. Four o'clock came too soon, and with it the three hours of evening stables: then supper at seven and another day nearly done.

For most of the time I thought about Humber's name cropping up three times in the typescript. I couldn't really see that it was of more significance than that four of the eleven horses had been fed on horse cubes at the time of their doping. What was disturbing was that I should have missed it entirely on my first two reading. I realised that I had had no reason to notice the name Humber before seeing him and his horse and talking to his lad at Leicester, but if I had missed one name occurring three times, I could have missed others as well. The thing to do would be to make lists of every single name mentioned in the typescript, and see if any other turned up in association with several of the horses. An electric computer could have done it in seconds. For me, it looked like another night in the bathroom.

There were more than a thousand names in the typescript. I listed half of them on the Wednesday night, and slept a bit, and finished them on Thursday night, and slept some more.

On Friday the sun shone for a change, and the morning was beautiful on the moor. I trotted Sparking Plug along the track somewhere in the middle of the string and thought about the lists. No names except Humber's and one other occurred in connection with more than two of the horses. But the one other was a certain Paul J. Adams, and he had at one time or another owned six of them. Six out of eleven. It couldn't be a coincidence. The odds against it were phenomenal. I was certain I had made my first really useful discovery, yet I couldn't see why the fact that P. J. Adams, Esq. had owned a horse for a few months once should enable it to be doped a year or two later. I puzzled over it all morning without a vestige of understanding.

As it was a fine day, Wally said, it was a good time for me to scrub some rugs. This meant laying the rugs the horses wore to keep them warm in their boxes flat on the concrete in the yard, soaking them with the aid of a hose pipe, scrubbing them with a long-handled broom and detergent, hosing them off again, and hanging the wet rugs on the fence to drip before they were transferred to the warm tack room to finish drying thoroughly. It was an unpopular job, and Wally, who had treated me even more coldly since Sparking Plug's disgrace (though he had not gone so far as to accuse me of engineering it), could hardly conceal his dislike when he told me that it was my turn to do it.

However, I reflected, as I laid out five rugs after lunch and thoroughly soaked them with water, I had two hours to be alone and think. And as so often happens, I was wrong.

At three o'clock, when the horses were dozing and the lads were either copying them or had made quick trips to Harrogate with their new pay packets; when stable life was at its siesta and only I with my broom showed signs of reluctant activity, Patty Tarren walked in through the gate, across the tarmac, and slowed to a halt a few feet away.

She was wearing a straightish dress of soft looking knobbly green tweed with a row of silver buttons from throat to hem. Her chestnut hair hung in a clean shining bob on her shoulders and was held back from her forehead by a wide green band, and with her fluffy eyelashes and pale pink mouth she looked about as enticing an interruption as a hard worked stable hand could ask for.

'Hullo, Danny boy,' she said.

'Good afternoon, miss.'

'I saw you from my window,' she said.

I turned in surprise, because I had thought October's house entirely hidden by trees, but sure enough, up the slope, one stone corner and a window could be seen through a gap in the leafless boughs. It was, however, a long way off. If Patty had recognised me from that distance she had been using binoculars.

'You looked a bit lonely, so I came down to talk to you.'

'Thank you, miss.'

'As a matter of fact,' she said, lowering the eyelashes, 'the rest of the family don't get here until this evening, and I had nothing to do in that barn of a place all by myself, and I was bored. So I thought I'd come down and talk to you.'

'I see.' I leant on the broom, looking at her lovely face and thinking that there was an expression in her eyes too old for her years.

'It's rather cold out here, don't you think? I want to talk to you about something . . . don't you think we could stand in the shelter of that doorway?' Without waiting for an answer she walked towards the doorway in question, which was that of the hay barn, and went inside. I followed her, resting the broom against the door post on the way.

'Yes, miss?' I said. The light was dim in the barn.

It appeared that talking was not her main object after all.

She put her hands round the back of my neck and offered her mouth for a kiss. I bent my head and kissed her. She was no virgin, October's daughter. She kissed with her tongue and with her teeth, and she moved her stomach rhythmically against mine. My muscles turned to knots. She smelled sweetly of fresh soap, more innocent than her behaviour.

'Well . . . that's all right, then,' she said with a giggle, disengaging herself and heading for the bulk of the bales of hay which half filled the barn.

'Come on,' she said over her shoulder, and climbed up the bales to the flat level at the top. I followed her slowly. When I got to the top I sat looking down at the hay barn floor with the broom, the bucket and the rug touched with sunshine through the doorway. On top of the hay had been Philip's favourite play place for years when he was little . . . and this is a fine time to think of my family, I thought.

Patty was lying on her back three feet away from me. Her eyes were wide and glistening, and her mouth curved open in an odd little smile. Slowly, holding my gaze, she undid all the silver buttons down the front of her dress to a point well below her waist. Then she gave a little shake so that the edges of the dress fell apart

She had absolutely nothing on underneath.

I looked at her body, which was pearl pink and slender, and very desirable; and she gave a little rippling shiver of anticipation.

I looked back at her face. Her eyes were big and dark, and the odd way in which she was smiling suddenly struck me as being half furtive, half greedy; and wholly sinful. I had an abrupt vision of myself as she must see me, as I had seen myself in the long mirror in October's London house, a dark, flashy looking stable boy with an air of deceitfulness and an acquaintance with dirt.

I understood her smile, then.

I turned round where I sat until I had my back to her, and felt a flush of anger and shame spread all over my body.

'Do your dress up,' I said.

'Why? Are you impotent after all, Danny boy?'

'Do your dress up,' I repeated. 'The party's over.'

I slid down the hay, walked across the floor and out of the door without looking back. Twitching up the broom and cursing under my breath I let out my fury against myself by scrubbing the rug until my arms ached.

After a while I saw her (green dress re-buttoned) come slowly out of the hay barn, look around her, and go across to a muddy puddle on the edge of the tarmac. She dirtied her shoes thoroughly in it, then childishly walked on to the rug I had just cleaned, and wiped all the mud off carefully in the centre.

Her eyes were wide and her face expressionless as she looked at me.

'You'll be sorry, Danny boy,' she said simply, and without haste strolled away down the yard, the chestnut hair swinging gently on the green tweed dress.

I scrubbed the rug again. Why had I kissed her? Why, after knowing about her from that kiss, had I followed her up into the hay? Why had I been such a stupid, easily roused, lusting fool? I was filled with useless dismay.

One didn't have to accept an invitation to dinner, even if the appetiser made one hungry. But having accepted, one should not so brutally reject what was offered. She had every right to be angry.

And I had every reason to be confused. I had been for nine years a father to two girls, one of whom was nearly Patty's age. I had taught them when they were little not to take lifts from strangers and when they were bigger how to avoid more subtle snares. And here I was, indisputably on the other side of the parental fence.

I felt an atrocious sense of guilt towards October, for I had had the intention, and there was no denying it, of doing what Patty wanted.

Chapter Seven

It was Elinor who rode out on my horse the following morning, and Patty, having obviously got her to change mounts, studiously refused to look at me at all.

Elinor, a dark scarf protecting most of the silver blonde hair, accepted a leg up with impersonal grace, gave me a warm smile of thanks and rode away at the head of the string with her sister. When we got back after the gallops, however, she led the horse into its box and did half of the jobs for it while I was attending to Sparking Plug, I didn't know what she was doing until I walked down the yard, and was surprised to find her there, having grown used to Patty's habit of bolting the horse into the box still complete with saddle, bridle, and mud.

'You go and get the hay and water,' she said. 'I'll finish getting the dirt off, now I've started.'

I carried away the saddle and bridle to the tack room, and took back the hay and water. Elinor gave the horse's mane a few final strokes with the brush, and I put on his rug and buckled the roller round his belly. She watched while I tossed the straw over the floor to make a comfortable bed, and waited until I had bolted the door.

'Thank you,' I said. 'Thank you very much.'

She smiled faintly, 'It's a pleasure. It really is. I like horses. Especially race horses. Lean and fast and exciting.'

'Yes,' I agreed. We walked down the yard together, she to go to the gate and I to the cottage which stood beside it.

'They are so different from what I do all the week,' she said.

'What do you do all the week?'

'Oh . . . study. I'm at Durham University.' There was a sudden, private, recollecting grin. Not for me. On level terms, I thought, one might find more in Elinor than good manners.

'It's really extraordinary how well you ride,' she said suddenly. 'I heard Mr. Inskip telling Father this morning that it would be worth getting a licence for you. Have you ever thought of racing?'

'I wish I could,' I said fervently, without thinking.

'Well, why not?'

'Oh . . . I might be leaving soon.'

'What a pity.' It was polite; nothing more.

We reached the cottage. She gave me a friendly smile and walked straight on, out of the yard, out of sight. I may not ever see her again, I thought; and was mildly sorry.

When the horse box came back from a day's racing (with a winner, a third, and an also-ran) I climbed up into the cab and borrowed the map again. I wanted to discover the location of the village where Mr. Paul Adams lived, and after some searching I found it. As its significance sank in I began to smile with astonishment. There was, it seemed, yet another place where I could apply for a job.

I went back into the cottage into Mrs. Allnut's cosy kitchen, and ate Mrs. Allnut's delicious egg and chips and bread and butter and fruit cake, and later slept dreamlessly on Mrs. Allnut's lumpy mattress, and in the morning bathed luxuriously in Mrs. Allnut's shining bathroom. And in the afternoon I went up beside the stream with at last something worthwhile to tell October.

He met me with a face of granite, and before I could say a word he hit me hard and squarely across the mouth. It was a back-handed expert blow which started from the waist, and I didn't see it coming until far too late.

'What the hell's that for?' I said, running my tongue round my teeth and being pleased to find that none of them was broken off.

He glared at me. 'Patty told me . . .' He stopped as if it were too difficult to go on.

'Oh,' I said blankly.

'Yes, oh,' he mimicked savagely. He was breathing deeply and I thought he was going to hit me again. I thrust my hands into my pockets and his stayed where they were, down by his side, clenching and unclenching.

'What did Patty tell you?'

'She told me everything.' His anger was almost tangible. 'She came to me this morning in tears . . . she told me how you made her go into the hay barn . . . and held her there until she was worn out with struggling to get away . . . she told the . . . the disgusting things you did to her with your hands ... and then how you forced her ... forced her to ...' He couldn't say it.

I was appalled. 'I didn't,' I said vehemently. 'I didn't do anything like that. I kissed her ... and that's all. She's making it up.'

'She couldn't possibly have made it up. It was too detailed ... She couldn't know such things unless they had happened to her.'

I opened my mouth and shut it again. They had happened to her, right enough; somewhere, with someone else, more than once, and certainly also with her willing co-operation. And I could see that to some extent at least she was going to get away with her horrible revenge, because there are some things you can't say about a girl to her father, especially if you like him.

October said scathingly, 'I have never been so mistaken in a man before. I thought you were responsible ... or at least able to control yourself. Not a cheap lecherous jackanapes who would take my money – and my regard – and amuse yourself behind my back, debauching my daughter.'

There was enough truth in that to hurt, and the guilt I felt over my stupid behaviour didn't help. But I had to put up some kind of defence, because I would never have harmed Patty in any way, and there was still the investigation into the doping to be carried on. Now I had got so far, I did not want to be packed off home in disgrace.

I said slowly, 'I did go with Patty into the hay barn. I did kiss her. Once. Only once. After that I didn't touch her. I literally didn't touch any part of her, not her hand, not her dress ... nothing.'

He looked at me steadily for a long time while the fury slowly died out of him and a sort of weariness took its place.

At length he said, almost calmly, 'One of you is lying. And I have to believe my daughter.' There was an unexpected flicker of entreaty in his voice.

'Yes,' I said. I looked away, up the gully. 'Well ... this solves one problem, anyway.'

'What problem?'

'How to leave here with the ignominious sack and without a reference.'

It was so far away from what he was thinking about that it was several moments before he showed any reaction at all, and then he gave me an attentive, narrow-eyed stare which I did not try to avoid.

'You intend to go on with the investigation, then?'

'If you are willing.'

'Yes,' he said heavily, at length. 'Especially as you are moving on and will have no more opportunities of seeing Patty. In spite of what I personally think of you, you do still represent our best hope of success, and I suppose I must put the good of racing first.'

He fell silent. I contemplated the rather grim prospect of continuing to do that sort of work for a man who hated me. Yet the thought of giving up was worse. And that was odd.

Eventually he said, 'Why do you want to leave without a reference? You won't get a job in any of these three stables without a reference.'

'The only reference I need to get a job in the stable I am going to is no reference at all.'

'Whose stable?'

'Hedley Humber's.'

'Humber!' He was sombrely incredulous. 'But why? He's a very poor trainer and he didn't train any of the doped horses. What's the point of going there?'

'He didn't train any of the horses when they won,' I agreed, 'but he had three of them through his hands earlier in their careers. There is also a man called P. J. Adams who at one time or another owned six more of them. Adams lives, according to the map, less than ten miles from Humber. Humber lives at Posset, in Durham, and Adams at Tellbridge, just over the Northumberland border. That means that nine of the eleven horses spent some time in that one small area of the British Isles. None of them stayed long. The dossiers of Transistor and Rudyard are much less detailed than the others on the subject of their earlier life, and I have now no doubt that checking would show that they too, for a short while, came under the care of either Adams or Humber.'

'But how could the horses having spent some time with Adams or Humber possibly affect their speed months or years later?'

'I don't know,' I said. 'But I'll go and find out.'

There was a pause.

'Very well,' he said heavily. 'I'll tell Inskip that you are dismissed. And I'll tell him it is because you pestered Patricia.'

'Right.'

He looked at me coldly. 'You can write me reports. I don't want to see you again.'

I watched him walk away strongly up the gully. I didn't know whether or not he really believed any more that I had done what Patty said; but I did know that he needed to believe it. The alternative, the truth, was so much worse. What father wants to discover that his beautiful eighteen-year-old daughter is a lying slut?

And as for me, I thought that on the whole I had got off lightly; if I had found that anyone had assaulted Belinda or Helen I'd have half killed him.

After second exercise the following day Inskip told me exactly what he thought of me, and I didn't particularly enjoy it.

After giving me a public dressing down in the centre of the tarmac (with the lads grinning in sly amusement as they carried their buckets and hay nets with both ears flapping) he handed back the insurance card and income tax form – there was still a useful muddle going on over the illegible Cornish address on the one October had originally provided me with – and told me to pack my bags and get out of the yard at once. It would be no use my giving his name as a reference he said, because Lord October had expressly forbidden him to vouch for my character, and it was a decision with which he thoroughly agreed. He gave me a week's wages in lieu of notice, less Mrs. Allnut's share, and that was that.

I packed my things in the little dormitory, patted goodbye to the bed

I had slept in for six weeks, and went down to the kitchen where the lads were having their midday meal. Eleven pairs of eyes swivelled in my direction. Some were contemptuous, some were surprised, one or two thought it funny. None of them looked sorry to see me go. Mrs. Allnut gave me a thick cheese sandwich, and I ate it walking down the hill to Slaw to catch the two o'clock bus to Harrogate.

And from Harrogate, where?

No lad in his senses would go straight from a prosperous place like Inskip's to ask for a job at Humber's, however abruptly he had been thrown out; there had to be a period of some gentle sliding downhill if it were to look unsuspicious. In fact, I decided, it would be altogether much better if it were Humber's head travelling lad who offered me work, and not I who asked for it. It should not be too difficult. I could turn up at every course where Humber had a runner, looking seedier and seedier and more and more ready to take any job at all, and one day the lad-hungry stable would take the bait.

Meanwhile I needed somewhere to live. The bus trundled down to Harrogate while I thought it out. Somewhere in the north east, to be near Humber's local meetings. A big town, so that I could be anonymous in it. An alive town, so that I could find ways of passing the time between race meetings. With the help of maps and guide books in Harrogate public library I settled on Newcastle, and with the help of a couple of tolerant lorry drivers I arrived there late that afternoon and found myself a room in a back-street hotel.

It was a terrible room with peeling, coffee coloured walls, tatty printed linoleum wearing out on the floor, a narrow, hard divan bed, and some scratched furniture made out of stained plywood. Only its unexpected cleanliness and a shiny new washbasin in one corner made it bearable, but it did, I had to admit, suit my appearance and purpose admirably.

I dined in a fish and chip shop for three and six, and went to a cinema, and enjoyed not having to groom three horses or think twice about every word I said. My spirits rose several points at being free again and I succeeded in forgetting the trouble I was in with October.

In the morning I sent off to him in a registered package the second seventy-five pounds, which I had not given him in the gully on Sunday, together with a short formal note explaining why there would have to be a delay before I engaged myself to Humber.

From the post office I went to a betting shop and from their calendar copied down all the racing fixtures for the next month. It was the beginning of December, and I found there were very few meetings in the north before the first week in January; which was, from my point of view, a waste of time and a nuisance. After the following Saturday's programme at Newcastle itself there was no racing north of Nottinghamshire until Boxing Day, more than a fortnight later.

Pondering this set-back I next went in search of a serviceable second-hand motor-cycle. It took me until late afternoon to find exactly what I wanted, a souped-up 500 c.c. Norton four years old and the ex-property of a now one-legged young man who had done the ton once too often on the Great North Road. The salesman gave me those details with relish as he took my money and assured me that the bike would still do a hundred at a push. I thanked him politely and left the machine with him to have a new silencer fitted, along with some new hand grips, brake cables and tyres.

Lack of private transport at Slaw had not been a tremendous drawback, and I would not have been concerned about my mobility at Posset were it not for the one obtrusive thought that I might at some time find it advisable to depart in a hurry. I could not forget the journalist, Tommy Stapleton. Between Hexham and Yorkshire he had lost nine hours, and turned up dead. Between Hexham and Yorkshire lay Posset.

The first person I saw at Newcastle races four days later was the man with the black moustache who had offered me steady employment as a stable spy. He was standing in an unobtrusive corner near the entrance, talking to a big-eared boy whom I later saw leading round a horse from one of the best-known gambling stables in the country.

From some distance away I watched him pass to the boy a white envelope and receive a brown envelope in return. Money for information, I thought, and so openly done as to appear innocent.

I strolled along behind Black Moustache when he finished his transaction and made his way to the bookmakers' stands in Tattersalls. As before he appeared to be doing nothing but examining the prices offered on the first race: and as before I staked a few shillings on the favourite in case I should be seen to be following him. In spite of his survey he placed no bets at all, but strolled down to the rails which separated the enclosure from the course itself. There he came to an unplanned looking halt beside an artificial red-head wearing a yellowish leopard skin jacket over a dark grey skirt.

She turned her head towards him, and they spoke. Presently he took the brown envelope from his breast pocket and slipped it into his race card: and after a few moments he and the woman unobtrusively exchanged race cards. He wandered away from the rails, while she put the card containing the envelope into a large shiny black handbag and snapped it shut. From the shelter of the last row of bookies I watched her walk to the entrance into the Club and pass through on to the Members' lawn. I could not follow her there, but I went up on to the stands and watched her walk across the next-door enclosure. She appeared to be well-known. She stopped and spoke to several people . . . a bent old man with a big floppy hat, an obese young man who patted her arm repeatedly, a pair of women in mink cocoons, a group of three men who laughed loudly and hid her from my view so that I could not see if she had given any of them the envelope from her handbag.

The horses cantered down the course and the crowds moved up on to the stands to watch the race. The redhead disappeared among the throng on the Members' stand, leaving me frustrated at losing her. The race was run, and the favourite cantered in by ten lengths. The crowd roared with approval. I stood where I was while people round me flowed down from the stands, waiting without too much hope to see if the leopard-skin redhead would reappear.

Obligingly, she did. She was carrying her handbag in one hand and her race card in the other. Pausing to talk again, this time to a very short fat man, she eventually made her way over to the bookmakers who stood along the rails separating Tattersalls from the Club and stopped in front of one nearest the stands, and nearest to me. For the first time I could see her face clearly: she was younger than I had thought and plainer of feature, with gaps between her top teeth.

She said in a piercing, tinny voice, 'I'll settle my account, Bimmo dear,' and opening her handbag took out a brown envelope and gave it to a small man in spectacles, who stood on a box beside a board bearing the words Bimmo Bognor (est. 1920), Manchester and London.

Mr. Bimmo Bognor took the envelope and put it in his jacket pocket, and his hearty 'Ta, love,' floated up to my attentive ears.

I went down from the stands and collected my small winnings, thinking that while the brown envelope that the red-head had given to Bimmo Bognor *looked* like the envelope that the big-eared lad had given to Black Moustache, I could not be a hundred per cent sure of it. She might have given the lad's envelope to any one of the people I had watched her talk to, or to anyone on the stands while she was out of my sight: and she might then have gone quite honestly to pay her bookmaker.

If I wanted to be certain of the chain, perhaps I could send an urgent message along it, a message so urgent that there would be no wandering among the crowds, but an unconcealed direct line between a and b, and b and c. The urgent message, since Sparking Plug was a runner in the fifth race, presented no difficulty at all; but being able to locate Black Moustache at exactly the right moment entailed keeping him in sight all the afternoon.

He was a creature of habit, which helped. He always watched the races from the same corner of the stand, patronized the same bar between times, and stood inconspicuously near the gate on to the course when the horses were led out of the parade ring. He did not bet.

Humber had two horses at the meeting, one in the third race and one in the last; and although it meant leaving my main purpose untouched until late in the afternoon, I let the third race go by without making any attempt to find his head travelling lad. I padded slowly along behind Black Moustache instead.

After the fourth race I followed him into the bar and jogged his arm violently as he began to drink. Half of his beer splashed over his hand and ran down his sleeve, and he swung round cursing, to find my face nine inches from his own.

'Sorry,' I said. 'Oh, it's you.' I put as much surprise into my voice as I could.

His eyes narrowed. 'What are you doing here? Sparking Plug runs in this race.'

I scowled. 'I've left Inskip's.'

'Have you got one of the jobs I suggested? Good.'

'Not yet. There might be a bit of a delay there, like.'

'Why? No vacancies?'

'They don't seem all that keen to have me since I got chucked out of Inskip's.'

'You got what?' he said sharply.

'Chucked out of Inskip's,' I repeated.

'Why?'

'They said something about Sparking Plug losing last week on the day you spoke to me . . said they could prove nothing but they didn't want me around no more, and to get out.'

'That's too bad,' he said, edging away.

'But I got the last laugh,' I said, sniggering and holding on to his arm. 'I'll tell you straight, I got the bloody last laugh.'

'What do you mean?' He didn't try to keep the contempt out of his voice, but there was interest in his eyes.

'Sparking Plug won't win today neither,' I stated. 'He won't win because he'll feel bad in his stomach.'

'How do you know?'

'I soaked his salt-lick with liquid paraffin,' I said. 'Every day since I left on Monday he's been rubbing his tongue on a laxative. He won't be feeling like racing. He won't bloody win, he won't.' I laughed.

Black Moustache gave me a sickened look, prised my fingers off his arm, and hurried out of the bar. I followed him carefully. He almost ran down into Tattersalls, and began frantically looking around. The red-headed woman was nowhere to be seen, but she must have been watching, because presently I saw her walking briskly down the rails, to the same spot where they had met before. And there, with a rush she was joined by Black Moustache. He talked vehemently. She listened and nodded. He then turned away more calmly, and walked away out of Tattersalls and back to the parade ring. The woman waited until he was out of sight: then she walked firmly into the Members' enclosure and along the rails until she came to Bimmo Bognor. The little man leant forward over the rails as she spoke earnestly into his ear. He nodded several times and she began to smile, and when he turned round to talk to his clerks I saw that he was smiling broadly too.

Unhurriedly I walked along the rows of bookmakers, studying the odds they offered. Sparking Plug was not favourite, owing to his waterlogged defeat last time out, but no one would chance more than five to one. At that price I staked forty pounds – my entire earnings at Inskip's – on my old charge, choosing a prosperous, jolly-looking bookmaker in the back row.

Hovering within earshot of Mr. Bimmo Bognor a few minutes later I heard him offer seven to one against Sparking Plug to a stream of clients, and watched him rake in their money, confident that he would not have to pay them out.

Smiling contentedly I climbed to the top of the stands and watched Sparking Plug make mincemeat of his opponents over the fences and streak insultingly home by twenty lengths. It was a pity, I reflected, that I was too far away to hear Mr. Bognor's opinion of the result.

My jolly bookmaker handed me two hundred and forty pounds in fivers without a second glance. To avoid Black Moustache and any reprisals he might be thinking of organizing, I then went over to the cheap enclosure in the centre of the course for twenty boring minutes; returning through the horse gate when the runners were down at the start for the last race, and slipping up the stairs to the stand used by the lads.

Humber's head travelling lad was standing near the top of the stands. I pushed roughly past him and tripped heavily over his feet.

'Look where you're bloody going,' he said crossly, focusing a pair of shoe-button eyes on my face.

'Sorry mate. Got corns, have you?'

'None of your bloody business,' he said, looking at me sourly. He would know me again, I thought.

I bit my thumb nail. 'Do you know which of this lot is Martin Davies' head travelling lad?' I asked.

He said, 'That chap over there with the red scarf. Why?'

'I need a job,' I said: and before he could say anything I left him and pushed along the row to the man in the red scarf. His stable had one horse in the race. I asked him quietly if they ran two, and he shook his head and said no.

Out of the corner of my eye I noticed that this negative answer had not been wasted on Humber's head lad. He thought, as I had hoped, that I had asked for work, and had been refused. Satisfied that the seed was planted, I watched the race (Humber's horse finished last) and slipped quietly away from the racecourse via the paddock rails and the Members' car park, without any interception of Black Moustache or a vengeful Bimmo Bognor.

A Sunday endured half in my dreary room and half walking round the empty streets was enough to convince me that I could not drag through the next fortnight in Newcastle doing nothing, and the thought of a solitary Christmas spent staring at coffee-coloured peeling paint was unattractive. Moreover I had two hundred pounds of bookmakers' money packed into my belt alongside what was left of October's: and Humber had no horses entered before the Stafford meeting on Boxing Day. It took me only ten minutes to decide what to do with the time between.

On Sunday evening I wrote to October a report on Bimmo Bognor's intelligence service, and at one in the morning I caught the express to London. I spent Monday shopping and on Tuesday evening, looking civilized in some decent new clothes and equipped with an extravagant pair of Kastle skis I signed the register of a comfortable, bright little hotel in a snow-covered village in the Dolomites.

The fortnight I spent in Italy made no difference one way or another to the result of my work for October, but it made a great deal of difference to me. It was the first real holiday I had had since my parents died, the first utterly carefree, purposeless, self-indulgent break for nine years.

I grew younger. Fast strenuous days on the snow slopes and a succession of evenings dancing with my ski-ing companions peeled away the years of responsibility like skins, until at last I felt twenty-seven instead of fifty, a young man instead of a father; until the unburdening process, begun when I left Australia and slowly fermenting through the weeks of Inskip's, suddenly seemed complete.

There was also a bonus in the shape of one of the receptionists, a rounded glowing girl whose dark eyes lit up the minute she saw me and who, after a minimum of persuasion, uninhibitedly spent a proportion of her nights in my bed. She called me her Christmas box of chocolates. She said I was the happiest lover she had had for a long time, and that I pleased her. She was probably doubly as promiscuous as Patty but she was much more wholesome; and she made me feel terrific instead of ashamed.

On the day I left, when I gave her a gold bracelet, she kissed me and told me not to come back, as things were never as good the second time. She was God's gift to bachelors, that girl.

I flew back to England on Christmas night feeling as physically and mentally fit as I had ever been in my life, and ready to take on the worst that Humber could dish out. Which, as it happened, was just as well.

Chapter Eight

At Stafford on Boxing Day one of the runners in the first race, the selling chase, threw off his jockey a stride after landing in fourth place over the last fence, crashing through the rails, and bolted away across the rough grass in the centre of the course.

A lad standing near me on the draughty steps behind the weighing room ran off cursing to catch him; but as the horse galloped crazily from one end of the course to the other it took the lad, the trainer, and about ten assorted helpers a quarter of an hour to lay their hands on his bridle. I watched them as with worried faces they led the horse, an undistinguished bay, off the course and past me towards the racecourse stables.

The wretched animal was white and dripping with sweat and in obvious distress; foam covered his nostrils and muzzle, and his eyes rolled wildly in their sockets. His flesh was quivering, his ears lay flat on his head, and he was inclined to lash out at anyone who came near him.

His name, I saw from the race card, was Superman. He was not one of the eleven horses I had been investigating: but his hotted up appearance and frantic behaviour, coupled with the fact that he had met trouble at Stafford in a selling chase, convinced me that he was the twelfth of the series. The twelfth; and he had come unstuck. There was, as Beckett had said, no mistaking the effect of whatever had pepped him up. I had never before seen a horse in such a state, which seemed to me much worse than the descriptions of 'excited winners,' I had read in the press cuttings: and I came to the conclusion that Superman was either suffering from an overdose, or had reacted excessively to whatever the others had been given.

Neither October nor Beckett nor Macclesfield had come to Stafford.
I could only hope that the precautions October had promised had been
put into operation in spite of its being Boxing Day, because I could not,
without blowing open my role, ask any of the officials if the pre-race
dope tests had been made or other precautions taken, nor insist that the
jockey be asked at once for his impressions, that unusual bets should be
investigated, and that the horse be thoroughly examined for punctures.

The fact that Superman had safely negotiated all the fences inclined
me more and more to believe that he could not have been affected by the
stimulant until he was approaching, crossing, or landing over the last.
It was there that he had gone wild and, instead of winning, thrown his
jockey and decamped. It was there that he had been given the power to
sprint the four hundred yards, that long run-in which gave him time and
room to overhaul the leading horses.

The only person on the racecourse to whom I could safely talk was
Superman's lad, but because of the state of his horse it was bound to be
some time before he came out of the stables. Meanwhile there were more
steps to be taken towards getting myself a job with Humber.

I had gone to the meeting with my hair unbrushed, pointed shoes
unpolished, leather collar turned up, hands in pockets, sullen expression
in place. I looked, and felt, a disgrace.

Changing back that morning into stable lad clothes had not been a
pleasant experience. The sweaters stank of horses, the narrow cheap
trousers looked scruffy, the under-clothes were grey from insufficient
washing and the jeans were still filthy with mud and muck. Because of
the difficulty of getting them back on Christmas night I had decided
against sending the whole lot to the laundry while I was away, and in
spite of my distaste in putting them on again, I didn't regret it. I looked
all the more on the way to being down and out.

I changed and shaved in the cloakroom at the West Kensington Air
Terminal, parked my skis and grip of ski clothes in the Left Luggage
department on Euston Station, slept uneasily on a hard seat for an hour
or two, breakfasted on sandwiches and coffee from the auto-buffet, and
caught the race train to Stafford. At this rate, I thought wryly, I would
have bundles of belongings scattered all over London; because neither on
the outward nor return journeys had I cared to go to October's London
house to make use of the clothes I had left with Terence. I did not want
to meet October. I liked him, and saw no joy in facing his bitter resentment
again unless I absolutely had to.

Humber had only one runner on Boxing Day, a weedy looking hurdler
in the fourth race. I hung over the rails by the saddling boxes and
watched his head travelling lad saddle up, while Humber himself leant
on his knobbed walking stick and gave directions. I had come for a good
close look at him, and what I saw was both encouraging from the angle
that one could believe him capable of any evil, and discouraging from the
angle that I was going to have to obey him.

His large body was encased in a beautifully cut short camel-hair
overcoat, below which protruded dark trousers and impeccable shoes. On
his head he wore a bowler, set very straight, and on his hands some pale

unsoiled pigskin gloves. His face was large, not fat, but hard. Unsmiling eyes, a grim trap of a mouth, and deep lines running from the corners of his nose to his chin gave his expression a look of cold wilfulness.

He stood quite still, making no unnecessary fussy movements, the complete opposite of Inskip, who was for ever walking busily from side to side of his horse, checking straps and buckles, patting and pulling at the saddle, running his hand down legs, nervously making sure over and over that everything was in order.

In Humber's case it was the boy who held the horse's head who was nervous. Frightened, I thought, was hardly too strong a word for it. He kept giving wary, startled-animal glances at Humber, and stayed out of his sight on the far side of the horse as much as possible. He was a thin, ragged-looking boy of about sixteen, and not far, I judged, from being mentally deficient.

The travelling head lad, middle-aged, with a big nose and an unfriendly air, unhurriedly adjusted the saddle and nodded to the lad to lead the horse off into the parade ring. Humber followed. He walked with a slight limp, more or less disguised by the use of the walking stick, and he proceeded in a straight line like a tank, expecting everyone else to get out of his way.

I transferred myself to the parade ring rails in his wake and watched him give instructions to his jockey, an allowance-claimer who regarded his mount with justified disillusion. It was the head travelling lad, not Humber, who gave the jockey a leg up, and who picked up and carried off with him the horse's rug. Round at the lads' stand I carefully stood directly in front of the head travelling lad and in the lull before the race started I turned sideways and tried to borrow some money from the lad standing next to me, whom I didn't know. Not unexpectedly, but to my relief, the lad refused indignantly and more than loudly enough for Humber's head lad to hear. I hunched my shoulders and resisted the temptation to look round and see if the message had reached its destination.

Humber's horse ran out of energy in the straight and finished second to last. No one was surprised.

After that I stationed myself outside the stable gate to wait for Superman's lad, but he didn't come out for another half an hour, until after the fifth race. I fell into step beside him as if by accident, saying 'Rather you than me, chum, with one like that to look after.' He asked me who I worked for; I said Inskip, and he loosened up and agreed that a cup of char and a wad would go down a treat, after all that caper.

'Is he always that het up after a race?' I said, half-way through the cheese sandwiches.

'No. Usually, he's dog-tired. There's been all hell breaking loose this time, I can tell you.'

'How do you mean?'

'Well, first they came and took some tests on all the runners before the race. Now I ask you, why before? It's not the thing, is it? Not before. You ever had one done before?'

I shook my head.

'Then, see, old Super, he was putting up the same sort of job he always does, looking as if he is going to come on into a place at least and then packing it in going to the last. Stupid basket. No guts, I reckon. They had his heart tested, but it ticks O.K. So it's no guts, sure enough. Anyway, then at the last he suddenly kicks up his heels and bolts off as if the devil was after him. I don't suppose you saw him? He's a nervy customer always, really, but he was climbing the wall when we finally caught him. The old man was dead worried. Well, the horse looked as though he had been got at, and he wanted to stick his oar in first and get a dope test done so that the Stewards shouldn't accuse him of using a booster and take away his ruddy licence. They had a couple of vets fussing over him taking things to be analysed ... dead funny it was, because old Super was trying to pitch them over the stable walls ... and in the end they gave him a jab of something to quieten him down. But how we're going to get him home I don't know.'

'Have you looked after him long?' I asked sympathetically.

'Since the beginning of the season. About four months, I suppose. He's a jumpy customer, as I said, but before this I had just about got him to like me. Gawd, I hope he calms down proper before the jabs wear off, I do straight.'

'Who had him before you?' I asked casually.

'Last year he was in a little stable in Devon with a private trainer called Beaney, I think. Yes, Beaney, that's where he started, but he didn't do any good there.'

'I expect they made him nervous there, breaking him in,' I said.

'No, now that's a funny thing, I said that to one of Beaney's lads when we were down in Devon for one of the August meetings, and he said I must be talking about the wrong horse because Superman was a placid old thing and no trouble. He said if Superman was nervous it must have been on account of something that had happened during the summer after he left their place and before he came to us.'

'Where did he go for the summer?' I asked, picking up the cup of orange-coloured tea.

'Search me. The old man bought him at Ascot sales, I think, for a cheap horse. I should think he will shuffle him off again after this if he can get more than knacker's price for him. Poor old Super. Silly nit.' The lad stared gloomily into his tea.

'You don't think he went off his rocker today because he was doped then?'

'I think he just went bonkers,' he said. 'Stark, staring, raving bonkers. I mean, no one had a chance to dope him, except me and the old man and Chalky, and I didn't, and the old man didn't, because he's not that sort, and you wouldn't think Chalky would either, he's so darn proud being promoted head travelling lad only last month ...'

We finished our tea and went round to watch the sixth race still talking about Superman, but his lad knew nothing else which was of help to me.

After the race I walked the half mile into the centre of Stafford, and from a telephone box sent two identical telegrams to October, one to London and one to Slaw, as I did not know where he was. They read, 'Request urgent information re Superman, specifically where did he go from Beaney, permit holder, Devon, last May approximately. Answer care Post Restante, Newcastle-on-Tyne.'

I spent the evening, incredibly distant from the gaiety of the day before, watching a dreary musical in a three-quarters empty cinema, and slept that night in a dingy bed-and-breakfast hotel where they looked me up and down and asked for their money in advance. I paid, wondering if I would ever get used to being treated like dirt. I felt a fresh shock every time. I supposed I had been too accustomed to the respect I was offered in Australia even to notice it, far less appreciate it. I would appreciate some of it now, I ruefully thought, following the landlady into an unwelcoming little room and listening to her suspicious lectures on no cooking, no hot water after eleven, and no girls.

The following afternoon I conspicuously mooched around in front of Humber's head travelling lad with a hang-dog and worried expression, and after the races went back by bus and train to Newcastle for the night. In the morning I collected the motor-cycle, fitted with the new silencer and other parts, and called at the post office to see if there was a reply from October.

The clerk handed me a letter. Inside, without salutation or signature, there was a single sheet of typescript, which read; 'Superman was born and bred in Ireland. Changed hands twice before reaching John Beaney in Devon. He was then sold by Beaney to H. Humber, Esq. of Posset. Co. Durham, on May 3rd. Humber sent him to Ascot Sales in July, where he was bought by his present trainer for two hundred and sixty guineas.

'Investigations re Superman at Stafford yesterday are all so far uninformative; dope analyses have still to be completed but there is little hope they will show anything. The veterinary surgeon at the course was as convinced as you apparently were that this is another "joker", and made a thorough examination of the horse's skin. There were no visible punctures except the ones he made himself giving the horse sedation.

'Superman was apparently in a normal condition before the race. His jockey reports all normal until the last fence, when the horse seemed to suffer a sort of convulsion, and ejected him from the saddle.

'Further enquiries re Rudyard revealed he was bought four winters ago by P. J. Adams of Telbridge, Northumberland, and sold again within a short time at Ascot. Transistor was bought by Adams at Doncaster three years ago, sold Newmarket Dispersal Sales three months later.

'Enquiries re thirty consecutive five pound notes reveal they were issued by Barclays Bank, Birmingham New Street branch, to a man called Lewis Greenfield, who corresponds exactly to your description of the man who approached you in Slaw. Proceedings against Greenfield and T. N. Tarleton are in hand, but will be held in abeyance until after your main task is completed.

'Your report on Bimmo Bognor is noted, but as you say, the buying of stable information is not a punishable offence in law. No proceedings are at present contemplated, but warning that a spy system is in operation will be given privately to certain trainers.'

I tore the page up and scattered it in the litter basket, then went back to the motor-cycle and put it through its paces down the A1 to Catterick. It handled well, and I enjoyed the speed and found it quite true that it would still do a hundred.

At Catterick that Saturday Humber's head travelling lad rose like a trout to the fly.

Inskip had sent two runners, one of which was looked after by Paddy; and up on the lads' stand before the second race I saw the sharp little Irishman and Humber's head lad talking earnestly together. I was afraid that Paddy might relent towards me enough to say something in my favour, but I needn't have worried. He put my mind at rest himself.

'You're a bloody young fool,' he said, looking me over from my unkempt head to my grubby toes. 'And you've only got what you deserve. That man of Humber's was asking me about you, why you got the kick from Inskip's, and I told him the real reason, not all that eye-wash about messing about with his nibs' daughter.'

'What real reason?' I asked, surprised.

His mouth twisted in contempt. 'People talk, you know. You don't think they keep their traps shut, when there's a good bit of gossip going round? You don't think that Grits didn't tell me how you got drunk at Cheltenham and blew your mouth off about Inskip's? And what you said at Bristol about being willing to put the finger on a horse's box in the yard, well, that got round to me too. And thick as thieves with that crook Soupy, you were, as well. And there was that time when we all put our wages on Sparking Plug and he didn't go a yard . . . I'd lay any money that was your doing. So I told Humber's man he would be a fool to take you on. You're poison, Dan, and I reckon any stable is better off without you, and I told him so.'

'Thanks.'

'You can ride,' said Paddy disgustedly, 'I'll say that for you. And it's an utter bloody waste. You'll never get a job with a decent stable again, it would be like putting a rotten apple into a box of good ones.'

'Did you say all that to Humber's man?'

'I told him no decent stable would take you on,' he nodded. 'And if you ask me it bloody well serves you right.' He turned his back on me and walked away.

I sighed, and told myself I should be pleased that Paddy believed me such a black character.

Humber's head travelling lad spoke to me in the paddock between the last two reaces.

'Hey, you,' he said, catching my arm. 'I hear you're looking for a job.'

'That's right.'

'I might be able to put you in the way of something. Good pay, better than most.'

'Whose stable?' I asked. 'And how much?'

'Sixteen quid a week.'

'Sounds good,' I admitted. 'Where?'

'Where I work. For Mr. Humber. Up in Durham.'

'Humber,' I repeated sourly.

'Well, you want a job, don't you? Of course if you are so well off you can do without a job, that's different.' He sneered at my unprosperous appearance.

'I need a job,' I muttered.

'Well, then?'

'He might not have me,' I said bitterly. 'Like some others I could mention.'

'He will if I put in a word for you, we're short of a lad just now. There's another meeting here next Wednesday. I'll put in a word for you before that and if it is O.K. you can see Mr. Humber on Wednesday and he'll tell you whether he'll have you or not.'

'Why not ask him now?' I said.

'No. You wait till Wednesday.'

'All right,' I said grudgingly. 'If I've got to.'

I could almost see him thinking that by Wednesday I would be just that much hungrier, just that much more anxious to take any job that was offered and less likely to be frightened off by rumours of bad conditions.

I had spent all the bookmaker's two hundred, as well as half of the money I had earned at Inskip's, on my Italian jaunt (of which I regretted not one penny), and after paying for the motor-cycle and the succession of dingy lodgings I had almost nothing left of October's original two hundred. He had not suggested giving me any more for expenses, and I was not going to ask him for any: but I judged that the other half of my Inskip pay could be spent how I liked, and I despatched nearly all of it in the following three days on a motor-cycle trip to Edinburgh, walking round and enjoying the city and thinking myself the oddest tourist in Scotland.

On Tuesday evening, when Hogmanay was in full swing, I braved the head waiter of L'Aperitif, who to his eternal credit treated me with beautifully self-controlled politeness, but quite reasonably checked, before he gave me a little table in a corner, that I had enough money to pay the bill. Impervious to scandalized looks from better dressed diners, I slowly ate, with Humber's establishment in mind, a perfect and enormous dinner of lobster, duck bigarade, lemon soufflé and brie, and drank most of a bottle of Château Leauville Lescases 1948.

With which extravagant farewell to being my own master I rode down the A1 to Catterick on New Year's Day and in good spirits engaged myself to the worst stable in the country.

Chapter Nine

Rumour had hardly done Hedley Humber justice. The discomfort in which the lads were expected to live was so methodically devised that I had been there only one day before I came to the conclusion that its sole purpose was to discourage anyone from staying too long. I discovered that only the head lad and the head travelling lad, who both lived out in Posset, had worked in the yard for more than three months, and that the average time it took for an ordinary lad to decide that sixteen pounds a week was not enough was eight to ten weeks.

This meant that none of the stable hands except the two head lads knew what had happened to Superman the previous summer, because none of them had been there at the time. And caution told me that the only reason the two top men stayed was because they knew what was going on, and that if I asked *them* about Superman I might find myself following smartly in Tommy Stapleton's footsteps.

I had heard all about the squalor of the living quarters at some stables, and I was aware also that some lads deserved no better – some I knew of had broken up and burned their chairs rather than go outside and fetch coal, and others had stacked their dirty dishes in the lavatory and pulled the chain to do the washing up. But even granted that Humber only employed the dregs, his arrangements were very nearly inhuman.

The dormitory was a narrow hayloft over the horses. One could hear every bang of their hooves and the rattle of chains, and through cracks in the plank floor one could see straight down into the boxes. Upwards through the cracks rose a smell of dirty straw and an icy draught. There was no ceiling to the hayloft except the rafters and the tiles of the roof, and no way up into it except a ladder through a hole in the floor. In the one small window a broken pane of glass had been pasted over with brown paper, which shut out the light and let in the cold.

The seven beds, which were all the hayloft held in the way of furniture, were stark, basic affairs made of a piece of canvas stretched tautly on to a tubular metal frame. On each bed there was supposed to be one pillow and two grey blankets, but I had to struggle to get mine back because they had been appropriated by others as soon as my predecessor left. The pillow had no cover, there were no sheets, and there were no mattresses. Everyone went to bed fully dressed to keep warm, and on my third day there it started snowing.

The kitchen at the bottom of the ladder, the only other room available to the lads, was nothing more than the last loose box along one side of the yard. So little had been done to make it habitable as to leave a powerful suggestion that its inmates were to be thought of, and treated, as animals. The bars were still in place over the small window, and there were still bolts on the outside of the split stable door. The floor was still of bare concrete criss-crossed with drainage grooves; one side wall was of rough boards with kick marks still in them and the other three were of bare bricks. The room was chronically cold and damp and dirty; and although it may have been big enough as a home for one horse, it was uncomfortably cramped for seven men.

The minimal furniture consisted of rough benches around two walls, a wooden table, a badly chipped electric cooker, a shelf for crockery, and an old marble wash stand bearing a metal jug and a metal basin, which was all there was in the way of a bathroom. Other needs were catered for in a wooden hut beside the muck heap.

The food, prepared by a slatternly woman perpetually in curlers, was not up to the standard of the accommodation.

Humber, who had engaged me with an indifferent glance and a nod, directed me with equal lack of interest, when I arrived in the yard, to look after four horses, and told me the numbers of their boxes. Neither he nor anyone else told me their names. The head lad, who did one horse himself, appeared to have very little authority, contrary to the practice in most other training stables, and it was Humber himself who gave the orders and who made sure they were carried out.

He was a tyrant, not so much in the quality of the work he demanded, as in the quantity. There were some thirty horses in the yard. The head lad cared for one horse, and the head travelling lad, who also drove the horse box, did none at all. That left twenty-nine horses for seven lads, who were also expected to keep the gallops in order and do all the cleaning and maintenance work of the whole place. On racing days, when one or two lads were away, those remaining often had six horses to see to. It made my stint at Inskip's seem like a rest cure.

At the slightest sign of shirking Humber would dish out irritating little punishments and roar in an acid voice that he paid extra wages for extra work, and anyone who didn't like it could leave. As everyone was there because better stables would not risk employing them, leaving Humber's automatically meant leaving racing altogether. And taking whatever they knew about the place with them. It was very very neat.

My companions in this hell hole were neither friendly nor likeable. The best of them was the nearly half-witted boy I had seen at Stafford on Boxing Day. His name was Jerry, and he came in for a lot of physical abuse because he was slower and more stupid than anyone else.

Two of the others had been to prison and their outlook on life made Soupy Tarleton look like a Sunday-school favourite. It was from one of these, Jimmy, that I had had to wrench my blankets and from the other, a thickset tough called Charlie, my pillow. They were the two bullies of the bunch, and in addition to the free use they made of their boots, they could always be relied upon to tell lying tales and wriggle themselves out of trouble, seeing to it that someone else was punished in their stead.

Reggie was a food stealer. Thin, white faced, and with a twitch in his left eyelid, he had long prehensile hands which could whisk the bread off your plate faster than the eye could follow. I lost a lot of my meagre rations to him before I caught him at it, and it always remained a mystery why, when he managed to eat more than anyone else, he stayed the thinnest.

One of the lads was deaf. He told me phlegmatically in a toneless mumble that his dad had done it when he was little, giving him a few clips too many over the earholes. His name was Bert, and as he occasionally wet himself in bed, he smelled appalling.

The seventh, Geoff, had been there longest, and even after ten weeks never spoke of leaving. He had a habit of looking furtively over his shoulder, and any mention by Jimmy or Charlie about their prison experiences brought him close to tears, so that I came to the conclusion that he had committed some crime and was terrified of being found out. I supposed ten weeks at Humber's might be preferable to jail, but it was debatable.

They knew all about me from the head travelling lad, Jud Wilson. My general dishonesty they took entirely for granted, but they thought I was lucky to have got off without going inside if it was true about October's daughter, and they sniggered about it unendingly, and made merciless obscene jibes that hit their target all too often.

I found their constant closeness a trial, the food disgusting, the work exhausting, the beds relentless, and the cold unspeakable. All of which rather roughly taught me that my life in Australia had been soft and easy, even when I thought it most demanding.

Before I went to Humber's I had wondered why anyone should be foolish enough to pay training fees to a patently unsuccessful trainer, but I gradually found out. The yard itself, for one thing, was a surprise. From the appearance of the horses at race meetings one would have expected their home surroundings to be weedy gravel, broken-hinged boxes and flaked-off paint: but in fact the yard was trim and prosperous looking, and was kept that way by the lads, who never had time off in the afternoons. This glossy window-dressing cost Humber nothing but an occasional gallon of paint and a certain amount of slave driving.

His manner with the owners who sometimes arrived for a look round was authoritative and persuasive, and his fees, I later discovered, were lower than anyone else's, which attracted more custom than he would otherwise have had. In addition some of the horses in the yard were not racehorses at all, but hunters at livery, for whose board, lodging and exercise he received substantial sums without the responsibility of having to train them.

I learned from the other lads that only seven of the stable's inmates had raced at all that season, but that those seven had been hard worked, with an average of a race each every ten days. There had been one winner, two seconds and a third, among them.

None of those seven was in my care. I had been allotted to a quartet consisting of two racehorses which belonged, as far as I could make out, to Humber himself, and two hunters. The two racehorses were bays, about seven years old; one of them had a sweet mouth and no speed and the other a useful sprint over schooling fences but a churlish nature. I pressed Cass, the head lad, to tell me their names, and he said they were Dobbin and Sooty. These unraceman-like names were not to be found in the form book, nor in Humber's list in 'Horses in Training'; and it seemed to me highly probable that Rudyard, Superman, Charcoal and the rest had all spent their short periods in the yard under similar uninformative pseudonyms.

A lad who had gone out of racing would never connect the Dobbin or Sotty he had once looked after with the Rudyard who won a race for another trainer two years later.

But why, *why* did he win two years later? About that, I was as ignorant as ever.

The cold weather came and gripped, and stayed. But nothing, the other lads said, could be as bad as the fearsome winter before; and I reflected that in that January and February I had been sweltering under the midsummer sun. I wondered how Belinda and Helen and Phillip were enjoying their long vacation, and what they would think if they could see me in my dirty down-trodden sub-existence, and what the men would think, to see their employer brought so low. It amused me a good deal to imagine it: and it not only helped the tedious hours to pass more quickly, but kept me from losing my own inner identity.

As the days of drudgery mounted up I began to wonder if anyone who embarked on so radical a masquerade really knew what he was doing.

Expression, speech and movement had to be unremittingly schooled into a convincing show of uncouth dullness. I worked in a slovenly fashion and rode, with a pang, like a mutton-fisted clod; but as time passed all these deceptions became easier. If one pretended long enough to be a wreck, did one finally become one, I wondered. And if one stripped oneself continuously of all human dignity would one in the end be unaware of its absence? I hoped the question would remain academic: and as long as I could have a quiet laugh at myself now and then, I supposed I was safe enough.

My belief that after three months in the yard a lad was given every encouragement to leave was amply borne out by what happened to Geoff Smith.

Humber never rode out to exercise with his horses, but drove in a van to the gallops to watch them work, and returned to the yard while they were still walking back to have a poke round to see what had been done and not done.

One morning, when we went in with the second lot, Humber was standing in the centre of the yard radiating his frequent displeasure.

'You, Smith, and you, Roke, put those horses in their boxes and come here.'

We did so.

'Roke.'

'Sir.'

'The mangers of all your four horses are in a disgusting state. Clean them up.'

'Yes, sir.'

'And to teach you to be more thorough in future you will get up at five-thirty for the next week.'

'Sir.'

I sighed inwardly, but this was to me one of his more acceptable forms of pinprick punishment, since I didn't particularly mind getting up early. It entailed merely standing in the middle of the yard for over an hour, doing nothing. Dark, cold and boring. I don't think he slept much himself. His bedroom window faced down the yard, and he always knew if one were not standing outside by twenty to six, and shining a torch to prove it.

'And as for you.' He looked at Geoff with calculation. 'The floor of number seven is caked with dirt. You'll clean out the straw and scrub the floor with disinfectant before you get your dinner.'

'But sir,' protested Geoff incautiously, 'if I don't go in for dinner with the others, they won't leave me any.'

'You should have thought of that before, and done your work properly in the first place. I pay half as much again as any other trainer would, and I expect value for it. You will do as you are told.'

'But, sir,' whined Geoff, knowing that if he missed his main meal he would go very hungry, 'Can't I do it this afternoon?'

Humber casually slid his walking stick through his hand until he was holding it at the bottom. Then he swung his arm and savagely cracked the knobbed handle across Geoff's thigh.

Geoff yelped and rubbed his leg.

'Before dinner,' remarked Humber: and walked away, leaning on his stick.

Geoff missed his share of the watery half-stewed lumps of mutton, and came in panting to see the last of the bread-and-suet pudding spooned into Charlie's trap-like mouth.

'You bloody sods,' he yelled miserably, 'You bloody lot of sods.'

He stuck it for a whole week. He stood six more heavy blows on various parts of his body, and missed his dinner three more times, and his breakfast twice, and his supper once. Long before the end of it he was in tears, but he didn't want to leave.

After five days Cass came into the kitchen at breakfast and told Geoff, 'The boss has taken against you, I'm afraid. You won't ever do anything right for him again from now on. Best thing you can do, and I'm telling you for your own good, mind, is to find a job somewhere else. The boss gets these fits now and then when one of the lads can't do anything right, and no one can change him when he gets going. You can work until you're blue in the face, but he won't take to you any more. You don't want to get yourself bashed up any more, now do you? All I'm telling you is that if you stay here you'll find that what has happened so far is only the beginning. See? I'm only telling you for your own good.'

Even so, it was two more days before Geoff painfully packed his old army kit bag and sniffed his way off the premises.

A weedy boy arrived the next morning as a replacement, but he only stayed three days as Jimmy stole his blankets before he came and he was not strong enough to get them back. He moaned piteously through two freezing nights, and was gone before the third.

The next morning, before breakfast, it was Jimmy himself who collected a crack from the stick.

He came in late and cursing and snatched a chunk of bread out of Jerry's hand.

'Where's my bloody breakfast?'

We had eaten it, of course.

'Well,' he said, glaring at us, 'you can do my ruddy horses, as well. I'm off. I'm not bloody well staying here. This is worse than doing bird. You won't catch me staying here to be swiped at, I'll tell you that.'

Reggie said, 'Why don't you complain?'

'Who to?'

'Well . . . the bluebottles.'

'Are you out of your mind?' said Jimmy in amazement. 'You're a bloody nit, that's what you are. Can you see me, with my form, going into the cop house and saying I got a complaint to make about my employer, he hit me with his walking stick? For a start, they'd laugh. They'd laugh their bleeding heads off. And then what? Supposing they come here and asked Cass if he's seen anyone getting the rough end of it? Well, I'll tell you, that Cass wants to keep his cushy job. Oh no, he'd say, I ain't seen nothing. Mr Humber, he's a nice kind gentleman with a heart of gold, and what can you expect from an ex-con but a pack of bull? Don't ruddy well make me laugh. I'm off, and if the rest of you've got any sense, you'll be out of it too.'

No one, however, took his advice.

I found out from Charlie that Jimmy had been there two weeks longer than he, which made it, he thought, about eleven weeks.

As Jimmy strode defiantly out of the yard I went rather thoughtfully about my business. Eleven weeks, twelve at the most, before Humber's arm started swinging. I had been there already three: which left me a maximum of nine more in which to discover how he managed the doping. It wasn't that I couldn't probably last out as long as Geoff if it came to the point, but that if I hadn't uncovered Humber's method before he focused his attention on getting rid of me, I had very little chance of doing it afterwards.

Three weeks, I thought, and I had found out nothing at all except that I wanted to leave as soon as possible.

Two lads came to take Geoff's and Jimmy's places, a tall boy called Lenny who had been to Borstal and was proud of it, and Cecil, a far-gone alcoholic of about thirty-five. He had, he told us, been kicked out of half the stables in England because he couldn't keep his hands off the bottle. I don't know where he got the liquor from or how he managed to hide it, but he was certainly three parts drunk every day by four o'clock, and snored in a paralytic stupor every night.

Life, if you could call it that, went on.

All the lads seemed to have a good reason for having to earn the extra wages Humber paid. Lenny was repaying some money he had stolen from another employer, Charlie had a wife somewhere drawing maintenance, Cecil drank, Reggie was a compulsive saver, and Humber sent Jerry's money straight off to his parents. Jerry was proud of being able to help them.

I had let Jud Wilson and Cass know that I badly needed to earn sixteen pounds a week because I had fallen behind on hire purchase payments on the motor-cycle, and this also gave me an obvious reason for needing to spend some time in the Posset post office on Saturday afternoons.

Public transport from the stables to Posset, a large village a mile and a half away, did not exist. Cass and Jud Wilson both had cars, but would give no lifts. My motor-cycle was the only other transport available, but to the lads' fluently expressed disgust I refused to use it on the frosty snow-strewn roads for trips down to the pub in the evenings. As a result we hardly ever went to Posset except on the two hours we had off on Saturday afternoons, and also on Sunday evenings, when after a slightly less relentless day's work everyone had enough energy left to walk for their beer.

On Saturdays I unwrapped the motor-cycle from its thick plastic cocoon and set off to Posset with Jerry perched ecstatically on the pillion. I always took poor simple-minded Jerry because he got the worst of everything throughout the week; and we quickly fell into a routine. First we went to the post office for me to post off my imaginary hire purchase. Instead, leaning on the shelf among the telegram forms and scraps of pink blotting paper, I wrote each week a report to October, making sure that no one from the stables looked over my shoulder. Replies, if any, I collected, read, and tore up over the litter basket.

Jerry accepted without question that I would be at least a quarter of an hour in the post office, and spent the time unsuspiciously at the other end of the shop inspecting the stock in the toy department. Twice he bought a big friction-drive car and played with it, until it broke, on the dormitory floor: and every week he bought a children's fourpenny comic, over whose picture strips he giggled contentedly for the next few days. He couldn't read a word, and often asked me to explain the captions, so that I became intimately acquainted with the doings of Micky the Monkey and Flip McCoy.

Leaving the post office we climbed back on to the motor-cycle and rode two hundred yards down the street to have tea. This ritual took place in a square bare café with margarine coloured walls, cold lighting, and messy table tops. For decoration there were pepsi-cola advertisements, and for service a bored looking girl with no stockings and mousy hair piled into a matted, wispy mountain on top of her head.

None of this mattered. Jerry and I ordered and ate with indescribable enjoyment a heap of lamb chops, fried eggs, flabby chips and bright green peas. Charlie and the others were to be seen doing the same at adjoining tables. The girl knew where we came from, and looked down on us, as her father owned the café.

On our way out Jerry and I packed our pockets with bars of chocolate to supplement Humber's food, a hoard which lasted each week exactly as long as it took Reggie to find it.

By five o'clock we were back in the yard, the motor-cycle wrapped up again, the week's highlight nothing but a memory and a belch, the next seven days stretching drearily ahead.

There were hours, in that life, in which to think. Hours of trotting the horses round and round a straw track in a frozen field, hours brushing the dust out of their coats, hours cleaning the muck out of their boxes and carrying their water and hay, hours lying awake at night listening to the stamp of the horses below and the snores and mumblings from the row of beds.

Over and over again I thought my way through all I had seen or read or heard since I came to England: and what emerged as most significant was the performance of Superman at Stafford. He had been doped: he was the twelfth of the series: but he had not won.

Eventually I changed the order of these thoughts. He had been doped, and he had not won; but was he, after all, the twelfth of the series? He might be the thirteenth, the fourteenth ... there might have been others who had come to grief.

On my third Saturday, when I had been at Humber's just over a fortnight, I wrote asking October to look out the newspaper cutting which Tommy Stapleton had kept, about a horse going beserk and killing a woman in the paddock at Cartmel races. I asked him to check the horse's history.

A week later I read his typewritten reply.

'Old Etonian, destroyed at Cartmel, Lancashire, at Whitsun this year, spent the previous November and December in Humber's yard. Humber claimed him in a selling race, and sold him again at Leicester sales seven weeks later.

'*But:* Old Etonian went beserk in the parade ring *before* the race; he was due to run in a handicap, not a seller; and the run-in at Cartmel is short. None of these facts conform to the pattern of the others.

'Dope tests were made on Old Etonian, but proved negative.

'No one could explain why he behaved as he did.'

Tommy Stapleton, I thought, must have had an idea, or he would not have cut out the report, yet he could not have been sure enough to act on it without checking up. And checking up had killed him. There could be no more doubt of it.

I tore up the paper and took Jerry along to the café, more conscious than usual of the danger breathing down my neck. It didn't, however, spoil my appetite for the only edible meal of the week.

At supper a few days later, in the lull before Charlie turned on his transistor radio for the usual evening of pops from Luxembourg (which I had grown to enjoy) I steered the conversation round to Cartmel races. What, I wanted to know, were they like?

Only Cecil, the drunk, had ever been there.

'It's not like it used to be in the old days,' he said owlishly, not noticing Reggie filch a hunk of his bread and margarine.

Cecil's eyes had a glazed, liquid look, but I had luckily asked my question at exactly the right moment, in the loquacious half-hour between the silent bleariness of the afternoon's liquor and his disappearance to tank up for the night.

'What was it like in the old days?' I prompted.

'They had a fair there.' He hiccuped. 'A fair with roundabouts and swings and side-shows and all. Bank Holiday, see? Whitsun and all that.

Only place outside the Derby you could go on the swings at the races. Course, they stopped it now. Don't like no one to have a good time, they don't. It weren't doing no harm, it weren't, the fair.'

'Fairs,' said Reggie scornfully, his eyes flicking to the crust Jerry held loosely in his hand.

'Good for dipping,' commented Lenny, with superiority.

'Yeah,' agreed Charlie, who hadn't yet decided if Borstal qualified Lenny as a fit companion for one from the higher school.

'Eh?' said Cecil, lost.

'Dipping. Working the pockets,' Lenny said.

'Oh. Well, it can't have been that with the hound trails and they stopped them too. They were good sport, they were. Bloody good day out, it used to be, at Cartmel, but now it's the same as any other ruddy place. You might as well be at Newton Abbot or somewhere. Nothing but ordinary racing like any other day of the week.' He belched.

'What were the hound trails?' I asked.

'Dog races,' he said, smiling foolishly. 'Bloody dog races. They used to have one before the horse races, and one afterwards, but they've ruddy well stopped it now. Bloody kill-joys, that's all they are. Still,' he leered triumphantly, 'if you know what's what you can still have a bet on the dogs. They have the hound trail in the morning now, on the other side of the village from the race-track, but if you get your horse bedded down quick enough you can get there in time for a bet.'

'Dog races?' said Lenny disbelievingly. 'Dogs won't race round no horse track. There ain't no bloody electric hare, for a start.'

Cecil swivelled his head unsteadily in his direction.

'You don't have a track for hound trails,' he said earnestly, in his slurred voice. 'It's a *trail*, see?' Some bloke sets off with a bag full of aniseed and paraffin, or something like that, and drags it for miles and miles round the hills and such. Then they let all the dogs loose and the first one to follow all round the trail and get back quickest is the winner. Year before last someone shot at the bloody favourite half a mile from home and there was a bleeding riot. They missed him, though. They hit the one just behind, some ruddy outsider with no chance.'

'Reggie's ate my crust,' said Jerry sadly.

'Did you go to Cartmel this year too?' I asked.

'No,' Cecil said regretfully. 'Can't say I did. A woman got killed there, and all.'

'How?' asked Lenny, looking avid.

'Some bloody horse bolted in the paddock, and jumped the rails of the parade ring and landed on some poor bloody woman who was just having a nice day out. She backed a loser all right, she did that day. I heard she was cut to bits, time that crazy animal trampled all over her trying to get out through the crowd. He didn't get far, but he kicked out all over the place and broke another man's leg before they got the vet to him and shot him. Mad, they said he was. A mate of mine was there, see, leading one round in the same race, and he said it was something awful, that poor woman all cut up and bleeding to death in front of his eyes.'

The others looked suitably impressed at this horrific story, all except Bert, who couldn't hear it.

'Well,' said Cecil, getting up, 'it's time for my little walk.'

He went out for his little walk, which was presumably to wherever he had hidden his alcohol, because as usual he came back less than an hour later and stumbled up the ladder to his customary oblivion.

Chapter Ten

Towards the end of my fourth week Reggie left (complaining of hunger) and in a day or two was duly replaced by a boy with a soft face who said in a high pitched voice that his name was Kenneth.

To Humber I clearly remained one insignificant face in this endless procession of human flotsam; and as I could safely operate only as long as that state of affairs continued I did as little as possible to attract his attention. He gave me orders, and I obeyed them: and he cursed me and punished me, but not more than anyone else, for the things I left undone.

I grew to recognise his moods at a glance. There were days when he glowered silently all through first and second exercise and turned out again to make sure that no one skimped the third, and on these occasions even Cass walked warily and only spoke if he were spoken to. There were days when he talked a great deal but always in sarcasm, and his tongue was so rough that everyone preferred the silence. There were occasional days when he wore an abstracted air and overlooked our faults, and even rarer days when he looked fairly pleased with life.

At all times he was impeccably turned out, as if to emphasize the difference between his state and ours. His clothes, I judged, were his main personal vanity, but his wealth was also evident in his car, the latest type of Cunard-sized Bentley. It was fitted with back-seat television, plush carpets, radio telephone, fur rugs, air conditioning, and a built-in drinks cabinet holding in racks six bottles, twelve glasses, and a glittering array of chromiumed cork screws, ice picks and miscellaneous objects like swizzle sticks.

I knew the car well, because I had to clean it every Monday afternoon. Bert had to clean it on Fridays. Humber was proud of his car.

He was chauffeured on long journeys in this above-his-status symbol by Jud Wilson's sister Grace, a hard faced amazon of a woman who handled the huge car with practised ease but was not expected to maintain it. I never once spoke to her: she bicycled in from wherever she lived, drove as necessary, and bicycled away again. Frequently the car had not been cleaned to her satisfaction, but her remarks were relayed to Bert and me by Jud.

I looked into every cranny every time while cleaning the inside, but

Humber was neither so obliging nor so careless as to leave hypodermic syringes or phials of stimulants lying about in the glove pockets.

All through my first month there the freezing weather was not only a discomfort but also a tiresome delay. While racing was suspended Humber could dope no horses, and there was no opportunity for me to see what difference it made to his routine when the racing was scheduled for any of the five courses with long run-ins.

On top of that, he and Jud Wilson and Cass were always about in the stables. I wanted to have a look round inside Humber's office, a brick hut standing across the top end of the yard, but I could not risk a search when any one of them might come in and find me at it. With Humber and Jud Wilson away at the races, though, and with Cass gone home to his midday meal, I reckoned I could go into the office to search while the rest of the lads were eating.

Cass had a key to the office, and it was he who unlocked the door in the morning and locked it again at night. As far as I could see he did not bother to lock up when he went home for lunch, and the office was normally left open all day, except on Sunday. This might mean, I thought, that Humber kept nothing there which could possibly be incriminating: but on the other hand he could perhaps keep something there which was apparently innocent but would be incriminating if one understood its significance.

However, the likelihood of solving the whole mystery by a quick look round an unlocked stable office was so doubtful that it was not worth risking discovery, and I judged it better to wait with what patience I could until the odds were in my favour.

There was also Humber's house, a whitewashed converted farm house adjoining the yard. A couple of stealthy surveys, made on afternoons when I was bidden to sweep snow from his garden path, showed that this was an ultra-neat soulless establishment like a series of rooms in shop windows, impersonal and unlived-in. Humber was not married, and downstairs at least there seemed to be nowhere at all snug for him to spend his evenings.

Through the windows I saw no desk to investigate and no safe in which to lock away secrets: all the same I decided it would be less than fair to ignore his home, and if I both drew a blank and got away with an entry into the office, I would pay the house a visit at the first opportunity.

At last it began to thaw on a Wednesday night and continued fast all day Thursday and Friday, so that by Saturday morning the thin slush was disintegrating into puddles, and the stables stirred with the re-awakening of hunting and racing.

Cass told me on Friday night that the man who owned the hunters I looked after required them both to be ready for him on Saturday, and after second exercise I led them out and loaded them into the horse box which had come for them.

Their owner stood leaning against the front wing of a well polished Jaguar. His hunting boots shone like glass, his cream breeches were perfection, his pink coat fitted without a wrinkle, his stock was smooth and snowy. He held a sensible leather-covered riding stick in his hand and slapped it against his boot. He was tall, broad and bare-headed, about forty years old, and, from across the yard, handsome. It was only when one was close to him that one could see the dissatisfied look on his face and the evidence of dissipation in his skin.

'You,' he said, pointing at me with his stick. 'Come here.'

I went. He had heavy lidded eyes and a few purple thread veins on his nose and cheeks. He looked at me with superior bored disdain. I am five feet nine inches tall; he was four inches taller, and he made the most of it.

'You'll pay for it if those horses of mine don't last the day. I ride them hard. They need to be fit.'

His voice had the same expensive timbre as October's.

'They're as fit as the snow would allow,' I said calmly.

He raised his eyebrows.

'Sir,' I added.

'Insolence,' he said, 'will get you nowhere.'

'I am sorry, sir, I didn't mean to be insolent.'

He laughed unpleasantly. 'I'll bet you didn't. It's not so easy to get another job, is it? You'll watch your tongue when you speak to me in future, if you know what's good for you.'

'Yes sir.'

'And if those horses of mine aren't fit, you'll wish you'd never been born.'

Cass appeared at my left elbow, looking anxious.

'Is everything all right, sir?' he asked. 'Has Roke done anything wrong, Mr Adams?'

How I managed not to jump out of my skin I am not quite sure. Mr Adams. Paul James Adams, sometime owner of seven subsequently doped horses?

'Is this bloody gipsy doing my horses any good?' said Adams offensively.

'He's no worse than any of the other lads,' said Cass soothingly.

'And that's saying precious little.' He gave me a mean stare. 'You've had it easy during the freeze. Too damned easy. You'll have to wake your ideas up now hunting has started again. You won't find me as soft as your master, I can tell you that.'

I said nothing. He slapped his stick sharply against his boot.

'Do you hear what I say? You'll find me harder to please.'

'Yes, sir,' I muttered.

He opened his fingers and let his stick fall at his feet.

'Pick it up,' he said.

As I bent to pick it up, he put his booted foot on my shoulder and gave me a heavy, over-balancing shove, so that I fell sprawling on to the soaking, muddy ground.

He smiled with malicious enjoyment.

'Get up, you clumsy lout, and do as you are told. Pick up my stick.'

I got to my feet, picked up his stick and held it out to him. He twitched it out of my hand, and looking at Cass said, 'You've got to show them you won't stand any nonsense. Stamp on them whenever you can. This one,' he looked me coldly up and down, 'needs to be taught a lesson. What do you suggest?'

Cass looked at me doubtfully. I glanced at Adams. This, I thought, was not funny. His greyish blue eyes were curiously opaque, as if he were drunk: but he was plainly sober. I had seen that look before, in the eyes of a stable hand I had once for a short time employed, and I knew what it could mean. I had got to guess at once, and guess right, whether he preferred bullying the weak or the strong. From instinct, perhaps because of his size and evident worldliness, I guessed that crushing the weak would be too tame for him. In which case it was definitely not the moment for any show of strength. I drooped in as cowed and unresisting a manner as I could devise.

'God,' said Adams in disgust. 'Just look at him. Scared out of his bloody wits.' He shrugged impatiently. 'Well Cass, just find him some stinking useless occupation like scrubbing the paths and put him to work. There's no sport for me here. No backbone for me to break. Give me a fox any day, at least they've got some cunning and some guts.'

His gaze strayed sideways to where Humber was crossing the far end of the yard. He said to Cass, 'Tell Mr. Humber I'd like to have a word with him,' and when Cass had gone he turned back to me.

'Where did you work before this?'

'At Mr. Inskip's, sir.'

'And he kicked you out?'

'Yes, sir.'

'Why?'

'I . . . er . . .' I stuck. It was incredibly galling to have to lay oneself open to such a man; but if I gave him answers he could check in small things he might believe the whopping lies without question.

'When I ask a question, you will answer it,' said Adams coldly. 'Why did Mr. Inskip get rid of you?'

I swallowed. 'I got the sack for er . . . for messing about with the boss's daughter.'

'For messing about . . .' he repeated. 'Good God.' With lewd pleasure he said something which was utterly obscene, and which struck clear home. He saw me wince and laughed at my discomfiture. Cass and Humber returned. Adams turned to Humber, still laughing, and said, 'Do you know why this cockerel got chucked out of Inskip's?'

'Yes,' said Humber flatly. 'He seduced October's daughter.' He wasn't interested. 'And there was also the matter of a favourite that came in last. He looked after it.'

'October's daughter!' said Adams, surprised, his eyes narrowing. 'I thought he meant Inskip's daughter.' He casually dealt me a sharp clip on the ear. 'Don't try lying to me.'

'Mr. Inskip hasn't got a daughter,' I protested.

'And don't answer back.' His hand flicked out again. He was rather adept at it. He must have indulged in a lot of practice.

'Hedley,' he said to Humber, who had impassively watched this one-sided exchange. 'I'll give you a lift to Nottingham races on Monday if you like. I'll pick you up at ten.'

'Right,' agreed Humber.

Adams turned to Cass. 'Don't forget that lesson for this lily-livered Romeo. Cool his ardour a bit.'

Cass sniggered sycophantically and raised goose pimples on my neck.

Adams climbed coolly into his Jaguar, started it up and followed the horse box containing his two hunters out of the yard.

Humber said, 'I don't want Roke out of action Cass. You've got to leave him fit for work. Use some sense this time.' He limped away to continue his inspection of the boxes.

Cass looked at me, and I looked steadily down at my damp, muddy clothes, very conscious that the head lad counted among the enemy, and not wanting to risk his seeing that there was anything but submissiveness in my face.

He said, 'Mr. Adams don't like to be crossed.'

'I didn't cross him.'

'Nor he don't like to be answered back to. You mind your lip.'

'Has he any more horses here?' I asked.

'Yes,' said Cass, 'And it's none of your business. Now, he told me to punish you, and he won't forget. He'll check up later.'

'I've done nothing wrong,' I said sullenly, still looking down. What on earth would my foreman say about this, I thought; and nearly smiled at the picture.

'You don't need to have done nothing wrong,' said Cass. 'With Mr. Adams it is a case of punish first so that you won't do anything wrong after. Sense, in a way.' He gave a snort of laughter. 'Saves trouble, see?'

'Are his horses all hunters?' I asked.

'No,' said Cass, 'but the two you've got are, and don't you forget it. He rides those himself, and he'll notice how you look after every hair on their hides.'

'Does he treat the lads who look after his other horses so shockingly unfair?'

'I've never heard Jerry complaining. And Mr. Adams won't treat you too bad if you mind your p's and q's. Now that lesson he suggested . . .'

I had hoped he had forgotten it.

'You can get down on your knees and scrub the concrete paths round the yard. Start now. You can break for dinner, and then go on until evening stables.'

I went on standing in a rag-doll attitude of dejectedness, looking at the ground, but fighting an unexpectedly strong feeling of rebellion. What the hell, I thought, did October expect of me? Just how much was I to take? Was there any point at which, if he were there, he would say 'Stop; all right; that's enough. That's too much. Give it up.' But remembering how he felt about me, I supposed not!

Cass said, 'There's a scrubbing brush in the cupboard in the tack room. Get on with it.' He walked away.

The concrete pathways were six feet wide and ran round all sides of the yard in front of the boxes. They had been scraped clear of snow throughout the month I had been there so that the feed trolley could make its usual smooth journey from horse to horse, and as in most modern stables, including Inskip's and my own, they would always be kept clean of straw and excessive dust. But scrubbing them on ones knees for nearly four hours on a slushy day at the end of January was a miserable, back-breaking, insane waste of time. Ludicrous, besides.

I had a clear choice of scrubbing the paths or getting on the motorcycle and going. Thinking firmly that I was being paid at least ten thousand pounds for doing it, I scrubbed: and Cass hung around the yard all day to watch that I didn't rest.

The lads, who had spent much of the afternoon amusing themselves by jeering at my plight as they set off for and returned from the café in Posset, made quite sure during evening stables that the concrete paths ended the day even dirtier than they had begun. I didn't care a damn about that; but Adams had sent his hunters back caked with mud and sweat and it took me two hours to clean them because by the end of that day many of my muscles were trembling with fatigue.

Then, to crown it all, Adams came back. He drove his Jaguar into the yard, climbed out, and after having talked to Cass, who nodded and gestured round the paths, he walked without haste towards the box where I was still struggling with his black horse.

He stood in the doorway and looked down his nose at me; and I looked back. He was superbly elegant in a dark blue pin-striped suit with a white shirt and a silver-grey tie. His skin looked fresh, his hair well brushed, his hands clean and pale. I imagined he had gone home after hunting and enjoyed a deep hot bath, a change of clothes, a drink . . . I hadn't had a bath for a month and was unlikely to get one as long as I stayed at Humber's. I was filthy and hungry and extremely tired. I wished he would go away and leave me alone.

No such luck.

He took a step into the box and surveyed the mud still caked solid on the horse's hind legs.

'You're slow,' he remarked.

'Yes, sir.'

'This horse must have been back here three hours ago. What have you been doing?'

'My three other horses, sir.'

'You should do mine first.'

'I had to wait for the mud to dry, sir. You can't brush it out while it's still wet.'

'I told you this morning not to answer back.' His hand lashed out across the ear he had hit before. He was smiling slightly. Enjoying himself. Which was more than could be said for me.

Having, so to speak, tasted blood, he suddenly took hold of the front of my jersey, pushed me back against the wall, and slapped me twice in the face, forehand and backhand. Still smiling.

What I wanted to do was to jab my knee into his groin and my fist into his stomach; and refraining wasn't easy. For the sake of realism I knew I should have cried out loudly and begged him to stop, but when it came to the point I couldn't do it. However, one could act what one couldn't say, so I lifted both arms and folded them defensively round my head.

He laughed and let go, and I slid down on to one knee and cowered against the wall.

'You're a proper little rabbit, aren't you, for all your fancy looks.'

I stayed where I was, in silence. As suddenly as he had begun, he lost interest in ill-treating me.

'Get up, get up,' he said irritably. 'I didn't hurt you. You're not worth hurting. Get up and finish this horse. And make sure it is done properly or you'll find yourself scrubbing again.'

He walked out of the box and away across the yard. I stood up, leaned against the doorpost, and with uncharitable feelings watched him go up the path to Humber's house. To a good dinner, no doubt. An arm-chair. A fire. A glass of brandy. A friend to talk to. Sighing in depression, I went back to the tiresome job of brushing off the mud.

Shortly after a supper of dry bread and cheese, eaten to the accompaniment of crude jokes about my day's occupation and detailed descriptions of the meals which had been enjoyed in Posset, I had had quite enough of my fellow workers. I climbed the ladder and sat on my bed. It was cold upstairs. I had had quite enough of Humber's yard. I had had more than enough of being kicked around. All I had to do, as I had been tempted to do that morning, was to go outside, unwrap the motor-cycle, and make tracks for civilization. I could stifle my conscience by paying most of the money back to October and pointing out that I had done at least half of the job.

I went on sitting on the bed and thinking about riding away on the motor-bike. I went on sitting on the bed. And not riding away on the motor-bike.

Presently I found myself sighing. I knew very well I had never had any real doubts about staying, even if it meant scrubbing those dreadful paths every day of the week. Quite apart from not finding myself good company in future if I ran away because of a little bit of eccentric charring, there was the certainty that it was specifically in Mr. P. J. Adams' ruthless hands that the good repute of British racing was in danger of being cracked to bits. It was he that I had come to defeat. It was no good decamping because the first taste of him was unpleasant.

His name typed on paper had come alive as a worse menace than Humber himself had ever seemed. Humber was merely harsh, greedy, bad-tempered and vain, and he beat his lads for the sole purpose of making them leave. But Adams seemed to enjoy hurting for its own sake. Beneath that glossy crust of sophistication, and not far beneath, one glimpsed an irresponsible savage. Humber was forceful; but Adams, it now seemed to me, was the brains of the partnership. He was a more complex man and a far more fearsome adversary. I had felt equal to Humber. Adams dismayed me.

Someone started to come up the ladder. I thought it would be Cecil, reeling from his Saturday night orgy, but it was Jerry. He came and sat on the bed next to mine. He looked downcast.

'Dan?'

For Kicks

'Yes.'

'It weren't . . . it weren't no good in Posset today, without you being there.'

'Wasn't it?'

'No.' He brightened. 'I bought my comic though. Will you read it to me?'

'Tomorrow,' I said tiredly.

There was a short silence while he struggled to organise his thoughts.

'Dan.'

'Mm?'

'I'm sorry, like.'

'What for?'

'Well, for laughing at you, like, this afternoon. It wasn't right . . . not when you've took me on your motor-bike and all. I do ever so like going on your bike.'

'It's all right, Jerry.'

'The others were ribbing you, see, and it seemed the thing, like, to do what they done. So they would . . . would let me go with them, see?'

'Yes, Jerry, I see. It doesn't matter, really it doesn't.'

'You never ribbed me, when I done wrong.'

'Forget it.'

'I've been thinking,' he said, wrinkling his forehead, 'about me Mam. She tried scrubbing some floors once. In some offices, it was. She came home fair whacked, she did. She said scrubbing floors was wicked. It made your back ache something chronic, she said, as I remember.'

'Did she?'

'Does your back ache, Dan?'

'Yes, a bit.'

He nodded pleased. 'She knows a thing or two, does my Mam.' He lapsed into one of his mindless silences, rocking himself gently backwards and forwards on the creaking bed.

I was touched by his apology.

'I'll read your comic for you,' I said.

'You ain't too whacked?' he asked eagerly.

I shook my head.

He fetched the comic from the cardboard box in which he kept his few belongings and sat beside me while I read him the captions of Mickey the Monkey, Beryl and Peril, Julius Cheeser, the Bustom Boys, and all the rest. We went through the whole thing at least twice, with him laughing contentedly and repeating the words after me. By the end of the week he would know most of them by heart.

At length I took the comic out of his hands and put it down on the bed.

'Jerry,' I said, 'which of the horses you look after belongs to Mr. Adams?'

'Mr. Adams?'

'The man whose hunters I've got. The man who was here this morning, with a grey Jaguar, and a scarlet coat.'

'Oh, that Mr. Adams.'

'Why, is there another one?'

'No, that's Mr. Adams, all right.' Jerry shuddered.

'What do you know about him?' I asked.

'The chap what was here before you came, Dennis, his name was, Mr. Adams didn't like him, see? He cheeked Mr. Adams, he did.'

'Oh,' I said. I wasn't sure I wanted to hear what had happened to Dennis.

'He weren't here above three weeks,' said Jerry reflectively. 'The last couple of days, he kept on falling down. Funny, it was, really.'

I cut him short. 'Which of your horses belongs to Mr. Adams?' I repeated.

'None of them do,' he said positively.

'Cass said so.'

He looked surprised, and also scared. 'No, Dan, I don't want none of Mr. Adams' horses.'

'Well, who do your horses belong to?'

'I don't rightly know. Except of course Pageant. He belongs to Mr. Byrd.'

'That's the one you take to the races?'

'Uh huh, that's the one.'

'How about the others?'

'Well, Mickey . . .' His brow furrowed.

'Mickey is the horse in the box next to Mr. Adams' black hunter, which I do?'

'Yeah.' He smiled brilliantly, as if I had made a point.

'Who does Mickey belong to?'

'I dunno.'

'Hasn't his owner ever been to see him?'

He shook his head doubtfully. I wasn't sure whether or not he would remember if an owner had in fact called.

'How about your other horse?' Jerry had only three horses to do, as he was slower than everyone else.

'That's Champ,' said Jerry triumphantly.

'Who owns him?'

'He's a hunter.'

'Yes, but who owns him?'

'Some fellow.' He was trying hard. 'A fat fellow. With sort of sticking out ears.' He pulled his own ears forward to show me.

'You know him well?'

He smiled widely. 'He gave me ten bob for Christmas.'

So it was Mickey, I thought, who belonged to Adams, but neither Adams nor Humber nor Cass had let Jerry know it. It looked as though Cass had let it slip out by mistake.

I said, 'How long have you worked here, Jerry?'

'How long?' he echoed vaguely.

'How many weeks were you here before Christmas?'

He put his head on one side and thought. He brightened. 'I came on the day after the Rovers beat the Gunners. My Dad took me to the match, see? Near our house, the Rovers' ground is.'

I asked him more questions, but he had no clearer idea than that about when he had come to Humber's.

'Well,' I said, 'was Mickey here already, when you came?'

'I've never done no other horses since I've been here,' he said. When I asked him no more questions he placidly picked up the comic again and began to look at the pictures. Watching him, I wondered what it was like to have a mind like his, a brain like cotton wool upon which the accumulated learning of the world could make no dent, in which reason, memory, and awareness were blanketed almost out of existence.

He smiled happily at the comic strips. He was, I reflected, none the worse off for being simple-minded. He was good at heart, and what he did not understand could not hurt him. There was a lot to be said for life on that level. If one didn't realise one was an object of calculated humiliations, there would be no need to try to make oneself be insensitive to them. If I had his simplicity, I thought, I would find life at Humber's very much easier.

He looked up suddenly and saw me watching him, and gave me a warm, contented, trusting smile.

'I like you,' he said; and turned his attention back to the paper.

There was a raucous noise from downstairs and the other lads erupted up the ladder, pushing Cecil among them as he was practically unable to walk. Jerry scuttled back to his own bed and put his comic carefully away; and I, like all the rest, wrapped myself in two grey blankets and lay down, boots and all, on the inhospitable canvas. I tried to find a comfortable position for my excessively weary limbs, but unfortunately failed.

Chapter Eleven

The office was as cold and unwelcoming as Humber's personality, with none of the ostentation of his car. It consisted of a long narrow room with the door and the single smallish window both in the long wall facing down the yard. At the far end, away to the left as one entered, there was a door which opened into a washroom: this was whitewashed and lit by three slit-like, frosted glass windows, and led through an inner door into a lavatory. In the washroom itself there was a sink, a plastic topped table, a refrigerator, and two wall cupboards. The first of these on investigation proved to hold all the bandages, linaments and medicines in common use with horses.

Careful not to move anything from its original position I looked at every bottle, packet, and tin. As far as I could see there was nothing of a stimulating nature among them.

The second cupboard however held plenty of stimulant in the shape of alcohol for human consumption, an impressive collection of bottles with a well stocked shelf of glasses above them. For the entertainment of owners, not the quickening of their horses. I shut the door.

There was nothing in the refrigerator except four bottles of beer, some milk, and a couple of trays of ice cubes.

I went back into the office.

Humber's desk stood under the window, so that when he was sitting at it he could look straight out down the yard. It was a heavy flat-topped knee-hole desk with drawers at each side, and it was almost aggressively tidy. Granted Humber was away at Nottingham races and had not spent long in the office in the morning, but the tidiness was basic, not temporary. None of the drawers was locked, and their contents (stationery, tax tables and so on) could be seen at a glance. On top of the desk there was only a telephone, an adjustable reading lamp, a tray of pens and pencils, and a green glass paper weight the size of a cricket ball. Trapped air bubbles rose in a frozen spray in its depths.

The single sheet of paper which it held down bore only a list of duties for the day and had clearly been drawn up for Cass to work from. I saw disconsolately that I would be cleaning tack that afternoon with baby-voiced Kenneth, who never stopped talking, and doing five horses at evening stables, this last because the horses normally done by Bert, who had gone racing, had to be shared out among those left behind.

Apart from the desk the office contained a large floor-to-ceiling cupboard in which form books and racing colours were kept; too few of those for the space available. Three dark green filing cabinets, two leather arm-chairs, and an upright wooden chair with a leather seat stood round the walls.

I opened the unlocked drawers of the filing cabinet one by one and searched quickly through the contents. They contained racing calendars, old accounts, receipts, press cuttings, photographs, papers to do with the horses currently in training, analyses of form, letters from owners, records of saddlery and fodder transactions; everything that could be found in the office of nearly every trainer in the country.

I looked at my watch. Cass usually took an hour off for lunch. I had waited five minutes after he had driven out of the yard, and I intended to be out of the office ten minutes before he could be expected back. This had given me a working time of three-quarters of an hour, of which nearly half had already gone.

Borrowing a pencil from the desk and taking a sheet of writing paper from a drawer, I applied myself to the drawer full of current accounts. For each of seventeen race-horses there was a separate hard-covered blue ledger, in which was listed every major and minor expense incurred in its training. I wrote a list of their names, few of which were familiar to me, together with their owners and the dates when they had come into the yard. Some had been there for years, but three had arrived during the past three months, and it was only these, I thought, which were of any real interest. None of the horses which had been doped had stayed at Humber's longer than four months.

The names of the three newest horses were Chin-Chin, Kandersteg and Starlamp. The first was owned by Humber himself and the other two by Adams.

I put the account books back where I had found them and looked at my watch. Seventeen minutes left. Putting the pencil back on the desk I folded the list of horses and stowed it away in my money belt. The webbing pockets were filling up again with fivers, as I had spent little of my pay, but the belt still lay flat and invisible below my waist under my jeans: and I had been careful not to let any of the lads know it was there, so as not to be robbed.

I riffled quickly through the drawers of press cuttings and photographs, but found no reference to the eleven horses or their successes. The racing calendars bore more fruit in the shape of a pencilled cross against the name of Superman in the Boxing Day selling chase, but there was no mark against the selling chase scheduled for a coming meeting at Sedgefield.

It was at the back of the receipts drawer that I struck most gold. There was another blue accounts ledger there, with a double page devoted to each of the eleven horses. Among these eleven were interspersed nine others who had in various ways failed in their purpose. One of these was Superman and another Old Etonian.

In the left hand page of each double spread had been recorded the entire racing career of the horse in question, and on the right hand pages of my eleven old friends were details of the race they each won with assistance. Beneath were sums of money which I judged must be Humber's winnings of them. His winnings had run into thousands on every successful race. On Superman's page he had written 'Lost: three hundred pounds.' On Old Etonian's right hand page there was no race record: only the single word 'Destroyed.'

A cross-out line had been drawn diagonally across all the pages except those concerning a horse called Six-Ply; and two new double pages had been prepared at the end, one for Kandersteg, and one for Starlamp. The left-hand pages for these three horses were written up: the right-hand pages were blank.

I shut the book and put it back. It was high time to go, and with a last look round to make sure that everything was exactly as it had been when I came in, I let myself quietly, unnoticed, out of the door, and went back to the kitchen to see if by some miracle the lads had left me any crumbs of lunch. Naturally, they had not.

The next morning Jerry's horse Mickey disappeared from the yard while we were out at second exercise, but Cass told him Jud had run him down to a friend of Humber's on the coast, for Mickey to paddle in the sea water to strengthen his legs, and that he would be back that evening. But the evening came, and Mickey did not.

On Wednesday Humber ran another horse, and I missed my lunch to have a look inside his house while he was away. Entry was easy through an open ventilator, but I could find nothing whatever to give me any clue as to how the doping was carried out.

All day Thursday I fretted about Mickey being still away at the coast.

It sounded perfectly reasonable. It was what a trainer about twelve miles from the sea could be expected to arrange. Sea water was good for horses' legs. But something happened to horses sometimes at Humber's which made it possible for them to be doped later, and I had a deeply disturbing suspicion that whatever it was was happening to Mickey at this moment, and that I was missing my only chance of finding it out.

According to the accounts books Adams owned four of the racehorses in the yard, in addition to his two hunters. None of his racehorses was known in the yard by its real name: therefore Mickey could be any one of the four. He could in fact be Kandersteg or Starlamp. It was an even chance that he was one or the other, and was due to follow in Superman's footsteps. So I fretted.

On Friday morning a hired box took the stable runner to Haydock races, and Jud and Humber's own box remained in the yard until lunch time. This was a definite departure from normal; and I took the opportunity of noting the mileage on the speedometer.

Jud drove the box out of the yard while we were still eating the midday sludge, and we didn't see him come back as we were all out on the gallop furthest away from the stables sticking back into place the divots kicked out of the soft earth that week by the various training activities; but when we returned for evening stables at four, Mickey was back in his own quarters.

I climbed up into the cab of the horse box and looked at the mileage indicator. Jud had driven exactly sixteen and a half miles. He had not, in fact, been as far as the coast. I thought some very bitter thoughts.

When I had finished doing my two racehorses I carried the brushes and pitch forks along to see to Adams' black hunter, and found Jerry leaning against the wall outside Mickey's next door box with tears running down his cheeks.

'What's the matter?' I said, putting down my stuff.

'Mickey . . . bit me,' he said. He was shaking with pain and fright.

'Let's see.'

I helped him slide his left arm out of his jersey, and took a look at the damage. There was a fierce red and purple circular weal on the fleshy part of his upper arm near the shoulder. It had been a hard, savage bite.

Cass came over.

'What's going on here?'

But he saw Jerry's arm, and didn't need to be told. He looked over the bottom half of the door into Mickey's box, then turned to Jerry and said, 'His legs were too far gone for the sea water to cure them. The vet said he would have to put on a blister, and he did it this afternoon when Mickey got back. That's what's the matter with him. Feels a bit off colour, he does, and so would you if someone slapped a flaming plaster on your legs. Now you just stop this stupid blubbing and get right back in there and see to him. And you, Dan, get on with that hunter and mind your own bloody business.' He went off along the row.

'I can't,' whispered Jerry, more to himself than to me.

'You'll manage it,' I said cheerfully.

He turned to me a stricken face. 'He'll bite me again.'

'I'm sure he won't.'

'He tried lots of times. And he's kicking out something terrible. I daren't go into his box . . .' He stood stiffly, shivering with fright, and I realized that it really was beyond him to go back.

'All right,' I said, 'I'll do Mickey and you do my hunter. Only do him well, Jerry, very well. Mr. Adams is coming to ride him again tomorrow and I don't want to spend another Saturday on my knees.'

He looked dazed. 'Ain't no one done nothing like that for me before.'

'It's a swop,' I said brusquely. 'You mess up my hunter and I'll bite you worse than Mickey did.'

He stopped shivering and began to grin, which I had intended, and slipping his arm painfully back inside his jersey he picked up my brushes and opened the hunter's door.

'You won't tell Cass?' he asked anxiously.

'No,' I reassured him; and unbolted Mickey's box door.

The horse was tied up safely enough, and wore on his neck a long wooden barred collar called a cradle which prevented his bending his head down to bite the bandages off his fore legs. Under the bandages, according to Cass, Mickey's legs were plastered with 'blister', a sort of caustic paste used to contract and strengthen the tendons. The only trouble was that Mickey's legs had not needed treatment. They had been, to my eyes, as sound as rocks. But now, however, they were definitely paining him; at least as much as with a blister, and possibly more.

As Jerry had indicated, Mickey was distinctly upset. He could not be soothed by hand or voice, but lashed forwards with his hind feet whenever he thought I was in range, and made equal use of his teeth. I was careful not to walk behind him, though he did his best to turn his quarters in my direction while I was banking up his straw bed round the back of the box. I fetched him hay and water, but he was not interested, and changed his rug, as the one he wore was soaked with sweat and would give him a chill during the night. Changing his rug was a bit of an obstacle race, but by warding off his attacks with the pitchfork I got it done unscathed.

I took Jerry with me to the feed bins where Cass was doling out the right food for each horse, and when we got back to the boxes we solemnly exchanged bowls. Jerry grinned happily. It was infectious. I grinned back.

Mickey didn't want food either, not, that is, except lumps of me. He didn't get any. I left him tied up for the night and took myself and Jerry's sack of brushes to safety on the far side of the door. Mickey would, I hoped, have calmed down considerably by the morning.

Jerry was grooming the black hunter practically hair by hair, humming tonelessly under his breath.

'Are you done?' I said.

'Is he all right?' he asked anxiously.

I went in to have a look.

'Perfect,' I said truthfully. Jerry was better at strapping a horse than at most things; and the next day, to my considerable relief, Adams passed both hunters without remark and spoke hardly a word to me. He was in a hurry to be off to a distant meet, but all the same it seemed I had succeeded in appearing too spineless to be worth tormenting.

Mickey was a good deal worse, that morning. When Adams had gone I stood with Jerry looking over the half-door of Mickey's box. The poor animal had managed to rip one of the bandages off in spite of the cradle, and we could see a big raw area over his tendon.

Mickey looked round at us with baleful eyes and flat ears, his neck stretched forward aggressively. Muscles quivered violently in his shoulders and hind quarters. I had never seen a horse behave like that except when fighting; and he was, I thought, dangerous.

'He's off his head,' whispered Jerry, awestruck.

'Poor thing.'

'You ain't going in?' he said. 'He looks like he'd kill you.'

'Go and get Cass,' I said. 'No, I'm not going in, not without Cass knowing how things are, and Humber too. You go and tell Cass that Mickey's gone mad. That ought to fetch him to have a look.'

Jerry trotted off and returned with Cass, who seemed to be alternating between anxiety and scorn as he came within earshot. At the sight of Mickey anxiety abruptly took over, and he went to fetch Humber, telling Jerry on no account to open Mickey's door.

Humber came unhurriedly across the yard leaning on his stick, with Cass, who was a short man, trotting along at his side. Humber looked at Mickey for a good long time. Then he shifted his gaze to Jerry, who was standing there shaking again at the thought of having to deal with a horse in such a state, and then further along to me, where I stood at the door of the next box.

'That's Mr. Adams' hunter's box,' he said to me.

'Yes, sir, he went with Mr. Adams just now, sir.'

He looked me up and down, and then Jerry the same, and finally said to Cass, 'Roke and Webber had better change horses. I know they haven't an ounce of guts between them, but Roke is much bigger, stronger and older.' And also, I thought with a flash of insight, Jerry has a father and mother to make a fuss if he gets hurt, whereas against Roke in the next-of-kin file was the single word 'none'.

'I'm not going in there alone, sir,' I said. 'Cass will have to hold him off with a pitchfork while I muck him out.' And even then, I thought, we'd both be lucky to get out without being kicked.

Cass, to my amusement, hurriedly started telling Humber that if I was too scared to do it on my own he would get one of the other lads to help me. Humber however took no notice of either of us, but went back to staring sombrely at Mickey.

Finally he turned to me and said, 'Fetch a bucket and come over to the office.'

'An empty bucket, sir?'

'Yes,' he said impatiently, 'an empty bucket.' He turned and gently limped over to the long brick hut. I took the bucket out of the hunter's box, followed him, and waited by the door.

He came out with a small labelled glass-stoppered chemist's jar in one

hand and a teaspoon in the other. The jar was three-quarters full of
white powder. He gestured to me to hold out the bucket, then he put half
a teaspoonful of the powder into it.

'Fill the bucket only a third full of water,' he said. 'And put it in
Mickey's manger, so that he can't kick it over. It will quieten him down,
once he drinks it.'

He took the jar and spoon back inside the office, and I picked a good
pinch of the white powder out of the bottom of the bucket and dropped
it down inside the list of Humber's horses in my money belt. I licked my
fingers and thumb afterwards; the particles of powder clinging there had
a faintly bitter taste. The jar, which I had seen in the cupboard in the
washroom, was labelled 'Soluble phenobarbitone', and the only surprising
factor was the amount of it that Humber kept available.

I ran water into the bucket, stirred it with my hand and went back to
Mickey's box. Cass had vanished. Jerry was across the yard seeing to his
third horse. I looked round for someone to ask for help, but everyone was
carefully keeping out of sight. I cursed. I was not going into Mickey
alone: it was just plain stupid to try it.

Humber came back across the yard.

'Get on in,' he said.

'I'd spill the water dodging him, sir.'

'Huh.'

Mickey's hoofs thudded viciously against the wall.

'You mean you haven't got the guts.'

'You'd need to be a bloody fool to go in there alone, sir,' I said sullenly.

He glared at me, but he must have seen it was no use insisting. He
suddenly picked up the pitchfork from where it stood against the wall
and transferred it to his right hand and the walking stick to his left.

'Get on with it then,' he said harshly. 'And don't waste time.'

He looked incongruous, brandishing his two unconventional weapons
while dressed like an advertisement for *Country Life*. I hoped he was
going to be as resolute as he sounded.

I unbolted Mickey's door and we went in. It had been an injustice to
think Humber might turn tail and leave me there alone: he behaved as
coldly as ever, as if fear were quite beyond his imagination. Efficiently
he kept Mickey penned first to one side of the box and then to the other
while I mucked out and put down fresh straw, remaining steadfastly at
his post while I cleaned the uneaten food out of the manger and wedged
the bucket of doped water in place. Mickey didn't make it easy for him,
either. The teeth and hooves were busier and more dangerous than the
night before.

It was especially aggravating in the face of Humber's coolness to have
to remember to behave like a bit of a coward myself, though I minded
less than if he had been Adams.

When I had finished the jobs Humber told me to go out first, and he
retreated in good order after me, his well-pressed suit scarcely rumpled
from his exertions.

I shut the door and bolted it, and did my best to look thoroughly
frightened. Humber looked me over with disgust.

'Roke,' he said sarcastically, 'I hope you will feel capable of dealing with Mickey when he is half asleep with drugs?'

'Yes sir,' I muttered.

'Then in order not to strain your feeble stock of courage I suggest we keep him drugged for some days. Every time you fetch him a bucket of water you can get Cass or me to put some sedative in it. Understand?'

'Yes sir,'

'Right.' He dismissed me with a chop of his hand.

I carried the sack of dirty straw round to the muck heap, and then took a close look at the bandage which Mickey had dislodged. Blister is a red paste. I had looked in vain for red paste on Mickey's raw leg; and there was not a smear of it on the bandage. Yet from the size and severity of the wound there should have been half a cupful.

I took Jerry down to Posset on the motor-cycle again that afternoon and watched him start to browse contentedly in the toy department of the post office.

There was a letter for me from October.

'Why did we receive no report from you last week? It is your duty to keep us informed of the position.'

I tore the page up, my mouth twisting. Duty. That was just about enough to make me lose my temper. It was not from any sense of duty that I stayed at Humber's to endure a minor version of slavery. It was because I was obstinate, and liked to finish what I started, and although it sounded a bit grandiose, it was because I really wanted, if I could, to remove British steeple chasing from Adams' clutches. If it had been only a matter of duty I would have repaid October his money and cleared out.

'It is your duty to keep us informed of the position.'

He was still angry with me about Patty, I thought morosely, and he wrote that sentence only because he knew I wouldn't like it.

I composed my report.

'Your humble and obedient servant regrets that he was unable to carry out his duty last week by keeping you informed of the position.

'The position is still far from clear, but a useful fact has been ascertained. None of the original eleven horses will be doped again: but a horse called Six-Ply is lined up to be the next winner. He is now owned by a Mr. Henry Waddington, of Lewes, Sussex.

'May I please have the answers to the following questions:

1. Is the powder in the enclosed twist of paper soluble phenobarbitone?

2. What are in detail the registered physical characteristics of the racehorses Chin-Chin, Kandersteg and Starlamp?

3. On what date did Blackburn, playing at home, beat Arsenal?'

And that, I thought, sticking down the envelope and grinning to myself, that will fix him and his duty.

Jerry and I gorged ourselves at the café. I had been at Humber's for five weeks and two days, and my clothes were getting looser.

When we could eat no more I went back to the post office and bought a large-scale hiker's map of the surrounding district, and a cheap pair of compasses. Jerry spent fifteen shillings on a toy tank which he had resisted before, and, after checking to see if my goodwill extended so far, a second comic for me to read to him. And we went back to Humber's.

Days passed. Mickey's drugged water acted satisfactorily, and I was able to clean his box and look after him without much trouble. Cass took the second bandage off, revealing an equal absence of red paste. However, the wounds gradually started healing.

As Mickey could not be ridden and showed great distress if one tried to lead him out along the road, he had to be walked round the yard for an hour each day, which exercised me more than him, but gave me time to think some very fruitful thoughts.

Humber's stick landed with a resounding thump across Charlie's shoulders on Tuesday morning, and for a second it looked as though Charlie would hit him back. But Humber coldly stared him down, and the next morning delivered an even harder blow in the same place. Charlie's bed was empty that night. He was the fourth lad to leave in the six weeks I had been there (not counting the boy who stayed only three days) and of my original half dozen dormitory companions, only Bert and Jerry remained. The time was getting perceptibly closer when I would find myself at the top of the queue for walking the plank.

Adams came with Humber when he made his usual rounds on Thursday evening. They stopped outside Mickey's box but contented themselves with looking over the half-door.

'Don't go in, Paul,' said Humber warningly. 'He's still very unpredictable, in spite of drugs.'

Adams looked at me where I stood by Mickey's head.

'Why is the gipsy doing this horse? I thought it was the moron's job.' He sounded angry and alarmed.

Humber explained that as Mickey had bitten Jerry, he had made me change places with him. Adams still didn't like it, but looked as if he would save his comments until he wouldn't be overheard.

He said, 'What is the gipsy's name?'

'Roke,' said Humber.

'Well, Roke, come here, out of that box.'

Humber said anxiously, 'Paul, don't forget we're one lad short already.'

These were not particularly reassuring words to hear. I walked across the box, keeping a wary eye on Mickey, let myself out through the door, and stood beside it, drooping and looking at the ground.

'Roke,' said Adams in a pleasant sounding voice, 'what do you spend your wages on?'

'The never-never on my motor-bike, sir.'

'The never-never? Oh, yes. And how many instalments have you still to pay?'

'About – er – fifteen, sir.'

'And you don't want to leave here until you've finished paying them off.'

'No, sir.'

'Will they take your motor-cycle away if you stop paying?'

'Yes sir, they might do.'

'So Mr. Humber doesn't need to worry about you leaving him?'

I said slowly, unwillingly, but as it happened, truthfully, 'No, sir.'

'Good,' he said briskly. 'Then that clears the air, doesn't it. And now you can tell me where you find the guts to deal with an unstable, half-mad horse.'

'He's drugged, sir.'

'You and I both know, Roke, that a drugged horse is not necessarily a safe horse.'

I said nothing. If there was ever a time when I needed an inspiration, this was it: and my mind was a blank.

'I don't think, Roke,' he said softly, 'that you are as feeble as you make out. I think there is a lot more stuffing in you than you would have us believe.'

'No, sir,' I said helplessly.

'Let's find out, shall we?'

He stretched out his hand to Humber, and Humber gave him his walking stick. Adams drew back his arm and hit me fairly smartly across the thigh.

If I were to stay in the yard I had got to stop him. This time the begging simply had to be done. I slid down the door, gasping, and sat on the ground.

'No sir, don't,' I shouted. 'I got some pills, I was dead scared of Mickey, and I asked the chemist in Posset on Saturday if he had any pills to make me brave, and he sold me some, and I've been taking them regular ever since.'

'What pills?' said Adams disbelieving.

'Tranquil something he said. I didn't rightly catch the wood.'

'Tranquillizers.'

'Yes, that's it, tranquillizers. Don't hit me any more sir, please sir. It was just that I was so dead scared of Mickey. Don't hit me any more, sir.'

'Well I'm damned.' Adams began to laugh. 'Well I'm damned. What will they think of next?' He gave the stick back to Humber, and the two of them walked casually away along to the next box.

'Take tranquillizers to help you out of a blue funk. Well, why not?' Still laughing, they went in to see the next horse.

I got up slowly and brushed the dirt off the seat of my pants. Damn it, I thought miserably, what else could I have done? Why was pride so important, and abandoning it so bitter?

It was more clear than ever that weakness was my only asset. Adams had this fearful kink of seeing any show of spirit as a personal challenge to his ability to crush it. He dominated Humber, and exacted instant obedience from Cass, and they were his allies. If I stood up to him even mildly I would get nothing but a lot of bruises and he would start wondering why I stayed to collect still more. The more tenaciously I stayed, the more incredible he would find it. Hire purchase on the motor-bike wouldn't convince him for long. He was quick. He knew, if he began to think about it, that I had come from October's stables. He must know that October was a Steward and therefore his natural enemy.

He would remember Tommy Stapleton. The hyper-sensitivity of the hunted to danger would stir the roots of his hair. He could check and find out from the post office that I did not send money away each week, and discover that the chemist had sold me no tranquillizers. He was in too deep to risk my being a follow-up to Stapleton; and at the very least, once he was suspicious of me, my detecting days would be over.

Whereas if he continued to be sure of my utter spinelessness he wouldn't bother about me, and I could if necessary stay in the yard up to five or six weeks more. And heaven forbid, I thought, that I would have to.

Adams, although it had been instinct with him, not reason, was quite right to be alarmed that it was I and not Jerry who was now looking after Mickey.

In the hours I had spent close to the horse I had come to understand what was really the matter with him, and all my accumulated knowledge about the affected horses, and about all horses in general, had gradually shaken into place. I did by that day know in outline how Adams and Humber had made their winners win.

I knew in outline, but not in detail. A theory, but no proof. For detail and proof I still needed more time, and if the only way I could buy time was to sit on the ground and implore Adams not to beat me, then it had to be done. But it was pretty awful, just the same.

Chapter Twelve

October's reply was unrelenting.

'Six-Ply, according to his present owner, is not going to be entered in any selling races. Does this mean that he will not be doped?

'The answers to your questions are as follows:

1. The powder is soluble phenobarbitone.

2. The physical characteristics of Chin-Chin are: bay gelding, white blaze down nose, white sock, off-fore. Kandersteg: gelding, washy chestnut, three white socks, both fore-legs and near hind. Starlamp: brown gelding, near hind white heel.

3. Blackburn beat Arsenal on November 30th.

'I do not appreciate your flippancy. Does your irresponsibility now extend to the investigation?'

Irresponsibility. Duty. He could really pick his words.

I read the descriptions of the horses again. They told me that Starlamp was Mickey. Chin-Chin was Dobbin, one of the two racehorses I did which belonged to Humber. Kandersteg was a pale shambling creature looked after by Bert, and known in the yard as Flash.

If Blackburn beat Arsenal on November 30th, Jerry had been at Humber's eleven weeks already.

I tore up October's letter and wrote back.

'Six-Ply may now be vulnerable whatever race he runs in, as he is the only shot left in the locker since Old Etonian and Superman both misfired.

'In case I fall on my nut out riding, or get knocked over by a passing car, I think I had better tell you that I have this week realised how the scheme works, even though I am as yet ignorant of most of the details.'

I told October that the stimulant Adams and Humber used was in fact adrenalin; and I told him how I believed it was introduced into the blood stream.

'As you can see, there are two prime facts which must be established before Adams and Humber can be prosecuted. I will do my best to finish the job properly, but I can't guarantee it, as the time factor is a nuisance.'

Then, because I felt very alone, I added impulsively, jerkily, a postscript. 'Believe me. Please believe me. I did nothing to Patty.'

When I had written it, I looked at this *cri de coeur* in disgust. I am getting as soft as I pretend, I thought. I tore the bottom of the sheet of paper and threw the pitiful words away, and posted my letter in the box.

Thinking it wise actually to buy some tranquillizers in case anyone checked, I stopped at the chemist's and asked for some. The chemist absolutely refused to sell me any, as they could only be had on a doctor's or dentist's prescription. How long would it be, I wondered ruefully, before Adams or Humber discovered this awkward fact.

Jerry was disappointed when I ate my meal in the café very fast, and left him alone to finish and walk back from Posset, but I assured him that I had jobs to do. It was high time I took a look at the surrounding countryside.

I rode out of Posset and, stopping the motor-cycle in a lay-by, got out the map over which I had pored intermittently during the week. I had drawn on it with pencil and compasses two concentric circles: the outer circle had a radius of eight miles from Humber's stables, and the inner circle a radius of five miles. If Jud had driven straight there and back when he had gone to fetch Mickey, the place he had fetched him from would lie in the area between the circles.

Some directions from Humber's were unsuitable because of open-cast coal-mines: and eight miles to the south-east lay the outskirts of the sprawling mining town called Clavering. All round the north and west sides, however, there was little but moorland interspersed with small valleys like the one in which Humber's stable lay, small fertile pockets in miles and miles of stark windswept heath.

Tellbridge, the village where Adams lived, lay outside the outer circle by two miles, and because of this I did not think Mickey could have been lodged there during his absence from Humber's. But all the same the area on a line from Humber's yard to Adams' village seemed the most sensible to take a look at first.

As I did not wish Adams to find me spying out the land round his house, I fastened on my crash helmet, which I had not worn since the trip to Edinburgh, and pulled up over my eyes a large pair of goggles, under which even my sisters wouldn't have recognised me. I didn't, as it happened, see Adams on my travels; but I did see his house which was a square, cream-coloured Georgian pile with gargoyle heads adjoining the gate-posts. It was the largest, most imposing building in the tiny group of a church, a shop, two pubs and a gaggle of cottages which made up Tellbridge.

I talked about Adams to the boy who filled my petrol tank in the Tellbridge garage.

'Mr. Adams? Yes, he bought old Sir Lucas' place three-four years ago. After the old man died. There weren't no family to keep it on.'

'And Mrs. Adams?' I suggested.

'Blimey, there isn't any Mrs. Adams,' he said, laughing and pushing his fair hair out of his eyes with the back of his wrist. 'But a lot of birds, he has there sometimes. Often got a houseful there, he has. Nobs, now, don't get me wrong. Never has anyone but nobs in his house, doesn't Mr. Adams. And anything he wants, he gets, and quick. Never mind anyone else. He woke the whole village up at two in the morning last Friday because he got into his head that he'd like to ring the church bells. He smashed a window to get in . . . I ask you! Of course, no one says much, because he spends such a lot of money in the village. Food and drink and wages, and so on. Everyone's better off, since he came.'

'Does he often do things like that – ringing the church bells?'

'Well, not that exactly, but other things, yes. I shouldn't think you could believe all you hear. But they say he pays up handsome if he does any damage, and everyone just puts up with it. High spirits, that's what they say it is.'

But Adams was too old for high spirits of that sort.

'Does he buy his petrol here?' I asked idly, fishing in my pocket for some money.

'Not often he doesn't, he has his own tank.' The smile died out of the boy's open face. 'In fact, I only served him once, when his supplies had run out.'

'What happened?'

'Well, he trod on my foot. In his hunting boots, too. I couldn't make out if he did it on purpose, because it seemed like that really, but why would he do something like that?'

'I can't imagine.'

He shook his head wondering. 'He must have thought I'd moved out of his way, I suppose. Put his heel right on top of my foot, he did, and leaned back. I only had sneakers on. Darn nearly broke my bones, he did. He must weigh getting on for sixteen stone, I shouldn't wonder.' He sighed and counted my change into my palm, and I thanked him and went on my way thinking that it was extraordinary how much a psychopath could get away with if he was big enough and clever and well-born.

It was a cold afternoon, and cloudy, but I enjoyed it. Stopping on the highest point of a shoulder of moorland I sat straddling the bike and looking round at rolling distances of bare bleak hills and at the tall chimneys of Clavering pointing up on the horizon. I took off my helmet and goggles and pushed my fingers through my hair to let the cold wind in to my scalp. It was invigorating.

There was almost no chance, I knew, of my finding where Mickey had been kept. It could be anywhere, in any barn, outhouse or shed. It didn't have to be a stable, and quite likely was not a stable: and indeed all I was sure of was that it would be somewhere tucked away out of sight and sound of any neighbours. The trouble was that in that part of Durham, with its widely scattered villages, its sudden valleys, and its miles of open heath, I found there were dozens of places tucked away out of sight and sound of neighbours.

Shrugging, I put my helmet and goggles on again, and spent what little was left of my free time finding two vantage points on high ground, from one of which one could see straight down the valley into Humber's yard, and from the other a main cross roads on the way from Humber's to Tellbridge, together with good stretches of road in all directions from it.

Kandersteg's name being entered in Humber's special hidden ledger, it was all Durham to a doughnut that one day he would take the same trail that Mickey-Starlamp had done. It was quite likely that I would still be unable to find out where he went, but there was no harm in getting the lie of the land clear in my head.

At four o'clock I rolled back into Humber's yard with the usual lack of enthusiasm, and began my evening's work.

Sunday passed, and Monday. Mickey got no better; the wounds on his legs were healing but he was still a risky prospect, in spite of the drugs, and he was beginning to lose flesh. Although I had never seen or had to deal with a horse in this state before, I gradually grew certain that he would not recover, and that Adams and Humber had another misfire on their hands.

Neither Humber nor Cass liked the look of him either, though Humber seemed more annoyed than anxious, as time went on. Adams came one morning, and from across the yard in Dobbin's box I watched the three of them standing looking in at Mickey. Presently Cass went into the box for a moment or two, and came out shaking his head. Adams looked furious. He took Humber by the arm and the two of them walked across to the office in what looked like an argument. I would have given much to have overheard them. A pity I couldn't lip-read, I thought, and that I hadn't come equipped with one of those long-range listening devices. As a spy, I was really a dead loss.

On Tuesday morning at breakfast there was a letter for me, post-marked Durham, and I looked at it curiously because there were so few people who either knew where I was or would bother to write to me. I put it in my pocket until I could open it in private and I was glad I had, for to my astonishment it was from October's elder daughter.

She had written from her University address, and said briefly,

'Dear Daniel Roke,
   I would be glad if you could call to see me for a few moments sometime this week. There is a matter I must discuss with you.
                                        Yours sincerely,
                                        Elinor Tarren.'

October, I thought, must have given her a message for me, or something he wanted me to see, or perhaps he intended to be there to meet me himself, and had not risked writing to me direct. Puzzled, I asked Cass for an afternoon off, and was refused. Only Saturday, he said, and Saturday only if I behaved myself.

I thought Saturday might be too late, or that she would have gone to Yorkshire for the week-end, but I wrote to her that I could come only on that day, and walked into Posset after the evening meal on Tuesday to post the letter.

Her reply came on Friday, brief again and to the point, with still no hint of why I was to go.

'Saturday afternoon will do very well. I will tell the porter you are coming: go to the side door of the College (this is the door used by students and their visitors) and ask to be shown to my room.'

She enclosed a pencilled sketch to show me where to find the college, and that was all.

On Saturday morning I had six horses to do, because there was still no replacement for Charley, and Jerry had gone with Pageant to the races. Adams came as usual to talk to Humber and to supervise the loading up of his hunters, but wasted no attention or energy on me, for which I was thankful. He spent half of the twenty minutes he was in the yard looking into Mickey's box with a scowl on his handsome face.

Cass himself was not always unkind, and because he knew I particularly wanted the afternoon free he even went so far as to help me get finished before the midday meal. I thanked him, surprised, and he remarked that he knew there had been a lot extra for everyone (except himself incidentally) to do, as we were still a lad short, and that I hadn't complained about it as much as most of the others. And that, I thought, was a mistake I would not have to make too often.

I washed as well as the conditions would allow; one had to heat all washing water in a kettle on the stove and pour it into the basin on the marble washstand; and shaved more carefully than usual, looking into the six-by-eight-inch flyblown bit of looking glass, jostled by the other lads who wanted to be on their way to Posset.

None of the clothes I had were fit for visiting a women's college. With a sigh I settled for the black sweater, which had a high collar, the charcoal drainpipe trousers, and the black leather jacket. No shirt, because I had no tie. I eyed the sharp-pointed shoes, but I had not been able to overcome my loathing for them, so I scrubbed my jodhpur boots under the tap in the yard, and wore those. Everything else I was wearing needed cleaning, and I supposed I smelled of horses, though I was too used to it to notice.

I shrugged. There was nothing to be done about it. I unwrapped the motor-bike and made tracks for Durham.

Chapter Thirteen

Elinor's college stood in a tree-lined road along with other sturdy and learned looking buildings. It had an imposing front entrance and a less-imposing tarmacked drive entrance along to the right. I wheeled the motor-cycle down there and parked it beside a long row of bicycles. Beyond the bicycles stood six or seven small cars, one of which was Elinor's little scarlet two-seater.

Two steps led up to a large oak door embellished with the single words 'Students'. I went in. There was a porter's desk just inside on the right, with a mournful looking middle-aged man sitting behind it looking at a list.

'Excuse me,' I said, 'could you tell me where to find Lady Elinor Tarren?'

He looked up and said 'You visiting? You expected?'

'I think so,' I said.

He asked my name, and thumbed down the list painstakingly. 'Daniel Roke to visit Miss Tarren, please show him her room. Yes, that's right. Come on, then.' He got down off his stool, came round from behind his desk, and breathing noisily began to lead me deeper into the building.

There were several twists in the corridors and I could see why it was necessary to have a guide. On every hand were doors with their occupant or purpose written up on small cards let into metal slots. After going up two flights of stairs and round a few more corners, the porter halted outside one more door just like the rest.

'Here you are,' he said unemotionally. 'This is Miss Tarren's room.' He turned away and started to shuffle back to his post.

The card on the door said Miss E. C. Tarren. I knocked. Miss E. C. Tarren opened it.

'Come in,' she said. No smile.

I went in. She shut the door behind me. I stood still, looking at her room. I was so accustomed to the starkness of the accommodation at Humber's that it was an odd, strange sensation to find myself again in a room with curtains, carpet, sprung chairs, cushions and flowers. The colours were mostly blues and greens, mixed and blending, with a bowl of daffodils and red tulips blazing against them.

There was a big desk with books and papers scattered on it; a bookshelf, a bed with a blue cover, a wardrobe, a tall built-in cupboard, and two easy chairs. It looked warm and friendly. A very good room for working in. If I had had more than a moment to stand and think about it, I knew I would be envious: this was what my father and mother's death had robbed me of, the time and liberty to study.

'Please sit down.' She indicated one of the easy chairs.

'Thank you.' I sat, and she sat down opposite me, but looking at the floor, not at me. She was solemn and frowning, and I rather gloomily wondered if what October wanted her to say to me meant more trouble.

'I asked you to come here,' she started. 'I asked you to come here because . . .' She stopped and stood up abruptly, and walked round behind me and tried again.

'I asked you to come,' she said to the back of my head, 'Because I have to apologise to you, and I'm not finding it very easy.'

'Apologise?' I said, astonished. 'What for?'

'For my sister.'

I stood up and turned towards her. 'Don't,' I said vehemently. I had been too much humbled myself in the past weeks to want to see anyone else in the same position.

She shook her head. 'I'm afraid,' she swallowed, 'I'm afraid that my family has treated you very badly.'

The silver-blonde hair shimmered like a halo against the pale sunshine which slanted sideways through the window behind her. She was wearing a scarlet jersey under a sleeveless dark green dress. The whole effect was colourful and gorgeous, but it was clearly not going to help her if I went on looking at her. I sat down again in the chair and said with some light-heartedness, as it appeared October had not after all despatched a dressing-down, 'Please don't worry about it.'

'Worry,' she exclaimed. 'What else can I do? I knew of course why you were dismissed, and I've said several times to Father that he ought to have had you sent to prison, and now I find none of it is true at all. How can you say there is nothing to worry about when everyone thinks you are guilty of some dreadful crime, and you aren't?'

Her voice was full of concern. She really minded that anyone in her family should have behaved as unfairly as Patty had. She felt guilty just because she was her sister. I liked her for it: but then I already knew she was a thoroughly nice girl.

'How did you find out?' I asked.

'Patty told me last week-end. We were just gossiping together, as we often do. She had always refused to talk about you, but this time she laughed, and told me quite casually, as if it didn't matter any more. Of course I know she's . . . well . . . used to men. She's just built that way. But this . . . I was so shocked. I couldn't believe her at first.'

'What exactly did she tell you?'

There was a pause behind me, then her voice went on, a little shakily. 'She said she tried to make you make love to her, but you wouldn't. She said . . . she said she showed you her body, and all you did was to tell her to cover herself up. She said she was so flamingly angry about that that she thought all next day about what revenge she would have on you, and on Sunday morning she worked herself up into floods of tears, and went and told Father . . . told Father . . .'

'Well,' I said good humouredly, 'yes, that is, I suppose, a slightly more accurate picture of what took place.' I laughed.

'It isn't funny,' she protested.

'No. It's relief.'

She came round in front of me and sat down and looked at me.

'You did mind, then, didn't you?'

My distaste must have shown. 'Yes. I minded.'

'I told Father she had lied about you. I've never told him before about her love affairs, but this was different . . . anyway, I told him on Sunday after lunch.' She stopped, hesitating. I waited. At last she went on, 'It was very odd. He didn't seem surprised, really. Not utterly overthrown, like I was. He just seemed to get very tired, suddenly, as if he had heard bad news. As if a friend had died after a long illness, that sort of sadness. I didn't understand it. And when I said that of course the only fair thing to do would be to offer you your job back, he utterly refused. I argued, but I'm afraid he is adamant. He also refuses to tell Mr. Inskip that you shouldn't have had to leave, and he made me promise not to repeat to him or anyone what Patty had said. It is so unfair,' she concluded passionately, 'and I felt that even if no one else is to know, at least you should. I don't suppose it makes it any better for you that my father and I have at last found out what really happened, but I wanted you to know that I am sorry, very, very sorry for what my sister did.'

I smiled at her. It wasn't difficult. Her colouring was so blazingly fair that it didn't matter if her nose wasn't entirely straight. Her direct grey eyes were full of genuine, earnest regret, and I knew she felt Patty's misbehaviour all the more keenly because she thought it had affected a stable lad who had no means of defending himself. This also made it difficult to know what to say in reply.

I understood, of course, that October couldn't declare me an injured innocent, even if he wanted to, which I doubted, without a risk of it reaching Humber's ears, and that the last thing that either of us wanted was for him to have to offer to take me back at Inskip's. No one in their right mind would stay at Humber's if they could go to Inskip's.

'If you knew,' I said slowly, 'how much I have wanted your father to believe that I didn't harm your sister, you would realise that what you have just said is worth a dozen jobs to me. I like your father. I respect him. And he is quite right. He cannot possibly give me my old job back, because it would be as good as saying publicly that his daughter is at least a liar, if not more. You can't ask him to do that. You can't expect it. I don't. Things are best left as they are.'

She looked at me for some time without speaking. It seemed to me that there was relief in her expression, and surprise, and finally puzzlement.

'Don't you want *any* compensation?'

'No.'

'I don't understand you.'

'Look,' I said, getting up, away from her enquiring gaze. 'I'm not as blameless as the snow. I did kiss your sister. I suppose I led her on a bit. And then I was ashamed of myself and backed out, and that's the truth of it. It wasn't all her fault. I did behave very badly. So please . . . please don't feel so much guilt on my account.' I reached the window and looked out.

'People shouldn't be hung for murders they decide not to commit,' she said dryly. 'You are being very generous, and I didn't expect it.'

'Then you shouldn't have asked me here,' I said idly. 'You were taking too big a risk.' The window looked down on to a quadrangle, a neat square of grass surrounded by broad paths, peaceful and empty in the early spring sunshine.

Risk . . . of what?' she said.

'Risk that I would raise a stink. Dishonour to the family. Tarnish to the Tarrens. That sort of thing. Lots of dirty linen and Sunday newspapers and your father losing face among his business associates.'

She looked startled, but also determined. 'All the same, a wrong had been done, and it had to be put right.'

'And damn the consequences?'

'And damn the consequences,' she repeated faintly.

I grinned. She was a girl after my own heart. I had been damning a few consequences too.

'Well,' I said reluctantly, 'I'd better be off. Thank you for asking me to come. I do understand that you have had a horrible week screwing yourself up for this, and I appreciate it more than I can possibly say.'

She looked at her watch, and hesitated. 'I know it's an odd time of day, but would you like some coffee? I mean, you've come quite a long way . . .'

'I'd like some very much,' I said.

'Well . . . sit down, and I'll get it.'

I sat down. She opened the built-in cupboard, which proved to hold a wash basin and mirror on one side and a gas ring and shelves for crockery on the other. She filled a kettle, lit the gas, and put some cups and saucers on the low table between the two chairs, moving economically and gracefully. Unselfconscious, I thought. Sure enough of herself to drop her title in a place where brains mattered more than birth. Sure enough of herself to have a man who looked like I did brought to her bed-sittingroom, and to ask him to stay for coffee when it was not necessary, but only polite.

I asked her what subject she was reading, and she said English. She assembled some milk, sugar, and biscuits on the table.

'May I look at your books?' I asked.

'Go ahead,' she said amiably.

I got up and looked along her bookshelves. There were the language text books – Ancient Icelandic, Anglo Saxon and Middle English – and a comprehensive sweep of English writings from Alfred the Great's Chronicles to John Betjeman's unattainable amazons.

'What do you think of my books?' she asked curiously.

I didn't know how to answer. The masquerade was damnably unfair to her.

'Very learned,' I said lamely.

I turned away from the bookshelves, and came suddenly face to face with my full-length reflection in the mirror door of her wardrobe.

I looked at myself moodily. It was the first comprehensive view of Roke the stable lad that I had had since leaving October's London house months before, and time had not improved things.

My hair was too long, and the sideburns flourished nearly down to the lobes of my ears. My skin was a sort of pale yellow now that the suntan had all faded. There was a tautness in the face and a wary expression in the eyes which had not been there before: and in my black clothes I looked disreputable and a menace to society.

Her reflection moved behind mine in the mirror, and I met her eyes and found her watching me.

'You look as if you don't like what you see,' she said.

I turned round. 'No,' I said wryly. 'Would anyone?'

'Well . . .' Incredibly she smiled mischievously. 'I wouldn't like to set you loose in this college, for instance. If you don't realize, though, the effect which you . . . you may have a few rough edges, but I do now see why Patty tried . . . er . . . I mean . . .' Her voice tailed off in the first confusion she had shown.

'The kettle's boiling,' I said helpfully.

Relieved, she turned her back on me and made the coffee. I went to the window and looked down into the deserted quad, resting my forehead on the cold glass.

It still happened, I thought. In spite of those terrible clothes, in spite of the aura of shadiness, it could still happen. What accident, I wondered for the thousandth time in my life, decided that one should be born with bones of a certain design? I couldn't help the shape of my face and head. They were a legacy from a pair of neat featured parents: their doing, not mine. Like Elinor's hair, I thought. Born in you. Nothing to be proud of. An accident, like a birth mark or a squint. Something I habitually forgot, and found disconcerting when anyone mentioned it. And it had been expensive, moreover. I had lost at least two prospective customers because they hadn't liked the way their wives looked at me instead of my horses.

With Elinor, I thought, it was a momentary attraction which wouldn't last. She was surely too sensible to allow herself to get tangled up with one of her father's ex-stable lads. And as for me, it was strictly hands off the Tarren sisters, both of them. If I was out of the frying-pan with one, I was not jumping into the fire with the other. It was a pity, all the same. I liked Elinor rather a lot.

'The coffee's ready,' she said.

I turned and went back to the table. She had herself very well controlled again. There was no mischievous revealing light in her face any more, and she looked almost severe, as if she very much regretted what she had said and was going to make quite certain I didn't take advantage of it.

She handed me a cup and offered the biscuits, which I ate because the lunch at Humber's had consisted of bread, margarine, and hard tasteless cheese, and the supper would be the same. It nearly always was, on Saturdays, because Humber knew we ate in Posset.

We talked sedately about her father's horses, I asked how Sparking Plug was getting on, and she told me, very well, thank you.

'I've a newspaper cutting about him, if you'd like to see it?' she said.

'Yes, I'd like to.'

I followed her to her desk while she looked for it. She shifted some papers to search underneath, and the top one fell on to the floor. I picked it up, put it back on the desk, and looked down at it. It seemed to be some sort of quiz.

'Thank you,' she said. 'I mustn't lose that, it's the Literary Society's competition, and I've only one more answer to find. Now where did I put that cutting?'

The competition consisted of a number of quotations to which one had to ascribe the author. I picked up the paper and began reading.

'That top one's a brute,' she said over her shoulder. 'No one's got it yet, I don't think.'

'How do you win the competition?' I asked.

'Get a complete, correct set of answers in first.'

'And what's the prize?'

'A book. But prestige, mostly. We only have one competition a term, and it's difficult.' She opened a drawer full of papers and oddments. 'I know I put that cutting somewhere.' She began shovelling things out on to the top of the desk.

'Please don't bother any more,' I said politely.

'No, I want to find it.' A handful of small objects clattered on to the desk.

Among them was a small chromium-plated tube about three inches long with a loop of chain running from one end to the other. I had seen something like it before, I thought idly. I had seen it quite often. It had something to do with drinks.

'What's that?' I asked, pointing.

'That? Oh, that's a silent whistle.' She went on rummaging. 'For dogs,' she explained.

I picked it up. A silent dog whistle. Why then did I think it was connected with bottles and glasses and . . . the world stopped.

With an almost physical sensation, my mind leaped towards its prey. I held Adams and Humber in my hand at last. I could feel my pulse racing.

So simple. So very simple. The tube pulled apart in the middle to reveal that one end was a thin whistle, and the other its cap. A whistle joined to its cap by a little length of chain. I put the tiny mouthpiece to my lips and blew. Only a thread of sound came out.

'You can't hear it very well,' Elinor said, 'but of course a dog can. And you can adjust that whistle to make it sound louder to human ears, too.' She took it out of my hand and unscrewed part of the whistle itself. 'Now blow.' She gave it back.

I blew again. It sounded much more like an ordinary whistle.

'Do you think I could possibly borrow this for a little while?' I asked. 'If you're not using it? I . . . I want to try an experiment.'

'Yes, I should think so. My dear old sheepdog had to be put down last spring, and I haven't used it since. But you will let me have it back? I am getting a puppy in the long vac, and I want to use it for his training.'

'Yes, of course.'

'All right, then. Oh, here's that cutting, at last.'

I took the strip of newsprint, but I couldn't concentrate on it. All I could see was the drinks compartment in Humber's monster car, with the rack of ice-picks, tongs and little miscellaneous chromium-plated objects. I had never given them more than a cursory glance; but one of them was a small tube with a loop of chain from end to end. One of them was a silent whistle for dogs.

I made an effort, and read about Sparking Plug, and thanked her for finding the cutting.

I stowed her whistle in my money belt and looked at my watch. It was already after half past three. I was going to be somewhat late back at work.

She had cleared me with October and shown me the whistle: two enormous favours. I wanted to repay her, and could think of only one way of doing it.

' "Nowhere either with more quiet or more freedom from trouble does a man retire than into his own soul . . ." ' I quoted.

She looked up at me, startled. 'That's the beginning of the competition.'

'Yes. Are you allowed help?'

'Yes. Anything. But . . .'

'It's Marcus Aurelius.'

'Who?' She was staggered.

'Marcus Aurelius Antoninus. Roman Emperor, 121 to 180 A.D. . . .'

'The Meditations?' I nodded.

'What language was it originally written in? We have to put that too. Latin, I suppose.'

'Greek.'

'This is fantastic . . . just where did you go to school?'

'I went to a village school in Oxfordshire.' So I had, for two years, until I was eight. 'And we had a master who perpetually crammed Marcus Aurelius down our throats.' But that master had been at Geelong.

I had been tempted to tell her the truth about myself all afternoon, but never more than at that moment. I found it impossible to be anything but my own self in her company, and even at Slaw I had spoken to her more or less in my natural accent. I hated having to pretend to her at all. But I didn't tell her where I had come from and why, because October hadn't, and I thought he ought to know his daughter better than I did. There were her cosy chats with Patty . . . whose tongue could not be relied on; and perhaps he thought it was a risk to his investigations. I didn't know. And I didn't tell her.

'Are you really sure it's Marcus Aurelius?' she said doubtfully. 'We only get one shot. If it's wrong, you don't get another.'

'I should check it then. It comes in a section about learning to be content with your lot. I suppose I remember it because it is good advice and I've seldom been able to follow it.' I grinned.

'You know,' she said tentatively, 'It's none of my business, but I would have thought you could have got on a bit in the world. You seem . . . you seem decidedly intelligent. Why do you work in a stable?'

'I work in a stable,' I told her with perfect, ironic truth, 'because it's the only thing I know how to do.'

'Will you do it for the rest of your life?'

'I expect so.'

'And will it content you?'

'It will have to.'

'I didn't expect this afternoon to turn out like this at all,' she said. 'To be frank, I was dreading it. And you have made it easy.'

'That's all right, then,' I said cheerfully.

She smiled. I went to the door and opened it, and she said, 'I'd better see you out. This building must have been the work of a maze-crazy architect. Visitors have been found wandering about the upper reaches dying of thirst days after they were supposed to have left.'

I laughed. She walked beside me back along the twisting corridors, down the stairs, and right back to the outside door, talking easily about her life in college, talking to me freely, as an equal. She told me that Durham was the oldest English University after Oxford and Cambridge, and that it was the only place in Britain which offered a course in Geophysics. She was indeed, a very nice girl.

She shook hands with me on the step.

'Goodbye,' she said. 'I'm sorry Patty was so beastly.'

'I'm not. If she hadn't been, I wouldn't have been here this afternoon.'

She laughed. 'But what a price to pay.'

'Worth it.'

Her grey eyes had darker grey flecks in them, I noticed. She watched me go over and sit on the motor-cycle and fasten on the helmet. Then she waved her hand briefly, and went back through the door. It closed with finality behind her.

Chapter Fourteen

I stopped in Posset on the return journey to see if there were any comment from October on the theory I had sent him the previous week, but there was no letter for me at all.

Although I was already late for evening stables, I stopped longer to write to him. I couldn't get Tommy Stapleton out of my head: he had died without passing on what he knew. I didn't want to make the same mistake. Or to die either, if it came to that. I scribbled fast.

'I think the trigger is a silent whistle, the sort used for dogs. Humber keeps one in the drinks compartment of his car. Remember Old Etonian? They hold hound-trails at Cartmel, on the morning of the races.'

Having posted that, I bought a large slab of chocolate for food, and also Jerry's comic, and slid as quietly as I could back into the yard. Cass caught me, however, and said sourly that I'd be lucky to get Saturday off next week as he would be reporting me to Humber. I sighed resignedly, started the load of evening chores, and felt the cold, dingy, sub-violent atmosphere of the place seep back into my bones.

But there was a difference now. The whistle lay like a bomb in my money belt. A death sentence, if they found me with it. Or so I believed. There remained the matter of making sure that I had not leaped to the wrong conclusion.

Tommy Stapleton had probably suspected what was going on and had walked straight into Humber's yard to tax him with it. He couldn't have known that the men he was dealing with were prepared to kill. But, because he had died, I did know. I had lived under their noses for seven weeks, and I had been careful: and because I intended to remain undetected to the end I spent a long time on Sunday wondering how I could conduct my experiment and get away with it.

On Sunday evening, at about five o'clock, Adams drove into the yard in his shining grey Jaguar. As usual at the sight of him, my heart sank. He walked round the yard with Humber when he made his normal tour of inspection and stopped for a long time looking over the door at Mickey. Neither he nor Humber came in. Humber had been into Mickey's box several times since the day he helped me take in the first lot of drugged water, but Adams had not been in at all.

Adams said, 'What do you think, Hedley?'

Humber shrugged, 'There's no change.'

'Write him off?'

'I suppose so.' Humber sounded depressed.

'It's a bloody nuisance,' said Adams violently. He looked at me. 'Still bolstering yourself up with tranquillizers?'

'Yes, sir.'

He laughed rudely. He thought it very funny. Then his face changed to a scowl, and he said savagely to Humber, 'It's useless, I can see that. Give him the chop, then.'

Humber turned away, and said, 'Right, I'll get it done tomorrow.'

Their footsteps moved off to the next box. I looked at Mickey. I had done my best for him, but he was too far gone, and had been from the beginning. After a fortnight what with his mental chaos, his continual state of druggedness, and his persistent refusal to eat, Mickey's condition was pitiable, and any one less stony than Humber would have had him put down long ago.

I made him comfortable for his last night and evaded yet another slash from his teeth. I couldn't say I was sorry not to have to deal with him any more, as a fortnight of looking after an unhinged horse would be enough for anyone; but the fact that he was to be put down the next day meant that I would have to perform my experiment without delay.

I didn't feel ready to do it. Thinking about it, as I put away my brushes for the night and walked across the yard towards the kitchen, I tried to find one good reason for putting it off.

The alacrity with which a good excuse for not doing it presented itself led me to the unwelcome, swingeing realization that for the first time since my childhood, I was thoroughly afraid.

I could get October to make the experiment, I thought, on Six-Ply. Or on any of the other horses. I hadn't got to do it myself. It would definitely be more prudent not to do it myself. October could do it with absolute safety, but if Humber found me out I was as good as dead: therefore I should leave it to October.

That was when I knew I was afraid, and I didn't like it. It took me most of the evening to decide to do the experiment myself. On Mickey. The next morning. Shuffling it off on to October doubtless would have been more prudent, but I had myself to live with afterwards. What had I really wanted to leave home for, if not to find out what I could or couldn't do?

When I took the bucket to the office door in the morning for Mickey's last dose of phenobarbitone, there was only a little left in the jar. Cass tipped the glass container upside down and tapped it on the bucket so that the last grains of white powder should not be wasted.

'That's his lot, poor bastard,' he observed, putting the stopper back in the empty jar. 'Pity there isn't a bit more left, we could have given him a double dose, just this once. Well, get on with it,' he added sharply. 'Don't·hang about looking mournful. It's not you that's going to be shot this afternoon.'

Well, I hoped not.

I turned away, went along to the tap, splashed in a little water, swilled round in it the instantly dissolved phenobarbitone, and poured it away down the drain. Then I filled the bucket with clean water and took it along for Mickey to drink.

He was dying on his feet. The bones stuck out more sharply under his skin and his head hung down below his shoulders. There was still a disorientated wildness in his eye, but he was going downhill so fast that he had little strength left for attacking anyone. For once he made no attempt to bite me when I put the bucket down at his head, but lowered his mouth into it and took a few half-hearted swallows.

Leaving him, I went along to the tack room and took a new head collar out of the basket of stores. This was strictly against the rules: only Cass was supposed to issue new tack. I took the head collar along to Mickey's box and fitted it on to him, removing the one he had weakened by constant fretting during his fortnight's illness and hiding it under a pile of straw, I unclipped the tethering chain from the old collar and clipped it on to the ring of the new one. I patted Mickey's neck, which he didn't like, walked out of his box, and shut and bolted only the bottom half of the door.

We rode out the first lot, and the second lot; and by then, I judged, Mickey's brain, without its morning dose, would be coming out of its sedation.

Leading Dobbin, the horse I had just returned on, I went to look at Mickey over the stable door. His head was weaving weakly from side to side, and he seemed very restless. Poor creature, I thought. Poor creature. And for a few seconds I was going to make him suffer more.

Humber stood at his office door, talking to Cass. The lads were bustling in and out looking after their horses, buckets were clattering, voices calling to each other: routine stable noise. I was never going to have a better opportunity.

I began to lead Dobbin across the yard to his box. Half way there I took the whistle out of my belt and pulled off its cap: then, looking round to make sure that no one was watching, I turned my head over my shoulder, put the tiny mouthpiece to my lips, and blew hard. Only a thread of sound came out, so high that I could hardly hear it above the clatter of Dobbin's feet on the ground.

The result was instantaneous and hideous.

Mickey screamed with terror.

His hooves threshed wildly against the floor and walls, and the chain which held him rattled as he jerked against it.

I walked Dobbin quickly the few remaining yards into his stall, clipped his chain on, zipped the whistle back into my belt, and ran across towards Mickey's box. Everyone else was doing the same. Humber was limping swiftly down the yard.

Mickey was still screaming and crashing his hooves against the wall as I looked into his box over the shoulders of Cecil and Lenny. The poor animal was on his hind legs, seemingly trying to beat his way through the bricks in front of him. Then suddenly, with all his ebbing strength, he dropped his forelegs to the ground and charged backwards.

'Look out,' shouted Cecil, instinctively retreating from the frantically bunching hind-quarters, although he was safely outside a solid door.

Mickey's tethering chain was not very long. There was a sickening snap as he reached the end of it and his backwards momentum was joltingly, appallingly stopped. His hind legs slid forward under his belly and he fell with a crash on to his side. His legs jerked stiffly. His head, still secured in the strong new head collar, was held awkwardly off the ground by the taut chain, and by its unnatural angle told its own tale. He had broken his neck. As indeed, to put him quickly out of his frenzy, I had hoped he might.

Everyone in the yard had gathered outside Mickey's box. Humber, having glanced perfunctorily over the door at the dead horse, turned and looked broodingly at his six ragged stable lads. The narrow eyed harshness of his expression stopped anyone asking him questions. There was a short silence.

'Stand in a line,' he said suddenly.

The lads looked surprised, but did as he said.

'Turn out your pockets,' said Humber.

Mystified, the lads obeyed. Cass went down the line, looking at what was produced and pulling the pockets out like wings to make sure they were empty. When he came to me I showed him a dirty handkerchief, a penknife, a few coins, and pulled my pockets inside out. He took the handkerchief from my hand, shook it out, and gave it back. The whistle at my waist was only an inch from his fingers.

I felt Humber's searching gaze on me from six feet away, but as I studied to keep my face vacantly relaxed and vaguely puzzled I was astonished to find that I was neither sweating nor tensing my muscles to make a run for it. In an odd way the nearness of the danger made me cool and clear headed. I didn't understand it, but it certainly helped.

'Back pocket?' asked Cass.

'Nothing in it,' I said casually, turning half round to show him.

'All right. Now you, Kenneth.'

I pushed my pockets in again, and replaced their contents. My hands were steady. Extraordinary, I thought.

Humber watched and waited until Kenneth's pockets had been innocently emptied: then he looked at Cass and jerked his head towards the loose boxes. Cass rooted around in the boxes of the horses we had just exercised. He finished the last, came back, and shook his head. Humber pointed silently towards the garage which sheltered his Bentley. Cass disappeared, reappeared, and again excitedly shook his head. In silence Humber limped away to his office, leaning on his heavy stick.

He couldn't have heard the whistle, and he didn't suspect that any of us had blown one for the sole purpose of watching its effect on Mickey, because if he had he would have had us stripped and searched from head to foot. He was still thinking along the lines of Mickey's death being an accident: and having found no whistle in any of the lad's pockets or in their horses' boxes he would conclude, I hoped, that it was none of that downtrodden bunch who had caused Mickey's brain-storm. If only Adams would agree with him, I was clear.

It was my afternoon for washing the car. Humber's own whistle was still there, tucked neatly into a leather retaining strap between a corkscrew and a pair of ice tongs. I looked, and left it where it was.

Adams came the next day.

Mickey had gone to the dog-meat man, who had grumbled about his thinness, and I had unobtrusively returned the new head collar to the store basket, leaving the old one dangling as usual from the tethering chain. Even Cass had not noticed the substitution.

Adams and Humber strolled along to Mickey's empty box and leaned on the half door, talking. Jerry poked his head out of the box next door, saw them standing there, and hurriedly disappeared again. I went normally about my business, fetching hay and water for Dobbin and carting away the muck sack.

'Roke,' shouted Humber, 'come here. At the double.'

I hurried over. 'Sir?'

'You haven't cleaned out this box.'

'I'm sorry sir. I'll do it this afternoon.'

'You will do it,' he said deliberately, 'before you have your dinner.'

He knew very well that this meant having no dinner at all. I glanced at his face. He was looking at me with calculation, his eyes narrowed and his lips pursed.

I looked down. 'Yes, sir,' I said meekly. Damn it, I thought furiously; this was too soon. I had been there not quite eight weeks, and I ought to have been able to count on at least three more. If he were already intent on making me leave, I was not going to be able to finish the job.

'For a start,' said Adams, 'you can fetch out that bucket and put it away.'

I looked into the box. Mickey's bucket still stood by the manger. I opened the door, walked over, picked it up, turned round to go back, and stopped dead.

Adams had come into the box after me. He held Humber's walking stick in his hand, and he was smiling.

I dropped the bucket and backed into a corner. He laughed.

'No tranquillizers today, eh, Roke?'

He swung his arm and the knobbed end of the stick landed on my ribs. It was hard enough, in all conscience. When he lifted his arm again I ducked under it and bolted out through the door. His roar of laughter floated after me.

I went on running until I was out of sight, and then walked and rubbed my chest. It was going to be a fair sized bruise, and I wasn't too keen on collecting many more. I supposed I should be thankful at least that they proposed to rid themselves of me in the ordinary way, and not over a hillside in a burning car.

All through that long, hungry afternoon I tried to decide what was best to do. To go at once, resigned to the fact that I couldn't finish the job, or to stay the few days I safely could without arousing Adams' suspicions. But what, I depressedly wondered, could I discover in three or four days that I had been unable to discover in eight weeks.

It was Jerry, of all people, who decided for me.

After supper (baked beans on bread, but not enough of it) we sat at the table with Jerry's comic spread open. Since Charlie had left no one had a radio, and the evenings were more boring than ever. Lenny and Kenneth were playing dice on the floor. Cecil was out getting drunk. Bert sat in his silent world on the bench on the other side of Jerry, watching the dice roll across the concrete.

The oven door was open, and all the switches on the electric stove were turned on as high as they would go. This was Lenny's bright idea for supplementing the small heat thrown out by the paraffin stove Humber had grudgingly provided. It wouldn't last longer than the arrival of the electricity bill, it was warm meanwhile.

The dirty dishes were stacked in the sink. Cobwebs hung like a cornice where the walls met the ceiling. A naked light bulb lit the brick-walled room. Someone had spilled tea on the table, and the corner of Jerry's comic had soaked it up.

I sighed. To think that I wasn't happy to be about to leave this squalid existence, now that I was being given no choice!

Jerry looked up from his comic, keeping his place with his finger.

'Dan?'

'Mmm?'

'Did Mr. Adams bash you?'

'Yes.'

'I thought he did.' He nodded several times, and went back to his comic.

I suddenly remembered his having looked out of the box next to Mickey's before Adams and Humber had called me over.

'Jerry,' I said slowly, 'did you hear Mr. Adams and Mr. Humber talking, while you were in the box with Mr. Adams' black hunter?'

'Yes,' he said, without looking up.

'What did they say?'

'When you ran away Mr. Adams laughed and told the boss you wouldn't stand it long. Stand it long,' he repeated vaguely, like a refrain, 'stand it long.'

'Did you hear what they said before that? When they first got there, and you looked out and saw them?'

This troubled him. He sat up and forgot to keep his place.

'I didn't want the boss to know I was still there, see? I ought to have finished that hunter a good bit before then.'

'Yes. Well, you're all right. They didn't catch you.'

He grinned and shook his head.

'What did they say?' I prompted.

'They were cross about Mickey. They said they would get on with the next one at once.'

'The next what?'

'I don't know.'

'Did they say anything else?'

He screwed up his thin little face. He wanted to please me, and I knew this expression meant he was thinking his hardest.

'Mr. Adams said you had been with Mickey too long, and the boss said yes it was a bad . . . a bad . . . um . . . oh, yes . . . risk, and you had better leave, and Mr. Adams said yes, get on with that as quick as you can and we'll do the next one as soon as he's gone.' He opened his eyes wide in triumph at this sustained effort.

'Say that again,' I said. 'The last bit, that's all.'

One thing Jerry could do, from long practice with the comics, was to learn by heart through his ears.

Obediently he repeated, 'Mr. Adams said get on with that as quick as you can and we'll do the next one as soon as he's gone.'

'What do you want most on earth?' I asked.

He looked surprised and then thoughtful, and finally a dreamy look spread over his face.

'Well?'

'A train,' he said. 'One you wind up. You know. And rails and things. And a signal.' He fell silent in rapture.

'You shall have them,' I said. 'As soon as I can get them.'

His mouth opened.

I said, 'Jerry, I'm leaving here. You can't stay when Mr. Adams starts bashing you, can you? So I'll have to go. But I'll send you that train. I won't forget, I promise.'

The evening dragged away as so many others had done, and we climbed the ladder to our unyielding beds, where I lay on my back in the dark with my hands laced behind my head and thought about Humber's stick crashing down somewhere on my body in the morning. Rather like going to the dentist for a drilling, I thought ruefully: the anticipation was worse than the event. I sighed, and went to sleep.

Operation Eviction continued much as expected, the next day.

When I was unsaddling Dobbin after the second exercise Humber walked into the box behind me and his stick landed with a thud across my back.

I let go of the saddle – which fell on a pile of fresh droppings – and swung round.

'What did I do wrong, sir?' I said, in an aggrieved voice. I thought I might as well make it difficult for him, but he had an answer ready.

'Cass tells me you were late back at work last Saturday afternoon. And pick up that saddle. What do you think you're doing, dropping it in that dirt?'

He stood with his legs planted firmly apart, his eyes judging his distance.

Well, all right, I thought. One more, and that's enough.

I turned round and picked up the saddle. I already had it in my arms and was straightening up when he hit me again, more or less in the same place, but much harder. The breath hissed through my teeth.

I threw the saddle down again in the dirt and shouted at him. 'I'm leaving. I'm off. Right now.'

'Very well,' he said coldly, with perceptible satisfaction. 'Go and pack. Your cards will be waiting for you in the office.' He turned on his heel and slowly limped away, his purpose successfully concluded.

How frigid he was, I thought. Unemotional, sexless and calculating. Impossible to think of him loving, or being loved, or feeling pity, or grief, or any sort of fear.

I arched my back, grimacing, and decided to leave Dobbin's saddle where it was, in the dirt. A nice touch, I thought. In character, to the bitter end.

Chapter Fifteen

I took the polythene sheeting off the motor-cycle and coasted gently out of the yard. All the lads were out exercising the third lot, with yet more to be ridden when they got back; and even while I was wondering how five of them were possibly going to cope with thirty horses, I met a shifty-looking boy trudging slowly up the road to Humber's with a kit bag slung over his shoulder. More flotsam. If he had known what he was going to, he would have walked more slowly still.

I biked to Clavering, a dreary mining town of mean back-to-back terraced streets jazzed up with chromium and glass in the shopping centre, and telephoned to October's London house.

Terence answered. Lord October, he said, was in Germany, where his firm were opening a new factory.

'When will he be back?'

'Saturday morning, I think. He went last Sunday, for a week.'

'Is he going to Slaw for the week-end?'

'I think so. He said something about flying back to Manchester, and he's given me no instructions for anything here.'

'Can you find the addresses and telephone numbers of Colonel Beckett and Sir Stuart Macclesfield for me?'

'Hang on a moment.' There was fluttering of pages, and Terence told me the numbers and addresses. I wrote them down and thanked him.

'Your clothes are still here, sir,' he said.

'I know,' I grinned. 'I'll be along to fetch them quite soon, I think.'

We rang off, and I tried Beckett's number. A dry, precise voice told me that Colonel Beckett was out, but that he would be dining at his Club at nine, and could be reached then. Sir Stuart Macclesfield, it transpired, was in a nursing home recovering from pneumonia. I had hoped to be able to summon some help in keeping a watch on Humber's yard so that when the horse-box left with Kandersteg on board it could be followed. It looked, however, as though I would have to do it myself, as I could visualise the local police neither believing my story nor providing anyone to assist me.

Armed with a rug and a pair of good binoculars bought in a pawn shop, and also with a pork pie, slabs of chocolate, a bottle of vichy water, and some sheets of foolscap paper, I rode the motor-cycle back through Posset and out along the road which crossed the top of the valley in which Humber's stables lay. Stopping at the point I had marked on my previous excursion, I wheeled the cycle a few yards down into the scrubby heathland, and found a position where I was off the sky line, more or less out of sight from passing cars, and also able to look down into Humber's yard through the binoculars. It was one o'clock, and there was nothing happening there.

I unbuckled the suitcase from the carrier and used it as a seat, settling myself to stay there for a long time. Even if I could reach Beckett on the telephone at nine, he wouldn't be able to rustle up reinforcements much before the next morning.

There was, meanwhile, a report to make, a fuller, more formal, more explanatory affair than the notes scribbled in Posset's post office. I took out the foolscap paper and wrote, on and off, for most of the afternoon, punctuating my work by frequent glances through the binoculars. But nothing took place down at Humber's except the normal routine of the stable.

I began . . .

'To The Earl of October.
   Sir Stuart Macclesfield.
   Colonel Roderick Beckett.
Sirs,
   The following is a summary of the facts which have so far come to light during my investigations on your behalf, together with some deductions which it seems reasonable to make from them.
   Paul James Adams and Hedley Humber started collaborating in a scheme for ensuring winners about four years ago, when Adams bought the Manor House and came to live at Tellbridge, Northumberland.
   Adams (in my admittedly untrained opinion) has a psychopathic personality, in that he impulsively gives himself pleasure and pursues his own ends without any consideration for other people or much apparent

anxiety about the consequences to himself. His intelligence seems to be above average, and it is he who gives the orders. I believe it is fairly common for psychopaths to be aggressive swindlers: it might be enlightening to dig up his life history.

Humber, though dominated by Adams, is not as irresponsible. He is cold and controlled at all times. I have never seen him genuinely angry (he uses anger as a weapon) and everything he does seems to be thought out and calculated. Whereas Adams may be mentally abnormal, Humber seems to be simply wicked. His comparative sanity may act as a brake on Adams, and have prevented their discovery before this.

Jud Wilson, the head travelling lad, and Cass, the head lad, are both involved, but only to the extent of being hired subordinates. Neither of them does as much stable work as their jobs would normally entail, but they are well paid. Both own big cars of less than a year old.

Adams' and Humber's scheme is based on the fact that horses learn by association and connect noises to events. Like Pavlov's dogs who would come to the sound of a bell because they had been taught it meant feeding time, horses hearing the feed trolley rattling across a stable yard know very well that their food is on the way.

If a horse is accustomed to a certain consequence following closely upon a certain noise, he automatically *expects* the consequence whenever he hears the noise. He reacts to the noise in anticipation of what is to come.

If something frightening were substituted – if, for instance, the rattle of the feed trolley were followed always by a thrashing and no food – the horse would soon begin to fear the noise, because of what it portended.

Fear is the stimulant which Adams and Humber have used. The appearance of all the apparently 'doped' horses after they had won – the staring, rolling eyes and the heavy sweat – was consistent with their having been in a state of terror.

Fear strongly stimulates the adrenal glands, so that they flood the bloodstream with adrenalin: and the effects of extra adrenalin, as of course you know, is to release the upsurge of energy needed to deal with the situation, either by fighting back or by running away. Running, in this case. At top speed, in panic.

The laboratory reports stated that the samples taken from all the original eleven horses showed a high adrenalin content, but that this was not significant because horses vary enormously, some always producing more adrenalin than others. I, however, think that it *was* significant that the adrenalin counts of those eleven horses were uniformly higher than average.

The noise which triggered off their fear is the high note of the sort of silent whistle normally used for training dogs. Horses can hear it well, though to human ears it is faint: this fact makes it ideal for the purpose, as a more obtrusive sound (a football rattle, for instance) would soon have been spotted. Humber keeps a dog whistle in the drinks compartment of his Bentley.

I do not yet know for sure how Adams and Humber frighten the horses, but I can make a guess.

For a fortnight I looked after a horse known in the yard as Mickey (registered name, Starlamp) who had been given the treatment. In Mickey's case, it was a disaster. He returned from three days' absence with large raw patches on his fore legs and in a completely unhinged mental state.

The wounds on his legs were explained by the head lad as having been caused by the application of a blister. But there was no blister paste to be seen, and I think they were ordinary burns caused by some sort of naked flame. Horses are more afraid of fire than of anything else, and it seems probable to me that it is expectation of being burnt that Adams and Humber have harnessed to the sound of a dog whistle.

I blew a dog whistle to discover its effect on Mickey. It was less than three weeks after the association had been planted, and he reacted violently and unmistakably. If you care to, you can repeat this trial on Six-Ply; but give him room to bolt in safety.

Adams and Humber chose horses which looked promising throughout their racing careers but had never won on account of running out of steam or guts at the last fence; and there are of course any number of horses like this. They bought them cheaply one at a time from auction sales or out of selling races, instilled into them a noise-fear association, and quietly sold them again. Often, far from losing on the deal, they made a profit (c.f. past histories of horses collected by officer cadets).

Having sold a horse with such a built-in accelerator, Adams and Humber then waited for it to run in a selling chase at one of five courses: Segefield, Haydock, Ludlow, Kelso and Stafford. They seem to have been prepared to wait indefinitely for this combination of place and event to occur, and in fact it has only occurred twelve times (eleven winners and Superman) since the first case twenty months ago.

These courses were chosen, I imagine, because their extra long run-in gave the most room for the panic to take effect. The horses were often lying fourth or fifth when landing over the last fence, and needed time to overhaul the leaders. If a horse were too hopelessly behind, Adams and Humber could just have left the whistle unblown, forfeited their stake money, and waited for another day.

Selling chases were preferred, I think, because horses are less likely to fall in them, and because of the good possibility of the winners changing hands yet again immediately afterwards.

At first sight it looks as if it would have been safer to have applied this scheme to Flat racing: but Flat racers do not seem to change hands so often, which would lessen the confusion. Then again Humber has never held a Flat licence, and probably can't get one.

None of the horses has been galvanised twice, the reason probably being that having once discovered they were not burnt after hearing the whistle they would be less likely to expect to be again. Their reaction would no longer be reliable enough to gamble on.

All the eleven horses won at very long odds, varying from 10–1 to 50–1, and Adams and Humber must have spread their bets thinly enough to raise no comment. I do not know how much Adams won on each race, but the least Humber made was seventeen hundred pounds, and the most was four thousand five hundred.

Details of all the processed horses, successful and unsuccessful, are recorded in a blue ledger at present to be found at the back of the third drawer down in the centre one of three green filing cabinets in Humber's stable office.

Basically, as you see, it is a simple plan. All they do is make a horse associate fire with a dog whistle, and then blow a whistle as he lands over the last fence.

No drugs, no mechanical contrivances, no help needed from owner, trainer or jockey. There was only a slight risk of Adams and Humber being found out, because their connection with the horses was so obscure and distant.

Stapleton, however, suspected them, and I am certain in my own mind that they killed him, although there is no supporting evidence.

They believe now that they are safe and undetected: and they intend, during the next few days, to plant fear in a horse called Kandersteg. I have left Humber's employ, and am writing this while keeping watch on the yard. I propose to follow the horse box when Kandersteg leaves in it, and discover where and how the heat is applied.'

I stopped writing and picked up the binoculars. The lads were bustling about doing evening stables and I enjoyed not being down there among them.

It was too soon, I thought, to expect Humber to start on Kandersteg, however much of a hurry he and Adams were in. They couldn't have known for certain that I would depart before lunch, or even that day, and they were bound to let my dust settle before making a move. On the other hand I couldn't risk missing them. Even the two miles to the telephone in Posset made ringing up Beckett a worrying prospect. It would take no longer for Kandersteg to be loaded up and carted off than for me to locate Beckett in his Club. Mickey-Starlamp had been both removed and brought back in daylight, and it might be that Humber never moved any horses by night. But I couldn't be sure. I bit the end of my pen in indecision. Finally, deciding not to telephone, I added a postscript to the report.

'I would very much appreciate some help in this watch, because if it continues for several days I could easily miss the horse box through falling asleep. I can be found two miles out of Posset on the Hexham road, at the head of the valley which Humber's stables lie in.'

I added the time, the date, and signed my name. Then I folded the report into an envelope, and addressed it to Colonel Beckett.

I raced down to Posset to put the letter in the box outside the post office. Four miles. I was away for just under six minutes. It was lucky, I think, that I met no traffic on either part of the trip. I skidded to a worried halt at the top of the hill, but all appeared normal down in the stables. I wheeled the motor-cycle off the road again, down to where I had been before, and took a long look through the binoculars.

It was beginning to get dark and lights were on in nearly all the boxes, shining out into the yard. The dark looming bulk of Humber's house, which lay nearest to me, shut off from my sight his brick office and all the top end of the yard, but I had a sideways view of the closed doors of the horse box garage, and I could see straight into the far end row of boxes, of which the fourth from the left was occupied by Kandersteg.

And there he was, a pale washy chestnut, moving across and catching the light as Bert tossed his straw to make him comfortable for the night. I sighed with relief, and sat down again to watch.

The routine work went on, untroubled, unchanged. I watched Humber, leaning on his stick, make his slow inspection round the yard, and absent-mindedly rubbed the bruises he had given me that morning. One by one the doors were shut and the lights went out until a single window glowed yellow, the last window along the right hand row of boxes, the window of the lads' kitchen. I put down the binoculars, and got to my feet and stretched.

As always on the moors the air was on the move. It wasn't a wind, scarcely a breeze, more like a cold current flowing round whatever it found in its path. To break its chilling persistence on my back I constructed a rough barricade of the motor-cycle with a bank of brushwood on its roadward, moorward side. In the lea of this shelter I sat on the suitcase, wrapped myself in the rug, and was tolerably warm and comfortable.

I looked at my watch. Almost eight o'clock. It was a fine, clear night, and the sky was luminous with the white blaze of the stars. I still hadn't learned the northern hemisphere patterns except for the Great Bear and Pole Star. And there was Venus dazzling away to the west-south-west. A pity that I hadn't thought of buying an astral map to pass the time.

Down in the yard the kitchen door opened, spilling out an oblong of light. Cecil's figure stayed there for a few seconds silhouetted; then he came out and shut the door, and I couldn't see him in the dark. Off to his bottle, no doubt.

I ate some pie, and a while later, a bar of chocolate.

Time passed. Nothing happened down in Humber's yard. Occasionally a car sped along the road behind me, but none stopped. Nine o'clock came and went. Colonel Beckett would be dining at his Club, and I could after all have gone safely down to ring him up. I shrugged in the darkness. He would get my letter in the morning, anyway.

The kitchen door opened again, and two or three lads came out, picking their way with a torch round to the elementary sanitation. Upstairs in the hay-loft a light showed dimly through that half of the window not pasted over with brown paper. Bed-time. Cecil reeled in, clutching the door post to stop himself from falling. The downstairs light went out, and finally the upper one as well.

The night deepened. The hours passed. The moon rose and shone brightly. I gazed out over the primeval rolling moors and thought some unoriginal thoughts, such as how beautiful the earth was, and how vicious the ape creature who inhabited it. Greedy, destructive, unkind, power-hungry old homo sapiens. Sapiens, meaning wise, discreet, judicious. What a laugh. So fair a planet should have evolved a sweeter-natured, saner race. Nothing that produced people like Adams and Humber could be termed a roaring success.

At four o'clock I ate some more chocolate and drank some water, and for some time thought about my stud farm sweltering in the afternoon sun twelve thousand miles away. A sensible, orderly life waiting for me when I had finished sitting on wintry hillsides in the middle of the night.

Cold crept through the blanket as time wore on, but it was no worse than the temperature in Humber's dormitory. I yawned and rubbed my eyes, and began to work out how many seconds had to pass before dawn. If the sun rose (as expected) at ten to seven, that would be a hundred and thirteen times sixty seconds, which made it six thousand seven hundred and eighty ticks to Thursday. And how many to Friday? I gave up. It was quite likely I would be sitting on the hillside, but with a little luck there would be a Beckett-sent companion to give me a pinch when things started moving.

At six fifteen the light went on again in the lads' quarters, and the stable woke up. Half an hour later the first string of six horses wound its way out of the yard and down the road to Posset. No gallops on the moors on Thursday. Road work day.

Almost before they were out of sight Jud Wilson drove into the yard in his substantial Ford and parked it beside the horse box shed. Cass walked across the yard to meet him, and the two of them stood talking together for a few minutes. Then through the binoculars I watched Jud Wilson go back to the shed and open its big double doors, while Cass made straight for Kandersteg's box, the fourth door from the end.

They were off.

And they were off very slickly. Jud Wilson backed the box into the centre of the yard and let down the ramp. Cass led the horse straight across and into the horse box, and within a minute was out helping to raise and fasten the ramp again. There was then a fractional pause while they stood looking towards the house, from where almost instantly the limping back-view of Humber appeared.

Cass stood watching while Humber and Jud Wilson climbed up into the cab. The horse box rolled forward out of the yard. The loading up had taken barely five minutes from start to finish.

During this time I dropped the rug over the suitcase and kicked the brushwood away from the bike. The binoculars I slung round my neck and zipped inside the leather jacket. I put on my crash helmet, goggles and gloves.

In spite of my belief that it would be to the north or the west that Kandersteg would be taken, I was relieved when this proved to be the case. The horse box turned sharply west and trundled up the far side of the valley along the road which crossed the one I was stationed on.

I wheeled the bike on to the road, started it, and abandoning (this time with pleasure) my third clump of clothes, rode with some despatch towards the cross-roads. There from a safe quarter of a mile away I watched the horse box slow down, turn right, northwards, and accelerate.

Chapter Sixteen

I crouched in a ditch all day and watched Adams, Humber and Jud Wilson scare Kandersteg into a lathering frenzy.

It was wicked.

The means they used were as simple in essence as the scheme, and consisted mainly in the special lay-out of a small two-acre field.

The thin high hedge round the whole field was laced with wire to about shoulder height, strong, but without barbs. About fifteen feet inside this there was a second fence, solidly made of posts and rails which had weathered to a pleasant greyish-brown.

At first glance it looked like the arrangement found at many stud farms, where young stock are kept from damaging themselves on wire by a wooden protective inner fence. But the corners of this inner ring had been rounded, so that what in effect had been formed was a miniature race track between the outer and inner fences.

It all looked harmless. A field for young stock, a training place for racehorses, a show ring ... take your pick. With a shed for storing equipment, just outside the gate at one corner. Sensible. Ordinary.

I half-knelt, half-lay in the drainage ditch which ran along behind the hedge, near the end of one long side of the field, with the shed little more than a hundred yards away in the far opposite corner, to my left. The bottom of the hedge had been cut and laid, which afforded good camouflage for my head, but from about a foot above the ground the leafless hawthorn grew straight up, tall and weedy; as concealing as a sieve. But as long as I kept absolutely still, I judged I was unlikely to be spotted. At any rate, although I was really too close for safety, too close even to need to use the binoculars, there was nowhere else which gave much cover at all.

Bare hillsides sloped up beyond the far fence and along the end of the field to my right; behind me lay a large open pasture of at least thirty acres; and the top end, which was screened from the road by a wedge of conifers, was directly under Adams' and Humber's eyes.

Getting to the ditch had entailed leaving the inadequate shelter of the last flattening shoulder of hillside and crossing fifteen yards of bare turf when none of the men was in sight. But retreating was going to be less pulse quickening, since I had only to wait for the dark.

The horse box was parked beside the shed, and almost as soon as I had worked my way round the hill to my present position there was a clattering of hooves on the ramp as Kandersteg was unloaded. Jud Wilson led him round through the gate and on to the grassy track. Adams, following, shut the gate and then unlatched a swinging section of the inner fence and fastened it across the track, making a barrier. Walking past Jud and the horse he did the same with another section a few yards further on, with the result that Jud and Kandersteg were now standing in a small pen in the corner. A pen with three ways out; the gate out of the field, and the rails which swung across like level crossing gates on either side.

Jud let go of the horse, which quietly began to eat the grass, and he and Adams let themselves out and disappeared into the shed to join Humber. The shed, made of weathered wood, was built like a single loose box, with a window and a split door, and I imagined it was there that Mickey had spent much of the three days he had been away.

There was a certain amount of clattering and banging in the shed, which went on for some time, but as I had only a sideways view of the door I could see nothing of what was happening.

Presently all three of them came out. Adams walked round behind the shed and reappeared beyond the field, walking up the hillside. He went at a good pace right to the top, and stood gazing about him at the countryside.

Humber and Wilson came through the gate into the field, carrying between them an apparatus which looked like a vacuum cleaner, a cylindrical tank with a hose attached to one end. They put the tank down in the corner, and Wilson held the hose. Kandersteg, quietly cropping the grass close beside them, lifted his head and looked at them, incurious and trusting. He bent down again to eat.

Humber walked the few steps to where the swinging rail was fastened to the hedge, seemed to be checking something, and then went back to stand beside Wilson, who was looking up towards Adams.

On top of the hill, Adams casually waved his hand.

Down in the corner of the field Humber had his hand to his mouth ... I was too far away to see with the naked eye if what he held there was a whistle, and too close to risk getting out the glasses for a better look. But even though try as I might I could hear no noise, there wasn't much room for doubt. Kandersteg raised his head, pricked his ears, and looked at Humber.

Flame suddenly roared from the hose in Wilson's hand. It was directed behind the horse, but it frightened him badly, all the same. He sat back on his haunches, his ears flattening. Then Humber's arm moved, and the swinging barrier, released by some sort of catch, sprang back to let the horse out on to the track. He needed no telling.

He stampeded round the field, skidding at the corners, lurching against the inner wooden rail, thundering past ten feet from my head. Wilson opened the second barrier, and he and Humber retired through the gate. Kandersteg made two complete circuits at high speed before his stretched neck relaxed to a more normal angle and his wildly thrusting hind quarters settled down to a more natural gallop.

Humber and Wilson stood and watched him, and Adams strolled down the hill to join them at the gate.

They let the horse slow down and stop of his own accord, which he did away to my right, after about three and a half circuits. Then Jud Wilson unhurriedly swung one of the barriers back across the track, and waving a stick in one hand and a hunting whip in the other, began to walk round to drive the horse in front of him along into the corner. Kandersteg trotted warily ahead, unsettled, sweating, not wanting to be caught.

Jud Wilson swung his stick and his whip and trudged steadily on. Kandersteg trotted softly past where I lay, his hooves swishing through the short grass: but I was no longer watching. My face was buried in the roots of the hedge, and I ached with the effort of keeping still. Seconds passed like hours.

There was a rustle of trouser leg brushing against trouser leg, a faint clump of boots on turf, a crack of the long thong of the whip . . . and no outraged yell of discovery. He went past, and on up the field.

The muscles which had been ready to expel me out of the ditch and away towards the hidden motor-cycle gradually relaxed. I opened my eyes and looked at leaf mould close to my face, and worked some saliva into my mouth. Cautiously, inch by inch, I raised my head and looked across the field.

The horse had reached the barrier and Wilson was unhooking and swinging the other one shut behind him, so that he was again penned into the small enclosure. There, for about half an hour, the three men left him. They themselves walked back into the shed, where I could not see them, and I could do nothing but wait for them to appear again.

It was a fine, clear, quiet morning, but a bit cold for lying in ditches, especially damp ones. Exercise, however, beyond curling and uncurling my toes and fingers, was a bigger risk than pneumonia; so I lay still, taking heart from the thought that I was dressed from head to foot in black, and had a mop of black hair as well, and was crouched in blackish brown rotting dead leaves. It was because of the protective colouring it offered that I had chosen the ditch in preference to a shallow dip in the hillside, and I was glad I had, because it was fairly certain that Adams from his look-out point would at once have spotted a dark intruder on the pale green hill.

I didn't notice Jud Wilson walk out of the shed, but I heard the click of the gate, and there he was, going into the little enclosure and laying his hand on Kandersteg's bridle, for all the world as if he were consoling him. But how could anyone who liked horses set about them with a flame thrower? And Jud, it was clear, was going to do it again. He left the horse, went over to the corner, picked up the hose and stood adjusting its nozzle.

Presently Adams appeared and climbed the hill, and then Humber, limping on his stick, joined Jud in the field.

There was a long wait before Adams waved his hand, during which three cars passed along the lonely moorland road. Eventually Adams was satisfied. His arm languidly rose and fell.

Humber's hand went immediately to his mouth.

Kandersteg already knew what it meant. He was running back on his haunches in fear before the flame shot out behind him and stopped him dead.

This time there was a fiercer, longer, closer burst of fire, and Kandersteg erupted in greater terror. He came scorching round the track . . . and round again . . . it was like waiting for the ball to settle in roulette with too much staked. But he stopped this time at the top end of the field, well away from my hiding place.

Jud walked across the middle of the field to come up behind him, not round the whole track. I sighed deeply with heartfelt relief.

I had folded my limbs originally into comfortable angles, but they were beginning to ache with inactivity, and I had cramp in the calf of my right leg, but I still didn't dare move while all three men were in my sight and I in theirs.

They shut Kandersteg into his little pen and strolled away into the shed, and cautiously, as quietly as I could in the rotting leaves, I flexed my arms and legs, got rid of the cramp, and discovered pins and needles instead. Ah well . . . it couldn't go on for ever.

They were, however, plainly going to repeat the process yet again. The flame thrower still lay by the hedge.

The sun was high in the sky by this time, and I looked at the gleam it raised on the leather sleeve of my left arm, close to my head. It was too shiny. Hedges and ditches held nothing as light-reflecting as black leather. Could Wilson possibly, *possibly* walk a second time within feet of me without coming close enough to the hedge to see a shimmer which shouldn't be there?

Adams and Humber came out of the shed and leaned over the gate, looking at Kandersteg. Presently they lit cigarettes and were clearly talking. They were in no hurry. They finished the cigarettes, threw them away, and stayed where they were for another ten minutes. Then Adams walked over to his car and returned with a bottle and some glasses. Wilson came out of the shed to join them and the three of them stood there in the sun, quietly drinking and gossiping in the most commonplace way.

What they were doing was, of course, routine to them. They had done it at least twenty times before. Their latest victim stood warily in his pen, unmoving, frightened, far too upset to eat.

Watching them drink made me thirsty, but that was among the least of my troubles. Staying still was becoming more and more difficult. Painful, almost.

At long last they broke it up. Adams put the bottle and glasses away and strolled off up the hill, Humber checked the quick release on the swinging barrier, and Jud adjusted the nozzle of the hose.

Adams waved. Humber blew.

This time the figure of Kandersteg was sharply, terrifyingly silhouetted against a sheet of flame. Wilson swayed his body, and the brilliant, spreading jet flattened and momentarily swept under the horse's belly and among his legs.

I nearly cried out, as if it were I that were being burned, not the horse. And for one sickening moment it looked as if Kandersteg were too terrified to escape.

Then, squealing, he was down the track like a meteor, fleeing from fire, from pain, from a dog whistle . . .

He was going too fast to turn the corner. He crashed into the hedge, bounced off, stumbled and fell. Eyes starting out of his head, lips retracted from his teeth, he scrambled frantically to his feet and bolted on, past my head, up the field, round again and round again.

He came to a jolting halt barely twenty yards away from me. He stood stock-still with sweat dripping from his neck and down his legs. His flesh quivered convulsively.

Jud Wilson, whip and stick in hand, started on his walk round the track. Slowly I put my face down among the roots and tried to draw some comfort from the fact that if he saw me there was still a heavily wired fence between us, and I should get some sort of start in running away. But the motor-cycle was hidden on rough ground two hundred yards behind me, and the curving road lay at least as far beyond that again, and Adams' grey Jaguar was parked on the far side of the horse box. Successful flight wasn't something I'd have liked to bet on.

Kandersteg was too frightened to move. I heard Wilson shouting at him and cracking the whip, but it was a full minute before the hooves came stumbling jerkily, in bursts and stamps, past my head.

In spite of the cold, I was sweating. Dear heavens, I thought, there was as much adrenalin pouring into my bloodstream as into the horse's; and I realized that from the time Wilson started his methodical walk round the track I had been able to hear my own heart thudding.

Jud Wilson yelled at Kandersteg so close to my ear that it felt like a blow. The whip cracked.

'Get on, get on, get on there.'

He was standing within feet of my head. Kandersteg wouldn't move. The whip cracked again. Jud shouted at the horse, stamping his boot on the ground in encouragement. The faint tremor came to me through the earth. He was a yard away, perhaps, with his eyes on the horse. He had only to turn his head . . . I began to think that anything, even discovery, was preferable to the terrible strain of keeping still.

Then, suddenly, it was over.

Kandersteg skittered away and bumped into the rails, and took a few more uneven steps back towards the top of the field. Jud Wilson moved away after him.

I continued to behave like a log, feeling exhausted. Slowly my heart subsided. I started breathing again . . . and unclamped my fingers from handfuls of leaf mould.

Step by reluctant step Jud forced Kandersteg round to the corner enclosure, where he swung the rails across and penned the horse in again. Then he picked up the flame thrower and took it with him through the gate. The job was done. Adams, Humber and Wilson stood in a row and contemplated their handiwork.

The pale coat of the horse was blotched with huge dark patches where the sweat had broken out, and he stood stiff legged, stiff necked, in the centre of the small enclosure. Whenever any of the three men moved he jumped nervously and then stood rigidly still again: and it was clearly going to be some long time before he had unwound enough to be loaded up and taken back to Posset.

Mickey had been away three days, but that, I judged, was only because his legs had been badly burned by mistake. As Kandersteg's indoctrination appeared to have gone without a hitch, he should be back in his own stable fairly soon.

It couldn't be too soon for me and my static joints. I watched the three men potter about in the sunlight, wandering between car and shed, shed and horse box, aimlessly passing the morning and managing never to be all safely out of sight at the same time. I cursed under my breath and resisted a temptation to scratch my nose.

At long last they made a move. Adams and Humber folded themselves into the Jaguar and drove off in the direction of Tellbridge. But Jud Wilson reached into the cab of the horse box, pulled out a paper bag, and proceeded to eat his lunch sitting on the gate. Kandersteg remained immobile in his little enclosure, and I did the same in my ditch.

Jud Wilson finished his lunch, rolled the paper bag into a ball, yawned, and lit a cigarette. Kandersteg continued to sweat, and I to ache. Everything was very quiet. Time passed.

Jud Wilson finished his cigarette, threw the stub away and yawned again. Then slowly, slowly, he climbed down from the gate, picked up the flame thrower, and took it into the shed.

He was scarcely through the door before I was slithering down into the shallow ditch, lying full length along it on my side, not caring about the dampness but thankfully, slowly, painfully, straightening one by one my cramped arms and legs.

The time, when I looked at my watch, was two o'clock. I felt hungry, and regretted that I hadn't had enough sense to bring some of the chocolate.

I lay in the ditch all afternoon, hearing nothing, but waiting for the horse box to start up and drive away. After a while in spite of the cold and the presence of Jud Wilson, I had great difficulty in keeping awake; a ridiculous state of affairs which could only be remedied by action. Accordingly I rolled over on to my stomach and inch by careful inch raised my head high enough to see across to Kandersteg and the shed.

Jud Wilson was again sitting on the gate. He must have seen my movements out of the corner of his eye, because he looked away from Kandersteg, who stood in front of him, and turned his head in my direction. For a fleeting second it seemed that he was looking straight into my eyes: then his gaze swept on past me, and presently, unsuspiciously, returned to Kandersteg.

I let my held breath trickle out slowly, fighting down a cough.

The horse was still sweating, the dark patches showing up starkly, but there was a less fixed look about him, and while I watched he swished his tail and restlessly shook his neck. He was over the hump.

More cautiously still, I lowered my head and chest down again on to my folded arms, and waited some more.

Soon after four Adams and Humber came back in the Jaguar, and again, like a rabbit out of his burrow, I edged up for a look.

They decided to take the horse home. Jud Wilson backed the horse box to the gate and let down the ramp, and Kandersteg, sticking in his feet at every step, was eventually pulled and prodded into it. The poor beast's distress was all too evident, even from across the field. I liked horses. I found I was wholly satisfied that because of me Adams and Humber and Wilson were going to be out of business.

Gently I lay down again, and after a short while I heard both the engines – first the Jaguar's and then the horse box's – start up and drive off, back towards Posset.

When the sound of them had died away I stood up, stretched, brushed the leaf mould from my clothes, and walked round the field to look at the shed.

It was fastened shut with a complicated looking padlock, but through the window I could see it held little besides the flame thrower, some cans presumably holding fuel, a large tin funnel and three garden chairs folded and stacked against one wall. There seemed little point in breaking in, though it would have been simple enough since the padlock fittings had been screwed straight on to the surface of the door and its surround. The screwdriver blade of my penknife could have removed the whole thing, fussy padlock intact. Crooks, I reflected, could be as fantastically dim in some ways as they were imaginative in others.

I went through the gate into Kandersteg's little enclosure. The grass where he had stood was scorched. The inside surfaces of the rails had been painted white, so that they resembled racecourse rails. I stood for a while looking at them, feeling a second-hand echo of the misery the horse had endured in that harmless looking place, and then let myself out and walked away, round past my hiding place in the ditch and off towards the motor-cycle. I picked it up, hooked the crash helmet on to the handle bars, and started the engine.

So that was the lot, I thought. My job was done. Safely, quietly, satisfactorily done. As it should be. Nothing remained but to complete yesterday's report and put the final facts at the Stewards' disposal.

I coasted back to the place from where I had kept a watch on Humber's yard, but there was no one there. Either Beckett had not got my letter or had not been able to send any help, or the help, if it had arrived, had got tired of waiting and departed. The rug, suitcase and remains of food lay where I had left them, undistured.

On an impulse, before packing up and leaving the area, I unzipped my jacket and took out the binoculars to have a last look down into the yard.

What I saw demolished in one second flat my complacent feeling of safety and completion.

A scarlet sports car was turning into the yard. It stopped beside Adams' grey Jaguar, a door opened, and a girl got out. I was too far away to distinguish her features but there was no mistaking that familiar car and that dazzling silver blonde hair. She slammed the car door and walked hesitantly towards the office, out of my sight.

I swore aloud. Of all damnable, unforeseeable, dangerous things to happen! I hadn't told Elinor anything. She thought I was an ordinary stable lad. I had borrowed a dog whistle from her. And she was October's daughter. What were the chances, I wondered numbly, of her keeping quiet on the last two counts and not giving Adams the idea that she was a threat to him.

She ought to be safe enough, I thought. Reasonably, she ought to be safe as long as she made it clear that it was I who knew the significance of dog whistles, and not her.

But supposing she didn't make it clear? Adams never behaved reasonably, to start with. His standards were not normal. He was psychopathic. He could impulsively kill a journalist who seemed to be getting too nosy. What was to stop him killing again, if he got it into his head that it was necessary?

I would give her three minutes, I thought. If she asked for me, and was told I had left, and went straight away again, everything would be all right.

I willed her to return from the office and drive away in her car. I doubted whether in any case if Adams were planning to harm her I could get her out safely, since the odds against, in the shape of Adams, Humber, Wilson and Cass, were too great for common sense. I wasn't too keen on having to try. But the three minutes went past, and the red car stood empty in the yard.

She had stayed to talk and she had no notion that there was anything which should not be said. If I had done as I had wanted and told her why I was at Humber's, she would not have come at all. It was my fault she was there. I had clearly got to do my best to see she left again in mint condition. There was no choice.

I put the binoculars in the suitcase and left it and the rug where it was. Then, zipping up the jacket and fastening on the crash helmet, I restarted the bike and rode it down and round and in through Humber's gate.

I left the bike near the gate and walked across towards the yard, passing the shed where the horse box was kept. The doors were shut, and there was no sign of Jud Wilson. Perhaps he had already gone home, and I hoped so. I went into the yard at the top end beside the wall of the office, and saw Cass at the opposite end looking over the door of the fourth box from the left. Kandersteg was home.

Adams' Jaguar and Elinor's T.R.4 stood side by side in the centre of the yard. Lads were hustling over their evening jobs, and everything looked normal and quiet.

I opened the office door, and walked in.

Chapter Seventeen

So much for my fears, I thought. So much for my melodramatic imagination. She was perfectly safe. She held a half empty glass of pink liquid in her hand, having a friendly drink with Adams and Humber, and she was smiling.

Humber's heavy face looked anxious, but Adams was laughing and enjoying himself. It was a picture which printed itself clearly on my mind before they all three turned and looked at me.

'Daniel!' Elinor exclaimed. 'Mr. Adams said you had gone.'

'Yes. I left something behind. I came back for it.'

'Lady Elinor Tarren,' said Adams with deliberation, coming round behind me, closing the door and leaning against it, 'came to see if you had conducted the experiment she lent you her dog whistle for.'

It was just as well, after all, that I had gone back.

'Oh, surely I didn't say that,' she protested. 'I just came to get the whistle, if Daniel had finished with it. I mean, I was passing, and I thought I could save him the trouble of sending it . . .'

I turned to him, 'Lady Elinor Tarren,' I said with equal deliberation, 'does not know what I borrowed her whistle for. I didn't tell her. She knows nothing about it.'

His eyes narrowed and then opened into a fixed stare. His jaw bunched. He took in the way I had spoken to him, the way I looked at him. It was not what he was used to from me. He transferred his stare to Elinor.

'Leave her alone,' I said. 'She doesn't know.'

'What on earth are you talking about?' said Elinor, smiling. 'What was this mysterious experiment, anyway?'

'It wasn't important,' I said. 'There's . . . er . . . there's a deaf lad here, and we wanted to know if he could hear high pitched noises, that's all.'

'Oh,' she said, 'and could he?'

I shook my head. 'I'm afraid not.'

'What a pity.' She took a drink, and ice tinkled against the glass. 'Well, if you've no more use for it, do you think I could have my whistle back?'

'Of course.' I dug into my money belt, brought out the whistle, and gave it to her. I saw Humber's astonishment and Adams' spasm of fury that Humber's search had missed so elementary a hiding place.

'Thank you,' she said, putting the whistle in her pocket. 'What are your plans now? Another stable job? You know,' she said to Humber, smiling, 'I'm surprised you let him go. He rode better than any lad we've ever had in Father's stables. You were lucky to have him.'

I had not ridden well for Humber. He began to say heavily, 'He's not all that good . . .' when Adams smoothly interrupted him.

'I think we have underestimated Roke, Hedley. Lady Elinor, I am sure Mr. Humber will take him back on your recommendation, and never let him go again.'

'Splendid,' she said warmly.

Adams was looking at me with his hooded gaze to make sure I had appreciated his little joke. I didn't think it very funny.

'Take your helmet off,' he said. 'You're indoors and in front of a lady. Take it off.'

'I think I'll keep it on,' I said equably. And I could have done with a full suit of armour to go with it. Adams was not used to me contradicting him, and he shut his mouth with a snap.

Humber said, puzzled, 'I don't understand why you bother with Roke, Lady Elinor. I thought your father got rid of him for ... well ... molesting you.'

'Oh no,' she laughed. 'That was my sister. But it wasn't true, you know. It was all made up.' She swallowed the last of her drink and with the best will in the world put the finishing touches to throwing me to the wolves. 'Father made me promise not to tell anyone that it was. all a story, but as you're Daniel's employer you really ought to know that he isn't anything like as bad as he lets everyone believe.'

There was a short, deep silence. Then I said, smiling, 'That's the nicest reference I've ever had ... you're very kind.'

'Oh dear,' she laughed. 'You know what I mean ... and I can't think why you don't stick up for yourself more.'

'It isn't always advisable,' I said, and raised an eyebrow at Adams. He showed signs of not appreciating my jokes either. He took Elinor's empty glass.

'Another gin and campari?' he suggested.

'No thank you, I must be going.'

He put her glass down on the desk with his own, and said, 'Do you think Roke would be the sort of man who'd need to swallow tranquillizers before he found the nerve to look after a difficult horse?'

'Tranquillizers? *Tranquillizers?* Of course not. I shouldn't think he ever took a tranquillizer in his life. Did you?' she said, turning to me and beginning to look puzzled.

'No,' I said. I was very anxious for her to be on her way before her puzzlement grew any deeper. Only while she suspected nothing and learned nothing was she safe enough.

'But you said ...' began Humber, who was still unenlightened.

'It was a joke. Only a joke,' I told him. 'Mr. Adams laughed about it quite a lot, if you remember.'

'That's true. I laughed,' said Adams sombrely. At least he seemed willing for her ignorance to remain undisturbed, and to let her go.

'Oh,' Elinor's face cleared. 'Well ... I suppose I'd better be getting back to college. I'm going to Slaw tomorrow for the week-end ... do you have any message for my father, Daniel?'

It was a casual, social remark, but I saw Adams stiffen.

I shook my head.

'Well ... it's been very pleasant, Mr. Humber. Thank you so much for the drink. I hope I haven't taken too much of your time.'

She shook Humber's hand, and Adams', and finally mine.

'How lucky you came back for something. I thought I'd missed you
. . . and that I could whistle for my whistle.' She grinned.

I laughed. 'Yes, it was lucky.'

'Goodbye then. Goodbye Mr. Humber,' she said, as Adams opened
the door for her. She said goodbye to him on the doorstep, where he
remained, and over Humber's shoulder I watched through the window
as she walked across to her car. She climbed in, started the engine, waved
gaily to Adams, and drove out of the yard. My relief at seeing her go was
even greater than my anxiety about getting out myself.

Adams stepped inside, shut the door, locked it, and put the key in his
pocket. Humber was surprised. He still did not understand.

He said, staring at me, 'You know, Roke doesn't seem the same. And
his voice is different.'

'Roke, damn him to hell, is God knows what.'

The only good thing in the situation that I could see was that I no
longer had to cringe when he spoke to me. It was quite a relief to be able
to stand up straight for a change. Even if it didn't last long.

'Do you mean it is Roke, and not Elinor Tarren after all, who knows
about the whistle?'

'Of course,' said Adams impatiently. 'For Christ's sake, don't you
understand anything? It looks as though October planted him on us,
though how in hell he knew . . .'

'But Roke is only a stable lad.'

'Only,' said Adams savagely. 'But that doesn't make it any better.
Stable lads have tongues, don't they? And eyes? And look at him. He's
not the stupid worm he's always seemed.'

'No one would take his word against yours,' said Humber.

'No one is going to take his word at all.'

'What do you mean.'

'I'm going to kill him,' said Adams.

'I suppose that might be more satisfactory.' Humber sounded as if he
were discussing putting down a horse.

'It won't help you,' I said. 'I've already sent a report to the Stewards.'

'We were told that once before,' said Humber, 'but it wasn't true.'

'It is, this time.'

Adams said violently, 'Report or no report, I'm going to kill him.
There are other reasons . . .' He broke off, glared at me and said, 'You
fooled me. *Me*. How?'

I didn't reply. It hardly seemed a good time for light conversation.

'This one,' said Humber reflectively, 'has a motor-cycle.'

I remembered that the windows in the office's wash room were all too
small to escape through. The door to the yard was locked, and Humber
stood in front of his desk, between me and the window. Yelling could
only bring Cass, not the poor rabble of lads who didn't even know I was
there, and wouldn't bother to help me in any case. Both Adams and
Humber were taller and heavier that I was, Adams a good deal so.
Humber had his stick and I didn't know what weapon Adams proposed

to use; and I had never been in a serious fight in my life. The next few minutes were not too delightful a prospect.

On the other hand I was younger than they, and, thanks to the hard work they had exacted, as fit as an athlete. Also I had the crash helmet. And I could throw things . . . perhaps the odds weren't impossible, after all.

A polished wooden chair with a leather seat stood by the wall near the door. Adams picked it up and walked towards me. Humber, remaining still, slid his stick through his hands and held it ready.

I felt appallingly vulnerable.

Adams' eyes were more opaque than I had ever seen them, and the smile which was growing on his mouth didn't reach them. He said loudly, 'We might as well enjoy it. They won't look too closely at a burnt-out smash.'

He swung the chair. I dodged it all right but in doing so got within range of Humber, whose stick landed heavily on top of my shoulder, an inch from my ear. I stumbled and fell, and rolled: and stood up just in time to avoid the chair as Adams crashed it down. One of the legs broke off as it hit the floor, and Adams bent down and picked it up. A solid, straight, square-edged chair leg with a nasty sharp point where it had broken from the seat.

Adams smiled more, and kicked the remains of the chair into a corner. 'Now,' he said, 'we'll have some sport.'

If you could call it sport, I suppose they had it.

Certainly after a short space of time they were still relatively unscathed, while I had added some more bruises to my collection, together with a fast bleeding cut on the forehead from the sharp end of Adams' chair leg. But the crash helmet hampered their style considerably, and I discovered a useful talent for dodging. I also kicked.

Humber, being a slow mover, stayed at his post guarding the window and slashed at me whenever I came within his reach. As the office was not large this happened too often. I tried from the beginning either to catch hold of one of the sticks, or to pick up the broken chair, or to find something to throw, but all that happened was that my hands fared badly, and Adams guessed my intentions regarding the chair and made sure I couldn't get hold of it. As for throwing things the only suitable objects in that bare office were on Humber's desk, behind Humber.

Because of the cold night on the hillside I was wearing two jerseys under my jacket, and they did act as some sort of cushion: but Adams particularly hit very hard, and I literally shuddered whenever he managed to connect. I had had some idea of crashing out through the window, glass and all, but they gave me no chance to get there, and there was a limit to the time I could spend trying.

In desperation I stopped dodging and flung myself at Humber. Ignoring Adams, who promptly scored two fearful direct hits, I grasped my ex-employer by the lapels, and with one foot on the desk for leverage, swung him round and threw him across the narrow room. He landed with a crash against the filing cabinets.

There on the desk was the green glass paper weight. The size of a cricket ball. It slid smoothly into my hand, and in one unbroken movement I picked it up, pivoted on my toes, and flung it straight at Humber where he sprawled off-balance barely ten feet away.

It took him centrally between the eyes. A sweet shot. It knocked him unconscious. He fell without a sound.

I was across the room before he hit the floor, my hand stretching out for the green glass ball which was a better weapon to me than any stick or broken chair. But Adams understood too quickly. His arm went up.

I made the mistake of thinking that one more blow would make no real difference and didn't draw back from trying to reach the paper weight even when I knew Adams' chair leg was on its way down. But this time, because I had my head down, the crash helmet didn't save me. Adams hit me below the rim of the helmet, behind the ear.

Dizzily twisting, I fell against the wall and ended up lying with my shoulders propped against it and one leg doubled underneath me. I tried to stand up, but there seemed to be no strength left in me anywhere. My head was floating. I couldn't see very well. There was a noise inside my ears.

Adams leaned over me, unsnapped the strap of my crash helmet, and pulled it off my head. That meant something, I thought groggily. I looked up. He was standing there smiling, swinging the chair leg. Enjoying himself.

In the last possible second my brain cleared a little and I knew that if I didn't do something about it, this blow was going to be the last. There was no time to dodge. I flung up my arm to shield my undefended head, and the savagely descending piece of wood crashed into it.

It felt like an explosion. My hand fell numb and useless by my side.

What was left? Ten seconds. Perhaps less. I was furious. I particularly didn't want Adams to have the pleasure of killing me. He was still smiling. Watching to see how I would take it, he slowly raised his arm for the *coup de grace*.

No, I thought, no. There was nothing wrong with my legs. What on earth was I thinking of, lying there waiting to be blacked out when I still had two good legs? He was standing on my right. My left leg was bent under me and he took no special notice when I disentangled it and crossed it over in front of him. I lifted both my legs off the ground, one in front and one behind his ankles, then I kicked across with my right leg, locked my feet tight together and rolled my whole body over as suddenly and strongly as I could.

Adams was taken completely by surprise. He overbalanced with wildly swinging arms and fell with a crash on his back. His own weight made the fall more effective from my point of view, because he was winded and slow to get up. I couldn't throw any longer with my numb right hand. Staggering to my feet, I picked the green glass ball up in my left and smashed it against Adams' head while he was still on his knees. It seemed to have no effect. He continued to get up. He was grunting.

Desperately I swung my arm and hit him again, low down on the back of the head. And that time he did go down; and stayed down.

I half fell beside him, dizzy and feeling sick, with pain waking up viciously all over my body and blood from the cut on my forehead dripping slowly on to the floor.

I don't know how long I stayed like that, gasping to get some breath back, trying to find the strength to get up and leave the place, but it can't really have been very long. And it was the thought of Cass, in the end, which got me to my feet. By that stage I would have been a pushover for a toddler, let alone the wiry little head lad.

Both of the men lay in heaps on the ground, not stirring. Adams was breathing very heavily; snoring, almost. Humber's chest scarcely moved.

I passed my left hand over my face and it came away covered with blood. There must be blood all over my face, I thought. I couldn't go riding along the road covered in blood. I staggered into the washroom to rinse it off.

There were some half melted ice cubes in the sink. Ice. I looked at it dizzily. Ice in the refrigerator. Ice clinking in the drinks. Ice in the sink. Good for stopping bleeding. I picked up a lump of it and looked in the mirror. A gory sight. I held the lump of ice on the cut and tried, in the classic phrase, to pull myself together. With little success.

After a while I splashed some water into the sink and rinsed all the blood off my face. The cut was then revealed as being only a couple of inches long and not serious, though still obstinately oozing. I looked round vaguely for a towel.

On the table by the medicine cupboard stood a glass jar with the stopper off and a teaspoon beside it. My glance flickered over it, looking for a towel, and then back, puzzled. I took three shaky steps across the room. There was something the jar should be telling me, I thought, but I wasn't grasping things very clearly.

A bottle of phenobarbitone in powder form, like the stuff I'd given Mickey every day for a fortnight. Only phenobarbitone, that was all. I sighed.

Then it struck me that Mickey had had the last dose in the bottle. The bottle should be empty. Tipped out. Not full. Not a new bottle full to the bottom of the neck, with the pieces of wax from the seal still lying in crumbs on the table beside it. Someone had just opened a new bottle of soluble phenobarbitone and used a couple of spoonfuls.

Of course. For Kandersteg.

I found a towel and wiped my face. Then I went back into the office and knelt down beside Adams to get the door key out of his pocket. He had stopped snoring.

I rolled him over.

There isn't a pretty way of saying it. He was dead.

Small trickles of blood had seeped out of his ears, eyes, nose and mouth. I felt his head where I had hit him, and the dented bones moved under my fingers.

Aghast and shaking, I searched in his pockets and found the key. Then I stood up and went slowly over to the desk to telephone to the police.

The telephone had been knocked on to the floor, where it lay with the receiver off. I bent down and picked it up clumsily left handed, and my head swam with dizziness. I wished I didn't feel so ill. Straightening up with an effort I put the telephone back on the desk. Blood started trickling down past my eyebrow. I hadn't the energy to wash it off again.

Out in the yard one or two lights were on, including the one in Kandersteg's box. His door was wide open and the horse himself, tied up by the head, was lashing out furiously in a series of kicks. He didn't look in the least sedated.

I stopped with my finger in the dial of the telephone, and felt myself go cold. My brain cleared with a click.

Kandersteg was not sedated. They wouldn't want his memory lulled. The opposite, in fact. Mickey had not been given any phenobarbitone until he was clearly deranged.

I didn't want to believe what my mind told me; that one or more teaspoonfuls of soluble phenobarbitone in a large gin and campari would be almost certainly fatal.

Sharply I remembered the scene I had found in the office, the drinks, the anxiety on Humber's face, the enjoyment on Adams'. It matched the enjoyment I had seen there when he thought he was killing me. He enjoyed killing. He had thought from what she had said that Elinor had guessed the purpose of the whistle, and he had wasted no time in getting rid of her.

No wonder he had raised no objections to her leaving. She would drive back to college and die in her room miles away, a silly girl who had taken an overdose. No possible connection with Adams or Humber.

And no wonder he had been so determined to kill me: not only because of what I knew about his horses, or because I had fooled him, but because I had seen Elinor drink her gin.

It didn't need too much imagination to picture the scene before I had arrived. Adams saying smoothly, 'So you came to see if Roke had used the whistle?'

'Yes.'

'And does your father know you're here? Does he know about the whistle?'

'Oh no, I only came on impulse. Of course he doesn't know.'

He must have thought her a fool, blundering in like that: but probably he was the sort of man who thought all women were fools anyway.

'You'd like some ice in your drink? I'll get some. No bother. Just next door. Here you are, my dear, a strong gin and phenobarbitone and a quick trip to heaven.'

He had taken the same reckless risk of killing Stapleton, and it had worked. And who was to say that if I had been found in the next county over some precipice, smashed up in the ruins of a motor-bike, and Elinor died in her college, that he wouldn't have got away with two more murders?

If Elinor died.

My finger was still in the telephone dial. I turned it three times, nine, nine, nine. There was no answer. I rattled the button, and tried again. Nothing. It was dead, the whole telephone was dead. Everything was dead, Mickey was dead, Stapleton was dead. Adams was dead, Elinor ... stop it, stop it. I dragged my scattering wits together. If the telephone wouldn't work, someone would have to go to Elinor's college and prevent her dying.

My first thought was that I couldn't do it. But who else? If I were right, she needed a doctor urgently, and any time I wasted on bumbling about finding another telephone or another person to go in my stead was just diminishing her chances. I could reach her in less than twenty minutes. By telephoning in Posset I could hardly get help for her any quicker.

It took me three shots to get the key in the keyhole. I couldn't hold the key at all in my right hand, and the left one was shaking. I took a deep breath, unlocked the door, walked out, and shut it behind me.

No one noticed me as I went out of the yard the way I had come and went back to the motor-bike. But it didn't fire properly the first time I kicked the starter, and Cass came round the end of the row of boxes to investigate.

'Who's that?' he called. 'Is that you, Dan? What are you doing back here?' He began to come towards me.

I stamped on the starter fiercely. The engine spluttered, coughed and roared. I squeezed the clutch and kicked the bike into gear.

'Come back,' yelled Cass. But I turned away from his hurrying figure, out of the gate and down the road to Posset, with gravel spurting under the tyres.

The throttle was incorporated into the hand grip of the right hand handle bar. One merely twisted it towards one to accelerate and away to slow down. Twisting the hand grip was normally easy. It was not easy that evening because once I had managed to grip it hard enough to turn it the numbness disappeared from my arm with a vengeance. I damned nearly fell off before I was through the gate.

It was ten miles north east to Durham. One and a half downhill to Posset, seven and a half across the moors on a fairly straight and unfrequented secondary road, one mile through the outskirts of the city. The last part, with turns and traffic and too much change of pace, would be the most difficult.

Only the knowledge that Elinor would probably die if I came off kept me on the motor-bike at all, and altogether it was a ride I would not care to repeat. I didn't know how many times I had been hit, but I didn't think a carpet had much to tell me. I tried to ignore it and concentrate on the matter in hand.

Elinor, if she had driven straight back to college, could not have been there long before she began to feel sleepy. As far as I could remember, never having taken much notice, barbiturates took anything up to an hour to work. But barbiturate dissolved in alcohol was a different matter. Quicker. Twenty minutes to half an hour, perhaps. I didn't know. Twenty minutes from the time she left the yard was easily enough for her to drive back safely. Then what? She would go up to her room: feel tired: lie down: and go to sleep.

During the time I had been fighting with Adams and Humber she had been on her way to Durham. I wasn't sure how long I had wasted dithering about in the washroom in a daze, but she couldn't have been back in college much before I started after her. I wondered whether she would have felt ill enough to tell a friend, to ask for help: but even if she had, neither she nor anyone else would know what was the matter with her.

I reached Durham: made the turns: even stopped briefly for a red traffic light in a busy street: and fought down an inclination to go the last half mile at walking pace in order to avoid having to hold the throttle any more. But my ignorance of the time it would take for the poison to do irreparable damage added wings to my anxiety.

Chapter Eighteen

It was getting dark when I swung into the College entrance, switched off the engine, and hurried up the steps to the door. There was no one at the porter's desk and the whole place was very quiet. I ran down the corridors, trying to remember the turns, found the stairs, went up two flights. And it was then that I got lost. I had suddenly no idea which way to turn to find Elinor's room.

A thin elderly women with pince nez was walking towards me carrying a sheaf of papers and a thick book on her arm. One of the staff, I thought.

'Please,' I said, 'which is Miss Tarren's room?'

She came close to me and looked at me. She did not approve of what she saw. What would I give, I thought, for a respectable appearance at the moment.

'Please,' I repeated. 'She may be ill. Which is her room?'

'You have blood on your face,' she observed.

'It's only a cut . . . please tell me . . .' I gripped her arm. 'Look, show me her room, then if she's all right and perfectly healthy I will go away without any trouble. But I think she may need help very badly. Please believe me . . .'

'Very well,' she said reluctantly. 'We will go and see. It is just round here . . . and round here.'

We arrived at Elinor's door. I knocked hard. There was no answer. I bent down to the low key-hole. The key was in the lock on her side, and I could not see in.

'Open it,' I urged the woman, who was still eyeing me dubiously. 'Open it, and see if she's all right.'

She put her hand on the knob and turned it. But the door didn't budge. It was locked.

I banged on the door again. There was no reply.

'Now please listen,' I said urgently. 'As the door is locked on the inside, Elinor Tarren is in there. She doesn't answer because she can't. She needs a doctor very urgently indeed. Can you get hold of one at once?'

The woman nodded, looking at me gravely through the pince nez. I wasn't sure that she believed me, but apparently she did.

'Tell the doctor she has been poisoned with phenobarbitone and gin. About forty minutes ago. And please, please hurry. Are there any more keys to this door?'

'You can't push out the key that's already there. We've tried on other doors, on other occasions. You will have to break the lock. I will go and telephone.' She retreated sedately along the corridor, still breathtakingly calm in the face of a wild looking man with blood on his forehead and the news that one of her students was half way to the coroner. A tough-minded university lecturer.

The Victorians who had built the place had not intended importunate men friends to batter down the girls' doors. They were a solid job. But in view of the thin woman's calm assumption that breaking in was within my powers, I didn't care to fail. I broke the lock with my heel, in the end. The wood gave way on the jamb inside the room, and the door opened with a crash.

In spite of the noise I had made, no students had appeared in the corridor. There was still no one about. I went into Elinor's room, switched on the light, and swung the door back into its frame behind me.

She was lying sprawled on top of her blue bedspread fast asleep, the silver hair falling in a smooth swathe beside her head. She looked peaceful and beautiful. She had begun to undress, which was why, I supposed, she had locked her door, and she was wearing only a bra and briefs under a simple slip. All these garments were white with pink rosebuds and ribbons. Pretty. Belinda would have liked them. But in these circumstances they were too poignant, too defenceless. They increased my grinding worry.

The suit which Elinor had worn at Humber's had been dropped in two places on the floor. One stocking hung over the back of a chair: the other was on the floor just beneath her slack hand. A clean pair of stockings lay on the dressing table, and a blue woollen dress on a hanger was hooked on to the outside of the wardrobe. She had been changing for the evening.

If she hadn't heard me kicking the door in she wouldn't wake by being touched, but I tried. I shook her arm. She didn't stir. Her pulse was normal, her breathing regular, her face as delicately coloured as always. Nothing looked wrong with her. I found it frightening.

How much longer, I wondered anxiously was the doctor going to be? The door had been stubborn – or I had been weak, whichever way you looked at it – and it must have been more than ten minutes since the thin woman had gone to telephone.

As if on cue the door swung open and a tidy solid-looking middle-aged man in a grey suit stood there taking in the scene. He was alone. He carried a suitcase in one hand and a fire hatchet in the other. Coming in, he looked at the splintered wood, pushed the door shut and put the axe down on Elinor's desk.

'That's saved time, anyway,' he said briskly. He looked me up and down without enthusiasm and gestured to me to get out of the way. Then he cast a closer glance at Elinor with her rucked up slip and her long bare legs, and said to me sharply, suspiciously, 'Did you touch her clothes?'

'No,' I said bitterly. 'I shook her arm. And felt her pulse. She was lying like that when I came in.'

Something, perhaps it was only my obvious weariness, made him give me a suddenly professional, impartial survey. 'All right,' he said, and bent down to Elinor.

I waited behind him while he examined her, and when he turned round I noticed he had decorously pulled down her rumpled slip so that it reached smoothly to her knees.

'Phenobarbitone and gin,' he said. 'Are you sure?'

'Yes.'

'Self-administered?' He started opening his case.

'No. Definitely not.'

'This place is usually teeming with women,' he said inconsequentially. 'But apparently they're all at some meeting or another.' He gave me another intent look. 'Are you fit to help?'

'Yes.'

He hesitated. 'Are you sure?'

'Tell me what to do.'

'Very well. Find me a good-sized jug and a bucket or large basin. I'll get her started first, and you can tell me how this happened later.'

He took a hypodermic syringe from his case, filled it, and gave Elinor an injection into the vein on the inside of her elbow. I found a jug and a basin in the built-in fitment.

'You've been here before,' he observed, eyes again suspicious.

'Once,' I said: and for Elinor's sake added, 'I am employed by her father. It's nothing personal.'

'Oh. All right then.' He withdrew the needle, dismantled the syringe and quickly washed his hands.

'How many tablets did she take, do you know?'

'It wasn't tablets. Powder. A teaspoonful, at least. Maybe more.'

He looked alarmed, but said, 'That much would be bitter. She'd taste it.'

'Gin and Campari . . . it's bitter anyway.'

'Yes. All right. I'm going to wash out her stomach. Most of the drug must have been absorbed already, but if she had as much as that . . . well, it's still worth trying.'

He directed me to fill the jug with tepid water, while he carefully slid a thickish tube down inside Elinor's throat. He surprised me by putting his ear to the long protruding end of it when it was in position, and he explained briefly that with an unconscious patient who couldn't swallow one had to make sure the tube had gone into the stomach and not into the lungs. 'If you can hear them breathe, you're in the wrong place,' he said.

He put a funnel into the end of the tube, held out his hand for the jug, and carefully poured in the water. When what seemed to me a fantastic amount had disappeared down the tube he stopped pouring, passed me the jug to put down, and directed me to push the basin near his foot. Then, removing the funnel, he suddenly lowered the end of the tube over the side of the bed and into the basin. The water flowed out again, together with all the contents of Elinor's stomach.

'Hm,' he said calmly. 'She had something to eat first. Cake, I should say. That helps.'

I couldn't match his detachment.

'Will she be all right?' My voice sounded strained.

He looked at me briefly and slid the tube out.

'She drank the stuff less than an hour before I got here?'

'About fifty minutes, I think.'

'And she'd eaten . . . Yes, she'll be all right. Healthy girl. The injection I gave her – megimide – is an effective antidote. She'll probably wake up in an hour or so. A night in hospital, and it will be out of her system. She'll be as good as new.'

I rubbed my hand over my face.

'Time makes of lot of difference,' he said calmly. 'If she'd lain here many hours . . . a teaspoonful; that might be thirty grains or more.' He shook his head. 'She would have died.'

He took a sample of the contents of the basin for analysis, and covered the rest with a hand towel.

'How did you cut your head?' he said suddenly.

'In a fight.'

'It needs stitching. Do you want me to do it?'

'Yes. Thank you.'

'I'll do it after Miss Tarren has gone to hospital. Dr. Pritchard said she would ring for an ambulance. They should be here soon.'

'Dr. Pritchard?'

'The lecturer who fetched me in. My surgery is only round the corner. She telephoned and said a violent blood-stained youth was insisting that Miss Tarren was poisoned, and that I'd better come and see.' He smiled briefly. 'You haven't told me how all this happened.'

'Oh . . . it's such a long story,' I said tiredly.

'You'll have to tell the police,' he pointed out.

I nodded. There was too much I would have to tell the police. I wasn't looking forward to it. The doctor took out pen and paper and wrote a letter to go with Elinor to the hospital.

There was a sudden eruption of girls' voices down the passage, and a tramp of many scholarly feet, and the opening and shutting of doors. The students were back from their meeting: from Elinor's point of view, too soon, as they would now see her being carried out.

Heavier footsteps came right up to her room and knuckles rapped. Two men in ambulance uniform had arrived with a stretcher, and with economy of movement and time they lifted Elinor between them, tucked her into blankets, and bore her away. She left a wake of pretty voices raised in sympathy and speculation.

The doctor swung the door shut behind the ambulance men and without more ado took from his case a needle and thread to sew up my forehead. I sat on Elinor's bed while he fiddled around with disinfectant and the stitching.

'What did you fight about?' he asked, tying knots.

'Because I was attacked,' I said.

'Oh?' He shifted his feet to sew from a different angle, and put his hand on my shoulder to steady himself. He felt me withdraw from the pressure and looked at me quizzically.

'So you got the worst of it?'

'No,' I said slowly. 'I won.'

He finished the stitching and gave a final snip with the scissors.

'There you are, then. It won't leave much of a scar.'

'Thank you.' It sounded a bit weak.

'Do you feel all right?' he said abruptly. 'Or is pale fawn tinged with grey your normal colouring?'

'Pale fawn is normal. Grey just about describes how I feel,' I smiled faintly. 'I got a bang on the back of the head, too.'

He explored the bump behind the ear and said I would live. He was asking me how many other tender spots I had about me when another heavy tramp of footsteps could be heard coming up the corridor, and presently the door was pushed open with a crash.

Two broad-shouldered businesslike policemen stepped into the room.

They knew the doctor. It appeared that he did a good deal of police work in Durham. They greeted each other politely and the doctor started to say that Miss Tarren was on her way to hospital. They interrupted him.

'We've come for him, sir,' said the taller of them, pointing at me. 'Stable lad, name of Daniel Roke.'

'Yes, he reported Miss Tarren's illness . . .'

'No, sir it's nothing to do with a Miss Tarren or her illness. We want him for questioning on another matter.'

The doctor said, 'He's not in very good shape. I think you had better go easy. Can't you leave it until later?'

'I'm afraid that's impossible, sir.'

They both came purposefully over to where I sat. The one who had done the talking was a red-headed man about my own age with an unsmiling wary face. His companion was slightly shorter, brown eyed, and just as much on guard. They looked as if they were afraid I was going to leap up and strangle them.

With precision they leaned down and clamped hard hands round my forearms. The red-head, who was on my right, dragged a pair of hand-cuffs from his pocket, and between them they fastened them on my wrists.

'Better take it quietly, chum,' advised the red-head, evidently mistaking my attempt to wrench my arm free of his agonising grip as a desire to escape in general.

'Let . . . go,' I said. 'I'm not . . . running anywhere.'

They did let go, and stepped back a pace, looking down at me. Most of the wariness had faded from their faces, and I gathered that they really had been afraid I would attack them. It was unnerving. I took two deep breaths to control the soreness of my arm.

'He won't give us much trouble,' said the dark one. 'He looks like death.'

'He was in a fight,' remarked the doctor.

'Is that what he told you, sir?' The dark one laughed.

I looked down at the hand-cuffs locked round my wrists: they were, I discovered, as uncomfortable as they were humiliating.

'What did he do?' asked the doctor.

The red-head answered, 'He ... er ... he'll be helping in enquiries into an attack on a race-horse trainer he worked for and who is still unconscious, and on another man who had his skull bust right in.'

'Dead?'

'So we are told, sir. We haven't actually been to the stables, though they say it's a shambles. We two were sent up from Clavering to fetch him in, and that's where we're taking him back to, the stables being in our area, you see.'

'You caught up with him very quickly,' commented the doctor.

'Yes,' said the red-head with satisfaction. 'It was a nice bit of work by some of the lads. A lady here telephoned to the police in Durham about half an hour ago and described *him*, and when they got the general call from Clavering about the job at the stables someone connected the two descriptions and told us about it. So we were sent up to see, and bingo ... there was his motor-bike, right number plate and all, standing outside the college door.'

I lifted my head. The doctor looked down at me. He was disillusioned, disenchanted. He shrugged his shoulders and said in a tired voice, 'You never know with them, do you? He seemed ... well ... not quite the usual sort of tearaway. And now this.' He turned away and picked up his bag.

It was suddenly too much. I had let too many people despise me and done nothing about it. This was one too many.

'I fought because they attacked me,' I said.

The doctor half turned round. I didn't know why I thought it was important to convince him, but it seemed so at the time.

The dark policeman raised an eyebrow and said to the doctor, 'The trainer was his employer, sir, and I understand the man who died is a rich gentleman whose horses were trained there. The head lad reported the killing. He saw Roke belting off on his motor-bike and thought it was strange, because Roke had been sacked the day before, and he went to tell the trainer about it, and found him unconscious and the other man dead.'

The doctor had heard enough. He walked out of the room without looking back. What was the use of trying? Better just do what the red-head said, and take it quietly, bitterness and all.

'Let's be going, chum,' said the dark one. They stood there, tense again, with watchful eyes and hostile faces.

I got slowly to my feet. Slowly, because I was perilously near to not being able to stand up at all, and I didn't want to seem to be asking for a sympathy I was clearly not going to get. But it was all right: once upright I felt better; which was psychological as much as physical because they were then not two huge threatening policemen but two quite ordinary young men of my own height doing their duty, and very concerned not to make any mistakes.

It worked the other way with them, of course. I think they had subconsciously expected a stable lad to be very short, and they were taken aback to discover I wasn't. They became visibly more aggressive: and I realized in the circumstances, and in those black clothes, I probably seemed to them, as Terence had once put it, a bit dangerous and hard to handle.

I didn't see any sense in getting roughed up any more, especially by the law, if it could be avoided.

'Look,' I sighed, 'like you said, I won't give you any trouble.'

But I suppose they had been told to bring in someone who had gone berserk and smashed a man's head in, and they were taking no chances. Red-head took a fierce grip of my right arm above the elbow and shoved me over to the door, and once outside in the passage the dark one took a similar grip on the left.

The corridor was lined with girls standing in little gossiping groups. I stopped dead. The two policemen pushed me on. And the girls stared.

That old saying about wishing the floor would open and swallow one up suddenly took on a fresh personal meaning. What little was left of my sense of dignity revolted totally against being exhibited as a prisoner in front of so many intelligent and personable young women. They were the wrong age. The wrong sex. I could have stood it better if they had been men.

But there was no easy exit. It was a good long way from Elinor's room to the outside door, along those twisting corridors and down two flights of stairs, and every single step was watched by interested female eyes.

This was the sort of thing one wouldn't be able to forget. It went too deep. Or perhaps, I thought miserably, one could even get accustomed to being hauled around in hand-cuffs if it happened often enough. If one were used to it, perhaps one wouldn't care . . . which would be peaceful.

I did at least manage not to stumble, not even on the stairs, so to that extent something was saved from the wreck. The police car however, into which I was presently thrust, seemed a perfect haven in contrast.

I sat in front, between them. The dark one drove.

'Phew,' he said, pushing his cap back an inch. 'All those girls.' He had blushed under their scrutiny and there was a dew of sweat on his forehead.

'He's a tough boy, is this,' said Red-head, mopping his neck with a white handkerchief as he sat sideways against the door and stared at me. 'He didn't turn a hair.'

I looked straight ahead through the windscreen as the lights of Durham began to slide past and thought how little could be told from a face. That walk had been a torture. If I hadn't shown it, it was probably only because I had by then had months of practice in hiding my feelings and thoughts, and the habit was strong. I guessed – correctly – that it was a habit I would find strength in clinging to for some time to come.

I spent the rest of the journey reflecting that I had got myself into a proper mess and that I was going to have a very unpleasant time getting out. I had indeed killed Adams. There was no denying or ducking that. And I was not going to be listened to as a respectable solid citizen but as a murdering villain trying every dodge to escape the consequences. I was going to be taken at my face value, which was very low indeed. That couldn't be helped. I had, after all, survived eight weeks at Humber's only because I looked like dregs. The appearance which had deceived Adams was going to be just as convincing to the police, and proof that in fact it already was sat on either side of me in the car, watchful and antagonistic.

Red-head's eyes never left my face.

'He doesn't talk much,' he observed, after a long silence.

'Got a lot on his mind,' agreed the dark one with sarcasm.

The damage Adams and Humber had done gave me no respite. I shifted uncomfortably in my seat, and the hand-cuffs clinked. The light-heartedness with which I had gone in my new clothes to Slaw seemed a long long time ago.

The lights of Clavering lay ahead. The dark one gave me a look of subtle enjoyment. A capture made. His purpose fulfilled. Red-head broke another long silence, his voice full of the same sort of satisfaction.

'He'll be a lot older when he gets out,' he said.

I emphatically hoped not: but I was all too aware that the length of time I remained in custody depended solely on how conclusively I could show that I had killed in self-defence. I wasn't a lawyer's son for nothing.

The next hours were abysmal. The Clavering police force were collectively a hardened cynical bunch suppressing as best they could a vigorous crime wave in a mining area with a high unemployment percentage. Kid gloves did not figure in their book. Individually they may have loved their wives and been nice to their children, but if so they kept their humour and humanity strictly for leisure.

They were busy. The building was full of bustle and hurrying voices. They shoved me still hand-cuffed from room to room under escort and barked out intermittent questions. 'Later,' they said. 'Deal with that one later. We've got all night for him.'

I thought with longing of a hot bath, a soft bed, and a handful of aspirins. I didn't get any of them.

At some point late in the evening they gave me a chair in a bare brightly lit little room, and I told them what I had been doing at Humber's and how I had come to kill Adams. I told them everything which had happened that day. They didn't believe me, for which one couldn't blame them. They immediately, as a matter of form, charged me with murder. I protested. Uselessly.

They asked me a lot of questions. I answered them. They asked them again. I answered. They asked the questions like a relay team, one of them taking over presently from another, so that they all appeared to remain full of fresh energy while I grew more and more tired. I was glad

I did not have to maintain a series of lies in that state of continuing discomfort and growing fatigue, as it was hard to keep a clear head, even for the truth, and they were waiting for me to make a mistake.

'Now tell us what really happened.'

'I've told you.'

'Not all that cloak and dagger stuff.'

'Cable to Australia for a copy of the contract I signed when I took on the job.' For the fourth time I repeated my solicitor's address, and for the fourth time they didn't write it down.

'Who did you say engaged you?'

'The Earl of October.'

'And no doubt we can check with him too?'

'He's in Germany until Saturday.'

'Too bad.' They smiled nastily. They knew from Cass that I had worked in October's stable. Cass had told them I was a slovenly stable lad, dishonest, easily frightened and not very bright. As he believed what he said, he had carried conviction.

'You got into trouble with his Lordship's daughter, didn't you?'

Damn Cass, I thought bitterly, damn Cass and his chattering tongue.

'Getting your own back on him for sacking you, aren't you, by dragging his name into this?'

'Like you got your own back on Mr. Humber for sacking you yesterday.'

'No. I left because I had finished my job there.'

'For beating you, then?'

'No.'

'The head lad said you deserved it.'

'Adams and Humber were running a crooked racing scheme. I found them out, and they tried to kill me.' It seemed to me it was the tenth time that I had said that without making the slightest impression.

'You resented being beaten. You went back to get even ... It's a common enough pattern.'

'No.'

'You brooded over it and went back and attacked them. It was a shambles. Blood all over the place.'

'It was my blood.'

'We can group it.'

'Do that. It's my blood.'

'From that little cut? Don't be so stupid.'

'It's been stitched.'

'Ah yes, that brings us back to Lady Elinor Tarren. Lord October's daughter. Got her into trouble, did you?'

'No.'

'In the family way ...'

'No. Check with the doctor.'

'So she took sleeping pills ...'

'No. Adams poisoned her.' I had told them twice about the bottle of phenobarbitone, and they must have found it when they had been at the stables, but they wouldn't admit it.

'You got the sack from her father for seducing her. She couldn't stand the disgrace. She took sleeping pills.'

'She had no reason to feel disgraced. It was not she, but her sister Patricia, who accused me of seducing her. Adams poisoned Elinor in gin and Campari. There are gin and Campari and phenobarbitone in the office and also in the sample from her stomach.'

They took no notice. 'She found you had deserted her on top of everything else. Mr. Humber consoled her with a drink, but she went back to college and took sleeping pills.'

'No.'

They were sceptical, to put it mildly, about Adams' use of the flame thrower.

'You'll find it in the shed.'

'This shed, yes. Where did you say it was?'

I told them again, exactly. 'The field probably belongs to Adams. You could find out.'

'It only exists in your imagination.'

'Look and you'll find it, and the flame thrower.'

'That's likely to be used for burning off the heath. Lots of farmers have them, round here.'

They had let me make two telephone calls to try to find Colonel Beckett. His manservant in London said he had gone to stay with friends in Berkshire for Newbury races. The little local exchange in Berkshire was out of action, the operator said, because a water main had burst and flooded a cable. Engineers were working on it.

Didn't my wanting to talk to one of the top brass of steeplechasing convince them, I wanted to know?

'Remember that chap we had in here once who'd strangled his wife? Nutty as a fruit cake. Insisted on ringing up Lord Bertrand Russell, didn't he, to tell him he'd struck a blow for peace.'

At around midnight one of them pointed out that even if (and, mind you, he didn't himself believe it) even if all I had said about being employed to find out about Adams and Humber were against all probability true, that still didn't give me the right to kill them.

'Humber isn't dead,' I said.

'Not yet.'

My heart lurched. Dear God, I thought, not Humber too. Not Humber too.

'You clubbed Adams with the walking stick then?'

'No, I told you, with a green glass ball. I had it in my left hand and I hit him as hard as I could. I didn't mean to kill him, just knock him out. I'm right handed ... I couldn't judge very well how hard I was hitting with my left.'

'Why did you use your left hand then?'

'I told you.'

'Tell us again.'

I told them again.

'And after your right arm was put out of action you got on a motor-cycle and rode ten miles to Durham? What sort of fools do you take us for?'

'The fingerprints of both my hands are on that paper-weight. The right ones from when I threw it at Humber, and the left ones on top, from where I hit Adams. You have only to check.'

'Fingerprints, now,' they said sarcastically.

'And while you're on the subject, you'll also find the fingerprints of my left hand on the telephone. I tried to call you from the office. My left hand prints are on the tap in the washroom . . . and on the key, and on the door handle, both inside and out. Or at least, they were . . .'

'All the same, you rode that motor-bike.'

'The numbness had gone by then.'

'And now?'

'It isn't numb now either.'

One of them came round beside me, picked up my right wrist, and pulled my arm up high. The hand-cuffs jerked and lifted my left arm as well. The bruises had all stiffened and were very sore. The policeman put my arm down again. There was a short silence.

'That hurt,' one of them said at last, grudgingly.

'He's putting it on.'

'Maybe . . .'

They had been drinking endless cups of tea all evening and had not given me any. I asked if I could have some then, and got it; only to find that the difficulty I had in lifting the cup was hardly worth it.

They began again.

'Granted Adams struck your arm, but he did it in self-defence. He saw you throw the paper-weight at your employer and realized you were going to attack him next. He was warding you off.'

'He had already cut my forehead open . . . and hit me several times on the body, and once on the head.'

'Most of that was yesterday, according to the head lad. That's why you went back and attacked Mr. Humber.'

'Humber hit me only twice yesterday. I didn't particularly resent it. The rest was today, and it was mostly done by Adams.' I remembered something. 'He took my crash helmet off when he had knocked me dizzy. His fingerprints must be on it.'

'Fingerprints again.'

'They spell it out,' I said.

'Let's begin again at the beginning. How can we believe a yob like you?'

Yob. One of the leather boys. Tearaway. Rocker. I knew all the words. I knew what I looked like. What a millstone of a handicap.

I said despairingly, 'There's no point in pretending to be a disreputable, dishonest stable lad if you don't look the part.'

'You look the part all right,' they said offensively. 'Born to it, you were.'

I looked at their stony faces, their hard, unimpressed eyes. Tough efficient policemen who were not going to be conned. I could read their thoughts like glass: if I convinced them and they later found out it was all a pack of lies, they'd never live it down. Their instincts were all dead against having to believe. My bad luck.

The room grew stuffy and full of cigarette smoke and I became too hot in my jerseys and jacket. I knew they took the sweat on my forehead to be guilt, not heat, not pain.

I went on answering all their questions. They covered the ground twice more with undiminished zeal, setting traps, sometimes shouting, walking round me, never touching me again, but springing the questions from all directions. I was really much too tired for that sort of thing because apart from the wearing-out effect of the injuries I had not slept for the whole of the previous night. Towards two o'clock I could hardly speak from exhaustion, and after they had woken me from a sort of dazed sleep three times in half an hour, they gave it up.

From the beginning I had known that there was only one logical end to that evening, and I had tried to shut it out of my mind, because I dreaded it. But there you are, you set off on a primrose path and if it leads to hell that's just too bad.

Two uniformed policemen, a sergeant and a constable, were detailed to put me away for the night, which I found involved a form of accommodation to make Humber's dormitory seem a paradise.

The cell was cubic, eight feet by eight by eight, built of glazed bricks, brown to shoulder height and white above that. There was a small barred window too high to see out of, a narrow slab of concrete for a bed, a bucket with a lid on it in a corner and a printed list of regulations on one wall. Nothing else. Bleak enough to shrink the guts; and I had never much cared for small enclosed spaces.

The two policemen brusquely told me to sit on the concrete. They removed my boots and the belt from my jeans, and also found and unbuckled the money belt underneath. They took off the hand-cuffs. Then they went out, shut the door with a clang, and locked me in.

The rest of that night was in every way rock bottom.

Chapter Nineteen

It was cool and quiet in the corridors of Whitehall. A superbly mannered young man deferentially showed me the way and opened a mahogany door into an empty office.

'Colonel Beckett will not be long sir. He has just gone to consult a colleague. He said I was to apologise if you arrived before he came back, and to ask if you would like a drink. And cigarettes are in this box, sir.'

'Thank you,' I smiled. 'Would coffee be a nuisance?'

'By no means. I'll have some sent in straight away. If you'll excuse me?' He went out and quietly closed the door.

It rather amused me to be called 'sir' again, especially by smooth civil servants barely younger than myself. Grinning, I sat down in the leather chair facing Beckett's desk, crossed my elegantly trousered legs, and lazily settled to wait for him.

I was in no hurry. It was eleven o'clock on Tuesday morning, and I had all day and nothing to do but buy a clockwork train for Jerry and book an air ticket back to Australia.

No noise filtered into Beckett's office. The room was square and high, and was painted a restful pale greenish grey colour, walls, door and ceiling alike. I supposed that here the furnishings went with rank; but if one were an outsider one would not know how much to be impressed by a large but threadbare carpet, an obviously personal lamp-shade, or leather, brass-studded chairs. One had to belong, for these things to matter.

I wondered about Colonel Beckett's job. He had given me the impression that he was retired, probably on a full disability pension since he looked so frail in health, yet here he was with a well established niche at the Ministry of Defence.

October had told me that in the war Beckett had been the sort of supply officer who never sent all left boots or the wrong ammunition. Supply Officer. He had supplied me with Sparking Plug and the raw material containing the pointers to Adams and Humber. He'd had enough pull with the Army to despatch in a hurry eleven young officer cadets to dig up the past history of obscure steeplechasers. What, I wondered, did he supply nowadays, in the normal course of events?

I suddenly remembered October saying, 'We thought of planting a stable lad . . .' not 'I thought', but 'We'. And for some reason I was now sure that it had been Beckett, not October, who had originally suggested the plan; and that explained why October had been relieved when Beckett approved me at our first meeting.

Unexcitedly turning these random thoughts over in my mind I watched two pigeons fluttering round the window sill and tranquilly waited to say goodbye to the man whose staff work had ensured the success of the idea.

A pretty young woman knocked and came in with a tray on which stood a coffee pot, cream jug, and pale green cup and saucer. She smiled, asked if I needed anything else, and when I said not, gracefully went away.

I was getting quite good at left-handedness. I poured the coffee and drank it black, and enjoyed the taste.

Snatches of the past few days drifted idly in and out of my thoughts . . .

Four nights and three days in a police cell trying to come to terms with the fact that I had killed Adams. It was odd, but although I had often considered the possibility of being killed, I had never once thought that I myself might kill. For that, as for so much else, I had been utterly unprepared; and to have caused another man's death, however much he might have asked for it, needed a bit of getting over.

Four nights and three days of gradually finding that even the various ignominies of being locked up were bearable if one took them quietly, and feeling almost like thanking Red-head for his advice.

On the first morning, after a magistrate had agreed that I should stay where I was for seven days, a police doctor came and told me to strip. I couldn't, and he had to help. He looked impassively at Adams' and Humber's widespread handiwork, asked a few questions, and examined my right arm, which was black from the wrist to well above the elbow. In spite of the protection of two jerseys and a leather jacket, the skin was broken where the chair leg had landed. The doctor helped me dress again and impersonally departed. I didn't ask him for his opinion, and he didn't give it.

For most of the four nights and three days I just waited, hour after silent hour. Thinking about Adams: Adams alive and Adams dead. Worrying about Humber. Thinking of how I could have done things differently. Facing the thought that I might not get out without a trial . . . or not get out at all. Waiting for the soreness to fade from the bruises and failing to find a comfortable way of sleeping on concrete. Counting the number of bricks from the floor to the ceiling and multiplying by the length of the walls (subtract the door and window). Thinking about my stud farm and my sisters and brother, and about the rest of my life.

On Monday morning there was the by then familiar scrape of the door being unlocked, but when it opened it was not as usual a policeman in uniform, but October.

I was standing up, leaning against the wall. I had not seen him for three months. He stared at me for a long minute, taking in with obvious shock my extremely dishevelled appearance.

'Daniel,' he said. His voice was low and thick.

I didn't think I needed any sympathy. I hooked my left thumb into my pocket, struck a faint attitude, and raised a grin.

'Hullo, Edward.'

His face lightened, and he laughed.

'You're so bloody tough,' he said. Well . . . let him think so.

I said, 'Could you possibly use your influence to get me a bath?'

'You can have whatever you like as soon as you are out.'

'Out? For good?'

'For good,' he nodded. 'They are dropping the charge.'

I couldn't disguise my relief.

He smiled sardonically. 'They don't think it would be worth wasting public funds on trying you. You'd be certain of getting an absolute discharge. Justifiable homicide, quite legitimate.'

'I didn't think they believed me.'

'They've done a lot of checking up. Everything you told them on Thursday is now the official version.'

'Is Humber . . . all right?'

'He regained consciousness yesterday, I believe. But I understand he isn't lucid enough yet to answer questions. Didn't the police tell you that he was out of danger?'

I shook my head. 'They aren't a very chatty lot, here. How is Elinor?'

'She's well. A bit weak, that's all.'

'I'm sorry she got caught up in things. If was my fault.'

'My dear chap, it was her own,' he protested. 'And Daniel . . . about Patty . . . and the things I said . . .'

'Oh, nuts to that,' I interrupted. 'It was a long time ago. When you said "Out" did you mean "out" now, this minute?'

He nodded. 'That's right.'

'Then let's not hang around in here any more, shall we? If you don't mind?'

He looked about him and involuntarily shivered. Meeting my eyes he said apologetically, 'I didn't foresee anything like this.'

I grinned faintly. 'Nor did I.'

We went to London, by car up to Newcastle and then by train. Owing to some delay at the police station discussing the details of my return to attend Adams' inquest, any cleaning up processes would have meant our missing the seats October had reserved on the non-stop Flying Scotsman, so I caught it as I was.

October led the way into the dining car, but as I was about to sit down opposite him a waiter caught hold of my elbow.

'Here you,' he said roughly, 'clear out. This is first-class only.'

'I've got a first-class ticket,' I said mildly.

'Oh yes? Let's see it, then.'

I produced from my pocket the piece of white cardboard.

He sniffed and gestured with his head towards the seat opposite October. 'All right then.' To October he said, 'If he makes a nuisance of himself, just tell me, sir, and I'll have him chucked out, ticket or no ticket.' He went off, swaying to the motion of the accelerating train.

Needless to say, everyone in the dining car had turned round to have a good view of the rumpus.

Grinning, I sat down opposite October. He looked exceedingly embarrassed.

'Don't worry on my account,' I said, 'I'm used to it.' And I realized that I was indeed used to it at last and that no amount of such treatment would ever trouble me again. 'But if you would rather pretend you don't know me, go ahead.' I picked up the menu.

'You are insulting.'

I smiled at him over the menu. 'Good.'

'For deviousness, Daniel, you are unsurpassed. Except possibly by Roddy Beckett.'

'My dear Edward . . . have some bread.'

He laughed, and we travelled amicably to London together, as ill-assorted looking a pair as ever rested heads on British Railways' starched white antimacassars.

I poured some more coffee and looked at my watch. Colonel Beckett was twenty minutes late. The pigeons sat peacefully on the window sill and I shifted gently in my chair, but with patience, not boredom, and thought about my visit to October's barber, and the pleasure with which I had had my hair cut short and sideburns shaved off. The barber himself (who had asked me to pay in advance) was surprised, he said, at the results.

'We look a lot more like a gentleman, don't we? But might I suggest . . . a shampoo?'

Grinning, I agreed to a shampoo, which left a high water mark of cleanliness about midway down my neck. Then, at October's house, there was the fantastic luxury of stepping out of my filthy disguise into a deep hot bath, and the strangeness with which I afterwards put on my own clothes. When I had finished dressing I took another look in the same long mirror. There was the man who had come from Australia four months ago, a man in a good dark grey suit, a white shirt and a navy blue silk tie: there was his shell anyway. Inside I wasn't the same man, nor ever would be again.

I went down to the crimson drawing-room where October walked solemnly all round me, gave me a glass of bone dry sherry and said, 'It is utterly unbelievable that you are the young tyke who just came down with me on the train.'

'I am,' I said dryly, and he laughed.

He gave me a chair with its back to the door, where I drank some sherry and listened to him making social chit-chat about his horses. He was hovering round the fireplace not entirely at ease, and I wondered what he was up to.

I soon found out. The door opened and he looked over my shoulder and smiled.

'I want you both to meet someone,' he said.

I stood up and turned round.

Patty and Elinor were there, side by side.

They didn't know me at first. Patty held out her hand politely and said, 'How do you do?' clearly waiting for her father to introduce us.

I took her hand in my left one and guided her to a chair.

'Sit down,' I suggested. 'You're in for a shock.'

She hadn't seen me for three months, but it was only four days since Elinor had made her disastrous visit to Humber's. She said hesitantly, 'You don't look the same . . . but you're Daniel.' I nodded, and she blushed painfully.

Patty's bright eyes looked straight into mine, and her pink mouth parted.

'You . . . are you really? Danny boy?'

'Yes.'

'Oh,' A blush as deep as her sister's spread up from her neck, and for Patty that was shame indeed.

October watched their discomfiture. 'It serves them right,' he said, 'for all the trouble they have caused.'

'Oh no,' I exclaimed, 'it's too hard on them . . . and you still haven't told them anything about me, have you?'

'No,' he agreed uncertainly, beginning to suspect there was more for his daughters to blush over than he knew, and that his surprise meeting was not an unqualified success.

'Then tell them now, while I go and talk to Terence . . . and Patty . . . Elinor . . .' They looked surprised at my use of their first names and I smiled briefly, 'I have a very short and defective memory.'

They both looked subdued when I went back, and October was watching them uneasily. Fathers, I reflected, could be very unkind to their daughters without intending it.

'Cheer up,' I said. 'I'd have had a dull time in England without you two.'

'You were a beast,' said Patty emphatically, sticking to her guns.

'Yes . . . I'm sorry.'

'You might have told us,' said Elinor in a low voice.

'Nonsense,' said October. 'He couldn't trust Patty's tongue.'

'I see,' said Elinor, slowly. She looked at me tentatively. 'I haven't thanked you, for . . . for saving me. The doctor told me . . . all about it.' She blushed again.

'Sleeping beauty,' I smiled. 'You looked like my sister.'

'You have a sister?'

'Two,' I said. 'Sixteen and seventeen.'

'Oh,' she said, and looked comforted.

October flicked me a glance. 'You are far too kind to them Daniel. One of them made me loathe you and the other nearly killed you, and you don't seem to care.'

I smiled at him. 'No. I don't. I really don't. Let's just forget it.'

So in spite of a most unpromising start it developed into a good evening, the girls gradually losing their embarrassment and even, by the end, being able to meet my eyes without blushing.

When they had gone to bed October put two fingers into an inner pocket, drew out a slip of paper, and handed it to me without a word. I unfolded it. It was a cheque for ten thousand pounds. A lot of noughts. I looked at them in silence. Then, slowly, I tore the fortune in half and put the pieces in an ash-tray.

'Thank you very much,' I said. 'But I can't take it.'

'You did the job. Why not accept the pay?'

'Because . . .' I stopped. Because what? I was not sure I could put it into words. It had something to do with having learned more than I had bargained for. With diving too deep. With having killed. All I was sure of was that I could no longer bear the thought of receiving money for it.

'You must have a reason,' said October, with a touch of irritation.

'Well, I didn't really do it for the money, to start with, and I can't take that sort of sum from you. In fact, when I get back I am going to repay you all that is left of the first ten thousand.'

'No,' he protested. 'You've earned it. Keep it. You need it for your family.'

'What I need for my family, I'll earn by selling horses.'

He stubbed out his cigar. 'You're so infuriatingly independent that I don't know now how you could face being a stable lad. If it wasn't for the money, why did you do it?'

I moved in my chair. The bruises still felt like bruises. I smiled faintly, enjoying the pun.

'For kicks, I suppose.'

The door of the office opened, and Beckett unhurriedly came in. I stood up. He held out his hand, and remembering the weakness of his grasp I put out my own. He squeezed gently and let go.

'It's been a long time, Mr. Roke.'

'More than three months,' I agreed.

'And you completed the course.'

I shook my head, smiling. 'Fell at the last fence, I'm afraid.'

He took off his overcoat and hung it on a knobbed hat rack, and unwound a grey woollen scarf from his neck. His suit was nearly black, a colour which only enhanced his extreme pallor and emphasized his thinness: but his eyes were as alive as ever in the gaunt shadowed sockets. He gave me a long observant scrutiny.

'Sit down,' he said. 'I am sorry to have kept you waiting. I see they've looked after you all right.'

'Yes, thank you.' I sat down again in the leather chair, and he walked round and sank carefully into the one behind his desk. His chair had a high back and arms, and he used them to support his head and elbows.

'I didn't get your report until I came back to London from Newbury on Sunday morning,' he said. 'It took two days to come from Posset and didn't reach my house until Friday. When I had read it I telephoned to Edward at Slaw and found he had just been rung up by the police at Clavering. I then telephoned to Clavering myself. I spent a good chunk of Sunday hurrying things up for you in various conversations with ever higher ranks, and early on Monday it was decided finally in the office of the Director of Public Prosecutions that there was no charge for you to answer.'

'Thank you very much,' I said.

He paused, considering me. 'You did more towards extricating yourself than Edward or I did. We only confirmed what you had said and had you freed a day or two sooner than you might have been. But it appeared that the Clavering police had already discovered from a thorough examination of the stable office that everything you had told them was borne out by the facts. They had also talked to the doctor who had attended Elinor, and to Elinor herself, and taken a look at the shed with the flame thrower, and cabled to your solicitor for a summary of the contract you signed with Edward. By the time I spoke to them they were taking the truth of your story for granted, and were agreeing that you had undoubtedly killed Adams in self-defence.'

'Their own doctor – the one who examined you – had told them straight away that the amount of crushing your right forearm had sustained was entirely consistent with its having been struck by a force strong enough to have smashed in your skull. He was of the opinion that the blow had landed more or less along the inside of your arm, not straight across it, thus causing extensive damage to muscles and blood vessels, but no bone fracture; and he told them that it was perfectly possible for you to have ridden a motor-bike a quarter of an hour later if you had wanted to enough.'

'You know,' I said, 'I didn't think they had taken any notice of a single word I said.'

'Mmm. Well, I spoke to one of the C.I.D. men who questioned you last Thursday evening. He said they brought you in as a foregone conclusion, and that you looked terrible. You told them a rigmarole which they thought was nonsense, so they asked a lot of questions to trip you up. They thought it would be easy. The C.I.D. man said it was like trying to dig a hole in a rock with your finger nails. They all ended up by believing you, much to their own surprise.'

'I wish they'd told me,' I sighed.

'Not their way. They sounded a tough bunch.'

'They seemed it, too.'

'However, you survived.'

'Oh yes.'

Beckett looked at his watch. 'Are you in a hurry?'

'No.' I shook my head.

'Good . . . I've rather a lot to say to you. Can you lunch?'

'Yes. I'd like to.'

'Fine. Now, this report of yours.' He dug the hand-written foolscap pages out of his inside breast pocket and laid them on the table. 'What I'd like you to do now is to lop off the bit asking for reinforcements and substitute a description of the flame-thrower operation. Right? There's a table and chair over there. Get to work, and when it's done I'll have it typed.'

When I had finished the report he spent some time outlining and discussing the proceedings which were to be taken against Humber, Cass and Jud Wilson, and also against Soupy Tarleton and his friend Lewis Greenfield. He then looked at his watch again and decided it was time to go out for lunch. He took me to his Club, which seemed to me to be dark brown throughout, and we ate steak, kidney and mushroom pie which I chose because I could manage it unobtrusively with a fork. He noticed though.

'That arm still troubling you?'

'It's much better.'

He nodded and made no further comment. Instead, he told me of a visit he had paid the day before to an elderly uncle of Adams, whom he had discovered living in bachelor splendour in Piccadilly.

'Young Paul Adams, according to his uncle, was the sort of child who would have been sent to an approved school if he hadn't had rich parents. He was sacked from Eton for forging cheques and from his next school for persistent gambling. His parents bought him out of scrape after scrape and were told by a psychiatrist that he would never change, or at least not until late middle age. He was their only child. It must have been terrible for them. The father died when Adams was twenty-five, and his mother struggled on, trying to keep him out of too disastrous trouble. About five years ago she had to pay out a fortune to hush up a scandal in which Adams had apparently broken a youth's arm for no reason at all, and she threatened to have him certified if he did anything like that again. And a few days later she fell out of her bedroom window and died. The uncle, her brother, says he has always thought that Adams pushed her.'

'Very likely, I should think,' I agreed.

'So you were right about him being psychopathic.'

'Well, it was pretty obvious.'

'From the way he behaved to you personally?'

'Yes.'

We had finished the pie and were on to cheese. Beckett looked at me curiously and said, 'What sort of life did you really have at Humber's stable?'

'Oh,' I grinned. 'You could hardly call it a holiday camp.'

He waited for me to go on and when I didn't, he said, 'Is that all you've got to say about it?'

'Yes, I think so. This is very good cheese.'

We drank coffee and a glass of brandy out of a bottle with Beckett's name on it, and eventually walked slowly back to his office.

As before he sank gratefully into his chair and rested his head and arms, and I as before sat down opposite him on the other side of his desk.

'You are going back to Australia soon, I believe?' he said.

'Yes.'

'I expect you are looking forward to getting back into harness.'

I looked at him. His eyes stared straight back, steady and grave. He waited for an answer.

'Not altogether.'

'Why not?'

I shrugged; grinned. 'Who likes harness?'

There was no point, I thought, in making too much of it.

'You are going back to prosperity, good food, sunshine, your family, a beautiful house and a job you do well . . . isn't that right?'

I nodded. It wasn't reasonable not to want to go to all that.

'Tell me the truth,' he said abruptly. 'The unvarnished honest truth. What is wrong?'

'I'm a discontented idiot, that's all,' I said lightly.

'Mr. Roke.' He sat up slightly in the chair. 'I have a good reason for asking these questions. Please give me truthful answers. What is wrong with your life in Australia?'

There was a pause, while I thought and he waited. When at last I answered, I was aware that whatever his good reason was it would do no harm to speak plainly.

'I do a job which I ought to find satisfying, and it leaves me bored and empty.'

'A diet of milk and honey, when you have teeth,' he observed.

I laughed. 'A taste for salt, perhaps.'

'What would you have been had your parents not died and left you with three children to bring up?'

'A lawyer, I think, though possibly . . .' I hesitated.

'Possibly what?'

'Well . . . it sounds a bit odd, especially after the last few days . . . a policeman.'

'Ah,' he said softly, 'that figures.' He leant his head back again and smiled.

'Marriage might help you feel more settled,' he suggested.

'More ties,' I said, 'Another family to provide for. The rut for ever.'

'So that's how you look at it. How about Elinor?'

'She's a nice girl.'

'But not for keeps?'

I shook my head.

'You went to a great deal of trouble to save her life,' he pointed out.

'It was only because of me that she got into danger at all.'

'You couldn't know that she would be so strongly attracted to you and find you so . . . er . . . irresistible that she would drive out to take another look at you. When you went back to Humber's to extricate her, you had already finished the investigation, tidily, quietly and undiscovered. Isn't that right?'

'I suppose so. Yes.'

'Did you enjoy it?'

'Enjoy it?' I repeated, surprised.

'Oh, I don't mean the fracas at the end, or the hours of honest toil you had to put in,' he smiled briefly, 'But the . . . shall we say, the chase?'

'Am I, in fact, a hunter by nature?'

'Are you?'

'Yes.'

There was a silence. My unadorned affirmative hung in the air, bald and revealing.

'Were you afraid at all?' His voice was matter of fact.

'Yes.'

'To the point of incapacity?'

I shook my head.

'You knew Adams and Humber would kill you if they found you out. What effect did living in perpetual danger have on you?' His voice was so clinical that I answered with similar detachment.

'It made me careful.'

'Is that all?'

'Well, if you mean was I in a constant state of nervous tension, then no, I wasn't.'

'I see.' Another of his small pauses. Then he said, 'What did you find hardest to do?'

I blinked, grinned, and lied. 'Wearing those loathsome pointed shoes.'

He nodded as if I had told him a satisfying truth. I probably had. The pointed shoes had hurt my pride, not my toes.

And pride had got the better of me properly when I visited Elinor in her college and hadn't been strong enough to play an oaf in her company. All that stuff about Marcus Aurelius was sheer showing off, and the consequences had been appalling. It didn't bear thinking of, let alone confessing.

Beckett said idly, 'Would you ever consider doing something similar again?'

'I should think so. Yes. But not like that.'

'How do you mean?'

'Well . . . I didn't know enough, for one thing. For example, it was just luck that Humber always left his office unlocked, because I couldn't have got in if he hadn't. I don't know how to open doors wihout keys. I would have found a camera useful . . . I could have taken films of the blue ledger in Humber's office, and so on, but my knowledge of photography is almost nil. I'd have got the exposures wrong. Then I had never fought anyone in my life before. If I'd known anything at all about unarmed combat I probably wouldn't have killed Adams or been so much battered myself. Apart from all that there was nowhere where I could send you or Edward a message and be sure you would receive it quickly. Communications, in fact, were pretty hopeless.'

'Yes. I see. All the same, you did finish the job in spite of those disadvantages.'

'It was luck. You couldn't count on being lucky twice.'

'I suppose not.' He smiled. 'What do you plan to do with your twenty thousand pounds?'

'I . . . er . . . plan to let Edward keep most of it.'

'What do you mean?'

'I can't take that sort of money. All I ever wanted was to get away for a bit. It was he who suggested such a large sum, not me. I don't think he thought I would take on the job for less, but he was wrong . . . I'd have done it for nothing if I could. All I'll accept from him is the amount it has cost for me to be away. He knows, I told him last night.'

There was a long pause. Finally Beckett sat up and picked up a telephone. He dialled and waited.

'This is Beckett,' he said. 'It's about Daniel Roke . . . yes, he's here.' He took a postcard out of an inner pocket. 'Those points we were discussing this morning . . . I have had a talk with him. You have your card?'

He listened for a moment, and leaned back again in his chair. His eyes were steady on my face.

'Right?' He spoke into the telephone. 'Numbers one to four can all have an affirmative. Number five is satisfactory. Number six, his weakest spot . . . he didn't maintain his role in front of Elinor Tarren. She said he was good mannered and intelligent. No one else thought so . . . yes, I should say so, sexual pride . . . apparently only because Elinor is clever as well as pretty, since he kept it up all right with her younger sister . . . yes . . . oh undoubtedly it was his intellect as much as his physical appearance which attracted her . . . yes, very good looking: I believe you sometimes find that useful . . . no, he doesn't. He didn't look in the mirror in the washroom at the Club or in the one on the wall here . . . no, he didn't admit it today, but I'd say he is well aware he failed on that point . . . yes, rather a harsh lesson . . . it may still be a risk, or it may have been sheer unprofessionalism . . . your Miss Jones could find out, yes.'

I didn't particularly care for this dispassionate vivisection, but short of walking out there seemed to be no way of avoiding it. His eyes still looked at me expressionlessly.

'Number seven . . . normal reaction. Eight, slightly obsessive, but that's all the better from your point of view.' He glanced momentarily down at the card he held in his hand 'Nine . . . well, although he is British by birth and spent his childhood here, he is Australian by inclination, and

I doubt whether subservience comes easily . . . I don't know, he wouldn't
talk about it . . . no, I wouldn't say he had a vestige of a martyr complex,
he's clear on that. . . . Of course you never get a perfect one . . . it's
entirely up to you . . . Number ten? The three B's. I should say definitely
not the first two, much too proud. As for the third, he's the type to shout
for help. Yes, he's still here. Hasn't moved a muscle . . . yes, I do think
so . . . all right . . . I'll ring you again later.'

He put down the receiver. I waited. He took his time and I refrained
consciously from fidgeting under his gaze.

'Well?' he said at last.

'If you're going to ask what I think, the answer is no.'

'Because you don't want to, or because of your sisters and brother?'

'Philip is still only thirteen.'

'I see.' He made a weak-looking gesture with his hand. 'All the same,
I'd better make sure you know what you are turning down. The colleague
who kept me late this morning, and to whom I was talking just now,
runs one of the counter-espionage departments – not only political but
scientific and industrial, and anything else which crops up. His section
are rather good at doing what you have done – becoming an inconspicuous
part of the background. It's amazing how little notice even agents take
of servants and workmen . . . and his lot have had some spectacular
results. They are often used to check on suspected immigrants and
political refugees who may not be all they seem, not by watching from
afar, but by working for or near them day by day. And recently, for
instance, several of the section have been employed as labourers on
top-secret construction sites . . . there have been some disturbing leaks of
security; complete site plans of secret installations have been sold abroad;
and it was found that a commercial espionage firm was getting information
through operatives actually putting brick on brick and photographing
the buildings at each stage.'

'Philip,' I said, 'is only thirteen.'

'You wouldn't be expected to plunge straight into such a life. As you
yourself pointed out, you are untrained. There would be at least a year's
instruction in various techniques before you were given a job.'

'I can't,' I said.

'Between jobs all his people are given leave. If a job takes as long as
four months, like the one you have just done, they get about six weeks
off. They never work more than nine months in a year, if it can be
helped. You could often be home in the school holidays.'

'If I am not there all the time, there won't be enough money for fees
and there won't be any home.'

'It is true that the British Government wouldn't pay you as much as
you earn now,' he said mildly, 'but there are such things as full-time stud
managers.'

I opened my mouth and shut it again.

'Think about it,' he said gently. 'I've another colleague to see . . . I'll
be back in an hour.'

He levered himself out of the chair and slowly walked out of the room.
The pigeons fluttered peaceably on the window sill. I thought of the

years I had spent building up the stud farm, and what I had achieved there. In spite of my comparative youth the business was a solid success, and by the time I was fifty I could with a bit of luck put it among the top studs in Australia and enjoy a respected, comfortably-off, influential middle-age.

What Beckett was offering was a lonely life of unprivileged jobs and dreary lodgings, a life of perpetual risk which could very well end with a bullet in the head.

Rationally, there was no choice. Belinda and Helen and Philip still needed a secure home with the best I could do for them as a father substitute. And no sensible person would hand over to a manager a prosperous business and become instead a sort of sweeper-up of some of the world's smaller messes . . . one couldn't put the job any higher than that.

But irrationally . . . With very little persuasion I had already left my family to fend for themselves, for as Beckett said, I wasn't of the stuff of martyrs; and the prosperous business had already driven me once into a pit of depression.

I knew now clearly what I was, and what I could do.

I remembered the times when I had been tempted to give up, and hadn't. I remembered the moment when I held Elinor's dog whistle in my hand and my mind made an almost muscular leap at the truth. I remembered the satisfaction I felt in Kandersteg's scorched enclosure, knowing I had finally uncovered and defeated Adams and Humber. No sale of any horse had ever brought so quiet and complete a fulfilment.

The hour passed. The pigeons defecated on the window and flew away. Colonel Beckett came back.

'Well?' he said. 'Yes or no?'

'Yes.'

He laughed aloud. 'Just like that? No questions or reservations?'

'No reservations. But I will need time to arrange things at home.'

'Of course.' He picked up the telephone receiver. 'My colleague will wish you to see him before you go back.' He rested his fingers on the dial. 'I'll make an appointment.'

'And one question.'

'Yes?'

'What are the three Bs of number ten?'

He smiled secretly, and I knew he had intended that I should ask: which meant that he wanted me to know the answer. Devious, indeed. My nostrils twitched as if at the scent of a whole new world. A world where I belonged.

'Whether you could be bribed or bludgeoned or blackmailed,' he said casually, 'into changing sides.'

He dialled the number, and altered my life.

FLYING FINISH

Flying Finish

With my thanks to

THE BRITISH BLOODSTOCK AGENCY

BRUCE DAGLISH
Of Lep Transport

PETER PALMER
Airline Captain

JOHN MERCER
Of C.S.E. Aviation, Oxford Airport

I assure them that everyone in this book is imaginary

Chapter One

'You're a spoilt bad-tempered bastard,' my sister said, and jolted me into a course I nearly died of.

I carried her furious unattractive face down to the station and into the steamed-up compartment of Monday gloom and half done crosswords and all across London to my unloved office.

Bastard I was not: not with parents joined by bishop with half Debrett and Burke in the pews. And if spoilt, it was their doing, their legacy to an heir born accidentally at the last possible minute when earlier intended pregnancies had produced five daughters. My frail eighty-six year old father in his second childhood saw me chiefly as the means whereby a much hated cousin was to be done out of an earldom he had coveted: my father delighted in my existence and I remained to him a symbol.

My mother had been forty-seven at my birth and was now seventy-three. With a mind which had to all intents stopped developing round about Armistice Day 1918, she had been for as long as I could remember completely batty. Eccentric, her aquaintances more kindly said. Anyway, one of the first things I ever learnt was that age had nothing to do with wisdom.

Too old to want a young child around them, they had brought me up and educated me at arms length – nurse-maids, prep school and Eton – and in my hearing had regretted the length of the school holidays. Our relationship was one of politeness and duty, but not of affection. They didn't even seem to expect me to love them, and I didn't. I didn't love anyone. I hadn't had any practice.

I was first at the office as usual. I collected the key from the caretaker's cubbyhole, walked unhurriedly down the long echoing hall, up the gritty stone staircase, down a narrow dark corridor, and at the far end of it unlocked the heavily brown varnished front door of the Anglia Bloodstock Agency. Inside, typical of the old London warren-type blocks of offices, comfort took over from barracks. The several rooms opening right and left from the passage were close carpeted, white painted, each with the occupant's name in neat black on the door. The desks ran to extravagances like tooled leather tops, and there were sporting prints on the wall. I had not yet, however, risen to this success bracket.

The room where I had worked (on and off) for nearly six years lay at the far end, past the reference room and the pantry. 'Transport' it said, on the half-open door. I pushed it wide. Nothing had changed from Friday. The three desks looked the same as usual: Christopher's, with thick uneven piles of papers held down by cricket balls; Maggie's with the typewriter cover askew, carbons screwed up beside it, and a vase of dead chrysanthemums dropping petals into a scummy teacup; and mine, bare.

I hung up my coat, sat down, opened my desk drawers one by one and uselessly straightened the already tidy contents. I checked that it was precisely eight minutes to nine by my accurate watch, which made the office clock two minutes slow. After this activity I stared straight ahead unseeingly at the calendar on the pale green wall.

A spoilt bad-tempered bastard, my sister said.

I didn't like it. I was not bad-tempered, I assured myself defensively. I was not. But my thoughts carried no conviction. I decided to break with tradition and refrain from reminding Maggie that I found her slovenly habits irritating.

Christopher and Maggie arrived together, laughing, at ten past nine.

'Hullo,' said Christopher cheerfully, hanging up his coat. 'I see you lost on Saturday.'

'Yes,' I agreed.

'Better luck next time,' said Maggie automatically, blowing the sodden petals out of the cup on to the floor. I bit my tongue to keep it still. Maggie picked up the vase and made for the pantry, scattering petals as she went. Presently she came back with the vase, fumbled it, and left a dripping trail of Friday's tea across my desk. In silence I took some white blotting paper from the drawer, mopped up the spots, and threw the blotting paper in the waste basket. Christopher watched in sardonic amusement, pale eyes crinkling behind thick spectacles.

'A short head, I believe?' he said, lifting one of the cricket balls and going through the motions of bowling it through the window.

'A short head,' I agreed. All the same if it had been ten lengths, I thought sourly. You got no present for losing, whatever the margin.

'My uncle had a fiver on you.'

'I'm sorry,' I said formally.

Christopher pivoted on one toe and let go: the cricket ball crashed into the wall, leaving a mark. He saw me frowning at it and laughed. He had come straight into the office from Cambridge two months before, robbed of a cricket blue through deteriorating eyesight and having failed his finals into the bargain. He remained always in better spirits than I, who had suffered no similar reverses. we tolerated each other. I found it difficult, as always, to make friends, and he had given up trying.

Maggie came back from the pantry, sat down at her desk, took her nail varnish out of the stationery drawer and begun brushing on the silvery pink. She was a large assured girl from Surbiton with a naturally unkind tongue and a suspect talent for registering remorse immediately after the barbs were in.

The cricket ball slipped out of Christopher's hand and rolled across Maggie's desk. Lunging after it, he brushed one of his heaps of letters into a fluttering muddle on the floor, and the ball knocked over Maggie's bottle of varnish, which scattered pretty pink viscous blobs all over the 'We have received yours of the fourteenth ult.'

'God-damn,' said Christopher with feeling.

Old Cooper who dealt with insurance came into the room at his doddery pace and looked at the mess with cross disgust and pinched nostrils. He held out to me the sheaf of papers he had brought.

'Your pigeon, Henry. Fix it up for the earliest possible.'

'Right.'

As he turned to go he said to Christopher and Maggie in a complaining voice certain to annoy them, 'Why can't you two be as efficient as Henry? He's never late, he's never untidy, his work is always correct and always done on time. Why don't you try to be more like him?'

I winced inwardly and waited for Maggie's inevitable retaliation. She would be in good form: it was Monday morning.

'I wouldn't want to be like Henry in a thousand years,' she said sharply. 'He's a prim, dim, sexless *nothing*. He's not alive.'

Not my day, definitely.

'He rides those races though,' said Christopher in mild defence.

'And if he fell off and broke both his legs, all he'd care about would be seeing they got the bandages straight.'

'The bones,' I said.

'What?'

'The bones straight.'

Christopher blinked and laughed. 'Well, well, what do you know? The still waters of Henry might just possibly be running deep.'

'Deep, nothing,' said Maggie. 'A stagnant pond, more like.'

'Slimy and smelly?' I suggested.

'No . . . oh dear . . . I mean, I'm sorry . . .'

'Never mind,' I said. 'Never mind.' I looked at the paper in my hand and picked up the telephone.

'Henry . . .' said Maggie desperately. 'I didn't mean it.'

Old Cooper tut-tutted and doddered away along the passage, and Christopher began sorting his varnished letters. I got through to Yardman Transport and asked for Simon Searle. 'Four yearlings from the Newmarket sales to go to Buenos Aires as soon as possible,' I said.

'There might be a delay.'

'Why?'

'We've lost Peters.'

'Careless,' I remarked.

'Oh ha-ha.'

'Has he left?'

Simon hesitated perceptibly. 'It looks like it.'

'How do you mean?'

'He didn't come back from one of the trips. Last Monday. Just never turned up for the flight back, and hasn't been seen or heard of since.'

'Hospitals?' I said.

'We checked those, of course. And the morgue, and the jail. Nothing. He just vanished. And as he hasn't done anything wrong the police aren't interested in finding him. No police would be, it isn't criminal to leave your job without notice. They say he fell for a girl, very likely, and decided not to go home.'

'Is he married?'

'No.' He sighed. 'Well, I'll get on with your yearlings, but I can't give you even an approximate date.'

'Simon,' I said slowly. 'Didn't something like this happen before?'

'Er . . . do you mean Ballard?'

'One of your liaison men,' I said.

'Yes. Well . . . I suppose so.'

'In Italy?' I suggested gently.

There was a short silence the other end. 'I hadn't thought of it,' he said. 'Funny coincidence. Well . . . I'll let you know about the yearlings.'

'I'll have to get on to Clarksons if you can't manage it.'

He sighed. 'I'll do my best. I'll ring you back tomorrow.'

I put down the receiver and started on a large batch of customs declarations, and the long morning disintegrated towards the lunch hour. Maggie and I said nothing at all to each other and Christopher cursed steadily over his letters. At one sharp I beat even Maggie in the rush to the door.

Outside, the December sun was shining. On impulse I jumped on to a passing bus, got off at Marble Arch, and walked slowly through the park to the Serpentine. I was still there, sitting on a bench, watching the sun ripple on the water, when the hands on my watch read two o'clock. I was still there at half past. At a quarter to three I threw some stones with force into the lake, and a park keeper told me not to.

A spoilt bad-tempered bastard. It wouldn't have been so bad if she had been used to saying things like that, but she was a gentle see-no-evil person who had been made to wash her mouth out with soap for swearing as a child and had never taken the risk again. She was my youngest sister, fifteen years my elder, unmarried, plain, and quietly intelligent. She had reversed roles with our parents: she ran the house and managed them as her children. She also to a great extent managed me, and always had.

A repressed, quiet, 'good' little boy I had been: and a quiet, withdrawn, secretive man I had become. I was almost pathologically tidy and methodical, early for every appointment, controlled alike in behaviour, hand-writing and sex. A prim dim nothing, as Maggie had said. The fact that for some months now I had not felt in the least like that inside was confusing, and getting more so.

I looked up into the blue gold-washed sky. Only there, I thought with a fleeting inward smile, only there am I my own man. And perhaps in steeplechases. Perhaps there too, sometimes.

She had been waiting for me as usual at breakfast, her face fresh from her early walk with the dogs. I had seen little of her over the week end: I'd been racing on Saturday, and on Sunday I'd left home before breakfast and gone back late.

'Where did you go yesterday?' she asked.

I poured some coffee and didn't answer. She was used to that, however.

'Mother wanted to speak to you.'

'What about?'

'She has asked the Filyhoughs to lunch next Sunday.'

I tidily ate my bacon and egg. I said calmly, 'That coy spotty Angela. It's a waste of time. I won't be here anyway.'

'Angela will inherit half a million,' she said earnestly.

'And we have beetles in the roof,' I agreed dryly.

'Mother wants to see you married.'

'Only to a very rich girl.'

My sister acknowledged that this was true, but saw nothing particularly wrong in it. The family fortunes were waning: as my parents saw it, the swop of a future title for a future fortune was a suitable bargain. They didn't seem to realise that a rich girl nowadays had more sense than to hand over her wealth to her husband, and could leave with it intact if she felt like it.

'Mother told Angela you would be here.'

'That was silly of her.'

'Henry!'

'I do not like Angela,' I said coldly. 'I do not intend to be here for lunch next Sunday. Is that quite clear?'

'But you must . . . you can't leave me to deal with them all alone.'

'You'll just have to restrain Mother from issuing these stupid invitations. Angela is the umpteenth unattractive heiress she's invited this year. I'm fed up with it.'

'We need . . .'

'I am not,' I said stiffly, 'a prostitute.'

She stood up bitterly offended. 'That's unkind.'

'And while we are at it, I wish the beetles good luck. This damp decaying pile of a house eats up every penny we've got and if it fell down tomorrow we'd all be far better off.'

'It's our home,' she said, as if that was the final word.

When it was mine, I would get rid of it; but I didn't say that, and encouraged by my silence she tried persuasion. 'Henry, please be here for the Filyhoughs.'

'No,' I said forcefully. 'I won't. I want to do something else next Sunday. You can count me right out.'

She suddenly and completely lost her temper. Shaking she said, 'I cannot stand much more of your damned autistic behaviour. You're a spoilt, bad-tempered *bastard* . . .'

Hell, I thought by the Serpentine, was I really? And if so, why?

At three, with the air growing cold, I got up and left the park, but the office I went to was not the elegant suite of Anglia Bloodstock in Hanover Square. There, I thought, they could go on wondering why the ever-punctual Henry hadn't returned from lunch. I went instead by taxi to a small dilapidated rubbish-strewn wharf down in the Pool, where the smell of Thames mud at low tide rose earthily into my nostrils as I paid the fare.

At one end of the wharf, on an old bombed site, a small square concrete building had been thrown up shortly after the war and shoddily maintained ever since. Its drab walls, striped by rust from leaking gutters, badly needed a coat of 'Snowcem'; its rectangular metal windows were grimed and flaking, and no one had polished the brass door fittings since my previous visit six months ago. There was no need to put on a plushy front for the customers; the customers were not expected to come.

I walked up the uncarpeted stairs, across the eight foot square of linoleumed landing and through the open door of Simon Searle's room. He looked up from some complicated doodling on a memo pad, lumbered to his feet and greeted me with a large handshake and a wide grin. As he was the only person who ever gave me this sort of welcome I came as near to unbending with him as with anyone. But we had never done more than meet now and again on business and occasionally repair to a pub afterwards. There he was inclined to lots of beer and bonhomie, and I to a single whisky, and that was that.

'You haven't trekked all the way down here about those yearlings?' he protested. 'I told you . . .'

'No,' I said, coming to the point abruptly. 'I came to find out if Yardman would give me a job.'

'*You*,' said Simon, 'want to work *here?*'

'That's right.'

'Well I'm damned.' Simon sat down on the edge of his desk and his bulk settled and spread comfortably around him. He was a vast shambling man somewhere in the doldrums between thirty-five and forty-five, bald on top, bohemian in dress and broad of mind.

'Why, for God's sake?' he said, looking me up and down. A more thorough contrast than me in my charcoal worsted to him in his baggy green corduroys would have been hard to find.

'I need a change.'

'For the worse?' He was sardonic.

'Of course not. And I'd like the chance of a bit of globe-trotting now and then.'

'You can afford to do that in comfort. You don't have to do it on a horse transport.'

Like so many other people, he took it for granted that I had money. I hadn't. I had only my salary from Anglia, and what I could earn by being frankly, almost notoriously, a shamateur jockey. Every penny I got was earmarked. From my father I took only my food and the beetle infested roof over my head, and neither expected nor asked for anything else.

'I imagine I would like a horse transport,' I said equably. 'What are the chances?'

'Oh,' Simon laughed. 'You've only to ask. I can't see him turning you down.'

But Yardman very nearly did turn me down, because he couldn't believe I really meant it.

'My dear boy, now think carefully, I beg you. Anglia Bloodstock is surely a better place for you? However well you might do here, there isn't any power or any prestige . . . We must face facts, we must indeed.'

'I don't particularly care for power and prestige.'

He sighed deeply. 'There speaks one to whom they come by birth. Others of us are not so fortunate as to be able to despise them.'

'I don't despise them. Also I don't want them. Or not yet.'

He lit a dark cigar with slow care. I watched him, taking him in. I hadn't met him before, and as he came from a different mould from the top men at Anglia I found that I didn't instinctively know how his mind worked. After years of being employed by people of my own sort of background, where much that was understood never needed to be stated, Yardman was a foriegn country.

He was being heavily paternal, which somehow came oddly from a thin man. He wore black-rimmed spectacles on a strong beaky nose. His cheeks were hollowed, and his mouth in consequence seemed to have to stretch to cover his teeth and gums. His lips curved downwards strongly at the corners, giving him at times a disagreeable and at times a sad expression. He was bald on the crown of his head, which was not noticeable at first sight, and his skin looked unhealthy. But his voice and his fingers were strong, and as I grew to acknowledge, his will and his character also.

He puffed slowly at the cigar, a slim fierce looking thing with an aroma to match. From behind the glasses his eyes considered me without haste. I hadn't a clue as to what he was thinking.

'All right,' he said at last. 'I'll take you on as an assistant to Searle, and we'll see how it goes.'

'Well . . . thank you,' I answered. 'But what I really came to ask for was Peters's job.'

'*Peters's* . . .' His mouth literally fell open, revealing a bottom row of regular false teeth. He shut it with a snap. 'Don't be silly, my boy. You can't have Peters's job.'

'Searle says he has left.'

'I dare say, but that's not the point, is it?'

I said calmly, 'I've been in the Transport Section of Anglia for more than five years, so I know all the technical side of it, and I've ridden horses all my life, so I know how to look after them. I agree that I haven't any practical experience, but I could learn very quickly.'

'Lord Grey,' he said, shaking his head. 'I don't think you realise just what Peters's job was.'

'Of course I do,' I said. 'He travelled on the planes with the horses and saw they arrived safely and well. He saw that they passed the Customs all right at both ends and that the correct people collected them, and where necessary saw that another load of horses was brought safely back again. It is a responsible job and it entails a lot of travelling and I am seriously applying for it.'

'You don't understand,' he said with some impatience. 'Peters was a travelling head groom.'

'I know.'

He smoked, inscrutable. Three puffs. I waited, quiet and still.

'You're not . . . er . . . in any trouble, at Anglia?'

'No. I've grown tired of a desk job, that's all.' I had been tired of it from the day I started, to be exact.

'How about racing?'

'I have Saturdays off at Anglia, and I take my three weeks annual holiday in seperate days during the winter and spring. And they have been very considerate about extra half-days.'

'Worth it to them in terms of trade, I dare say.' He tapped off the ash absentmindedly into the inkwell. 'Are you thinking of giving it up?'

'No.'

'Mm . . . if you work for me, would I get any increase in business from your racing connections?'

'I'd see you did,' I said.

He turned his head away and looked out of the window. The river tide was sluggishly at the ebb, and away over on the other side a row of cranes stood like red meccano toys in the beginnings of dusk. I couldn't even guess then at the calculations clicking away at high speed in Yardman's nimble brain, though I've often thought about those few minutes since.

'I think you are being unwise, my dear boy. Youth . . . youth . . .' He sighed, straightened his shoulders and turned the beaky nose back in my direction. His shadowed greenish eyes regarded me steadily from deep sockets, and he told me what Peters had been earning; fifteen pounds a trip plus three pounds expenses for each overnight stop. He clearly thought that would deter me; and it nearly did.

'How many trips a week?' I asked frowning.

'It depends on the time of year. You know that, of course. After the yearling sales, and when the brood mares come over, it might be three trips. To France, perhaps even four. Usually two, sometimes none.'

There was a pause. We looked at each other. I learned nothing.

'All right,' I said abruptly. 'Can I have the job?'

His lips twisted in a curious expression which I later came to recognise as an ironic smile.

'You can try it,' he said. 'If you like.'

Chapter Two

A job is what you make it. Three weeks later, after Christmas, I flew to Buenos Aires with twelve yearlings, the four from Anglia and eight more from different bloodstock agencies, all mustered together at five o'clock on a cold Tuesday morning at Gatwick. Simon Searle had organised their arrival and booked their passage with a charter company; I took charge of them when they unloaded from their various horseboxes, installed them in the plane, checked their papers through Customs, and presently flew away.

With me went two of Yardman's travelling grooms, both of them fiercely resenting that I had been given Peter's job over their heads. Each of them had coveted the promotion, and in terms of human relationships the trip was a frost-bitten failure. Otherwise, it went well enough. We

arrived in Argentina four hours late, but the new owners' horseboxes
had all turned up to collect the cargo. Again I cleared the horses and
papers through the Customs, and made sure that each of the five new
owners had got the right horses and the certificates to go with them. The
following day the plane picked up a load of crated furs for the return
journey, and we flew back to Gatwick, arriving on Friday.

On Saturday I had a fall and a winner at Sandown Races, Sunday I
spent in my usual way, and Monday I flew with some circus ponies to
Germany. After a fortnight of it I was dying from exhaustion; after a
month I was acclimatised. My body got used to long hours, irregular
food, non-stop coffee, and sleeping sitting upright on bales of hay ten
thousand feet up in the sky. The two grooms, Timmie and Conker,
gradually got over the worst of their anger, and we developed into a
quick, efficient, laconic team.

My family were predictably horrified by my change of occupation and
did their best to pry me away from it. My sister anxiously retracted the
words I knew I'd earned, my father foresaw the earldom going to the
cousin after all, aeroplanes being entirely against nature and usually
fatal, and my mother had hysterics over what her friends would say.

'It's a labourer's job,' she wailed.

'A job is what you make it.'

'What will the Filyhoughs think?'

'Who the hell cares what they think?'

'It isn't a *suitable* job for you.' She wrung her hands.

'It's a job I like. It suits me, therefore it *is* suitable.'

'You know that isn't what I mean.'

'I know exactly what you mean, Mother, and I profoundly disagree
with you. People should do work they like doing; that's all that should
decide them. Whether it is socially O.K. or not shouldn't come into it.'

'But it does,' she cried, exasperated.

'It has for me for nearly six years,' I admitted, 'but not any more. And
ideas change. What I am doing now may be the top thing next year. If
I don't look out half the men I know will be muscling in on the act.
Anyway, it's right for me, and I'm going on with it.'

All the same she couldn't be won over, and could only face her own
elderly convention-bound circle by pretending my job was 'for the
experience, you know,' and by treating it as a joke.

It was a joke to Simon Searle too, at first.

'You won't stick it, Henry,' he said confidently. 'Not you and all that
dirt. You with your spotless dark suits and your snowy white shirts and
not a hair out of place. One trip will be enough.'

After a month, looking exactly the same, I turned up for my pay packet
late on Friday afternoon, and we sauntered along to his favourite pub,
a tatty place with stained glass doors and a chronic smell of fug. He
oozed onto a bar stool, his bulk drooping around him. A pint for him,
he said. I bought it, and a half for me, and he drank most of his off with
one much practised swallow.

'How's the globe-trotting, then?' He ran his tongue over his upper lip
for the froth.

'I like it.'

'I'll grant you,' he said, smiling amicably, 'that you haven't made a mess of it yet.'

'Thanks.'

'Though of course since I do all the spade work for you at both ends you bloody well shouldn't.'

'No,' I agreed. He was, in truth, an excellent organiser, which was mainly why Anglia often dealt with Yardman Transport instead of Clarkson Carriers, a much bigger and better known firm. Simon's arrangements were clear, simple, and always twice confirmed: agencies, owners and air-lines alike knew exactly where they stood and at what hours they were expected to be where. No one else in the business, that I had come across at any rate, was as consistently reliable. Being so precise myself, I admired his work almost as a work of art.

He looked me over, privately amused. 'You don't go on trips dressed like that?'

'I do, yes, more or less.'

'What does more or less mean?'

'I wear a sweater instead of my jacket, in and around the aircraft.'

'And hang up your jacket on a hanger for when you land?'

'Yes, I do.'

He laughed, but without mockery. 'You're a rum sort of chap, Henry.' He ordered more beer, shrugged when I refused, and drank deep again. 'Why are you so methodical?'

'It's safer.'

'Safer.' He choked on his beer, coughing and laughing. 'I suppose it doesn't strike you that to many people steeplechasing and air transport might not seem especially safe?'

'That wasn't what I meant.'

'What, then?'

But I shook my head and didn't explain.

'Tell me about Yardman,' I said.

'What about him?'

'Well, where he came from . . . anything.'

Simon hunched his great shoulders protectively around his pint, and pursed his lips.

'He joined the firm after the war, when he left the Army. He was a sergeant in an infantry regiment, I think. Don't know any details: never asked. Anyway he worked his way up through the business. It wasn't called Yardman Transport then, of course. Belonged to a family, the Mayhews, but they were dying out . . . nephews weren't interested, that sort of thing. Yardman had taken it over by the time I got there; don't know how really, come to think of it, but he's a bright lad, there's no doubt of that. Take switching to air, for instance. That was him. He was pressing the advantages of air travel for horses, whilst all the other transport agencies were going entirely by sea.'

'Even though the office itself is on a wharf,' I remarked.

'Yes. Very handy once. It isn't used much at all now since they clamped down on exporting horses to the continent for meat.'

'Yardman was in that?'

'Shipping agent,' he nodded. 'There's a big warehouse down the other end of the wharf where we used to collect them. They'd start being brought in three days before the ship came. Once a fortnight, on average. I can't say I'm sorry it's finished. It was a lot of work and a lot of mess and noise, and not much profit, Yardman said.'

'It didn't worry you, though, that they were going to be slaughtered?'

'No more than cattle or pigs.' He finished his beer. 'Why should it? Everything dies sometime.' He smiled cheerfully and gestured to the glasses. 'Another?'

He had one, I didn't.

'Has anyone heard any more of Peters?' I asked.

He shook his head. 'Not a murmur.'

'How about his cards?'

'Still in the office, as far as I know.'

'It's a bit odd isn't it?'

Simon shrugged. 'You never know, he might have wanted to duck someone, and did it thoroughly.'

'But did anyone ever come looking for him?'

'Nope. No police, no unpaid bookies, no rampaging females, no one.'

'He just went to Italy and didn't come back?'

'That's the size of it,' Simon agreed. 'He went with some brood mares to Milan and he should have come back the same day. But there was some trouble over an engine or something, and the pilot ran out of time and said he'd be in dead trouble if he worked too many hours. So they stayed there overnight and in the morning Peters didn't turn up. They waited nearly all day, then they came back without him.'

'And that's all?'

'That's the lot,' he agreed. 'Just one of life's little mysteries. What's the matter, are you afraid Peters will reappear and take back his job?'

'Something like that.'

'He was an awkward bastard,' he said thoughtfully. 'stood on his rights. Always arguing; that sort of chap. Belligerent. Never stood any nonsense from foreign customs officers.' He grinned. 'I'll bet they're quite glad to see you instead.'

'I dare say I'll be just as cussed in a year or two.'

'A year or two?' He looked surprised. 'Henry, it's all very well you taking Peters's job for a bit of a giggle but you surely can't mean to go on with it permanently?'

'You think it would be more suitable if I was sitting behind a nice solid desk at Anglia?' I asked ironically.

'Yes,' he said seriously. 'Of course it would.'

I sighed. 'Not you too. I thought you at least might understand ...' I stopped wryly.

'Understand what?'

'Well ... that who one's father is has nothing to do with the sort of work one is best suited for. And I am not fitted for sitting behind a desk. I came to that conclusion my first week at Anglia, but I stayed there because I'd kicked up a fuss and insisted on getting an ordinary job, and

I wasn't going to admit I'd made a mistake with it. I tried to like it. At any rate I got used to it, but now ... now ... I don't think I could face that nine-to-five routine ever again.'

'Your father's in his eighties, isn't he?' Simon said thoughtfully.

I nodded.

'And do you think that when he dies you will be allowed to go on carting horses around the world? And for how long *could* you do it without becoming an eccentric nut? Like it or not, Henry, it's easy enough to go up the social scale, but damn difficult to go down. And still be respected, that is.'

'And I could be respected sitting behind a desk at Anglia, transferring horses from owner to owner on paper, but not if I move about and do it on aeroplanes?'

He laughed. 'Exactly.'

'The world is mad,' I said.

'You're a romantic. But time will cure that.' He looked at me in a large tolerant friendship, finished his beer, and flowed down from the stool like a green corduroy amoeba.

'Come on,' he said, 'there's time for another along the road at the Saracen's Head.'

At Newbury Races the following afternoon I watched five races from the stands and rode in one.

This inactivity was not mine by choice, but thrust upon me by the Stewards. They had, by the time I was twenty, presented me with their usual ultimatum to regular amateur riders: either turn professional, or ride in only fifty open races each season. In other words, don't undercut the trade: stop taking the bread and butter out of the professionals mouths. (As if jockeys *ate* much bread and butter, to start with.)

I hadn't turned professional when I was twenty because I had been both too conventional and not really good enough. I was still not good enough to be a top rank professional, but I had long been a fully employed amateur. A big fish in a small pond. In the new-found freedom of my Yardman's job I regretted that I hadn't been bolder at twenty. I liked steeplechasing enormously, and with full-time professional application I might just have made a decent success. Earth-bound on the stands at Newbury I painfully accepted that my sister had brought me to my senses a lot too late.

The one horse I did ride was in the 'amateurs only' race. As there were no restrictions on the number of amateur events I could ride in, few were run without me. I rode regularly for many owners who grudged paying professional jockey's fees, for some who reckoned their horses stood more chance in amateur races, and a few who genuinely liked my work.

All of them knew very well that if I won either amateur or open races I expected ten per cent of the prize. The word had got around. Henry Grey rode for money, not love. Henry Grey was the shamateur to end all shamateurs. Because I was silent and discreet and they could trust my tongue, I had even been given cash presents by stewards: and solely because my father was the Earl of Creggan, my amateur permit survived.

In the changing room that afternoon I found that however different I might feel, I could not alter my long set pattern. The easy bantering chat flowed round me and as usual it was impossible to join in. No one expected me to. They were used to me. Half of them took my aloofness to be arrogant snobbery, and the rest shrugged it off as 'just Henry's way.' No one was actively hostile, and it was I, I, who had failed to belong. I changed slowly into my racing clothes and listened to the jokes and the warm earthy language, and I could think of nothing, not one single thing, to say.

I won the race. The well pleased owner gave me a public clap on the shoulder and a drink in the members' bar, and surreptitiously, round a private corner, forty pounds.

On the following day, Sunday, I spent the lot.

I started my little Herald in the garage in the pre-dawn dark, and as quietly as possible opened the doors and drifted away down the drive. Mother had invited yet another well-heeled presumptive virgin for the week-end, together with her slightly forbidding parents, and having dutifully escorted them all to Newbury Races the day before and tipped them a winner – my own – I felt I had done quite enough. They would be gone, I thought coolly, before I got back late that evening, and with a bit of luck my bad manners in disappearing would have discouraged them for ever.

A steady two and a half hours driving northwards found me at shortly before ten o'clock turning in through some inconspicuously signposted gates in Lincolnshire. I parked the car at the end of the row of others, climbed out, stretched, and looked up into the sky. It was a cold clear morning with maximum visibility. Not a cloud in sight. Smiling contentedly I strolled over to the row of white painted buildings and pushed open the glass door into the main hall of the Fenland Flying Club.

The hall was a big room with several passages leading off it and a double door on the far side opening to the airfield itself. Round the walls hung framed charts, Air Ministry regulations, a large map of the surrounding area, do's and don'ts for visiting pilots, a thumb-tacked weather report and a list of people wanting to enter for a ping-pong tournament. There were several small wooden tables and hard chairs at one end, half occupied, and across the whole width of the other end stretched the reception-cum-operations-cum-everything else desk. Yawning behind it and scratching between his shoulder blades stood a plump sleepy man of about my own age, sporting a thick sloppy sweater and a fair sized hangover. He held a cup of strong coffee and a cigarette in his free hand, and he was talking lethargically to a gay young spark who had turned up with a girl-friend he wanted to impress.

'I've told you, old chap, you should have given us a ring. All the planes are booked today. I'm sorry, no can do. You can hang about if you like, in case someone doesn't turn up . . .'

He turned towards me, casually.

'Morning, Harry,' he said. 'How's things?'

'Very O.K.,' I said. 'And you?'

'Ouch,' he grinned, 'don't cut me. The gin would run out.' He turned round and consulted the vast timetable charts covering most of the wall behind him. 'You've got Kilo November today, it's out by the petrol pumps, I think. Cross country again; is that right?'

'Uh-huh,' I nodded.

'Nice day for it.' He put a tick on his chart where it said H. Grey, solo cross.

'Couldn't be better.'

The girl said moodily, 'How about this afternoon, then?'

'No dice. All booked. And it gets dark so early . . . there'll be plenty of planes tomorrow.'

I strolled away, out of the door to the airfield and around to the petrol pumps.

There were six single engined aircraft lined up there in two rows of three, with a tall man in white overalls filling one up through the opening on the upper surface of the port wing. He waved when he saw me coming, and grinned.

'Just doing yours next, Harry. The boys have tuned her up special. They say you couldn't have done it better yourself.'

'I'm delighted to hear it,' I said smiling.

He screwed on the cap and jumped down.

'Lovely day,' he said, looking up. There were already two little planes in the air, and four more stood ready in front of the control tower. 'Going far?' he asked.

'Scotland,' I said.

'That's cheating.' He swung the hose away and began to drag it along to the next aircraft. 'The navigation's too easy. you only have to go west till you hit the A.1 and then fly up it.'

'I'm going to Islay,' I smiled. 'No roads, I promise.'

'Islay. That's different.'

'I'll land there for lunch and bring you back a bit of heather.'

'How far is it?'

'Two seventy nautical miles, about.'

'You'll be coming back in the dark.' It was a statement, not a question. He unscrewed the cap of Kilo November and topped up the tanks.

'Most of the way, yes.'

I did the routine checks all round the aircraft, fetched my padded jacket and my charts from the car, filed my flight plan, checked with the control tower for taxy clearance, and within a short while was up in the sky and away.

Air is curious stuff. One tends to think that because it is invisible it isn't there. What you can't see don't exist, sort of thing. But air is tough, elastic and resistant; and the harder you dig into it the more solid it becomes. Air has currents stronger than tides and turbulences which would make Charybdis look like bath water running away.

When I first went flying I rationalised the invisibility thing by thinking of an aircraft being like a submarine: in both one went up and down and sideways in a medium one couldn't see but which was very palpably around. Then I considered that if human eyes had been constructed differently it might have been possible to see the mixture of nitrogen and oxygen we breathe as clearly as the hydrogen and oxygen we wash in. After that I took the air's positive plastic existence for granted, and thought no more about it.

The day I went to Islay was pure pleasure. I had flown so much by then that the handling of the little aircraft was as normal as driving a car, and with the perfect weather and my route carefully worked out and handy on the empty passenger seat behind me, there was nothing to do but enjoy myself. And that I did, because I liked being alone. Specifically I liked being alone in a tiny noisy efficient little capsule at 25,000 revs a minute, four thousand five hundred feet above sea level, speed over the ground one hundred and ten miles an hour, steady on a course 313 degrees, bound north-west towards the sea and a Scottish island.

I found Islay itself without trouble, and tuned my radio to the frequency – 118.5 – of Port Ellen airfield.

I said, 'Port Ellen tower this is Golf Alpha Romeo Kilo November, do you read?'

A Scots accent cracked back, 'Golf Kilo November, good afternoon, go ahead.'

'Kilo November is approaching from the south-east, range fifteen miles, request joining instructions, over.'

'Kilo November is cleared to join right base for runway zero four, QFE 998 millibars. Surface wind zero six zero, ten knots, call field in sight.'

Following his instructions I flew in and round the little airfield on the circuit, cut the engine, turned into wind, glided in at eighty, touched down, and taxied across to the control tower to report.

After eating in a snack bar I went for a walk by the sea, breathing the soft Atlantic air, and forgot to look for some heather to take back with me. The island lay dozing in the sun, shut up close because it was Sunday. It was peaceful and distant and slowed the pulse; soul's balm if you stayed three hours, devitalising if you stayed for life.

The gold had already gone from the day when I started back, and I flew contentedly along in the dusk and the dark, navigating by compass and checking my direction by the radio beacons over which I passed. I dropped down briefly at Carlisle to refuel, and uneventfully returned to Lincolnshire, landing gently and regretfully on the well-known field.

As usual on Sundays the club room next to the main hall was bursting with amateur pilots like myself all talking at once about stalls and spins and ratings and slide slips and allowances for deviations. I edged round the crowd to the bar and aquired some whisky and water, which tasted dry and fine on my tongue and reminded me of where I had been.

Turning round I found myself directly beside the reception desk man and a red-haired boy he was talking to. Catching my eye he said to the boy, 'Now here's someone you ought to have a word with. Our Harry here, he's dead quiet, but don't let that fool you ... He could fly the pants off most of that lot.' He gestured round the room. 'You ask Harry, now. He started just like you, knowing nothing at all, only three or four years ago.'

'Four,' I said.

'There you are, then. Four years. Now he's got a commercial licence and enough ratings to fill a book and he can strip an engine down like a mechanic.'

'That's enough,' I interrupted mildly. The young man looked thoroughly unimpressed anyway, as he didn't understand what he was being told. 'I suppose the point is that once you start, you go on,' I said. 'One thing leads to another.'

'I had my first lesson today,' he said eagerly, and gave me a rev by rev account of it for the next fifteen minutes. I ate two thick ham sandwiches while he got it off his chest, and finished the whisky. You couldn't really blame him, I thought, listening with half an ear: if you liked it, your first flight took you by the throat and you were hooked good and proper. It had happened to him. It had happened to me, one idle day when I passed the gates of the airfield and then turned back and went in, mildly interested in going up for a spin in a baby aircraft just to see what it was like.

I'd been visiting a dying great-aunt, and was depressed. Certainly Mr. . . . ? 'Grey.' I said. Certainly Mr. Grey could go up with an instructor, the air people said: and the instructor, who hadn't been told I only wanted a sight-seeing flip, began as a matter of course to teach me to fly. I stayed all day and spent a week's salary in fees; and the next Sunday I went back. Most of my Sundays and most of my money had gone the same way since.

The red-head was brought to a full stop by a burly tweed-suited man who said 'Excuse me,' pleasantly but very firmly, and planted himself between us.

'Harry, I've been waiting for you to come back.'

'Have a drink?'

'Yes . . . all right, in a minute.'

His name was Tom Wells. He owned and ran a small charter firm which was based on the airfield, and on Sundays, if they weren't out on jobs, he allowed the flying club to hire his planes. It was one of his that I had flown to Islay.

'Have I done something wrong?' I asked.

'Wrong? Why should you, for God's sake? No, I'm in a spot and I thought you might be able to help me out.'

'If I can, of course.'

'I've overbooked next week-end and I'm going to be a pilot short. Will you do a flight for me next Sunday?'

'Yes,' I said: I'd done it before, several times.

He laughed. 'You never waste words, Harry boy. Well, thanks. When can I ring you to give you a briefing?'

I hesitated. 'I'd better ring you, as usual.'

'Saturday morning, then.'

'Right.'

We had a drink together, he talking discontentedly about the growing shortage of pilots and how it was now too expensive for a young man to take it up on his own account, it cost at least three thousand pounds to train a multi-engine pilot, and only the air lines could afford it. They trained their own men and kept them, naturally. When the generation who had learned flying in the R.A.F. during the war got too old, the smaller charter firms were going to find themselves in very sticky straits.

'You know,' he said, and it was obviously what he'd been working round to all along. 'You're an oddity. You've got a commercial licence and all the rest, and you hardly use it. Why not? Why don't you give up that boring old desk job and come and work for me?'

I looked at him for a long, long moment. It was almost too tempting, but apart from everything else, it would mean giving up steeplechasing, and I wasn't prepared to do that. I shook my head slowly, and said not for a few years yet.

Driving home I enjoyed the irony of the situation. Tom Wells didn't know what my desk job was, only that I worked in an office. I hadn't got around to telling him that I no longer did, and I wasn't going to. He didn't know where I came from or anything about my life away from the airfield. No one there did, and I liked it that way. I was just Harry who turned up on Sundays and flew if he had any money and worked on the engines in the hangars if he hadn't.

Tom Wells had offered me a job on my own account, not, like Yardman, because of my father, and that pleased me very much. It was rare for me to be sure of the motive behind things which were offered to me. But if I took the job my anonymity on the airfield would vanish pretty soon, and all the old problems would crowd in, and Tom Wells might very well retract, and I would be left with nowhere to escape to on one day a week to be myself.

My family did not know I was a pilot. I hadn't told them I had been flying that first day because by the time I got home my great-aunt had died and I was ashamed of having enjoyed myself while she did it. I hadn't told them afterwards because I was afraid that they would make a fuss and stop me. Soon after that I realised what a release it was to lead two lives and I deliberately kept them separate. It was quite easy, as I had always been untalkative: I just didn't answer when asked where I went on Sundays, and I kept my books and charts, slide rules and computers, securely locked up in my bedroom. And that was that.

Chapter Three

It was on the day after I went to Islay that I first met Billy.

With Conker and Timmie, once they had bitten down their resentment at my pinching their promotion, I had arrived at a truce. On trips they chatted exclusively to each other, not to me, but that was as usual my fault: and we had got as far as sharing things like sandwiches and chocolate – and the work – on a taken-for-granted basis.

Billy at once indicated that with him it would be quite quite different. For Billy the class war existed as a bloody battlefield upon which he was the most active and tireless warrior alive. Within five seconds of our first meeting he was sharpening his claws.

It was at Cambridge Airport at five in the morning. We were to take two consignments of recently sold racehorses from Newmarket to Chantilly near Paris, and with all the loading and unloading at each end it would be a long day. Locking my car in the car park I was just thinking how quickly Conker and Timmie and I were getting to be able to do things when Yardman himself drove up alongside in a dark Jaguar Mark 10. There were two other men in the car, a large indistinct shape in the back, and in front, Billy.

Yardman stepped out of his car, yawned, stretched, looked up at the sky, and finally turned to me.

'Good-morning my dear boy,' he said with great affability. 'A nice day for flying.'

'Very,' I agreed. I was surprised to see him: he was not given to early rising or to waving us bon voyage. Simon Searle occasionally came if there were some difficulty with papers but not Yardman himself. Yet here he was with his black suit hanging loosely on his too thin frame and the cold early morning light making uncomplimentary shadows on his stretched coarsely pitted skin. The black-framed spectacles as always hid the expression in his deep-set eyes. After a month in his employ, seeing him at the wharf building two or three times a week on my visits for instructions, reports, and pay, I knew him no better than on that first afternoon. In their own way his defence barriers were as good as mine.

He told me between small shut-mouthed yawns that Timmie and Conker weren't coming, they were due for a few days leave. He had brought two men who obligingly substituted on such occasions and he was sure I would do a good job with them instead. He had brought them, he explained, because public transport wasn't geared to five o'clock rendezvous at Cambridge Airport.

While he spoke the front passenger climbed out of his car.

'Billy Watkins,' Yardman said casually, nodding between us.

'Good-morning, Lord Grey,' Billy said. He was about nineteen, very slender, with round cold blue eyes.

'Henry,' I said automatically. The job was impossible on any other terms and these were in any case what I preferred.

Billy looked at me with eyes wide, blank, and insolent. He spaced his words, bit them out and hammered them down.

'Good . . . morning . . . Lord . . . Grey.'

'Good-morning then, Mr. Watkins.'

His eyes flickered sharply and went back to their wide stare. If he expected any placatory soft soaping from me, he could think again.

Yardman saw the instant antagonism and it annoyed him.

'I warned you, Billy,' he began swiftly, and then as quickly stopped. 'You won't, I am sure, my dear boy,' he said to me gently, 'allow any personal ... er ... clash of temperaments to interfere with the safe passage of your valuable cargo.'

'No,' I agreed.

He smiled, showing his greyish regular dentures back to the molars. I wondered idly why, if he could afford such a car, he didn't invest in more natural looking teeth. It would have improved his unprepossessing appearance one hundred per cent.

'Right then,' he said in brisk satisfaction. 'Let's get on.'

The third man levered himself laboriously out of the car. His trouble stemmed from a paunch which would have done a pregnant mother of twins proud. About him flapped a brown storeman's overall which wouldn't do up by six inches, and under that some bright red braces over a checked shirt did a load-bearing job on some plain dark trousers. He was about fifty, going bald, and looked tired, unshaven and sullen, and he did not then or at any time meet my eyes.

What a crew, I thought resignedly, looking from him to Billy and back. So much for a day of speed and efficiency. The fat man, in fact, proved to be even more useless than he looked, and treated the horses with the sort of roughness which is the product of fear. Yardman gave him the job of loading them from their own horse-boxes up the long matting-covered side-walled ramp into the aircraft, while Billy and I inside fastened them into their stalls.

John, as Yardman called him, was either too fat or too scared of having his feet trodden on to walk side by side with each horse up the ramp: he backed up it, pulling the horse after him, stretching its head forward uncomfortably. Not surprisingly they all stuck their toes in hard and refused to budge. Yardman advanced on them from behind, shouting and waving a pitch fork, and prodded them forward again. The net result was some thoroughly upset and frightened animals in no state to be taken flying.

After three of them had arrived in the plane sweating, rolling their eyes and kicking out, I went down the ramp and protested.

Let John help Billy, and I'll lead the horses,' I said to Yardman. 'I don't suppose you'll want them to arrive in such an unnerved state that their owners won't use the firm again? Always supposing that they don't actually kick the aircraft to bits en route.'

He knew very well that this had really happened once or twice in the history of bloodstock transport. There was always the risk that a horse would go berserk in the air at the best of times: taking off with a whole planeload of het-up thoroughbreds would be a fair way to commit suicide.

He hesitated only a moment, then nodded.

'All right. Change over.'

The loading continued with less fuss but no more speed. John was as useless at installing the horses as he was at leading them.

Cargo on aeroplanes has to be distributed with even more care than on ships. If the centre of gravity isn't kept to within fairly close specific limits the plane won't fly at all, just race at high speed to the end of the runway and turn into scrap metal. If the cargo shifts radically in mid-air it keels the plane over exactly as it would a ship, but with less time to put it right, and no lifeboats handy as a last resort.

From the gravity point of view, the horses had to be stowed down the centre of the plane, where for their own comfort and balance they had to face forwards. This meant, in a medium sized aircraft such as Yardman's usually chartered, four pairs of horses standing behind each other. From the balance point of view, the horses had to be fairly immobile, and they also had to be accessible, as one had to be able to hold their heads and soothe them at take-off and landing. Each pair was therefore boxed separately, like four little islands down the centre of the plane. There were narrow gangways between the boxes and up both sides the whole length of the aircraft so that one could easily walk round and reach every individual horse to look after him.

The horses stood on large trays of peat which were bolted to the floor. The boxes of half inch thick wood panels had to be built up round the horses when each pair was loaded: one erected the forward end wall and the two sides, led in the horses and tied them up, added the back wall, and made the whole thing solid with metal bars banding the finished box. The bars were joined at each corner by lynch pins. There were three bars, at the top, centre and bottom. To prevent the boxes from collapsing inwards, each side of each box had to be separately fixed to the floor with chains acting as guy ropes. When the loading was complete, the result looked like four huge packing cases chained down, with the horses' backs and heads showing at the open tops.

As one couldn't afford to have a box fall apart in the air, the making of them, though not difficult, demanded attention and thoroughness. John conspicuously lacked both. He was also unbelievably clumsy at hooking on and tightening the guy chains, and he dropped two lynch pins which we couldn't find again: we had to use wire instead, which wouldn't hold if a strong-minded horse started kicking. By the end Billy and I were doing the boxes alone, while John stood sullenly by and watched: and Billy throughout made my share as difficult as he could.

It all took such a time that at least the three frightened horses had calmed down again before the pilot climbed aboard and started the engines. I closed the first of the big double doors we had loaded the horses through, and had a final view of Yardman on the tarmac, the slipstream from the propellers blowing his scanty hair up round the bald patch like a black sea anemone. The light made silver window panes of his glasses. He lifted his hand without moving his elbow, an awkward little gesture of farewell. I put my own hand up in acknowledgement and reply, and fastened the second door as the plane began to move.

As usual there was a crew of three flying the aircraft, pilot, co-pilot and engineer. The engineer, on all the trips I had so far made, was the one who got landed with brewing the coffee and who could also be reasonably asked to hold a pair of horses' heads during take-off. This one did so with far more familiarity than John.

The trip was a relatively short one and there was a helpful following wind, but we were over an hour late at the French end. When we had landed the airport staff rolled another ramp up to the doors and I opened them from inside. The first people through them were three unsmiling businesslike customs officials. With great thoroughness they compared the horses we had brought against our list and their own. On the papers for each horse were details of its physical characteristics and colour: the customs men checked carefully every star, blaze and sock, guarding against the possibility that some poorer animal had been switched for the good one bought. France proved more hard to satisfy and more suspicious than most other countries.

Content at length that no swindle had been pulled this time, the chief customs man politely gave me back the papers and said that the unloading could begin.

Four horseboxes from French racing stables had turned up to collect the new purchases. The drivers, phlegmatically resigned to all delays, were engaged in digging round their mouths with tooth picks in a solid little group. I went down the ramp and across to them and told them in which order the horses would be unloaded. My French vocabulary, which was shaky on many subjects, covered at least all horse jargon and was fairly idiomatic when it came to racing or bloodstock: at Anglia I had done quite a bit of work on French horses, and after six years knew my way round the French stud book as well as I did the British.

The drivers nodded, sucked their teeth and drove up the boxes in the right order. The first horse off (the last loaded at Cambridge) was a nondescript brown filly who was led into the waiting horse-box by the driver himself. He took her casually from my hand, slapped her rump in a friendly fashion, and by the time I led out the second horse he had already loaded her up and was on his way.

The other drivers had, more usually, brought one or two grooms with them, as they were to collect more than one horse. Billy took over leading the horses from the ramp, and I dismantled the boxes with John. This very nearly meant, in effect, doing it by myself. He dropped the bars, tripped over the anchorages on the floor, caught his fingers in the chains, and because of the paunch could do nothing which entailed bending down. Why Yardman employed him at all, I thought in irritation, was an unfathomable mystery.

We were supposed to be taking four horses back on the return trip, but by the time the last of our cargo had departed, not one of the four had turned up. When they were more than half an hour overdue, I walked over to the airport buildings and rang up one of the trainers concerned. Certainly he was sending two horses today he said, two four-year-old hurdlers which he had sold to an English stable, but they were not due at the airport until three o'clock. Fifteen hundred hours: it was typed clearly on his notice from Yardman Transport. A second trainer, consulted, said the same: and although I had no phone number for the third, I took it for granted that his notice had been identical. Either Simon, or more likely his typist, had written five instead of nought on all three. It was a bore, as it meant unloading at the end of the last trip when we would all be tired.

The day's troubles, however, had barely warmed up. On my way back to the plane I saw Billy and John standing beside it engaged in a furious argument, but they broke off before I was close enough to hear what they were saying. John turned his back and kicked moodily at the bottom of the ramp and Billy gave me his best insulting stare.

'What's the matter?' I said.

Billy pursed his lips into an expression which said clearly that it was none of my business, but after a visible inner struggle he did answer.

'He's got a headache,' he said, nodding at John. 'From the noise.'

A headache. That hardly explained the fat man's hopeless inefficiency, his sullenness, his shifty manner or his row with Billy. Nor, I realised in some surprise, did it explain why he hadn't spoken a single word to me the whole trip. But as repeating the question was unlikely to get a more fruitful answer, I shrugged and didn't bother.

'Get on board,' I said instead. 'We're going back empty. There's been a mix-up and we'll have to take the French horses back next time.'

'—' said Billy calmly. He used a word so obscene that I wondered what he used for when he was annoyed.

'I dare say,' I said dryly. 'Let's not waste any more time.'

John lumbered unwillingly and morosely up the ramp. Billy followed him after a pause, and I too let Billy get well ahead before I started after him. The spaces between us, I thought sardonically, were symbolic.

The airport staff removed the ramp, the plane's crew returned from their coffee break, and we proceeded back to Cambridge. On the way we sat on three separate bales of straw along the length of the aircraft and didn't even look at each other. John put his elbows on his knee and held his head in his hands, and Billy looked steadily and sightlessly at the cloud-dotted sky.

With all the sides of the boxes lying flat and strapped down on the peat trays the body of the aircraft seemed large and empty. In that state it echoed and was much noisier than usual, and I had some small sympathy for John's head. The plane was adapted, by the charter company who owned it, for any purpose that was required. The regularly spaced anchorages on the floor were as often used for fastening passenger seats as boxes for animals, and the airline would fly sixty people on a coach tour type holiday to Europe one day and a load of pigs or cattle the next. In between they merely bolted or unbolted the rows of seats and swept out the relevant debris, either farmyard manure and straw or cigarette packets and bags full of vomit.

One was not allowed to sweep out manure on to foreign soil. The whole lot had to be solemnly carted back to England to comply with quarantine regulations. The odd thing was, I reflected again, that the peat trays never seemed to smell. Not even now that there was no live horse smell to mask it. Of course this plane was unpressurised, so that fresh air continually found its way in, but all the same it smelled less than an ordinary stable, even after a whole day in a hot climate.

The first person on the plane at Cambridge was a cheerful underworked bareheaded excise officer who had come there especially to clear the horses. He bounced in as soon as the cockpit ladder was in position, made a loud rude comment to the pilot and came back through the galley into the main cabin.

'What have you done with them, then?' he said, looking round at the emptiness. 'Dumped them in the Channel?'

I explained the situation.

'Damn,' he said. 'I wanted to get off early. Well, did any of you buy anything in France?'

John didn't answer. I shook my head. Billy said offensively, 'We weren't given a sodding minute to get off the sodding plane.'

The Customs man in his navy blue suit glanced at me sideways in amusement. I gathered that he had met Billy before.

'O.K.' he said. 'See you this afternoon, then.'

He opened the big double doors, beckoned to the men outside who were wheeling up the ramp, and as soon as it was in position walked jauntily down it and back across the tarmac towards the airport building. As we were now more or less up to schedule through not having to load and unload the French hurdlers, John and Billy and I followed him in order to have lunch. I sat at one table and Billy and John ostentatiously moved to another as far away as they could get. But if Billy thought he could distress me in that way, he was wrong. I felt relieved to be alone, not shunned.

By one o'clock the horseboxes bringing the next consignment had arrived, and we started the loading all over again. This time I got the groom who had brought the horses to lead them up to the plane. Billy and I made the boxes, and John belched and got in the way.

When I had finished I went into the airport building, checked the horses' export papers with the customs man and persuaded the pilot away from his fourth cup of coffee. Up we went again into the clear wintry sky, across the grey sea, and down again in France. The same French customs men came on board, checked every horse as meticulously as before, and as politely let them go. We took down the boxes, led out the horses, saw them loaded into their horseboxes, and watched them depart.

This time the French hurdlers for the return journey had already arrived and without a pause we began getting them on board. As there were only four we had only two boxes to set up, which by that point I found quite enough. John's sole contribution towards the fourth journey was to refill and hang the haynets for the hurdlers to pick from on their way, and even at that he was clumsy and slow.

With the horses at length unconcernedly munching in their boxes we went across to the airport buildings, Billy and John ahead, I following. The only word I heard pass between them as they left down the ramp was 'beer.'

There was a technical delay over papers in one of the airport offices. One of the things I had grown to expect in the racehorse export business was technical delays. A journey without one of some sort was a gift. With up to twenty horses sometimes carried on one aeroplane there only had to be a small query about a single animal for the whole load to be kept waiting for hours. Occasionally it was nothing to do with the horses themselves but with whether the airlines owed the airport dues for another plane or another trip: in which case the airport wouldn't clear the horse plane to leave until the dues were paid. Sometimes the quibbling was enough to get one near to jumping out of the window. I was growing very good indeed at keeping my temper when all around were losing theirs and blaming it on me. Kipling would have been proud.

This time it was some question of insurance which I could do nothing to smooth out as it involved the owner of one of the hurdlers, who was fighting a contested claim on a road accident it had been slightly hurt in. The insurance company didn't want the horse to leave France. I said it was a bit late, the horse was sold, and did the insurance company have the right to stop it anyway. No one was quite sure about that. A great deal of telephoning began.

I was annoyed, mainly because the horse in question was in the forward of the two boxes: if we had to take it off the plane it meant dismantling the rear box and unloading the back pair first in order to reach it; and then reloading those two again once we had got it off. And with Billy and John full of all the beer they were having plenty of time to ship, this was likely to be a sticky manoeuvre. The horses' own grooms and motor boxes had long gone home. The hurdlers were each worth thousands. Who, I wondered gloomily, was I going to trust not to let go of them if we had to have them standing about on the tarmac.

The pilot ran me to earth and said that if we didn't take off soon we would be staying all night as after six o'clock he was out of time. We had to be able to be back at Cambridge at six, or he couldn't start at all.

I relayed this information to the arguing officials. It produced nothing but some heavy gallic shrugs. The pilot swore and told me that until twenty to five I would find him having coffee and after that he'd be en route for Paris. And I would have to get another pilot as he had worked for maximum hours for a long spell and was legally obliged now to have forty-eight hours rest.

Looking morosely out of the window across to where the plane with its expensive cargo sat deserted on the apron, I reflected that this was the sort of situation I could do without. And if we had to stay all night, I was going to have to sleep with those horses. A delightful new experience every day, I thought in wry amusement. Join Yardman Transport and see the world, every discomfort thrown in.

With minutes to spare, the insurance company relented: the hurdler could go. I grabbed the papers, murmuring profuse thanks, raced to dig out the pilot, and ran Billy to earth behind a large frothy glass. It was clearly far from his first.

'Get John,' I said shortly. 'We've got to be off within ten minutes.'

'Get him yourself,' he said with sneering satisfaction. 'If you can.'

'Where is he?'

'Half way to Paris.' He drank unconcernedly. 'He's got some whore there. He said he'd come back tomorrow on a regular airline. There isn't a sodding thing you can do about it, so put that in your pipe and smoke it.'

John's presence, workwise, made little difference one way or another. I really cared not a bent sou if he wanted to pay his own fare back. He was free enough. He had his passport in his pocket, as we all did. Mine was already dog-eared and soft from constant use. We had to produce them whenever asked, though they were seldom stamped as we rarely went into the passengers' immigration section of airports. We showed them more like casual passes than weighty official documents, and most countries were so tolerant of people employed on aircraft that one pilot told me he had left his passport in a hotel bedroom in Madrid and had been going unhindered round the world for three weeks without it while he tried to get it back.

'Ten minutes,' I said calmly to Billy. 'Fifteen, and you'll be paying your own fare back too.'

Billy gave me his wide-eyed stare. He picked up his glass of beer and poured it over my foot. The yellow liquid ran away in a pool on the glossy stone floor, froth bubbles popping round the edges.

'What a waste,' I said, unmoving. 'Are you coming?'

He didn't answer. It was too much to expect him to get up meekly while I waited, and as I wanted to avoid too decisive a clash with him if I could I turned away and went back alone, squelching slightly, to the aircraft. He came as I had thought he would, but with less than two minutes in hand to emphasize his independence. The engines were already running when he climbed aboard, and we were moving as soon as the doors were shut.

As usual during take-off and landing, Billy stood holding the heads of two horses and I of the other two. After that, with so much space on the half loaded aircraft, I expected him to keep as far from me as he could, as he had done all day. But Billy by then was eleven hours away from Yardman's restraining influence and well afloat on airport beer. The crew were all up forward in the cockpit, and fat useless John was sexbent for Paris.

Billy had me alone, all to himself.

Billy intended to make the most of it.

Chapter Four

'Your kind ought not to be allowed,' he said, with charming directness. He had to say it very loudly, also, on account of the noise of the aircraft.

I sat on a hay bale with my back against the rear wall of the cabin and looked at him as he stood ten feet in front of me with his legs apart for balance.

'Your kind, of course,' I shouted back, 'are the salt of the earth.'

He took a step forward and the plane bumped hard in an air pocket. It lurched him completely off his balance and he fell rolling on to his side. With sizzling fury, though it wasn't I who had pushed him, he raised himself up on one knee and thrust his face close to mine.

'— you,' he said.

At close quarters I could see how very young he was. His skin was still smooth like a child's and he had long thick eyelashes round those vast pale blue-grey searchlight eyes. His hair, a fairish brown, curled softly close to his head and down the back of his neck, cut short and in the shape of a helmet. He had a soft, full lipped mouth and a strong straight nose. A curiously sexless face. Too unlined to be clearly male, too heavily boned to be female.

He wasn't so much a man, not even so much a person, as a force. A wild, elemental, poltergeist force trapped barely controllably in a vigorous steel-spring body. You couldn't look into Billy's cold eyes from inches away and not know it. I felt a weird unexpected primitive tingle away down somewhere in my gut, and at the same time realised on a conscious level that friendliness and reason couldn't help, that there would be no winning over, ever, of Billy.

He began mildly enough.

'Your sort,' he yelled. 'You think you own the bloody earth. You soft lot of out-of-date nincompoops, you and your lah-di-dah bloody Eton.'

I didn't answer. He put his sneering face even nearer.

'Think yourself something special, don't you? You and your sodding ancestors.'

'They aren't very usual,' I yelled in his ear.

'What aren't?'

'Sodding ancestors.'

He had no sense of humour. He looked blank.

'You didn't spring from an acorn,' I said resignedly. 'You've had as many ancestors as I have.'

He stood up and took a step back. 'Bloody typical,' he shouted, 'making fun of people you look down on.'

I shook my head, got to my feet, and went along the plane to check the horses. I didn't care for useless arguments at the best of times, let alone those which strained the larynx. All four hurdlers were standing quiet in the boxes, picking peacefully at the haynets, untroubled by the noise. I patted their heads, made sure everything was secure, hesitated about going forward to the galley and cockpit for more friendly company, and had the matter settled for me by Billy.

'Hey,' he shouted. 'Look at this.' He was pointing downwards with one arm and beckoning me with sweeps of the other. There was anxiety on his face.

I walked back between the last box and the side wall of the aircraft, into the open space at the back, and across to Billy. As soon as I got near enough to see what he was pointing at, the anxiety on his face changed to spite.

'Look at this,' he shouted again, and jabbed his clenched fist straight at my stomach.

The only flicker of talent I had shown in a thoroughly mediocre and undistinguished career at Eton had been for boxing. I hadn't kept it up afterwards, but all the same the defence reflex was still there even after eight years. Billy's unexpected blow landed on a twisting target and my head did not go forward to meet a punch on the jaw. Or more likely in this case, I thought fleetingly, a chop on the back of the neck. Instead,

I gave him back as good as I got, a short hard jolt to the lower ribs. He was surprised, but it didn't stop him. Just the reverse. He seemed pleased.

There are better places for fighting than the back of an aircraft. The floor of that one was banded by the rows of seat anchorages, so that it was only a matter of time before one of us caught his foot in them and overbalanced, and it happened to be me, dodging away from a hand stretched at my throat. I went down flat on my back, unable to stop myself.

Billy fell deliberately and heavily on top of me, grinning fiercely with his own private pleasure, stabbing his elbows sharply into my chest and pressing me down hard on to the rigid anchorages. It hurt, and he meant it to. I kicked and rolled over, trying to get him underneath for a taste of it, but he was off like a cat at the crucial point and already aiming his boot as I stood up. I took that on the thigh and lunged accurately in return at his head. He just shook it briefly and went on punching, hard, quick, and with no respect for convention; but the pleasure left his face when he continued to get everything back with interest.

Thankful at least that he had produced no flick knife or bicycle chain I battled on, knowing in a cold detached part of my brain that I would gain nothing even if I won. Billy's resentment would be greater, not less, for being slogged by what he despised.

I did win in the end, if anyone did, but only because he had a belly full of beer and I hadn't. We were both very near to a standstill. I hit him finally very hard just below the navel, my fist sinking in deep, and he fell against the aft box retching and clutching himself and sliding down on to his knees. I caught hold of one of his wrists and twisted his arm up across his back.

'Now you listen, Billy,' I said loudly in his ear, panting to get enough breath, 'I don't see any point in fighting you, but I will if you make me. You can forget I'm an earl's son, Billy, and take me as I am, and this is what I am ...' I jerked his arm. 'Hard, Billy, not soft. As tough as necessary. Remember it.'

He didn't answer, perhaps because he was showing signs of being sick. I yanked him to his feet, pushed him across to the lavatory compartment in the tail, opened the door for him, and shoved him through. As the only lock was on the inside I couldn't make sure he stayed there, but from the sounds which presently issued from the open door, he was in no state to leave.

My own body ached from head to foot from his punches and kicks and from brisk contact with many sharp and knobbled edges, not least those spaced regularly on the floor. I sat down weakly on a straw bale and rubbed at a few places which didn't do much good, and was suddenly struck by something very odd indeed.

My face was completely unmarked.

I had bashed my head against one of the metal bars on the rear box and there was a tender swelling a little above my right ear. But Billy, I remembered dinstinctly, had not once even aimed at my face; not at any point higher than my throat.

For someone in the grip of obsessive fury, surely that was extraordinary,

I thought. The usual impulse in such a case was to 'smash his face in'.
Billy had actually taken pains not to. I didn't understand why. I thought
about it all the way to Cambridge.

It was dark when we landed and the cabin lights were on. The cheerful
customs man made his way through the plane, raised his eyebrows, and
asked where my two mates were.

'Billy is in there,' I nodded towards the lavatory, 'and John stayed in
France. He said he was coming back tomorrow.'

'O.K.' He checked through the horses' papers perfunctorily. 'All clear,'
he said, and as an afterthought: 'Buy anything?'

I shook my head, and he grinned, helped me open the double doors,
and whistled away down the ramp as soon as it was in position.

Billy had locked himself into the lavatory and refused to come out, so
I had to get one of the box drivers who had arrived to collect the cargo
to help me unload the horses. Unloading was always quicker and easier
than loading, but I had begun to stiffen up all over with bruises, and I
was glad when it was done. The helpful box driver led out the last horse,
an undistinguished brown mare, and before turning back to tidy up I
watched them step and slither down the ramp. That mare, I thought
idly, was very like the one we had taken across in the morning, though
the rug she wore might be misleading. But it couldn't of course be the
same. No one would ship a horse out in the morning and back in the
afternoon.

I turned away and began slowly to stack the box sides and the bars,
wished painfully that Billy hadn't been quite so rough, and forgot about
it.

The following day I went down to the wharf building and hooked
Simon out for a liquid lunch. We shambled down the road to the usual
hideous pub and he buried his face in a pint like a camel at an oasis.

'That's better,' he said, sighing, when a scant inch remained. 'How
did yesterday's trip go?'

'All right.'

His eyes considered me thoughtfully. 'Did you have a fall on Saturday?'

'No. A winner. Why?'

'You're moving a bit carefully, that's all.'

I grinned suddenly. 'You should see the other fellow.'

His face melted in comprehension and he laughed. 'I imagine I have,'
he said. 'Billy has a sunset of a black eye.'

'You've seen him?' I was surprised.

Simon nodded. 'He was in the office this morning, talking to
Yardman.'

'Getting his version in first, I suppose.'

'What happened?' he asked interestedly.

'Billy picked a fight.' I shrugged. 'He resents my existence. It's
ridiculous. No one can help what his father is. You can't choose your
birth.'

'You feel strongly about it,' Simon observed, ordering another pint. I
shook my head to his invitation.

'So would you, if you had to live with it. I mostly get treated as a villain or a nit or a desirable match, and not much else.' I was exaggerating, but not unduly.

'That last doesn't sound too bad,' he grinned.

'You haven't had half the debs' mums in London trying to net you for their daughters,' I said gloomily, 'with your own mother egging them on.'

'It sounds a wow.' He had no sympathy for such a fate.

'It isn't me they want,' I pointed out. 'It's only my name. Which is no fun at all. And on the other end from the wedding ring I get bashed around for exactly the same reason.'

'Very few can feel as strongly as Billy.'

I looked at him. 'There were the French in seventeen eighty-nine, remember? And the Russians in nineteen-seventeen. They all felt as strongly as Billy.'

'The English like their aristocrats.'

'Don't you believe it. They don't mind them from the social point of view because titles make the scandal sheets juicier. But they make damn sure they have no effective power. They say we are a joke, an anachronism, out of date, and weak and silly. They pretend we are these things so that we are kept harmless, so that no one will take us seriously. Think of the modern attitude to the House of Lords, for example. And you — you still think it funny that I want this sort of job, but you wouldn't think so if my father was a . . . a farmer, or a pubkeeper, or a school-master. But I'm me, here and now, a man of now, not of some dim glorious past. I am not an anachronism. I'm Henry Grey, conceived and born like everyone else, into this present world. Well, I insist on living in it. I am not going to be shoved off into an unreal playboy existence where my only function is to s're the next in line, which is what my parents want.'

'You could renounce your title, when you get it,' Simon pointed out calmly. He spotted a pin on the bar counter and absent-mindedly tucked it into his lapel. It was such a habit with him that he sported a whole row of them, like a dressmaker.

'I could,' I said, 'but I won't. The only good reason for doing that is to stay in the House of Commons, and I'll never be a politician, I'm not the type. Renouncing for any other reason would be just a retreat. What I want is for people to acknowledge that an earl is as good as the next man, and give him an equal chance.'

'But if you get on, they say it's because of your title, not because you have talent.'

'You are so right. But there's a prince or two, a few dukes' sons, and some others like me, all in the same boat just now, and I reckon that our generation, if we try hard enough, might in the end be treated on our own terms. Have some more beer.'

He laughed and agreed.

'I've never heard you say so much,' he said smiling.

'It's Billy's fault. Forget it.'

'I don't think I will.'

'You know something odd? I'm covered with bruises, and there isn't a single one on my face.'

He considered, drinking.

'He'd have got into trouble if he'd marked you for all to see.'

'I suppose so.'

'I gather you haven't told Yardman?'

'No.'

'Why not?'

I shrugged. 'I think he expected it, or something like it. He was ironic when he gave me the job. He must have known that sooner or later I would come up against Billy. And yesterday, he knew Billy would be after me. He warned me, in his way.'

'What are you going to do about it?'

'Nothing.'

'But what if you find yourself on another trip with Billy? I mean, you're bound to, sometime.'

'Yes, I know. Well, it's up to him entirely. I wouldn't start anything. I didn't yesterday. But I did tell him plainly that I'd fight back any time. And I am not, repeat *not*, leaving here because of him.'

'And you look so quiet and mild.' He smiled one-sidedly, looking down into his again empty glass. 'I think,' he said slowly, almost it seemed to me sadly, 'that one or two people in Yardman Transport have miscalculated about you, Henry.'

But when I pressed him to explain, he wouldn't.

With no more export trips to be flown until Thursday, I went the next day, Wednesday, to the races. Someone offered me a spare ride in the novice chase and for some reason it fretted me more than ever to have to refuse. 'I can't,' I said, explaining thoroughly so that he wouldn't think I was being rude. 'I'm only allowed to ride in fifty open races a season, and I'm already over the forty mark, and I've got mounts booked for Cheltenham and the Whitbread and so on. And if I ride too much now I'll be out of those, but thank you very much for asking me.'

He nodded understandingly and hurried off to find someone else, and in irritation two hours later I watched his horse canter home to a ten lengths win. It was some consolation, however, when immediately afterwards I was buttonholed by a large shrewd-faced man I knew very slightly, the father of another well occupied amateur jockey. Between them, father and son owned and trained half a dozen good hunter 'chasers which they ran only in amateur events with notoriously satisfactory results. But on this particular afternoon Mr. Thackery, a large-scale farmer from Shropshire, showed signs both of worry and indecision.

'Look,' he said, 'I'll not beat about the bush, I'm a blunt man, so I'm told. Now, what do you say to riding all my horses until the end of the season?'

I was astonished. 'But surely Julian . . . I mean, he hasn't had a bad fall or anything, has he?'

He shook his head. The worry stayed in place. 'Not a fall. He's got jaundice. Got it pretty badly, poor chap. He won't be fit again for weeks.

But we've a grand lot of horses this year and he won't hear of them not running just because he can't ride them. He told me to ask you, it's his idea.'

'It's very good of him,' I said sincerely. 'And thank you, I'd like to ride for you very much, whenever I can.'

'Good, then.' He hesitated, and added, 'Er . . . Julian told me to tell you, to ask you, if ten per cent of the prize money would be in order?'

'Thank you,' I said. 'That will be fine.'

He smiled suddenly, his heavy face lightening into wrinkles which made him look ten years younger. 'I wasn't sure about asking you, I'll tell you that, only Julian insisted on it. There's no nonsense about Henry, he said, and I can see he's right. He said Henry don't drink much, don't talk much, gets on with the job and expects to be paid for it. A pro at heart, he says you are. Do you want expenses?'

I shook my head. 'Ten per cent for winning. Nothing else.'

'Fair enough.' He thrust out his hand and I shook it.

'I'm sorry about Julian's jaundice,' I said.

Mr. Thackery's lips twitched. 'He said if you said that, that he hoped for the sake of our horses you were being hypocritical.'

'Oh, subtle stuff.' I pondered. 'Tell him to get up too soon and have a relapse.'

The next afternoon I went on a flight to New York.

With Billy.

The ice between us was as cold as the rarefied air outside the pressurized stratocruiser which took us. Yardman, I reflected, wasn't showing much sense in pushing us off together so soon, and on a two-day journey at that.

The wide cold stare was somewhat marred by the blackish streaks and yellow smudges left by my fist, and Billy was distinctly warier than he had been on the French journeys. There were no elementary taunts this time; but at the end of everything he said to me he tacked on the words 'Lord Grey,' and made them sound like an insult.

He tried nothing so crude as punching to make my trip memorable; instead he smashed down one of the metal bars as I was fixing a guy chain during the loading. I looked up angrily, squeezing four squashed right fingers in my left hand, and met his watchful waiting eyes. He was looking down at me with interest, with faintly sneering calculation, to see what I would do.

If anyone else had dropped the bar, I would have known it was accidental. With Billy, apart from the force with which it had landed, I knew it wasn't. But the day had barely begun, and the cargo was much too valuable to jeopardise for personal reasons, which I dare say he was counting on. When he saw that I was not going to retaliate, or at least not instantly, he nodded in satisfaction, picked up the bar with a small cold private smile, and calmly began putting it into place.

The loading was finished and the plane took off. There were thick dark red marks across my fingers an inch below the nails, and they throbbed all the way to America.

With us on that trip, looking after a full load of twelve horses, we took two other grooms, an elderly deaf one supplied by Yardman, and another man travelling privately with one particular horse. Owners occasionally sent their own grooms instead of entrusting their valued or difficult animals entirely to Yardman's, and far from resenting it I had learned from Timmie and Conker to be glad of the extra help.

The horse involved on this occasion had come from Norway, stayed in England overnight, and was bound for a racing stable in Virginia. The new owner had asked for the Norwegian groom to go all the way, at his expense, so that the horse should have continuous care on the journey. It didn't look worth it, I reflected, looking over at it idly while I checked the horses in the next box. A weak-necked listless chestnut, it had a straggle of hair round the fetlocks which suggested there had been a cart horse not far enough back in its ancestry, and the acute-angled hocks didn't have the best conformation for speed. Norway was hardly famed for the quality of its racing any more, even though it was possibly the Vikings who had invented the whole sport. They placed heaps of valued objects (the prizes) at varying distances from the starting point: then all the competitors lined up, and with wild whoops the race began. The prizes nearest the start were the smallest, the furthest away, the richest, so each rider had to decide what suited his mount best, a quick sprint or a shot at stamina. Choosing wrong meant getting no prize at all. Twelve hundred years ago fast sturdy racing horses had been literally worth a fortune in Norway, but the smooth skinned long legged descendants of those tough shaggy ponies didn't count for much in the modern thoroughbred industry. It was sentiment, I supposed, which caused an American to pay for such an inferior looking animal to travel so far from home.

I asked the middle-aged Norwegian groom if he had everything he wanted, and he said, in halting, heavily accented English, that he was content. I left him sitting on his hay bale staring mindlessly into space, and went on with my rounds. The horses were all travelling quietly, munching peacefully at their haynets, oblivious to rocketing round the world at six hundred miles an hour. There is no sensation of speed if you can't see an environment rushing past.

We arrived without incident at Kennedy airport, where a gum-chewing customs man came on board with three helpers. He spoke slowly, every second word an 'uh', but he was sharply thorough with the horses. All their papers were in order however, and we began the unloading without more ado. There was the extra job of leading all the horses through a tray of disinfectant before they could set foot on American soil, and while I was seeing to it I heard the customs man asking the Norwegian groom about a work permit, and the halting reply that he was staying for a fortnight only, for a holiday, the kindness of the man who owned the horse.

It was the first time I too had been to the States, and I envied him his fortnight. Owing to the five hours time difference, it was only six in the evening, local time, when we landed at Kennedy, and we were due to leave again at six next morning; which gave me about nine free hours in which to see New York. Although to my body mechanism it was already bedtime, I didn't waste any of them in sleeping.

The only snag to this was having to start another full day's work with eyes requiring matchsticks. Billy yawned over making the boxes as much as I did and only the third member of the team, the deaf elderly Alf, had had any rest. Since even if one shouted he could hear very little, the three of us worked in complete silence like robots, isolated in our own thoughts, with gaps as unbridgeable between us as between like poles of magnets. Unlike poles attract, like poles repel. Billy and I were a couple of cold Norths.

There was a full load going back again, as was usual on Yardman trips from one continent to another. He hated wasting space, and was accustomed to telephone around the studs when a long flight was on the books, to find out if they had anything to send or collect. The customers all liked it, for on full long distance loads Yardman made a reduction in the fares. Timmie and Conker had less cheerful views of this practice, and I now saw why. One's body didn't approve of tricks with the clock. But at the point of no return way out over the Atlantic I shed my drowsiness in one leaping heartbeat, and with horror had my first introduction to a horse going berserk in mid-air.

Old Alf shook my shoulder, and the fright in his face brought me instantly to my feet. I went where he pointed, up towards the nose of the aircraft.

In the second to front box a solidly muscled three-year-old colt had pulled his head collar to pieces and was standing free and untied in the small wooden square. He had his head down, his forelegs straddled, and he was kicking out with his hind feet in a fixed, fearful rhythm. White foamy sweat stood out all over him, and he was squealing. The companion beside him was trying in a terrified way to escape, his eyes rolling and his body pushing hard against the wooden side of the box.

The colt's hooves thudded against the back wall of the box like battering rams. The wooden panels shook and rattled and began to splinter. The metal bars banding the sides together strained at the corner lynch pins, and it only needed one to break for the whole thing to start disintegrating.

I found the co-pilot at my elbow, yelling urgently.

'Captain says how do you expect him to fly the aircraft with all this thumping going on. He says to keep that horse still, it's affecting the balance.'

'How?' I asked.

'That's your affair,' he pointed out. 'And for God's sake do something about it quickly.'

The back wall of the colt's box cracked from top to bottom. The pieces were still held in place by the guy chains, but at the present rate they wouldn't hold more than another minute, and then we should have on our minds a maddened animal loose in a pressurised aircraft with certain death to us all if he got a hoof through a window.

'Have you got a humane killer on board?' I said.

'No. This is usually a passenger craft. Why don't you bring your own?'

There were no rules to say one had to take a humane killer in animal transport. There should be. But it was too late to regret it.

'We've got drugs in the first aid kit,' the co-pilot suggested.

I shook my head. 'They're unpredictable. Just as likely to make him worse.' It might even have been a tranquilliser which started him off, I thought fleetingly. They often backfired with horses. And it would be quite impossible in any case to inject even a safe drug through a fine needle designed for humans into a horse as wild as this.

'Get a carving knife or something from the galley,' I said. 'Anything long and sharp. And quick.'

He turned away, stumbling in his haste. The colt's hind feet smashed one broken half of the back wall clean out. He turned round balefully, thrust his head between the top and centre banding bars, and tried to scramble through. The panic in his eyes was pitiful.

From inside his jerkin Billy calmly produced a large pistol and pointed it towards the colt's threshing head.

'Don't be a bloody fool,' I shouted. 'We're thirty thousand feet up.'

The co-pilot came back with a white handled saw-edged bread knife, saw the gun, and nearly fainted.

'D . . . don't,' he stuttered. 'D . . . d . . . don't.'

Billy's eyes were very wide. He was looking fixedly at the heaving colt and hardly seemed to hear. All his mind seemed to be concentrated on aiming the gun that could kill us all.

The colt smashed the first of the lynch pins and lunged forwards, bursting out of the remains of the box like flood water from a dam. I snatched the knife from the co-pilot and as the horse surged towards me stuck the blade into the only place available, the angle where the head joined the neck.

I hit by some miracle the carotid artery. But I couldn't get out of his way afterwards. The colt came down solidly on top of me, pouring blood, flailing his legs and rolling desperately in his attempts to stand up again.

His mane fell in my mouth and across my eyes, and his heaving weight crushed the breath in and out of my lungs like some nightmare form of artificial respiration. He couldn't right himself over my body, and as his struggles weakened he eventually got himself firmly wedged between the remains of his own box and the one directly aft of it. The co-pilot bent down and put his hands under my arm-pits and in jerks dragged me out from underneath.

The blood went on pouring out, hot sticky gallons of it, spreading down the gangways in scarlet streams. Alf cut open one of the hay bales and began covering it up, and it soaked the hay into a sodden crimson brown mess. I don't know how many pints of blood there should be in a horse: the colt bled to death and his heart pumped out nearly every drop.

My clothes were soaked in it, and the sweet smell made me feel sick. I stumbled down the plane into the lavatory compartment and stripped to the skin, and washed myself with hands I found to be helplessly trembling. The door opened without ceremony, and the co-pilot thrust a pair of trousers and a sweater into my arms. His overnight civvies.

'Here,' he said. 'Compliments of the house.'

I nodded my thanks, put them on, and went back up the plane, soothing the restive frightened cargo on the way.

The co-pilot was arguing with Billy about whether Billy would really have pulled the trigger and Billy was saying a bullet from a revolver wouldn't make a hole in a metal aircraft. The co-pilot cursed, said you couldn't risk it, and mentioned richochets and glass windows. But what I wanted to know, though I didn't ask, was what was Billy doing carrying a loaded pistol round with him in an underarm holster as casually as a wallet.

Chapter Five

I slept like the dead when I finally got home, and woke with scant time the next morning to reach Kempton for the amateurs' chase. After such a mangling week I thought it highly probable I would crown the lot by falling off the rickety animal I had in a weak moment promised to ride. But though I misjudged where it was intending to take off at the last open ditch and practically went over the fence before it while it put in an unexpected short one, I did in fact cling sideways like a limpet to the saddle, through sheer disinclination to hit the ground.

Though I scrambled back on top, my mount, who wouldn't have won anyway, had lost all interest, and I trotted him back and apologised to his cantankerous owner, who considered I had spoilt his day and was churlish enough to say so. As he outranked my father by several strawberry leaves he clearly felt he had the right to be as caustic as he chose. I listened to him saying I couldn't ride in a cart with a pig-net over it and wondered how he treated the professionals.

Julian Thackery's father caught the tail end of these remarks as he was passing, and looked amused: and when I came out of the weighing room after changing he was leaning against the rails waiting for me. He had brought the list of entries of his horses, and at his suggestion we adjourned to the bar to discuss them. He bought me some lemon squash without a quiver, and we sat down at a small table on which he spread out several sheets of paper. I realised, hearing him discussing his plans and prospects, that the year by year success of his horses was no accident: he was a very able man.

'Why don't you take out a public licence?' I said finally.

'Too much worry,' he smiled. 'This way it's a hobby. If I make mistakes, I have no one on my conscience. No one to apologise to or smooth down. No need to worry about owners whisking their horses away at an hour's notice. No risk of them not paying my fees for months on end.'

'You know the snags,' I agreed dryly.

'There's no profit in training,' he said. 'I break even most years, maybe finish a little ahead. But I work the stable in with the farm, you see. A lot of the overheads come into the farm accounts. I don't see how half these public trainers stay in business, do you? They either have to be rich to start with, or farmers like me, or else they have to bet, if they want a profit.'

'But they don't give it up,' I pointed out mildly. 'And they all drive large cars. They can't do too badly.'

He shook his head and finished his whisky. 'They're good actors, some of them. They put on a smiling not-a-care-in-the-world expression at the races when they've got the bank manager camping on their door-step back home. Well, now,' he shuffled the papers together, folded them, and tucked them into a pocket. 'You think you can get next Thursday off to go to Stratford?'

'I'm pretty sure of it, yes.'

'Right. I'll see you there, then.'

I nodded and we stood up to go. Someone had left an *Evening Standard* on the next table, and I glanced at it casually as we passed. Then I stopped and went back for a closer look. A paragraph on the bottom of the front page started 'Derby Hope Dead,' and told a few bald words that Okinawa, entered for the Derby, had died on the flight from the United States, and was consequently scratched from all engagements.

I smiled inwardly. From the lack of detail or excitement, it was clear the report had come from someone like the trainer to whom Okinawa had been travelling, not from airport reporters sniffing a sensational story. No journalist who had seen or even been told of the shambles on that plane could have written so starkly. But the horse had been disposed of now, and I had helped wash out the plane myself, and there was nothing to see any more. Okinawa had been well insured, a vet had certified that destroying him was essential, and I had noticed that my name on the crew list was spelled wrongly; H. Gray. With a bit of luck, and if Yardman himself had his way, that was the end of it. 'My dear boy,' he'd said in agitation when hurriedly summoned to the airport, 'it does business no good to have horses go crazy on our flights. We will not broadcast it, will we?'

'We will not,' I agreed firmly, more for my sake than for his.

'It was unfortunate . .' he sighed and shrugged, obviously relieved.

'We should have a humane killer,' I said, striking the hot iron.

'Yes. Certainly. All right. I'll get one.'

I would hold him to that, I thought. Standing peacefully in the bar at Kempton I could almost feel the weight of Okinawa and the wetness of his blood, the twenty-four hour old memory of lying under a dying horse still much too vivid for comfort. I shook myself firmly back into the present and went out with Julian's father to watch a disliked rival ride a brilliant finish.

Saturday night I did my level best to be civil to Mother's youngest female week-end guest, while avoiding all determined manoeuvres to leave me alone with her, and Sunday morning I slid away before dawn northwards to Lincolnshire.

Tom Wells was out on the apron when I arrived, giving his planes a personal check. He had assigned me, as I had learned on the telephone the previous morning, to fly three men to Glasgow for a round of golf. I was to take them in an Aztec and do exactly what they wanted. They were good customers. Tom didn't want to lose them.

'Good-morning, Harry,' he said as I reached him. 'I've given you Quebec Bravo. You planned your route?'

I nodded.

'I've put scotch and champagne on board, in case they forget to bring any,' he said. 'You're fetching them from Coventry – you know that – and taking them back there. They may keep you late at Gleneagles until after dinner. I'm sorry about that.'

'Expensive game of golf,' I commented.

'Hm,' he said shortly. 'That's an alibi. They are three tycoons who like to compare notes in private. They stipulate a pilot who won't repeat what he hears, and I reckon you fit that bill, Harry my lad, because you've been coming here for four years and if a word of gossip has passed your lips in that time I'm a second class gas fitter's mate.'

'Which you aren't.'

'Which I'm not.' He smiled, a pleasant solid sturdy man of forty plus, a pilot himself who knew chartering backwards and ran his own little firm with the minimum of fuss. Ex-R.A.F., of course, as most flyers of his age were: trained on bombers, given a love for the air, and let down with a bang when the service chucked them out as redundant. There were too many pilots chasing too few jobs in the post-war years, but Tom Wells had been good, persistent and lucky, and had converted a toe-hole co-pilot's job in a minor private airline into a seat on the board, and finally, backed by a firm of light aircraft manufacturers, had started his present company on his own.

'Give me a ring when you're leaving Gleneagles,' he said, 'I'll be up in the Tower myself when you come back.'

'I'll try not to keep you too late.'

'You won't be the last.' He shook his head. 'Joe Wilkins is fetching three couples from a week-end in Le Touquet. A dawn job, that'll be, I shouldn't wonder . . .'

I picked up the three impressive business men as scheduled and conveyed them to Scotland. On the way up they drank Tom Wells' Black and White and talked about dividend equalisation reserves, unappropriated profits, and contingent liabilities: none of which I found in the least bit interesting. They moved on to exports and the opportunities available in the European market. There was some discussion about 'whether the one and three-quarters was any positive inducement,' which was the only point of their conversation I really understood.

The one and three quarters, as I had learned at Anglia Bloodstock, was a percentage one could claim from the Government on anything one sold for export. The three tycoons were talking about machine tools and soft drinks, as far as I could gather, but the mechanism worked for bloodstock also. If a stud sold a horse abroad for say twenty thousand pounds, it received not only that sum from the buyer, but also one and three quarters per cent of it – three hundred and fifty pounds – from the Government. A carrot before the export donkey. A bonus. A pat on the head for helping the country's economy. In effect, it did influence some studs to prefer foreign buyers. But racehorses were simple to export: they needed no after sales service, follow-up campaign or multi-lingual advertising, which the tycoons variously argued were or were not worth the trouble. Then they moved on to taxation and I lost them again, the more so as they were some lowish clouds ahead over the Cheviots and at their request I was flying them below three thousand feet so that they could see the countryside.

I went up above the cloud into the quadrantal system operating above three thousand feet, where to avoid collision one had to fly on a steady regulated level according to the direction one was heading: in our case, going north west, four thousand five hundred or six thousand five hundred or eight thousand five hundred, and so on up.

One of the passengers commented on the climb and asked the reason for it, and wanted to know my name.

'Grey.'

'Well, Grey, where are we off to? Mars?'

I smiled. 'High hills, low clouds.'

'My God,' said the weightiest and oldest tycoon, patting me heavily on the shoulder, 'What wouldn't I give for such succinctness in my boardroom.'

They were in good form, enjoying their day as well as making serious use of it. The smell of whisky in the warm luxurious little cabin overcame even that of hot oil, and the expensive cigar smoke swirled huskily in my throat. I enjoyed the journey, and for Tom's sake as well as my own pride, knowing my passengers were connoisseurs of private air travel, put them down on the Gleneagles strip like a whisper on a lake.

They played golf and drank and ate; and repeated the programme in the afternoon. I walked on the hills in the morning, had lunch, and in the late afternoon booked a room in the hotel, and went to sleep. I guess it was a satisfactory day all round.

It was half past ten when the reception desk woke me by telephone and said my passengers were ready to leave, and eleven before we got away. I flew back on a double dogleg, making for the St. Abbs radio beacon on the Northumberland coast and setting a course of one sixty degrees south south east from there on a one five two nautical mile straight course to Ottringham, and then south west across country to Coventry, coming in finally on their 122.70 homer signal.

The tycoons, replete, talked in mellow, rumbling, satisfied voices, no longer about business but about their own lives. The heaviest was having trouble over currency regulations with regard to a villa he had bought on the Costa del Sol: the government had slapped a two thousand pound ceiling on pleasure spending abroad, and two thousand would hardly buy the bath taps . . .

The man sitting directly behind me asked about decent yachts available for charter in the Aegean, and the other two told him. The third said it was really time his wife came back from Gstaad, she had been there for two months, and they were due to go to Nassau for Easter. They made me feel poverty-stricken, listening to them.

We landed safely at Coventry, where they shook my hand, yawning, thanked me for a smooth trip, and ambled off to a waiting Rolls, shivering in the chilly air. I made the last small hop back to Fenland and found Tom, as good as his word on duty in the control tower to help me down. He yelled out of the window to join him, and we drank coffee out of a thermos jug while he waited for his Le Touquet plane to come back. It was due in an hour: earlier than expected. Apparently the client had struck a losing streak and the party had fizzled out.

'Everything go all right with your lot?' Tom said.

'They seemed happy,' I nodded, filling in the flight details on his record chart and copying them into my own log book.

'I suppose you want your fee in flying hours, as usual?'

I grinned. 'How did you guess?'

'I wish you'd change your mind and work for me permanently.'

I put down the pen and stretched, lolling back on the wooden chair with my hands laced behind my head. 'Not yet. Give it three or four years; perhaps then.'

'I need you now.'

Need. The word was sweet. 'I don't know ... I'll think it over again, anyway.'

'Well, that's something I suppose.' He ruffled his thinning light brown hair and rubbed his hands down over his face, his skin itching with tiredness. 'Sandwich?'

'Thanks.' I took one. Ham, with French mustard, made in their bungalow by Tom's capable wife Janie, not from the airport canteen. The ham was thick and juicy, home cooked in beer. We ate in silence and drank the hot strong coffee. Outside the glass-walled high up square room the sky grew a thick matt black, with clouds drifting in to mask the stars. The wind was slowly backing, the atmospheric pressure falling. It was getting steadily colder. Bad weather on its way.

Tom checked his instruments, frowned, leaned back on his chair and twiddled his pencil. 'The forecast was right,' he said gloomily, 'Snow tomorrow.'

I grunted sympathetically. Snow grounded his planes and caused a hiatus in his income.

'Have to expect it in February, I suppose,' he sighed.

I nodded in agreement. I wondered if Stratford races would be snowed off on Thursday. I wondered if weather interfered much with Yardman's trips. I reflected that Janie Wells made good coffee, and that Tom was a sound sensible man. Untroubled, organised surface thoughts. And it was the last night I ever spent in my calm emotional deep-freeze.

The sky was a sullen orange grey when we took off at eight the next morning from Gatwick, the as yet unshed snow hanging heavily as spawn in a frog's belly. We were carrying eight brood mares in an old unpressurised D.C.4, flying away from the incoming storm, en route to Milan. Timmie and Conker were back to my relief, but neither had had a scintillating holiday, by the sound of it. I overheard Conker, a much harassed small father of seven large hooligans, complaining as he loaded the cargo that he'd done nothing but cook and wash up while his wife curled up in bed with what was, in his opinion, opportunist malingering influenza. Timmie showed his sympathy in his usual way: a hearty gear-changing sniff. A thick-set black haired square little Welshman, he suffered from interminable catarrh and everyone around him suffered also. It had been his sinuses, he unrepentantly said after one particularly repulsive spitting session, which had stopped him going down the mines like his pa. The February holiday, Timmie agreed, was not much cop.

'How many holidays do you have?' I asked, fixing chains.

'A week off every two months,' Conker said. 'Blimey mate, don't tell me you took this job without asking that.'

'I'm afraid I did.'

'You'll be exploited,' Conker said seriously. 'When you start a job, you want your terms cut and dried, wages, overtime, holidays with pay, bonuses, superannuation, the lot. If you don't stand up for your rights, no one else will, there isn't a union for us, you know, bar the agricultural workers, if you care for that which I don't. And old Yardman, he don't give nothing away you know. You want to make sure about your weeks off, mate, or you won't get any. I'm telling you.'

'Well . . . thank you. I'll ask him.'

'Aw, look man,' said Timmie in his soft Welsh voice, 'We get other times off too. You don't want to work yourself to death. Mr. Yardman don't hold you to more than two trips a week, I'll say that for him. If you don't want to go, that is.'

'I see,' I said. 'And if you don't go, Billy and Alf do?'

'That's about it,' agreed Conker. 'I reckon.' He fitted the last lynch pin on the last box and rubbed his hands down the sides of his trousers.

I remembered Simon saying that my predecessor Peters had been a belligerent stand-on-your-rights man, and I supposed that Conker had caught his anti-exploitation attitude from him, because it seemed to me, from what they'd said, that Conker and Timmie both had free time positively lavished up them. A day's return trip certainly meant working a continuous stretch of twelve hours or more, but two of those in seven days wasn't exactly penal servitude. Out of interest I had added up my hours on duty some weeks, and even at the most they had never touched forty. They just don't know when they are well off, I thought mildly, and signalled to the airport staff to take the ramp away.

The D.C.4 was noisy and very cramped. The gangways between and alongside the horses were too narrow for two people to pass, and in addition one had to go forward and backward along the length of the plane bent almost double. It was, as usual, normally a passenger ship, and it had low-hung luggage shelves along its length on both sides. There were catches to hold the racks up out of the way, but they were apt to shake open in flight and it was more prudent to start with all the racks down than have them fall on one's head. This, added to the angled guy chains cutting across at shin level, made walking about a tiresome process and provided the worst working conditions I had yet struck. But Conker, I was interested to notice, had no complaints. Peters, maybe, hadn't been with him on a D.C.4.

After take-off, the horses all being quiet and well behaved, we went forward into the galley for the first cup of coffee. The engineer, a tall thin man with a habit of raising his right eyebrow five or six times rather fast when he asked a question, was already dispensing it into disposable mugs. Two full ones had names pencilled on: Patrick and Bob. The engineer picked them up and took them forward to the pilot and co-pilot in the cockpit. Coming back, the engineer asked our names and wrote us each a mug.

'There aren't enough on board for us to throw them away every time,' he explained, handing me 'Henry'. 'Sugar?' He had a two-pound bag of granulated, and a red plastic spoon. 'I know the way you lot drink coffee. The skipper, too.'

We drank the scalding brown liquid: it didn't taste of coffee, but if you thought of it as a separate unnamed thirst quencher, it wasn't too bad. In the galley the engine noise made it necessary to shout loudly to be heard, and the vibration shook concentric ripples in the coffee. The engineer sipped his gingerly over the scrawled word 'Mike'.

'You've got a right load there,' he commented. 'A ship full of expectant mums, aren't they?'

Conker, Timmie and I nodded in unison.

'Are they Italian?'

Together we shook our heads. Music hall stuff.

'What are they going for, then?'

'They are English mares going to be mated with Italian sires,' explained Conker, who had once worked in a stud and would be positively happy if one of the mares foaled down prematurely on the flight.

'Pull the other one, it's got bells on,' said the engineer.

'No, it's right,' said Conker. 'They have to have the foals they are carrying now in the stud where their next mate is.'

'Why?' The agile eyebrow worked overtime.

'Ah,' said Conker seriously. 'The gestation period for horses is eleven months, right? And a brood mare has a foal every twelve months, right? So there's only four weeks left between production and – er – reproduction, do you see? And in those four weeks the new foal isn't fit for travelling hundreds of miles in the freezing cold, so the mares have to have the foals in the stud of their next mate, Get?'

'I get,' agreed the engineer. 'I get indeed.'

'That one,' said Conker admiringly, pointing out in the foremost box an elegant brown silky head which owing to the general lack of space was almost in the galley, 'that one's going to Molvedo.'

'How do you know?' asked Timmie interestedly.

'Horse box driver told me.'

The co-pilot came back from the cockpit and said the skipper wanted a refill.

'Already? That man's a tank.' The engineer poured into the Patrick mug.

'Here,' said the co-pilot, handing it to me. 'Take it to him, will you? I'm off to see a man about a dog.' He brushed under Molvedo's future wife's inquisitive nose and bent down for the obstructed walk down to the john.

I took the steaming mug forward into the cockpit. The pilot, flying in white-than-white shirtsleeves despite the zero temperature outside, stretched out a languid hand and nodded his thanks. I stayed for a second looking round at the banked instruments, and he glanced up at me and gestured to me to put my ear down to his mouth. The noise there made even ordinary shouting impossible.

'Are you the head chap with the horses?'

'Yes.'

'Like to sit there for a bit?' He pointed to the empty co-pilot's seat.

'Yes, I would.' He gestured permissively, and I edged sideways into the comfortable bucket seat beside him. The cockpit was tiny, considering how much had to be packed into it, and battered and dented with age. It was also, to me, very much my home.

I studied the instruments with interest. I had never flown a four engined craft, only one and two, for the excellent reason that there were no four engined planes at Fenland. As even small two engined jobs like the Aztec I had taken to Gleneagles the day before cost nearly thirty-five pounds per flying hour to hire from Tom, I thought it unlikely I would ever raise enough cash for a course on the really big stuff, even if I could use the qualification once I got it. You couldn't just go up alone for an afternoon's jolly in an airliner: they simply weren't to be had. None of which stopped me for a moment being intent on learning everything I could.

The pilot, Patrick, indicated that I should put on the combined set of earphones and mouthpiece which was hanging over the semi-circular wheel. I slid it on to my head, and through it he began to explain to me what all the switches and dials were for. He was the first pilot I'd flown with on Yardman's trips who had taken such trouble, and I listened and nodded and felt grateful, and didn't tell him I knew already most of what he was saying.

Patrick was a big striking looking man of about thirty, with straight dark auburn hair cut a bit theatrically in duck tails, and light amber eyes like a cat. His mouth turned naturally up at the corners so that even in repose he seemed to be smiling, as if everything in the world was delightful, with no evil to be found anywhere. Nor, I later proved, did the implication of that curve lie: he persisted in believing the best of everybody, even with villainy staring him in the face. He had the illogical faith in human goodness of a probation officer, though in that first half-hour all I learned about him was that he was a gentle, careful, self-assured and eminently safe pilot.

He tuned in to the frequency of the radio beacon at Dieppe, explaining it to me as he went, and took a weather report there before turning on to the course to Paris.

'We'll go down to the Med and fly along the coast,' he said. 'There's too much cloud over the Alps to go straight across. Not being pressurised we ought not to go above ten thousand feet but fourteen thousand or so doesn't hurt unless you've got a bad heart. Even that doesn't give us enough in hand over the Alps in the present conditions, so I'm going the long way round.'

I nodded, thoroughly approving.

He checked the de-icing equipment for a second time in ten minutes and said, 'This bird won't fly with more than a quarter of a ton of ice on her, and the de-icers were U.S. last week.' He grinned. 'It's O.K., I've checked them six times since they were repaired, they're doing all right.'

He peeled and ate one of a large bunch of bananas lying on the ledge over the instrument panel, then calmly unhinged the window beside him a few inches and threw the skin out. I laughed to myself in appreciation and began to like Patrick a good deal.

The co-pilot returned to claim his place, and I went back to the horses for the rest of the journey. Uneventfully we went down across France to Dijon, turned south down the Rhone valley, east at Saint Tropez, and north again at Albenga, landing at Malpensa Airport, Milan, in exactly four hours from Gatwick.

Italy was cold. Shivering as the open doors let in air thirty degrees below the cabin temperature we watched about ten airport men in royal blue battle dress push the wide top-class ramp into position, and waited while three customs men made their way over from the building. They came up the ramp, and the eldest of them said something in his own language.

'Non parlo italiano,' I said apologetically, which useful sentence was all I knew.

'Non importa,' he said. He took from me the mares' temporary import permits which had been made out in both English and Italian, and his two assistants began going from horse to horse calling out their descriptions.

All was in order. He gave me back the papers with a courteous nod of the head, and led his shadows away down the ramp. Again we went through the familiar routine of transferring the cargo from the plane to the waiting horse boxes, Conker making a great fuss of the mare going to Molvedo.

With an hour to spare before we set about loading another cargo of mares bound in the opposite direction for the same reason, Conker, Timmie and I walked across a quarter of a mile of tarmac to the airport building to have lunch. We were met at the door by Patrick, looking very official with gold-braided shoulder tabs on his navy uniform jacket, and wearing an expression of resignation.

'We can't go back today.' he said, 'so you chaps don't need to hurry over your beer.'

'What's up, then?' asked Timmie, sniffing loudly.

'A blizzard. Came down like a burst eiderdown in a wind tunnel after we left this morning. It's raging all over the south and half-way across the channel, and snowing clear up to John o' Groats. The bottom's dropped out of the barometer and . . . well, anyway, my instructions are not to go back.'

'All that pasta,' said Conker philosophically. 'It does my tripes no good.'

He and Timmie went off to the snack bar and Patrick showed me the telegraph office to send 'no go' messages to Yardman and the expectant studs. After that we went back to the aircraft, where he collected his overnight bag and I turned homewards the arriving convoy of Italian mares. He waited for me to finish and helped me shut the big double doors from inside at the top of the ramp, and we walked forward across the flattened dismantled boxes, through the galley, and down the staircase which had been wheeled up to the door just behind the cockpit.

'Where will you stay?' he said.

'Hotel, I suppose,' I said vaguely.

'If you like, you could come with me. There's a family in Milan I berth with when I'm stranded, and there's room for two.'

I had a strong inclination, as usual, to be by myself, but principally because I couldn't even ask for a hotel room in Italian let alone find entertainment except looking at architecture for the rest of the day, I accepted his offer, and thanked him.

'You'll like them,' he said.

We went two hundred yards in silence.

'Is it true,' he said, 'that you're a viscount?'

'No,' I said casually. 'A Boeing 707.'

He chuckled. 'A bleeding viscount, that little Welshman said you were, to be precise.'

'Would it make any difference to you if I were?'

'None whatever.'

'That's all right, then.'

'So you are?'

'On and off.'

We went through the glass doors into the hall of the airport. It was spacious, airy, glass-walled, stone floored. Along one side stretched a long gift counter with souvenir presents crowded in a row of display cases and stacked on shelves at the back. There were silk ties on a stand, and dolls in local dress scattered on the counter, and trays of paper-backed books and local view post-cards. In charge of this display stood a tall dark-haired girl in a smooth black dress. She saw us coming and her coolly solemn face lit into a delicious smile.

'Patrick,' she said. 'Hullo, Patrick, come sta?'

He answered her in Italian, and as an afterthought waved his hand at me and said 'Gabriella, . . . Henry.' He asked her a question, and she looked at me carefully and nodded.

'Si,' she said. 'Henry anche.'

'That's fixed, then,' said Patrick cheerfully.

'You mean,' I said incredulously, 'that we are going to stay with – er – Gabriella?'

He stiffened slightly. 'Do you object?'

I looked at Gabriella, and she at me.

'I think,' I said slowly, 'that it is too good to be true.'

It wasn't for another ten minutes, during which time she talked to Patrick while looking at me, that I realised that I spoke no Italian and the only English word that she knew was 'Hullo'.

Chapter Six

You couldn't say it was reasonable, it was just electric. I found out between one heartbeat and the next what all the poets throughout the ages had been going on about. I understood at last why Roman Anthony threw away his honour for Egyptian Cleopatra, why Trojan Paris caused a ten years war abducting Greek Helen, why Leander drowned on one of his risky nightly swims across the Dardanelles to see Hero. The distance from home, the mystery, the unknownness, were a part of it: one couldn't feel like that for the girl next door. But that didn't explain why it hadn't happened before: why it should be this girl, this one alone who fizzed in my blood.

I stood on the cool stone airport floor and felt as if I'd been struck by lightning: the world had tilted, the air was crackling, the grey February day blazed with light, and all because of a perfectly ordinary girl who sold souvenirs to tourists.

The same thing, fantastically, had happened to her as well. Perhaps it had to be mutual, to happen at all. I don't know. But I watched the brightness grow in her eyes, the excitement and gaiety in her manner, and I knew that against all probability it was for me. Girls were seldom moved to any emotion by my brown haired tidy unobtrusive self, and since I rarely set out to make an impression on them, I even more rarely did so. Even the ones who wanted to marry my title were apt to yawn in my face. Which made Gabriella's instant reaction doubly devastating.

'For God's sake,' said Patrick in amusement, when she didn't answer a twice repeated question, 'will you two stop gawping at each other?'

'Gabriella,' I said.

'Si?'

'Gabriella . . .'

Patrick laughed. 'You're not going to get far like that.'

'Parla francese?' she said anxiously.

Patrick translated. 'Do you speak French.'

'Yes.' I laughed with relief. 'Yes, more or less.'

'E bene,' she sighed smiling. 'E molto molto bene.'

Perhaps because we were unburdened by having to observe any French proprieties and because we both knew already that we would need it later on, we began right away using the intimate form tu instead of vous, for 'you'. Patrick raised his eyebrows and laughed again and said in three languages that we were nuts.

I *was* nuts, there was no getting away from it. Patrick endured the whole afternoon sitting at a table in the snack bar drinking coffee and telling me about Gabriella and her family. We could see her from where we sat, moving quietly about behind her long counter, selling trinkets to departing travellers. She was made of curves, which after all the flat hips, flat stomachs, and more or less flat chests of the skinny debs at home, was as warming as a night-watchman's fire on a snowy night. Her oval pale olive-skinned face reminded me of mediaeval Italian paintings, a type of bone structure which must have persisted through centuries, and her expression, except when she smiled, was so wholly calm as to be almost unfriendly.

It struck me after a while, when I watched her make two or three self-conscious customers nervous by her detached manner, that selling wasn't really suited to her character, and I said so, idly, to Patrick.

'I agree,' he said dryly. 'But there are few places better for a smuggler to work than an airport.'

'A . . . *smuggler?* I don't believe it.' I was aghast.

Patrick enjoyed his effect. 'Smuggler,' he nodded. 'Definitely.'

'No,' I said.

'So am I,' he added smiling.

I looked down at my coffee, very disturbed. 'Neither of you is the type.'

'You're wrong, Henry. I'm only one of many who brings . . . er . . . goods . . . in to Gabriella.'

'What,' I said slowly, fearing the answer, 'are the goods?'

He put his hand into his jacket pocket, pulled out a flat bottle about five inches high, and handed it to me. A printed chemist's label on the front said 'Two hundred aspirin tablets B.P.', and the brown glass bottle was filled to the brim with them. I unscrewed the top, pulled out the twist of cotton wool, and shook a few out on to my hand.

'Don't take one,' said Patrick, still smiling. 'It wouldn't do you any good at all.'

'They're not aspirins.' I tipped them back into the bottle and screwed on the cap.

'No.'

'Then what?'

'Birth control pills,' he said.

'*What?*'

'Italy is a Roman Catholic country,' he observed. 'You can't buy these pills here. But that doesn't stop women wanting to avoid being in a constant state of baby production, does it? And the pills are marvellous for them, they can take them without the devoutest husbands knowing anything about it.'

'Good God,' I said.

'My brother's wife collects them at home from her friends and so on, and when she has a bottle full I bring it to Gabriella and she passes them on at this end. I know for a fact that at least four other pilots do the same, not to mention a whole fleet of air hostesses, and she admitted to me once that a day seldom goes by without some supplies flying in.'

'Do you ... well ... sell ... them to Gabriella?'

He was quite shocked, which pleased me. 'Of course not. She doesn't sell them, either. They are a gift, a service if you like, from the women of one country to the women of another. My sister-in-law and her friends are really keen on it, they don't see why any woman in the world should have to risk having a child if she doesn't want one.'

'I've never thought about it,' I said, fingering the bottle.

'You've never had a sister who's borne six children in six years and collapsed into a shattering nervous break-down when she started the seventh.'

'Gabriella's sister?'

He nodded. 'That's why she got some pills, in the first place. And the demand just grew and grew.'

I gave him back the bottle and he put it in his pocket. 'Well?' he said, with a hint of challenge.

'She must be quite a girl,' I said, 'to do something like this.'

His curving mouth curved wider. 'If she smuggled the Crown Jewels you'd forgive her. Confess it.'

'Whatever she did,' I said slowly.

The amusement died right out of his face and he looked at me soberly. 'I've heard of this sort of thing,' he said. 'But I've never seen it happen before. And you didn't even need to speak to each other. In fact, it's just damn lucky you *can* speak to each other ...'

Three times during the afternoon I made sure of that. She would get into trouble, she said, if she just talked to me when she should be working, so I bought presents, separately, for my father, mother and sister, taking a long time over each choice. Each time she spoke and looked at me in a kaleidoscopic mixture of excitement, caution and surprise, as if she too found falling helplessly in love with a complete stranger an overwhelming and almost frightening business.

'I like that one.'

'It costs six thousand lire.'

'That is too dear.'

'This one is cheaper.'

'Show me some others.'

We began like that, like school-day text books, in careful stilted French, but by the end of the afternoon, when she locked the display cases and left with Patrick and me through the employees' entrance, we could talk with some ease. I perhaps knew most French of the three of us, then Gabriella, then Patrick; but his Italian was excellent, so between us everything could in one language or another be understood.

We left the airport in a taxi, and as soon as we were on the move Patrick gave her the aspirin bottle. She thanked him with a flashing smile and asked him if they were all the same sort. He nodded, and explained they'd come from some R.A.F. wives whose husbands were away on a three months overseas course.

From her large shoulder-sling bag of black leather she produced some of the bright striped wrapping paper from her airport gift shop and a large packet of sweets. The sweets and the aspirin bottle were expertly whisked into a ball shaped parcel with four corners sticking up on top like leaves on a pineapple, and a scrap of sticky tape secured them.

The taxi stopped outside a dilapidated narrow terrace house in a poor looking street. Gabriella climbed out of the taxi, but Patrick waved me back into my seat.

'She doesn't live here,' he said. 'She's just delivering the sweets.'

She was already talking to a tired looking young woman whose black dress accentuated the pallor of her skin, and whose varicose veins were the worst I had seen, like great dark blue knobbed worms networking just under the surface of her legs. Round her clung two small children with two or three more behind in the doorway, but she had a flat stomach in her skimpy dress and no baby in her arms. The look she gave Gabriella and her pretty present were all the reward that anyone would need. The children knew that there were sweets in the parcel. They were jumping up trying to reach it as their mother held it above their heads, and as we left she went indoors with them, and she was laughing.

'Now,' said Patrick, turning away from the window, 'we had better show Henry Milan.'

It was getting dark and was still cold, but not for us. I wouldn't have noticed if it had been raining ice. They began by marching me slowly around the Piazza del Duomo to see the great gothic cathedral and the Palazzo Reale, and along the high glass arcade into the Piazza della Scala to gaze at the opera house, which Gabriella solemnly told me was the second largest theatre in Europe, and could hold three thousand six hundred people.

'Where is the largest?' said Patrick.

'In Naples,' she said smiling. 'It is ours too.'

'I suppose Milan has the biggest cathedral, then,' he teased her.

'No,' she laughed, showing an unsuspected dimple, 'Rome.'

'An extravagant nation, the Italians.'

'We were ruling the world while you were still painting yourselves blue.'

'Hey, hey,' said Patrick.

'Leonardo da Vinci lived in Milan,' she said.

'Italy is undoubtedly the most beautiful country in the world and Milan is its pearl.'

'Patrick, you are a great idiot,' she said affectionately. But she was proud indeed of her native city, and before dinner that evening I learned that nearly a million and a half people lived there and that there were dozens of museums, and music and art schools, and that it was the best manufacturing town in the country, and the richest, and its factories made textiles and paper and railway engines and cars. And, in fact, aeroplanes.

We ate in a quiet warmly lit little restaurant which looked disconcertingly like Italian restaurants in London but smelled quite different, spicy and fragrant. I hardly noticed what I ate: Gabriella chose some sort of veal for us all, and it tasted fine, like everything else that evening. We drank two bottles of red local wine which fizzed slightly on the tongue, and unending little gold cups of black coffee. I knew even then that it was because we were all speaking a language not our own that I felt liberated from my usual self. It was so much easier to be uninhibited away from everything which had planted the inhibitions: another sky, another culture, a time out of time. But that only made the way simpler, it didn't make the object less real. It meant I didn't have chains on my tongue; but what I had said wasn't said loosely, it was still rooted in some unchanging inner core. On that one evening in Milan I learned what it was like to be gay deep into the spirit, and if for nothing else I would thank Gabriella for that all my life.

We talked for hours: not profoundly, I dare say, but companionably: at first about the things we had done and seen that day, then of ourselves, our childhood. Then of Fellini's films, and a little about travel, and then, in ever widening ripples, of religion, and our own hopes, and the state the world was in. There wasn't an ounce of natural reforming zeal among the three of us, as perhaps there ought to have been when so much needed reforming; but faith didn't move mountains any more, it got bogged down by committees, Patrick said, and the saints of the past would be smeared as psychological misfits today.

'Could you imagine the modern French army allowing itself to be inspired and led into battle by a girl who saw visions?' he said. 'You could not.'

It was true. You could not.

'Psychology,' Patrick said, with wine and candle light in his yellow eyes, 'is the death of courage.'

'I don't understand,' protested Gabriella.

'Not for girls,' he said. 'For men. It is now not considered sensible to take physical risks unless you can't avoid them. Ye gods, there's no quicker way to ruin a nation than to teach its young men it's foolish to take risks. Or worse than foolish, they would have you believe.'

'What do you mean?' she said.

'Ask Henry. He'll cheerfully go out and risk his neck on a racehorse any day of the week. Ask him why.'

'Why?' she said, half-serious, half-laughing, the glints of light in her dark eyes outpointing the stars.

'I like it,' I said. 'It's fun.'

Patrick shook his red head. 'You look out, pal, you mustn't go around admitting that sort of thing these days. You've got to say you do it only for the money, or you'll be labelled as a masochistic guilt complex before you can say . . . er . . . masochistic guilt complex.'

'Oh yeah?' I said, laughing.

'Yeah, damn it, and it's not funny. It's deadly serious. The knockers have had so much success that now it's fashionable to say you're a coward. You may not *be* one, mind, but you've got to *say* so, just to prove you're normal. Historically, it's fantastic. What other nation ever went around saying on television and in the press and at parties and things that cowardice is normal and courage is disgusting? Nearly all nations used to have elaborate tests for young men to prove they were brave. Now in England they are taught to settle down and want security. But bravery is built in somewhere in human nature and you can't stamp it out any more than the sex urge. So if you outlaw ordinary bravery it bursts out somewhere else, and I reckon that's what the increase in crime is due to. If you make enjoying danger seem perverted, I don't see how you can complain if it becomes so.'

This was too much for his French; he said it to me in hot English, and repeated it, when Gabriella protested, in cooler Italian.

'But,' she said wonderingly, 'I do not like a man to say he is a coward. Who wants that? A man is for hunting and for defending, for keeping his wife safe.'

'Back to the caves?' I said.

'Our instincts are still the same,' agreed Patrick. 'Basically good.'

'And a man is for loving,' Gabriella said.

'Yes, indeed,' I agreed with enthusiasm.

'If you like to risk your neck, I like that. If you risk it for me, I like it better.'

'You mustn't say so,' said Patrick smiling. 'There's probably some vile explanation for that too.'

We all laughed, and some fresh coffee came, and the talk drifted away to what girls in Italy wanted of life as opposed to what they could have. Gabriella said the gap was narrowing fast, and that she was content, particularly as she was an orphan and had no parental pressure to deal with. We discussed for some time the pros and cons of having parents after adolescence, and all maintained that what we had was best: Gabriella her liberty, Patrick a widowed mother who spoiled him undemandingly, and I, free board and lodging. Patrick looked at me sharply when I said that, and opened his mouth to blow the gaff.

'Don't tell her,' I said in English. 'Please don't.'

'She would like you even more.'

'No.'

He hesitated, but to my relief he left it, and when Gabriella asked, told her we had been arguing as to who should pay the bill. We shared it between us, but we didn't leave for some time after that. We talked, I remember, about loyalty: at first about personal loyalty, and then political.

Gabriella said that Milan had many communists, and she thought that for a Roman Catholic to be a communist was like an Arab saying he wanted to be ruled by Israel.

'I wonder who they would be loyal to, if Russia invaded Italy?' Patrick said.

'That's a big if,' I said smiling. 'Pretty impossible with Germany, Austria and Switzerland in between, not to mention the Alps.'

Gabriella shook her head. 'Communists begin at Trieste.'

I was startled and amused at the same time, hearing an echo of my die-hard father. 'Wogs begin at Calais.'

'Of course they do,' Patrick said thoughtfully. 'On your door-step.'

'But cheer up,' she said laughing. 'Yugoslavia also has mountains, and the Russians will not be arriving that way either.'

'They won't invade any more countries with armies,' I agreed mildly.

'Only with money and technicians. Italian and French and British communists can rely on never having to choose which side to shoot at.'

'And can go on undermining their native land with a clear conscience,' Patrick nodded smiling.

'Let's not worry about it,' I said, watching the moving shadows where Gabriella's smooth hair fell across her cheek. 'Not tonight.'

'It will never touch us, anyway,' Patrick agreed. 'And if we stay here much longer Gabriella's sister will lock us out.'

Reluctantly we went out into the cold street. When we had gone ten paces Patrick exclaimed that he had left his overnight bag behind, and went back for it, striding quickly.

I turned to Gabriella, and she to me. The street lights were reflected in her welcoming eyes, and the solemn mouth trembled on the edge of that transfiguring smile. There wasn't any need to say anything. We both knew. Although I stood with my body barely brushing hers and put my hands very gently on her arms just below the shoulders, she rocked as if I'd pushed her. It was the same for me. I felt physically shaken by a force so primitive and volcanic as to be frightening. How could just touching a girl, I thought confusedly, just touching a girl I'd been longing to touch all afternoon and all evening, sweep one headlong into such an uncivilised turbulence. And on a main street in Milan, where one could do nothing about it.

She let her head fall forward against my shoulder, and we were still standing like that, with my cheek on her hair, when Patrick came back with his bag. Without a word, smiling resignedly, he pulled her round, tucked her arm into his, and said briefly, 'Come on. You'll get run in if you stay here much longer like that.' She looked at him blindly for a moment, and then laughed shakily. 'I don't understand why this has happened,' she said.

'Struck by the Gods,' said Patrick ironically. 'Or chemistry. Take your pick.'

'It isn't sensible.'

'You can say that again.'

He began to walk down the road, pulling her with him. My feet unstuck themselves from the pavement and re-attached themselves to my watery legs and I caught them up. Gabriella put her other arm through mine, and we strolled the mile and a half to where her sister lived, gradually losing the heavy awareness of passion and talking normally and laughing, and finally ending up on her door-step in a fit of giggles.

Lisabetta, Gabriella's sister, was ten years older and a good deal fatter, though she had the same smooth olive skin and the same shaped fine dark eyes. Her husband, Giulio, a softly flabby man approaching forty with a black moustache, bags under his eyes, and less hair than he'd once had, lumbered ungracefully out of his arm-chair when we went into his sitting room and gave us a moderately enthusiastic welcome.

Neither he nor Lisabetta spoke English or French so while the two girls made yet more coffee, and Patrick talked to Giulio, I looked around with some interest at Gabriella's home. Her sister had a comfortable four bedroomed flat in a huge recently built tower, and all the furnishings and fabrics were uncompromisingly modern. The floors were some sort of reconstituted stone heated from underneath and without carpet or rugs, and there were blinds, not curtains, to cover the windows. I thought the total effect rather stark, but reflected idly that Milan in mid-summer must be an oven, and the flat had been planned for the heat.

Several children came and went, all indistinguishable to my eyes. Seven of them, there should be, I remembered. Four boys, three girls, Patrick had said. Although it was nearly midnight, none of them seemed to have gone to bed. They had all been waiting to see Patrick and tumbled about him like puppies.

When Lisabetta had poured the coffee and one of the children had handed it round Giulio asked Patrick a question, looking at me.

'He wants to know what your job is,' Patrick said.

'Tell him I look after the horses.'

'Nothing else?'

'Nothing else.'

Giulio was unimpressed. He asked another question.

Smiling faintly, Patrick said, 'He wants to know how much you earn?'

'My pay for a single trip to Milan is about one fifth of yours.'

'He won't like that.'

'Nor do I.'

He laughed. When he translated Giulio scowled.

Patrick and I slept in a room which normally belonged to two of the boys, now doubling with the other two. Gabriella shared a third bedroom with the two elder girls, while the smallest was in with her parents. There were toys all over the place in our room, and small shoes kicked off and clothes dumped in heaps, and the unchanged sheets on the boys' beds were wrinkled like elephant skins from their restless little bodies. Patrick had from long globe trotting habit come equipped with pyjamas, slippers, washing things, and a clean shirt for the morning. I eyed this splendour with some envy, and slept in my underpants.

'Why,' said Patrick in the dark, 'won't you tell them you have a title?'

'It isn't important.'

'It would be to Giulio.'

'That's the best reason for not telling him.'

'I don't see why you're so keen to keep it a secret.'

'Well, you try telling everyone you're an earl's son, and see what happens.'

'I'd love it. Everyone would be bowing and scraping in all directions. Priorities galore. Instant service. A welcome on every mat.'

'And you'd never be sure if anyone liked you for yourself.'

'Of course you would.'

'How many head grooms have you brought here before?' I asked mildly.

He drew in a breath audibly and didn't answer.

'Would you have offered me this bed if Timmie had kept his big mouth shut?'

He was silent.

I said, 'Remind me to kick your teeth in in the morning.'

But the morning, I found, was a long way off. I simply couldn't sleep. Gabriella's bed was a foot away from me on the far side of the wall, and I lay and sweated for her with a desire I hadn't dreamed possible. My body literally ached. Cold controlled Henry Grey, I thought helplessly. Grey by name and grey by nature. Cold controlled Henry Grey lying in a child's bed in a foreign city biting his arm to stop himself crying out. You could laugh at such hunger: ridicule it away. I tried that, but it didn't work. It stayed with me hour after wretched hour, all the way to the dawn, and I would have been much happier if I'd been able to go to sleep and dream about her instead.

She had kissed me good night in the passage outside her door, lightly, gaily, with Patrick and Lisabetta and about six children approvingly looking on. And she had stopped and retreated right there because it was the same as in the street outside the restaurant; even the lightest touch could start an earthquake. There just wasn't room for an earthquake in that crowded flat.

Patrick lent me his razor without a word, when we got up.

'I'm sorry,' I said.

'You were quite right. I would not have offered to take you with me if the Welshman hadn't said . . .'

'I know.' I put on my shirt and buttoned the cuffs.

'All the same I still wouldn't have asked you if I hadn't thought you looked all right.'

I turned towards him, surprised.

'What you need, Henry, is a bit more self-confidence. Why ever shouldn't people like you for yourself? Gabriella obviously does. So do I.'

'People often don't.' I pulled on my socks.

'You probably don't give them half a chance.' With which devastatingly accurate shot he went out of the door, shrugging his arms into his authoritative Captain's uniform.

Subdued by the raw steely morning, the three of us went back to the airport. Gabriella had dark shadows under her eyes and wouldn't look at me, though I could think of nothing I had done to offend her. She spoke only to Patrick, and in Italian, and he, smiling briefly, answered her in the same language. When we arrived at the airport, she asked me, hurriedly, not to come and talk to her at the gift counter, and almost ran away from me without saying good-bye. I didn't try to stop her. It would be hours before we got the horses loaded, and regardless of what she asked, I intended to see her again before I left.

I hung around the airport all the morning with Conker and Timmie, and about twelve Patrick came and found me and with a wide grin said I was in luck, traffic at Gatwick was restricted because of deep snow, and unessential freight flights were suspended for another day.

'You'd better telephone the studs again, and tell them we are taking the mares to England tomorrow at eight,' he said. 'Weather permitting.'

Gabriella received the news with such a flash of delight that my spirits rose to the ionosphere. I hesitated over the next question, but she made it easy for me.

'Did you sleep well?' she asked gravely, studying my face.

'I didn't sleep at all.'

She sighed, almost blushing. 'Nor did I.'

'Perhaps,' I said tentatively, 'if we spent the evening together, we could sleep tonight.'

'Henry!' She was laughing. 'Where?'

Where proved more difficult than I had imagined, as she would not consider a hotel, as we must not sleep there, but go back to her sister's before midnight. One must not be shameless, she said. She could not stay out all night. We ended up, of all unlikely places, inside the D.C.4, lying in a cosy nest hollowed in a heap of blankets stacked in the luggage bay alongside the galley.

There, where no one would ever find us, and with a good deal of the laughter of total happiness, we spent the whole of the evening in the age-old way: and were pleased and perhaps relieved to find that we suited each other perfectly.

Lying quietly cradled in my arms, she told me hesitantly that she had had a lover before, which I knew anyway by then, but that it was odd making love anywhere except in bed. She felt the flutter in my chest and lifted her head up to peer at my face in the dim reflected moonlight.

'Why are you laughing?' she said.

'It so happens that I have never made love *in* bed.'

'Where then?'

'In the grass.'

'Henry! Is that the custom in England?'

'Only at the end of parties in the summer.'

She smiled and put her head down contentedly again, and I stroked her hair and thought how wholesome she was, and how dreadful in comparison seemed the half-drunk nymphs taken casually down the deb-dance garden path. I would never do that again, I thought. Never again.

'I was ashamed, this morning,' she said, 'of wanting this so much. Ashamed of what I had been thinking all night.'

'There is no shame in it.'

'Lust is one of the seven deadly sins.'

'Love is a virtue.'

'They get very mixed up. Are we this evening being virtuous or sinful?' She didn't sound too worried about it.

'Doing what comes naturally.'

'Then it's probably sinful.'

She twisted in my arms, turning so that her face was close to mine. Her eyes caught a sheen in the soft near-darkness. Her teeth rubbed gently against the bare skin on the point of my shoulder.

'You taste of salt,' she said.

I moved my hand over her stomach and felt the deep muscles there contract. Nothing, I thought, shaken by an echoing ripple right down my spine, nothing was so impossibly potent as being wanted in return. I kissed her, and she gave a long soft murmuring sigh which ended oddly in a laugh.

'Sin,' she said, with a smile in her voice, 'is O.K.'

We went back to her sister's and slept soundly on each side of the wall. Early in the morning, in her dressing-gown, with tousled hair and dreaming eyes, she made coffee for Patrick and me before we set off for the airport.

'You'll come back?' she said almost casually, pouring my cup.

'As soon as I can.'

She knew I meant it. She kissed me good-bye without clinging, and Patrick also. 'For bringing him,' she said.

In the taxi on the way to the airport Patrick said, 'Why don't you just stay here with her? You easily could.'

I didn't answer him until we were turning into the airport road.

'Would you? Stay, I mean.'

'No. But then, I need to keep my job.'

'So do I. For different reasons, perhaps. But I need to keep it just the same.'

'It's none of my business,' he said, 'but I'm glad.'

We loaded the Italian mares and flew them to snowy England without another hitch. I soothed them on their way and thought about Gabriella, who seemed to have established herself as a warming knot somewhere under my diaphragm.

I thought about her with love and without even the conventional sort of anxiety, for as she had said with a giggle, it would be a poor smuggler who couldn't swallow her own contraband.

Chapter Seven

Stratford Races were off because of snow, which was just as well as Yardman squeezed in an extra trip on that day at very short notice. Seven three-year-olds to France, he said; but at loading time there were eight.

I was held up on the way to Cambridge by a lorry which had skidded sideways and blocked the icy road, and when I reached the airport all the cargo had already arrived, with the box drivers stamping their feet to keep warm and cursing me fluently. Billy, and it was Billy again, not Conker and Timmie, stood about with his hands in his pockets and a sneer permanently fixed like epoxy resin, enjoying the disapproval I had brought on myself. He had not, naturally, thought of beginning the work before I arrived.

We loaded the horses, he, I, and deaf old Alf, whom Billy had brought with him, and we worked in uncompanionable silence. There was a fourth groom on the trip, a middle-aged characterless man with a large straggly moustache and a bad cold, but he had come with one particular horse from an upper crust stud, and he refrained from offering to help with any others. Neither did he lend a hand on the journey, but sat throughout beside his own protégée, guarding it carefully from no visible danger. Billy dropped a handful of peat in my coffee and later poured his own, which was half full of sugar, over my head. I spent the rest of the journey in the washroom, awkwardly rinsing the stickiness out of my hair and vowing to get even with Billy one day when I hadn't thousands of pounds worth of bloodstock in my care.

During the unloading I looked closely at one inconspicuous brown mare, trying to memorise her thoroughly unmemorable appearance. She was definitely not a three-year-old, like all the others on the trip, and she was, I was sure, almost identical to the one we had taken to France the first day I flew with Billy. And very like the one we had brought back that afternoon on the second trip. Three mares, all alike . . . well, it was not impossible, especially as they had no distinct markings between them, none at all.

The special groom left us in Paris, escorting his own horse right through to its new home. He had been engaged, he said, to bring another horse back, a French stallion which his stud had bought, and we would be collecting him again the next week. We duly did collect him, the next Tuesday, complete with the stallion, a tight-muscled butty little horse with a fiery eye and a restless tail. He was squealing like a colt when we stored him on board, and this time there was some point in his straggly moustached keeper staying beside him all the way.

Among the cargo there was yet another undistinguished brown mare. I was leaning on the starboard side of her box, gazing over and down at her, not able to see her very clearly against the peat she stood on and the brown horse on her other side, when Billy crept up behind me and hit me savagely across the shoulders with a spare tethering chain. I turned faster than he expected and got in two hard quick kicks on his thigh. His lips went back with the pain and he furiously swung his arm, the short chain flickering and bending like an angry snake. I dodged it by ducking into one of the cross-way alleys between the boxes, and the chain wrapped itself with a vicious clatter round the corner where I had been standing. Unhesitatingly I skipped through to the port side of the plane and went forward at top speed to the galley. Hiding figuratively under the engineer's skirts may not have been the noblest course, but in the circumstances by far the most prudent, and I stayed with him, drinking coffee, until we were on the final approach to Cambridge.

I did a good deal of hard thinking that night and I didn't like my thought.

In the morning I waited outside Yardman's office, and fell into step with Simon as he shambled out to lunch.

'Hullo,' he said, beaming. 'Where did you spring from? Come and have a warmer up at the Angel.'

I nodded and walked beside him, shuffling on the thawing remains of the previous week's snow. Our breaths shot out in small sharp clouds. The day was misty and overcast; the cold, raw, damp, and penetrating, exactly matched my mood.

Simon pushed the stained glass and entered the fug; swam on to his accustomed stool, tugged free his disreputable corduroy jacket and hustled the willing barmaid into pouring hot water on to rum and lemon juice, a large glass each. There was a bright new modern electric fire straining at its kilowatts in the old brick fireplace, and the pulsating light from its imitation coal base lit warmly the big smiling face opposite me, and shone brightly on the friendliness in his eyes.

I had so few friends. So few.

'What's the matter then?' he said, sipping his steaming drink. 'You're excessively quiet today, even for you.'

I watched the fake flames for a while, but it couldn't be put off for ever.

'I have found out,' I said slowly, 'about the brown mare.'

He put down his glass with a steady hand but the smile drained completely away.

'What brown mare?'

I didn't answer. The silence lengthened hopelessly.

'What do you mean?' he said at last.

'I escorted a brown mare to France and back twice in a fortnight. The same brown mare every time.'

'You must be mistaken.'

'No.'

There was a pause. Then he said again, but without conviction, 'You are mistaken.'

'I noticed her the day she went over in the morning and came back the same afternoon. I wondered when she went over again last Thursday . . . and I was certain it was the same horse yesterday, when she came back.'

'You've been on several other trips. You couldn't remember one particular mare out of all those you dealt with . . .'

'I know horses,' I said.

'You're too quick,' he said, almost to himself. 'Too quick.'

'No,' I shook my head. 'You were. You shouldn't have done it again so soon; then I might not have realised . . .'

He shook himself suddenly, the bulk quivering in folds. 'Done what?' he said more firmly. 'What if a horse did go over and back twice? And what's it got to do with me?'

'There's no point in telling you what you already know.'

'Henry,' he leaned forward. 'I know what I know, but I don't know what you think you know. You've got some damn-fool notion in your head and I want to hear what it is.'

I watched the steam rise gently from my untouched drink and wished I hadn't come.

'Nice little fiddle,' I sighed. 'A sweet, neat little fraud. Easy as shelling peas. A few hundred quid every time you send the mare to France.'

He looked at me without speaking, waiting, making me say it all straight out.

'All right then. You sell a horse – the brown mare – to an accomplice in France. He arranges for his bank to transfer the purchase price to England and the bank over here certifies that it has been received. You put in a claim to the government that one thoroughbred has been exported

for x thousand francs: part of the great bloodstock industry. The grateful
government pays you the bonus, the one and three quarters per cent
bonus on exports, and you put it in your pocket. Meanwhile you bring
the horse back here and smuggle the money back as cash to France and
you're ready to start again.'

Simon sat like a stone, staring at me.

'All you really need is the working capital,' I said. 'A big enough sum
to make the one and three quarters per cent worth the trouble. Say twenty
thousand pounds, for argument's sake. Three hundred and fifty pounds
every time the mare goes across. If she went only once a month that
would make an untaxed dividend of over 20 per cent on the year. Four
thousand or more, tax free. You'd have a few expenses, of course, but
even so . . .'

'Henry!' his voice was low and stunned.

'It's not a big fraud,' I said. 'Not big. But pretty safe. And it had to
be you, Simon, because it's all a matter of filling up the right forms, and
you fill the forms at Yardman's. If anyone else, an outsider, tried it, he'd
have to pay the horse's air passage each way, which would make the
whole business unprofitable. No one would do it unless they could send
the horse for nothing. You can send one for nothing, Simon. You just put
one down on the flying list, but not on the office records. Every time
there's room on a flight to France, you send the mare. Yardman told me
himself there would be seven three-year-olds going over last Thursday,
but we took eight horses, and the eighth wasn't a three-year old, it was
the brown mare.

'The day we did two trips, when we took her over in the morning and
brought her back in the afternoon, that day it was no accident the return
horses weren't at the airport to come back on the first trip. Not even you
could risk unloading the mare and promptly loading her up again straight
away. So you made a "mistake" and put fifteen hundred hours on the
trainers' travelling instructions instead of ten hundred hours, you, who
never make such mistakes, whose accuracy is so phenomenal usually that
no one queries or checks up on what you do . . .'

'How,' he said dully. 'How did you work it out?'

'I came from Anglia Bloodstock,' I said gently. 'Don't you remember?
I used to fill up the same export forms as you do. I used to send them
to you from the transport section. But I might not have remembered
about the government bonus if I hadn't heard three business men
discussing it ten days ago, and last night while I was wondering how
anyone could gain from shuffling that mare over and back, the whole
thing just clicked.'

'Clicked,' he said gloomily.

I nodded. 'No markings on the mare, either. You couldn't keep sending
her in her own name, someone would have noticed at once. I would have
done, for a start. But all you had to do was go through the stud book, and
choose other unmarked mares of approximately the same age and fill up
the export forms accordingly. The customs certify a brown mare was
actually exported from here, and the French customs certify it was
imported there. No trouble at all. No one bothers to check with an owner

that he has sold his horse. Why ever should they? And coming back, you go through the same process with the French stud book, only this time you have to be a bit careful your faked mare isn't too well bred because you can't spend more than two thousand in sterling abroad without searching enquiries, which you couldn't risk.'

'Got it all buttoned up, haven't you?' he said bitterly.

'I was thinking about it nearly all night.'

'Who are you going to tell?'

I glanced at him and away, uncomfortably.

'Yardman?' he asked.

I didn't answer.

'The police?'

I looked at the flickering fire. I wouldn't have told anyone had it not been for . . .

'Did you,' I said painfully, 'did you *have* to get Billy to knock me about?'

'Henry!' He looked shattered. 'I didn't. How can you think I did that?'

I swallowed. 'He's been on all the trips with the mare, and he's never given me a moment's peace on any of them, except perhaps the first. He's punched me and poured syrupy coffee on my hair, and yesterday when I was looking at the mare he hit me with a chain. He's not doing it because he dislikes me . . . or not only. It's a smoke screen to keep me away from looking too closely at the horses. That's why he didn't smash my face in . . . he was fighting for a purpose, not from real fury.'

'Henry, I promise you, it isn't true.' He seemed deeply distressed. 'I wouldn't hurt you, for God's sake.'

He put out his hand for his drink and took a long swallow. There was no more steam: drink and friendship were both cold.

'Don't look like that,' he said shivering. 'Like an iceberg.' He drank again. 'All right, you've got it right about the mare. I'll admit that, but as God's my judge, I didn't put Billy on to you. I can't stand him. He's a young thug. Whatever he's been doing to you, it's from his own bloody nature. I promise you, Henry, I promise you . . .'

I looked at him searchingly, wanting very much to believe him, and feeling I'd merely be fooling myself if I did.

'Look,' he said anxiously, leaning forward, 'would you have sicked him on to me?'

'No.'

'Well, then.' He leaned back again. 'I didn't either.'

There was a long, long pause.

'What do you do with the money?' I asked, shelving it.

He hesitated. 'Pay my gambling debts.'

I shook my head. 'You don't gamble.'

'I do.'

'No.'

'You don't know everything.'

'I know that,' I said tiredly. 'I know that very well. You're not interested in racing. You never ask me for tips, never even ask me if I expect to win myself. And don't say you gamble at cards or something feeble like that . . . if you gambled enough to have to steal to pay your debts, you'd gamble on anything, horses as well. Compulsively.'

He winced. 'Steal is a hard word.' He leaned forward, picked up my untasted drink, and swallowed the lot.

'There's no pension at Yardman's,' he said.

I looked into his future, into his penurious retirement. I would have the remains of the Creggan fortune to keep me in cars and hot rums. He would have what he'd saved.

'You've banked it?'

'Only a third,' he said. 'A third is my cousin's. He's the one who keeps the mare on his small-holding and drives her to the airport at this end. And a third goes to a chap with a horse dealing business in France. He keeps the mare when she is over there, and drives her back and fore to the planes. They put up most of the stake, those two, when I thought of it. I hadn't anything like enough on my own.'

'You don't really make much out of it, then, yourself, considering the risks.'

'Double my salary,' he observed dryly. 'Tax free. And you underestimate us. We have two horses, and they each go about fifteen times a year.'

'Have I seen the other one?'

'Yes,' he nodded. 'There and back.'

'Once?'

'Once.'

'And how do you get the money back to France?'

'Send it in magazines. Weeklies. The *Horse and Hound*, things like that.'

'English money?'

'Yes. The chap in France has a contact who exchanges it.'

'Risky, sending it by post.'

'We've never lost any.'

'How long have you been doing it?'

'Since they invented the bonus. Shortly after, anyway.'

There was another long silence. Simon fiddled with his empty glass and didn't look like an embezzler. I wondered sadly if it was priggish to want one's friends to be honest, and found that I did still think of him as a friend, and could no longer believe that he had paid Billy to give me a bad time. Billy quite simply hated my pedigreed guts: and I could live with that.

'Well,' he said in the end. 'What are you going to do about it?'

He knew as well as I did that he'd have no chance in an investigation. Too many records of his transactions would still exist in various government and banking files. If I started any enquiry he would very likely end up in gaol. I stood up stiffly off the bar stool and shook my head.

'Nothing . . .' I hesitated.

'Nothing . . . as long as we stop?'

'I don't know.'

He gave me a twisted smile. 'All right, Henry. We'll pack it in.'

We went out of the pub and walked together through the slush back to the office, but it wasn't the same. There was no trust left. He must have been wondering whether I would keep my mouth shut permanently, and I knew, and hated the knowledge, that he could probably go on with his scheme in spite of saying he wouldn't. The brown mare wouldn't go again, but he could change her for another, and there was his second horse, which I hadn't even noticed. If he was careful, he could go on. And he was a careful man.

The travel schedules in the office, checked again, still showed no more trips to Milan till the Wednesday of the following week. Nor, as far as I could see, were there any flights at all before then; only a couple of sea passages booked for polo ponies, which weren't my concern. I knocked on Yardman's door, and went in and asked him if I could have the rest of the week off: my rights, Conker would have said.

'Milan next Wednesday,' he repeated thoughtfully. 'And there's nothing before that? Of course, my dear boy, of course you can have the time off. If you don't mind if I bring you back should an urgent trip crop up?'

'Of course not.'

'That's good, that's good.' The spectacles flashed as he glanced out of the window, the tight skin around his mouth lifting fleetingly into a skeletal smile. 'You still like the job, then?'

'Yes, thank you,' I said politely.

'Well, well, my dear boy, and I won't say that you're not good at it, I won't say that at all. Very reliable, yes, yes. I admire you for it, dear boy, I do indeed.'

'Well . . . thank you, Mr. Yardman.' I wasn't sure that underneath he wasn't laughing at me, and wondered how long it would be before he understood that I didn't look on my job as the great big joke everyone else seemed to think it.

I wrote to Gabriella to tell her I would be coming back the following week, and drove moderately home, thinking alternately of her and Simon in an emotional see-saw.

There was a message for me at home to ring up Julian Thackery's father, which I did. The weather forecast was favourable, he said, and it looked as though there would be racing on Saturday. He was planning to send a good hunter chaser up to Wetherby, and could I go and ride it.

'I could,' I said. 'Yes.'

'That's fine. She's a grand little mare, a real trier, with the shoulders of a champion and enough behind the saddle to take you over the best.'

'Wetherby fences are pretty stiff,' I commented.

'She'll eat them,' he said with enthusiasm. 'And she's ready. We gave her a mile gallop this morning, thinking she'd be backward after the snow, and she was pulling like a train at the end of it. Must thrive on being held up.'

'Sounds good.'

'A snip,' he said. 'I'll see you in the weighing room, just before the first. Right?'

I assured him I would be there, and was glad to be going, as I learned from a letter of acceptance lying beside the telephone that the Filyhoughs were again expected for the week-end. My sister Alice came along while I held the letter in my hand.

'I'm going up to Wetherby on Saturday,' I said, forestalling her.

'Sunday . . .' she began.

'No, Alice dear, no. I have no intention whatsoever of marrying Angela Fillyhough and there's no point in seeing her. I thought that we had agreed that Mother should stop this heiress hunting.'

'But you must marry someone, Henry,' she protested.

I thought of Gabriella, and smiled. Maybe her, once I was sure she'd be a friend for life, not just a rocket passion with no embers.

'I'll marry someone, don't you worry.'

'Well,' Alice said, 'if you're going as far north as Wetherby you might as well go on and see Louise and cheer her up a bit.'

'Cheer her up?' I said blankly. Louise was the sister just older than Alice. She lived in Scotland, nearly twice as far from Wetherby, as it happened, as Wetherby from home, but before I could point that out Alice replied.

'I told you yesterday evening,' she said in exasperation. 'Weren't you listening?'

'I'm afraid not.' I'd been thinking about brown mares.

'Louise has had an operation. She goes home from hospital today and she'll be in bed for two or three weeks more.'

'What's wrong with her?' But Alice either didn't know or wouldn't tell me, and though I hardly knew Louise in any deep sense I thought she would be far preferable to Angela Filyhough, and I agreed to go. Deciding, as I would be driving a long way after the races, to go up to Yorkshire on the Friday and spend the Saturday morning lazily, I set off northward at lunchtime and made a detour out of habit to Fenland.

'Hey, Harry, you're just the man I want. A miracle.' Tom Wells grabbed my arm as I walked in. 'Do me a short flight tomorrow? Two trainers and a jockey from Newmarket to Wetherby races.'

I nearly laughed. 'I'm awfully sorry. I can't, Tom. I really called in to cancel my booking for Sunday. I can't come then either. Got to go and visit a sick sister in Scotland. I'm on my way now.'

'Blast,' he said forcibly. 'Couldn't you put it off?'

'Afraid not.'

'You can have a plane to fly up, on Sunday.' He was cunning, looking at me expectantly. 'Free.'

I did laugh then. 'I can't.'

'I'll have to tell the trainers I can't fix them up.'

'I'm really sorry.'

'Yeah. Damn it all. Well, come and have a cup of coffee.'

We sat in the canteen for an hour and talked about aircraft, and I continued my journey to Wetherby thinking in amusement that my life was getting more and more like a juggling act, and that it would need skill to keep the racing, flying, horse-ferrying and Gabriella all spinning round safely in separate orbits.

At Wetherby the struggling sunshine lost to a fierce east wind, but the going was perfect, a surprise after the snow. Mr. Thackery's mare was all that he had promised, a tough workmanlike little chestnut with a heart as big as a barn, a true racer who didn't agree with giving up. She took me over the first two fences carefully, as she'd not been on the course before, but then with confidence attacked the rest. I'd seldom had a more solid feeling ride and enjoyed it thoroughly, finding she needed the barest amount of help when meeting a fence wrong and was not too pigheaded to accept it. Coming round the last bend into the straight she was as full of running as when she started, and with only a flicker of encouragement from me she began working her way up smoothly past the four horses ahead of us. She reached the leader coming into the last, pecked a bit on landing, recovered without breaking up her stride, and went after the only horse in sight with enviable determination. We caught him in time, and soared past the winning post with the pleasure of winning coursing like wine in the blood.

'Not bad,' said Julian's father beaming. 'Not bad at all,' and he gave me a sealed envelope he'd had the faith to prepare in advance.

With about three hundred and fifty miles to go I left soon after the race, and on the empty northern roads made good time to Scotland. My sister Louise lived in a dreary baronial hall near Elgin, a house almost as big as ours at home and just as inadequately heated. She had pleased our parents by marrying for money, and hadn't discovered her husband's fanatical tightfistedness until afterwards. For all she'd ever had to spend since, she'd have been better off in a semi-detached in Peckham. Her Christmas gifts to me as a child had been Everyman editions of the classics. I got none at all now.

Even so, when I went in to see her in the morning, having arrived after she was sleeping the night before, it was clear that some of her spirit had survived. We looked at each other as at strangers. She, after a seven-year gap, was much older looking than I remembered, older than forty-three, and pale with illness, but her eyes were bright and her smile truly pleased.

'Henry, my little brother, I'm so glad you've come . . .'

One had to believe her. I was glad too, and suddenly the visit was no longer a chore. I spent all day with her, looking at old photographs and playing Chinese chequers, which she had taught me as a child, and listening to her chat about the three sons away at boarding school and how poor the grouse had been this winter and how much she would like to see London again, it was ten years since she had been down. She asked me to do various little jobs for her, explaining that 'dear James' was apt to be irritated and the maids had too much else to do, poor things. I fetched things for her, packed up a parcel, tidied her room, filled her hot water bottle and found her some more toothpaste. After that she wondered if we couldn't perhaps turn out her medicine drawer while we had the opportunity.

The medicine drawer could have stocked a dispensary. Half of them, she said with relief, she would no longer need. 'Throw them away.' She sorted the bottles and boxes into two heaps. 'Put all those in the wastepaper basket.' Obediently I picked up a handful. One was labelled

'Conovid,' with some explanatory words underneath, and it took several seconds before the message got through. I picked that box out of the rubbish and looked inside. There was a strip of foil containing pills, each packed separately. I tore one square open and picked out the small pink tablet.

'Don't you want these?' I asked.

'Of course not. I don't need them any more, after the operation.'

'Oh . . . I see. No, of course not. Then may I have them?'

'What on earth for?'

'Don't be naïve, Louise.'

She laughed. 'You've got a girl friend at last? Of course you can have them. There's a full box lying around somewhere too, I think. In my top drawer, perhaps? Maybe some in the bathroom too.'

I collected altogether enough birth control pills to fill a bottle nearly as big as the one Patrick had given Gabriella, a square cornered brown bottle four inches high, which had held a prescription for penicillin syrup for curing the boys' throat infections. Louise watched with amusement while I rinsed it out, baked it dry in front of her electric fire, and filled it up, stuffing the neck with cotton wool before screwing on the black cap.

'Marriage?' she said. As bad as Alice.

'I don't know.' I put the drawer she had tidied back into the bedside table. 'And don't tell Mother.'

Wednesday seemed a long time coming, and I was waiting at Gatwick a good hour before the first horses turned up. Not even the arrival of Billy and Alf could damp my spirits and we loaded the horses without incident and faster than usual, as two of the studs had sent their own grooms as well, and for once they were willing.

It was one of the mornings that Simon came with last minute papers, and he gave them to me warily in the charter airline office when the plane was ready to leave.

'Good morning, Henry.'

'Good morning.'

One couldn't patch up a friendship at seven-thirty in the morning in front of yawning pilots and office staff. I took the papers with a nod, hesitated, and went out across the tarmac, bound for the aircraft and Milan.

There were running steps behind me and a hand on my arm.

'Lord Grey? You're wanted on the telephone. They say it's urgent.'

I picked up the receiver and listened, said 'All right,' and slowly put it down again. I was not, after all, going to see Gabriella. I could feel my face contract into lines of pain.

'What is it?' Simon said.

'My father . . . my father has died . . . sometime during the night. They have just found him . . . he was very tired, yesterday evening . . .'

There was a shocked silence in the office. Simon looked at me with great understanding, for he knew how little I wanted this day.

'I'm sorry,' he said, his voice thick with sincerity.

I spoke to him immediately, without thinking, in the old familiar way. 'I've got to go home.'

'Yes, of course.'

'But the horses are all loaded, and there's only Billy . . .'

'That's easy. I'll go myself.' He fished in his brief case and produced his passport.

It was the best solution. I gave him back the papers and took the brown bottle of pills out of my pocket. With a black ball point I wrote on the label, 'Gabriella Barzini, Souvenir Shop, Malpensa Airport.'

'Will you give this to the girl at the gift counter, and tell her why I couldn't come, and say I'll write?'

He nodded.

'You won't forget?' I said anxiously.

'No, Henry.' He smiled as he used to. 'I'll see she gets it, and the message. I promise.'

We shook hands, and after a detour through the passport office he shambled across the tarmac and climbed up the ramp into the plane. I watched the doors shut. I watched the aircraft fly away, taking my job, my friend and my gift, but not me.

Simon Searle went to Italy instead of me, and he didn't come back.

Chapter Eight

It was over a week before I found out. I went straight up to his room when I reached the wharf, and it was empty and much too tidy.

The dim teen-age secretary next door, in answer to my questions, agreed that Mr. Searle wasn't in today, and that no one seemed to know when he would be in at all . . . or whether.

'What do you mean?'

'He hasn't been in for a week. We don't know where he's got to.'

Disturbed, I went downstairs and knocked on Yardman's door.

'Come in.'

I went in. He was standing by the open window, watching colliers' tugs pulling heavy barges up the river. A Finnish freighter, come up on the flood, was manoeuvring alongside across the river under the vulture-like meccano cranes. The air was alive with hooter signals and the bang and clatter of dock work, and the tide was carrying the garbage from the lower docks steadily upstream to the Palace of Westminster. Yardman turned, saw me, carefully closed the window, and came across the room with both hands outstretched.

'My dear boy,' he said, squeezing one of mine. 'My condolences on your sad loss, my sincere condolences.'

'Thank you,' I said awkwardly. 'You are very kind. Do you . . . er . . . know where Simon Searle is?'

'Mr. Searle?' he raised his eyebrows so that they showed above the black spectacle frames.

'He hasn't been in for a week, the girl says.'

'No . . .' he frowned. 'Mr. Searle, for reasons best known to himself, chose not to return to this country. Apparently he decided to stay in Italy, the day he went to Milan in your place.'

'But why?' I said.

'I really have no idea. It is very inconvenient. Very. I am having to do his work until we hear from him.'

He shook his head. 'Well, my dear boy, I suppose our troubles no longer concern you. You'd better have your cards, though I don't expect you'll be needing them.' He smiled the twisted ironic smile and stretched out his hand to the inter-office phone.

'You're giving me the sack, then?' I said bluntly.

He paused, his hand in mid-air. 'My dear boy,' he protested. 'My dear boy. It simply hadn't occurred to me that you would want to stay on.'

'I do.'

He hesitated, and then sighed. 'It's against my better judgment, it is indeed. But with Searle and you both away, the agency has had to refuse business, and we can't afford much of that. No, we certainly can't. No, we certainly can't. Very well then, if you'll see us through at least until I hear from Searle, or find someone to replace him, I shall be grateful, very grateful indeed.'

If that was how he felt, I thought I might as well take advantage of it. 'Can I have three days off for Cheltenham races in a fortnight? I've got a ride in the Gold Cup.'

He nodded calmly. 'Let me have the exact dates, and I'll avoid them.'

I gave them to him then and there, and went back to Simon's room thinking that Yardman was an exceptionally easy employer, for all that I basically understood him as little as on our first meeting. The list of trips on Simon's wall showed that the next one scheduled was for the following Tuesday, to New York. Three during the past and present week had been crossed out, which as Yardman had said, was very bad for business. The firm was too small to stand much loss of its regular customers.

Yardman confirmed on the intercom that the Tuesday trip was still on, and he sounded so pleased that I guessed that he had been on the point of cancelling it when I turned up. I confirmed that I would fetch the relevant papers from the office on Monday afternoon, and be at Gatwick on the dot on Tuesday morning. This gave me a long week-end free and unbeatable ideas on how to fill it. With some relief the next day I drove determinedly away from the gloomy gathering of relations at home, sent a cable, picked up a stand-by afternoon seat with Alitalia, and flew to Milan to see Gabriella.

Three weeks and three days apart had changed nothing. I had forgotten the details of her face, shortened her nose in my imagination and lessened the natural solemnity of her expression, but the sight of her again and instantly did its levitation act. She looked momentarily anxious that I wouldn't feel the same, and then smiled with breathtaking brilliance when she saw that I did.

'I got your cable,' she said. 'One of the girls has changed her free day with me, and now I don't have to keep the shop tomorrow or Sunday.'

'That's marvellous.'

She hesitated, almost blushing. 'And I went home at lunch time to pack some clothes, and I have told my sister I am going to stay for two days with a girl friend near Genoa.'

'Gabriella!'

'Is that all right?' she asked anxiously.

'It's a miracle,' I said fervently, having expected only snatched unsatisfactory moments by day, and nights spent each side of a wall. 'It's unbelievable.'

When she had finished for the day we went to the station and caught a train, and on the principle of not telling more lies than could be helped, we did in fact go to Genoa. We booked separately into a large impersonal hotel full of incurious business men, and found our rooms were only four doors apart.

Over dinner in a warm obscure little restaurant she said, 'I'm sorry about your father, Henry.'

'Yes . . .' Her sympathy made me feel a fraud. I had tried to grieve for him, and had recognised that my only strong emotion was an aversion to being called by his name. I wished to remain myself. Relations and family solicitors clearly took it for granted, however, that having sown a few wild oats I would now settle down into his pattern of life. His death, if I wasn't careful, would be my destruction.

'I was pleased to get your letter,' Gabriella said, 'because it was awful when you didn't come with the horses. I thought you had changed your mind about me.'

'But surely Simon explained?'

'Who is Simon?'

'The big fat bald man who went instead of me. He promised to tell you why I couldn't come, and to give you a bottle . . .' I grinned, 'a bottle of pills.'

'So they were from you!'

'Simon gave them to you. I suppose he couldn't explain why I hadn't come, because he doesn't know Italian. I forgot to tell him to speak French.'

She shook her head.

'One of the crew gave them to me. He said he'd found them in the toilet compartment just after they had landed, and he brought them across to see if I had lost them. He is a tall man, in uniform. I've seen him often. It was not your bald, fat Simon.'

'And Simon didn't try to talk to you at all?'

'No.' She shook her head. 'I don't think so. I see hundreds of bald fat travellers, but no one tried to speak to me about you.'

'A friendly big man, with kind eyes,' I said. 'He was wearing a frightful old green corduroy jacket, with a row of pins in one lapel. He has a habit of picking them up.'

She shook her head again. 'I didn't see him.'

Simon had promised to give her my message and the bottle. He had done neither, and he had disappeared. I hadn't liked to press Yardman too hard to find out where Simon had got to because there was always the chance that too energetic spadework would turn up the export bonus fraud: and I had vaguely assumed that it was because of the fraud that Simon had chosen not to come back. But even if he had decided on the spur of the moment to duck out, he would certainly have kept his promise to see Gabriella. Or didn't a resuscitated friendship stretch that far?

'What's the matter?' Gabriella asked.

I explained.

'You are worried about him?'

'He's old enough to decide for himself . . .' But I was remembering like a cold douche that my predecessor Peters hadn't come back from Milan, and before him the liaison man Ballard.

'Tomorrow morning,' she said firmly, 'you will go back to Milan and find him.'

'I can't speak Italian.'

'Undoubtedly you will need an interpreter,' she nodded. 'Me.'

'The best,' I agreed, smiling.

We walked companionably back to the hotel.

'Were the pills all right?' I asked.

'Perfect, thank you very much. I gave them to the wife of our baker . . . She works in the bakery normally, but when she gets pregnant she's always sick for months, and can't stand the sight of dough, and he gets bad-tempered because he has to pay a man to help him instead. He is not a good Catholic.' She laughed. 'He makes me an enormous cake oozing with cream when I take the pills.'

No one took the slightest notice of us in the hotel. I went along the empty passage in my dressing-gown and knocked on her door, and she opened it in hers to let me in. I locked it behind me.

'If my sister could see us,' she said smiling, 'she'd have a fit.'

'I'll go away . . . if you like.'

'Could you?' She put her arms round my neck.

'Very difficult.'

'I don't ask it.'

I kissed her. 'It would be impossible to go now,' I said.

She sighed happily. 'I absolutely agree. We will just have to make the best of it.'

We did.

We went back to Milan in the morning sitting side by side in the railway carriage and holding hands surreptitiously under her coat, as if by this tiny area of skin contact we could keep alive the total union of the night. I had never wanted to hold hands with anyone before: never realised that it could feel like being plugged into a small electric current, warm, comforting, and vibrant, all at the same time.

Apart from being together, it was a depressing day. No one had seen Simon.

'He couldn't just vanish,' I said in exasperation, standing late in the afternoon in a chilly wind outside the last of the hospitals. We had drawn a blank there as everywhere else, though they had gone to some trouble to make sure for us. No man of his description had been admitted for any illness or treated for any accident during the past ten days.

'Where else can we look?' she said, the tiredness showing in her voice and in the droop of her rounded body. She had been splendid all day, asking questions unendingly from me and translating the replies, calm and business-like and effective. It wasn't her fault the answers had all been negative. Police, government departments, undertakers, we had tried them all. We had rung up every hotel in Milan and asked for him: he had stayed in none.

'I suppose we could ask the taxi drivers at the airport . . .' I said finally.

'There are so many . . . and who would remember one passenger after so long?'

'He had no luggage,' I said as I'd said a dozen times before. 'He didn't know he was coming here until fifteen minutes before he took off. He couldn't have made any plans. He doesn't speak Italian. He hadn't any Italian money. Where did he go? What did he do?'

She shook her head dispiritedly. There was no answer. We took a tram back to the station and with half an hour to wait made a few last enquiries from the station staff. They didn't remember him. It was hopeless.

Over dinner at midnight in the same café as the night before we gradually forgot the day's frustration; but the fruitless grind, though it hadn't dug up a trace of Simon, had planted foundations beneath Gabriella and me.

She drooped against me going back to the hotel, and I saw with remorse how exhausted she was. 'I've tired you too much.'

She smiled at the anxiety in my voice. 'You don't realise how much energy you have.'

'Energy?' I repeated in surprise.

'Yes. It must be that.'

'What do you mean?'

'You don't look energetic. You're quiet, and you move like machinery, oiled and smooth. No effort. No jerks. No awkwardness. And inside somewhere is a dynamo. It doesn't run down. I can feel its power. All day I've felt it.'

I laughed. 'You're too fanciful.'

'No. I'm right.'

I shook my head. There were no dynamos ticking away inside me. I was a perfectly ordinary and not too successful man, and the smoothness she saw was only tidiness.

She was already in bed and half asleep when I went along to her room. I locked the door and climbed in beside her, and she made a great effort to wake up for my sake.

'Go to sleep,' I said, kissing her lightly. 'There is always the morning.'

She smiled contentedly and snuggled into my arms, and I lay there cradling her sweet soft body, her head on my chest and her hair against

my mouth, and felt almost choked by the intensity with which I wanted
to protect her and share with her everything I had: Henry Grey, I
thought in surprise in the dark, was suddenly more than half way down
the untried track to honest-to-goodness love.

Sunday morning we strolled aimlessly round the city, talking and
looking at the mountains of leather work in the shops in the arcades;
Sunday afternoon we went improbably to a football match, an unexpected
passion of Gabriella's; and Sunday night we went to bed early because,
as she said with her innocent giggle, we would have to be up at six to
get her back to start work in the shop on time. But there was something
desperate in the way she clung to me during that night, as if it were our
last for ever instead of only a week or two, and when I kissed her there
were tears on her cheeks.

'Why are you crying?' I said, wiping them away with my fingers.
'Don't cry.'

'I don't know why.' She sniffed, half laughing. 'The world is a sad
place. Beauty bursts you. An explosion inside. It can only come out as
tears.'

I was impossibly moved. I didn't deserve her tears. I kissed them away
in humility and understood why people said love was painful, why Cupid
was invented with arrows. Love did pierce the heart, truly.

It wasn't until we were on the early train to Milan the next morning
that she said anything about money, and from her hesitation in beginning
I saw that she didn't want to offend me.

'I will repay you what you lent me for my bill,' she said matter of
factly, but a bit breathlessly. I had pushed the notes into her hand on the
way downstairs, as she hadn't wanted me to pay for her publicly, and
she hadn't enough with her to do it herself.

'Of course not,' I said.

'It was a much more expensive place than I'd thought of . . .'

'Big hotels ignore you better.'

She laughed. 'All the same . . .'

'No.'

'But you don't earn much. You can't possibly afford it all. The hotel
and the train fares, and the dinners.'

'I earned some money winning a race.'

'Enough?'

'I'll win another race . . . then it will be enough.'

'Giulio doesn't like it that you work with horses.' She laughed. 'He
says that if you were good enough to be a jockey you'd do it all the time
instead of being a groom.'

'What does Giulio do?'

'He works for the government in the taxation office.'

'Ah,' I said, smiling. 'Would it help if you told him my father has left
me some money? Enough to come to see you, anyway, when I get it.'

'I'm not sure I'll tell him. He judges people too much by how much
money they've got.'

'Do you want to marry a rich man?'

'Not to please Giulio.'

'To please yourself?'

'Not rich necessarily. But not too poor. I don't want to worry about how to afford shoes for the children.'

I smoothed her fingers with my own.

'I think I will have to learn Italian,' I said.

She gave me the flashing smile. 'Is English very difficult?'

'You can practise on me.'

'If you come back often enough. If your father's money should not be saved for the future.'

'I think,' I said slowly, smiling into her dark eyes, 'that there will be enough left. Enough to buy the children's shoes.'

I went to New York with the horses the following day in the teeth of furious opposition from the family. Several relatives were still staying in the house, including my three sharp tongued eldest sisters, none of whom showed much reserve in airing their views. I sat through a depressing lunch, condemned from all sides. The general opinion was, it seemed, that my unexplained absence over the week-end was disgraceful enough, but that continuing with my job was scandalous. Mother cried hysterical tears and Alice was bitterly reproving.

'Consider your *position*,' they all wailed, more or less in chorus.

I considered my position and left for Yardman's and Gatwick three hours after returning from Milan.

Mother had again brought up the subject of my early marriage to a suitable heiress. I refrained from telling her I was more or less engaged to a comparatively penniless Italian girl who worked in a gift shop, smuggled birth control pills, and couldn't speak English. It wasn't exactly the moment.

The outward trip went without a hitch. Timmie and Conker were along, together with a pair of grooms with four Anglia Bloodstock horses, and in consequence the work went quickly and easily. We were held up for thirty-six hours in New York by an engine fault, and when I rang up Yardman to report our safe return on the Friday morning he asked me to stay at Gatwick, as another bunch of brood mares was to leave that afternoon.

'Where for?'

'New York again,' he said briskly. 'I'll come down with the papers myself, early in the afternoon. You can send Timms and Chestnut home. I'm bringing Billy and two others to replace them.'

'Mr. Yardman . . .' I said.

'Yes?'

'If Billy tries to pick a fight, or molests me at all on the way, my employment with you ceases the instant we touch down in New York, and I will not help unload the horses or accept any responsibility for them.'

There was a shocked silence. He couldn't afford to have me do what I threatened, in the present sticky state of the business.

'My dear boy . . .' he protested sighing. 'I don't want you to have troubles. I'll speak to Billy. He's a thoughtless boy. I'll tell him not everyone is happy about his little practical jokes.'

'I'd appreciate it,' I said with irony at his view of Billy's behaviour.

Whatever Yardman said to him worked. Billy was sullen, unhelpful, and calculatingly offensive, but for once I completed a return trip with him without a bruise to show for it.

On the way over I sat for a time on a hay bale beside Alf and asked him about Simon's last trip to Milan. It was hard going, as the old man's deafness was as impenetratable as seven eighths cloud.

'Mr. Searle,' I shouted. 'Did he say where he was going?'

'Eh?'

After about ten shots the message got through, and he nodded.

'He came to Milan with us.'

'That's right, Alf. Where did he go then?'

'Eh?'

'Where did he go then?'

'I don't rightly know,' he said. 'He didn't come back.'

'Did he *say* where he was going?'

'Eh?'

I yelled again.

'No. He didn't say. Perhaps he told Billy. He was talking to Billy, see?'

I saw. I also saw that it was no use my ever asking Billy anything about anything. Yardman would have asked him, anyway, so if Simon had told Billy where he was going Yardman would have known. Unless, of course, Simon had asked Billy not to tell, and he hadn't. But Simon didn't like Billy and would never trust him with a secret.

'Where did Mr. Searle go, when you left the plane?'

I was getting hoarse before he answered.

'I don't know where he went. He was with Billy and the others. I went across on my own, like, to get a beer. Billy said they were just coming. But they never came.'

'None of them came?'

There had been the two grooms from the stud beside Simon and Billy, on that trip.

Eventually Alf shook his head. 'I finished my beer and went back to the plane. There was no one there as I ate my lunch.'

I left it at that because my throat couldn't stand any more.

Coming back we were joined by some extra help in the shape of a large pallid man who didn't know what to do with his hands and kept rubbing them over the wings of his jodhpurs as if he expected to find pockets there. He was ostensibly accompanying a two-year-old, but I guessed tolerantly he was some relation of the owner or trainer travelling like that to avoid a transatlantic fare. I didn't get around to checking on it, because the double journey had been very tiring, and I slept soundly nearly all the way back. Alf had to shake me awake as we approached Gatwick. Yawning I set about the unloading – it was by then well into Sunday morning – and still feeling unusually tired, drove home afterwards in a bee line to bed. A letter from Gabriella stopped me in the hall, and I went slowly upstairs reading it.

She had, she said, asked every single taxi driver and all the airport bus drivers if they had taken anywhere a big fat Englishman who couldn't speak Italian, had no luggage, and was wearing a green corduroy jacket. None of them could remember anyone like that. Also, she said, she had checked with the car hire firms which had agencies at the airport, but none of them had dealt with Simon. She had checked with all the airlines' passenger lists for the day he went to Milan, and the days after: he had not flown off anywhere.

I lay in a hot bath and thought about whether I should go on trying to find him. Bringing in any professional help, even private detectives, would only set them searching in England for a reason for his disappearance, and they'd all too soon dig it up. A warrant out for his arrest was not what I wanted. It would effectively stop him coming back at all. Very likely he didn't want to be found in the first place, or he wouldn't have disappeared so thoroughly, or stayed away so long. But supposing something had happened to him ... though what, I couldn't imagine. And I wouldn't have thought anything could have happened at all, were it not for Peters and Ballard.

There were Simon's partners in the fraud. His cousin, and the man in France. Perhaps I could ask them if they had heard from him ... I couldn't ask them, I thought confusedly: I didn't know their names. Simon had an elderly aunt somewhere, but I didn't know her name either ... the whole thing was too much ... and I was going to sleep in the bath.

I went to the wharf building the next morning at nine thirty to collect my previous week's pay and see what was on the schedule for the future. True to his word, Yardman had arranged no air trips for the following three days of Cheltenham races. There was a big question mark beside a trip for six circus horses for Spain that same afternoon, but no question mark, I was glad to see, about a flight to Milan with brood mares on Friday.

Yardman, when I went down to see him, said the circus horses were postponed until the following Monday owing to their trainer having read in his stars that it was a bad week to travel. Yardman was disgusted. Astrology was bad for business.

'Milan on Friday, now,' he said, sliding a pencil to and fro through his fingers. 'I might come on that trip myself, if I can get away. It's most awkward, with Searle's work to be done. I've advertised for someone to fill his place ... anyway, as I was saying, if I can get away I think I'd better go and see our opposite numbers out there. It always pays you know, my dear boy. I go to all the countries we export to. About once a year. Keeps us in touch, you know.'

I nodded. Good for business, no doubt.

'Will you ask them ... our opposite numbers ... if they saw Simon Searle any time after he landed?'

He looked surprised, the taut skin stretched over his jaw.

'I could, yes. But I shouldn't think he told them where he was going, if he didn't have the courtesy to tell me.'

'It's only an outside chance,' I agreed.

'I'll ask, though.' He nodded. 'I'll certainly ask.'

I went upstairs again to Simon's room, shut his door, sat in his chair, and looked out of his window. His room, directly over Yardman's, had the same panoramic view of the river, from a higher angle. I would like to live there, I thought idly. I liked the shipping, the noise of the docks, the smell of the river, the coming and going. Quite simply, I supposed, I liked the business of transport.

The Finnish ship had gone from the berth opposite and another small freighter had taken her place. A limp flag swung fitfully at her mast head, red and white horizontal stripes with a navy blue triangle and a white star. I looked across at the nationality chart on Simon's wall. Puerto Rico. Well, well, one lived and learned. Three alphabetical flags lower down, when checked, proved to be E, Q and M. Mildly curious, I turned them up in the international code of signals. 'I am delivering.' Quite right and proper. I shut the book, twiddled my thumbs, watched a police launch swoop past doing twenty knots on the ebb, and reflected not for the first time that the London river was a fast rough waterway for small boats.

After a while I picked up the telephone and rang up Fenland to book a plane for Sunday.

'Two o'clock?'

'That'll do me fine,' I said. 'Thanks.'

'Wait a minute, Harry. Mr. Wells said if you rang that he wanted a word with you.'

'O.K.'

There were some clicks, and then Tom's voice.

'Harry? Look, for God's sake, what is this job of yours?'

'I work for . . . a travel agency.'

'Well, what's so special about it? Come here, and I'll pay you more.' He sounded worried and agitated, not casually inviting as before.

'What's up?' I said.

'Everything's up except my planes. I've landed an excellent contract with a car firm in Coventry ferrying their executives, technicians, salesmen and so on all round the shop. They've a factory in Lancashire and tie-ups all over Europe, and they're fed-up with the airfield they've been using. They're sending me three planes. I'm to maintain them, provide pilots and have them ready when wanted.'

'Sounds good,' I said. 'So what's wrong?'

'So I don't want to lose them again before I've started. And not only can I not find any out-of-work pilots worth considering, but one of my three regulars went on a ski-ing holiday last week and broke his leg, the silly bastard. So how about it?'

'It's not as easy as you make it sound,' I said reluctantly.

'What's stopping you?'

'A lot of things . . . if you'll be around on Sunday, anyway, we could talk it over.'

He sighed in exasperation. 'The planes are due here at the end of the month, in just over a fortnight.'

'Get someone else, if you can,' I said.

'Yeah ... if I can.' He was depressed. 'And if I can't?'

'I don't know. I could do a day a week to help out, but even then ...'

'Even then, what?'

'There are difficulties.'

'Nothing to mine, Harry. Nothing to mine. I'll break you down on Sunday.'

Everyone had troubles, even with success. The higher the tougher, it seemed. I wiggled the button, and asked for another number, the charter airline which Patrick worked for. The Gatwick office answered, and I asked them if they could tell me how to get hold of him.

'You're in luck. He's actually here, in the office. Who's speaking?'

'Henry Grey, from Yardman Transport.'

I waited, and he came on the line.

'Hullo ... how's things? How's Gabriella?'

'She,' I said, 'is fine. Other things are not. Could you do me a favour?'

'Shoot.'

'Could you look up for me the name of the pilot who flew a load of horses to Milan for us a fortnight last Thursday? Also the names of the co-pilot and engineer, and could you also tell me how or when I could talk to one or all of them?'

'Trouble?'

'Oh, no trouble for your firm, none at all. But one of our men went over on that trip and didn't come back, and hasn't got in touch with us since. I just wanted to find out if the crew had any idea what became of him. He might have told one of them where he was going ... anyway, his work is piling up here and we want to find out if he intends to come back.'

'I see. Hang on then. A fortnight last Thursday?'

'That's it.'

He was away several minutes. The cranes got busy on the freighter from Puerto Rico. I yawned.

'Henry? I've got them. The pilot was John Kyle, co-pilot G. L. Rawlings, engineer V. N. Brede. They're not here, though; they've just gone to Arabia, ferrying mountains of luggage from London after some oil chieftain's visit. He brought about six wives, and they all went shopping.'

'Wow,' I said. 'When do they get back?'

He consulted someone in the background.

'Sometime Wednesday. They have Thursday off, then another trip to Arabia on Friday.'

'Some shopping,' I said gloomily. 'I can't get to see them on Wednesday or Thursday. I'm racing at Cheltenham. But I could ring them up on Wednesday night, if you can give me their numbers.'

'Well ...,' said Patrick slowly. 'John Kyle likes his flutter on the horses.'

'You don't think he'd come to Cheltenham, then?'

'He certainly might, if he isn't doing anything else.'

'I'll get him a member's badge, and the others too, if they'd like.'

'Fair enough. Let's see. I'm going to Holland twice tomorrow. I should think I could see them on Wednesday, if we all get back reasonably on schedule. I'll tell them what you want, and ring you. If they go to Cheltenham you'll see them, and if not you can ring them. How's that?'

'Marvellous. You'll find me at the Queen's Hotel at Cheltenham. I'll be staying there.'

'Right . . . and oh, by the way, I see I'm down for a horse transport flight on Friday to Milan. Is that your mob, or not?'

'Our mob,' I agreed. 'What's left of it.'

We rang off, and I leaned back in Simon's chair, pensively biting my thumbnail and surveying the things on his desk: telephone, tray of pens, blank notepad, and a pot of paper clips and pins. Nothing of any help. Then slowly, methodically, I searched through the drawers. They were predictably packed with export forms of various sorts, but he had taken little of a personal nature to work. Some indigestion tablets, a screwdriver, a pair of green socks, and a plastic box labelled 'spare keys'. That was the lot. No letters, no bills, no private papers of any sort.

I opened the box of keys. There were about twenty or more, the silt of years. Suitcase keys, a heavy old iron key, car keys. I stirred them up with my finger. A Yale key. I picked it out and looked at it. It was a duplicate, cut for a few shillings from a blank, and had no number. The metal had been dulled by time, but not smoothed, from use. I tapped it speculatively on the edge of the desk, thinking that anyway there would be no harm in trying.

Chapter Nine

Simon's home address, obtained off his insurance card via the dim typist, proved to be located in a dingy block of flats in the outer reaches of St. John's Wood. The grass on patchy lawns had remained uncut from about the previous August, which gave the graceless buildings a mournful look of having been thoughtlessly dumped in a hayfield. I walked through spotted glass entrance doors, up an uninspiring staircase, met no one, and came to a halt outside number fifteen in white twopenny plastic letters screwed on to cheap green painted deal.

The Yale key slid raspingly into the lock as if it had never been there before, but it turned under my pressure and opened the door. There was a haphazard foot-high pile of newspapers and magazines just inside. When I pushed the door against them they slithered away, and I stepped in and round them, and shut the door behind me.

The flat consisted only of a tiny entrance hall, a small bedroom, poky kitchen and bathroom and a slightly larger sitting-room. The prevailing colour was maroon, which I found depressing, and the furniture looked as if it had been bought piece by piece from second-class second-hand shops. The total effect could have been harmonious, but it wasn't: not so much through lack of taste as lack of imagination. He had spent the minimum trouble on his surroundings, and the result was gloomy. Cold dead air and a smell of mustiness seeped up my nose. There were unwashed, mould-growing dishes on the draining board in the kitchen, and crumpled thrown-back bedclothes on the bed. He had left his shaving water in the washbasin and the scum had dried into a hard grey line round the edge. Poor Simon, I thought forlornly, what an existence. No wife, no warmth: no wonder he liked pubs.

One wall in the sitting-room was lined with bookcases, and the newest, most obviously luxurious object in the flat was a big stereophonic radiogram standing behind the door. No television. No pictures on the dull coffee walls. Not a man of visual pleasures. Beside a large battered arm-chair, handy to perpetual reach, stood a wooden crate of bottled beer.

Wandering round his flat I realised what a fearful comment it was on myself that I had never been there before. This big tolerant dishonest man I would have counted my only real friend, yet I'd never seen where he lived. Never been asked; never thought of asking him to my own home. Even where I had wanted friendship, I hadn't known how to try. I felt as cold inside as Simon's flat; as uninhabited. Gabriella seemed very far away.

I picked up the heap of papers inside the front door and carried them into the sitting-room. Sorted into piles, they consisted of sixteen dailies, three Sundays, three *Horse and Hounds*, three *Sporting Life* weeklies and one *Stud and Stable*. Several letters in brown unstuck envelopes looked unpromising and with very little hesitation I opened all the rest. There were none from France, and none from the accomplice cousin. The only one of any help was written in spiky black hand on dark blue paper. It began 'Dear Simon,' thanked him for a birthday present, and was signed 'your loving aunt Edna.' The handwritten address at the top said 3 Gordon Cottages, East Road, Potter's Green, Berks., and there was no telephone number.

There was no desk as such in his flat. He kept his bills and papers clipped into labelled categories in the top drawer of a scratched chest in his bedroom, but if his cousin's name and address was among them, I couldn't recognise them. Alongside the papers lay a *Horse and Hound* rolled tightly into a tube and bound with wide brown sticky paper, ready to be posted. I picked it up and turned it round in my hands. It bore no address. The thick layers of brown sticky paper were tough, and even though I was careful with my penknife it looked as though a tiger had been chewing it when I finally hacked my way through. The magazine unrolled reluctantly, and I picked it up and shook it. Nothing happened. It wasn't until one looked at it page by page that the money showed, five pound notes stuck on with sellotape. They were used notes, not new, and there were sixty of them. I rolled the *Horse and Hound* up again and laid it back in the drawer, seeing a vivid mental picture, as I picked up the brown pieces of gummed strips and put them in the wastbasket, of Simon listening to his radiogram and sticking his money into the journals, night after night, an endless job, working for his old age.

Potter's Green turned out to be a large village spreading out into tentacles of development around the edges. East Road was a new one, and Gordon Cottages proved to be one of several identical strips of council-built bungalows for old people. Number three like all the rest still looked clean and fresh, with nothing growing yet in the bathmat sized flower bed under the front window. There was bright yellow paint clashing with pale pink curtains and a bottle of milk standing on the concrete doorstep.

I rang the bell. The pink curtains twitched, and I turned my head to see myself being inspected by a pair of mournful, faded eyes set in a large pale face. She flapped a hand at me in a dismissing movement, shooing me away, so I put my finger on the bell and rang again.

I heard her come round to the other side of the door.

'Go away,' she said. 'I don't want anything.'

'I'm not selling,' I said through the letter-box. 'I'm a friend of Simon's, your nephew Simon Searle.'

'Who are you? I don't know you.'

'Henry Grey . . . I work with Simon at Yardman's. Could I please talk to you inside, it's very difficult like this, and your neighbours will wonder what's going on.' There were in truth several heads at the front windows already, and it had its effect. She opened the door and beckoned me in.

The tiny house was crammed with the furniture she must have brought with her from a much larger place, and every available surface was covered with useless mass-produced ornaments. The nearest to me as I stood just inside the doorway was a black box decorated with 'A present from Brighton' in shells. And next to that a china donkey bore panniers of dried everlasting flowers. Pictures of all sorts crowded the walls, interspersed by several proverbs done in poker-work on wood. 'Waste not, Want not' caught my eye, and further round there was 'Take care of the pence and the pounds will take care of you'; an improvement on the original.

Simon's stout aunt had creaking corsets and wheezing breath and smelled of mentholated cough pastilles. 'Simon isn't here, you know. He lives in London, not here.'

'I know, yes.' Hesitatingly, I told her about Simon going away and not coming back. 'I wondered,' I finished, 'if by any chance he has written to you. Sent you a picture postcard. That sort of thing.'

'He will do. He's sure to.' She nodded several times. 'He always does, and brings me a little souvenir when he's been away. Very considerate is Simon.'

'But you haven't had a postcard yet.'

'Not yet. Soon, I expect.'

'If you do, would you write to me and let me know? You see, he hasn't

said when he'll be back, and Mr. Yardman is advertising for someone
to fill his job.'

'Oh, dear.' She was troubled. 'I hope nothing has happened to him.'

'I don't expect so: but if you hear from him, you will let us know?'

'Yes, yes, of course. Dear oh dear, I wonder what he is up to.'

Her choice of phrase reminded me of what in fact he was up to, and
I asked her if she knew Simon's cousin's name and address. Unhesitatingly
she reeled it off. 'He's my poor dead sister's son,' she said. 'But a surly
man. I don't get on with him at all. Not easy, like Simon, now. Simon
stayed with m e a lot when he was little, when I kept the village shop.
He never forgets my birthday, and always brings me nice little mementoes
like these.' She looked proudly round her overflowing possessions.
'Simon's very kind. I've only my old age pension, you know, and a little
bit put by and Simon's the only one who bothers with me much. Oh I've
got my two daughters, of course, but one's married in Canada and the
other's got enough troubles of her own. Simon's given me a hundred
pounds for my birthday every year for the last three years; what do you
think of that?'

'Absolutely splendid.' A hundred pounds of tax payers' money. Robin
Hood stuff. Oh well.

'You'll let me know, then,' I said, turning to go. She nodded, creaking
as she moved round me to open the street door. Facing me in the little
hall hung more time-worn poker work. 'See a pin and pick it up, all the
day you'll have good luck. See a pin and let it lie, you will want before
you die.' So there, I thought, smiling to myself, was the origin of Simon's
pin tidying habit, a proverb stretching back to childhood. He didn't
intend to want before he died.

The accomplice cousin farmed in Essex, reasonably handy for Cambridge airport, but a long haul for Gatwick. It was evident at once,
however, that I could expect no easy help from him.

'You,' he said forcefully, 'you're the interfering bastard who's fouled
up the works, aren't you? Well you can damn well clear off, that's what
you can do. It's no business of yours where Simon's gone and in future
you keep your bloody nose out of things that don't concern you.'

'If,' I said mildly, 'you prefer me to ask the police to find him, I will.'

He looked ready to explode, a large red faced man in khaki clothes
and huge gum boots, standing four square in a muddy yard. He struggled
visibly between the pleasure of telling me to go to hell and fear of the
consequences if he did so. Prudence just won.

'All right. All right. I don't know where he is and that's straight. He
didn't tell me he was going, and I don't know when he's coming back.'

Depressed, I drove home to Bedfordshire. The bulk and grandeur of
the great house lay there waiting as I rolled slowly up the long drive.
History in stone; the soul of the Creggans. Earl upon earl had lived there
right back to the pirate who brought Spanish gold to Queen Bess, and
since my father died I had only to enter to feel the chains fall heavily on
me like a net. I stopped in the sweep of gravel in front instead of driving
round to the garages as usual, and looked at what I had inherited. There
was beauty, I admitted, in the great façade with its pillars and pediments

and the two wide flights of steps sweeping up to meet at the door. The Georgian Palladian architect who had grafted a whole new mansion on to the Elizabethan and Stuart one already existing had produced a curiously satisfactory result, and as a Victorian incumbent had luckily confined his Gothic urges to a ruined folly in the garden, the only late addition had been a square red-bricked block of Edwardian plumbing. But for all its splendid outer show it had those beetles in the roof, miles of draughty passages, kitchens in the basement and twenty bedrooms mouldering into dust. Only a multi-millionaire could maintain and fill such a place now with servants and guests, whereas after death duties I would be hard put to it to find a case of champagne once the useless pile had voraciously gulped what it cost just to keep standing.

Opening it to the public might have been a solution if I had been any sort of a showman. But to someone solitary by nature that way meant a lifetime of horrifying square-peggery. Slavery to a building. Another human sacrifice on the altar of tradition. I simply couldn't face it. The very idea made me wilt.

Since it was unlikely anyone would simply let me pull the whole thing down, the National Trust, I thought, was the only hope. They could organise the sight-seeing to their heart's content and they might let Mother live there for the rest of her life, which she needed.

Mother usually used the front entrance while Alice and I drove on and went in through one of the doors at the side, near the garages. That early evening, however, I left my little car on the gravel and walked slowly up the shallow steps. At the top I leaned against the balustrade and looked back over the calm wide fields and bare branched trees just swelling into bud. I didn't really own all this, I thought. It was like the baton in a relay race, passed on from one, to be passed on to the next, belonging to none for more than a lap. Well, I wasn't going to pass it on. I was the last runner. I would escape from the track at a tangent and give the baton away. My son, if I ever had one, would have to lump it.

I pushed open the heavy front door and stepped into the dusk-filled house. I, Henry Grey, descendant of the sea pirate, of warriors and explorers and empire builders and of a father who'd been decorated for valour on the Somme, I, the least of them, was going to bring their way of life to an end. I felt one deep protesting pang for their sakes, and that was all. If they had anything of themselves to pass on to me, it was already in my genes. I carried their inheritance in my body, and I didn't need their house.

Not only did John Kyle and his engineer come to Cheltenham, but Patrick as well.

'I've never been before,' he said, his yellow eyes and auburn hair shining as he stood in the bright March sun.· 'These two are addicts. I just came along for the ride.'

'I'm glad you did,' I said, shaking hands with the other two. John Kyle was a bulky battered looking young man going prematurely thin on top. His engineer, tall and older, had three racing papers and a form sheet tucked under his arm.

'I see,' he said, glancing down at them, 'th . . . that you won the United Hunts Ch . . . Challenge Cup yesterday.' He managed his stutter unselfconsciously. 'W . . . w . . . well done.'

'Thank you,' I said. 'I was a bit lucky. I wouldn't have won if Century hadn't fallen at the last.'

'It d . . . d . . . d . . . does say that, in the p . . . p . . . paper,' he agreed disarmingly.

Patrick laughed and said, 'What are you riding in today?'

'The Gold Cup and the Mildmay of Flete Challenge Cup.'

'Clobber and Boathook,' said John Kyle readily.

'I'll back you,' Patrick said.

'M . . . m . . . money down the drain b . . . backing Clobber,' said the engineer seriously.

'Thanks very much,' I said with irony.

'F . . . form's all haywire. V . . . v . . . very inconsistent,' he explained.

'Do you think you've got a chance?' Patrick asked.

'No, not much. I've never ridden him before. The owner's son usually rides him, but he's got jaundice.'

'N . . . not a b . . . betting proposition,' nodded the engineer.

'For God's sake don't be so depressing, man,' protested Kyle.

'How about Boathook?' I asked, smiling.

The engineer consulted the sky. The result wasn't written there, as far as I could see.

'B . . . B . . . Boathook,' he remarked, coming back to earth, 'm . . . m . . . might just do it. G . . . good for a p . . . place anyway.'

'I shall back them both, just the same,' said Patrick firmly.

I took them all to lunch and sat with them while they ate

'Aren't you having any?' said Patrick.

'No. It makes you sick if you fall after eating.'

'How often do you fall then?' asked Kyle curiously, cutting into his cold red beef.

'On average, once in a dozen rides, I suppose. It varies. I've never really counted.'

'When did you fall last?'

'Day before yesterday.'

'Doesn't it bother you?' asked Patrick, shaking salt. 'The prospect of falling?'

'Well, no. You never think you're going to, for a start. And a lot of falls are easy ones; you only get a bruise, if that. Sometimes when the horse goes right down you almost step off.'

'And sometimes you break your bones,' Kyle said dryly.

I shook my head. 'Not often.'

Patrick laughed. I passed him the butter for his roll, looked at my watch, and said, 'I'll have to go and change soon. Do you think we could talk about the day you took Simon Searle to Milan?'

'Shoot,' said Kyle. 'What do you want to know?'

'Everything you can think of that happened on the way there and after you landed.'

'I don't suppose I'll be much help,' he said apologetically. 'I was in the cockpit most of the time, and I hardly spoke to him at all. I went aft to the karzy once, and he was sitting in one of those three pairs of sets that were bolted on at the back.'

I nodded. I'd bolted the seats on to the anchorages myself, after we had loaded all the horses. There was usually room for a few seats, and they made a change from hay bales.

'Was he alone?'

'No, there was a young fellow beside him. Your friend Searle was on the inside by the window, I remember, because this young chap had his legs sprawled out in the gangway and I had to step over them. He didn't move.'

'Billy,' I nodded.

'After I came out I asked them if they were O.K. and said we'd be landing in half an hour. The young one said "thanks Dad" as if he was bored to death, and I had to step over his legs again to get past. I can't say I took to him enormously.'

'You surprise me,' I said sardonically. 'Did Simon say anything?'

He hesitated. 'It's three weeks ago. I honestly can't remember, but I don't think so. Nothing special, anyway.'

I turned to the engineer. 'How about you?'

He chewed, shook his head, swallowed, and took a sip of beer.

'D . . . d . . . don't think I'm much better. I w . . . w . . . was talking to him q . . . q . . . quite a lot at the beginning. In the g . . . g . . . galley. He said he'd come at the l . . . l . . . last minute instead of you. He t . . . t . . . talked about you quite a lot.'

The engineer took a mouthful of salad and stuttered through it without embarrassment. A direct man, secure in himself. 'He's . . . said you were ice on a v . . . volcano. I said th . . . th . . . that didn't make sense, and he said it w . . . was the only w . . . way to describe you.'

Without looking up from his plate Patrick murmured, 'In a nutshell.'

'That's no help at all,' I said, disregarding him. 'Didn't he say anything about where he was going, or what he might do, when you got to Milan?'

The engineer shook his head. 'He m . . . m . . . meant to come straight back with us, in the afternoon, I'm sure of th . . . th . . . that.'

'We didn't come straight back, of course,' said Kyle matter-of-factly.

'You didn't?' I was surprised. 'I didn't know that.'

'We were supposed to. They got the return load of horses loaded up and then discovered there were no papers for one of the two they'd put in first. They had to get the whole lot out again, and they weren't very quick because there were only two of them, and by that time I said it was pointless loading again, as it would be too late to start, I'd be out of hours.'

'They should have checked they had all the papers before they loaded,' I said.

'Well, they didn't.'

'Only two of them,' I said, frowning.

'That's right. The young one – Billy, did you say? – and one other. Not you friend Simon. A deaf old fellow.'

'Alf,' I said. 'That's Alf. What about the two others who went over?

They were two specials going with horses from the studs they worked in.'

'From what I could make out from the old man, those two were going on with their horses right to their destination, somewhere further south.'

I thought it over. Simon obviously hadn't intended to come back at all, and it hadn't been the unexpected overnight stop which had given him the idea.

'You didn't see where Simon was headed, I suppose, when you got to Milan?' I spoke without much hope, and they both shook their heads.

'We got off the plane before him,' Kyle said.

I nodded The crew didn't have customs and unloading to see to.

'Well . . . that's that. Thank you for coming today, anyway. And thank you,' I said directly to the engineer, 'for delivering that bottle of pills to the girl in the souvenir shop.'

'P . . . pills? Oh yes, I remember.' He was surprised. 'How on earth d . . . d . . . did you know about that?'

'She told me a tall crew member brought them over for her.'

'I f . . . f . . . found them on the plane, standing on the w . . . w . . . washbasin in the k . . . k . . . karzy. I th . . . th . . . thought I might as well give them to her, as I was g . . . going across anyway. I did . . . didn't see how they got there, b . . . b . . . but they had her name on them.'

'Simon was taking them to her from me,' I explained.

'Oh, I s . . . see.'

Patrick said, grinning, 'Were they . . .?'

'Yes, they were.'

'He didn't go over to the airport building at all, then,' said Patrick flatly. 'He left the pills on board, hoping they would get to Gabriella somehow, and scooted from there.'

'It looks like it,' I agreed gloomily.

'You can get off that end of the airfield quite easily, of course. It's only that scrubland and bushes, and if you walk down that road leading away from the unloading area, the one the horseboxes often use, you're off the place in no time. I should think that explains pretty well why no one saw him.'

'Yes,' I sighed, 'that's what he must have done.'·

'But it doesn't explain why he went,' said Patrick gently.

There was a pause.

'He had . . . troubles,' I said at last.

'*In* trouble?' said Kyle.

'Looming. It might be because of something I discovered that he went. I wanted to find him, and tell him it was . . . safe . . . to come back.'

'On your conscience,' said Patrick.

'You might say so.'

They all nodded, acknowledging their final understanding of my concern for a lost colleague. The waiter brought their cheese and asked whether they would like coffee. I stood up.

'I'll see you again,' I said. 'How about after the fifth, outside the weighing room? After I've changed.'

'Sure thing,' said Patrick.

I ambled off to the weighing room and later got dressed in Mr. Thackery's red and blue colours. I'd never ridden in the Gold Cup before, and although I privately agreed with the engineer's assessment of the situation, there was still something remarkably stirring in going out in the best class race of the season. My human opponents were all handpicked professionals and all Clobber's bunch looked to have the beating of him, but nevertheless my mouth grew dry and my heart thumped.

I suspected Mr. Thackery had entered Clobber more for the prestige of having a Gold Cup runner than from any thought that he would win, and his manner in the parade ring confirmed it. He was enjoying himself enormously, untouched by the sort of anxious excitement characteristic of the hopeful.

'Julian's regards,' he said, beaming and shaking hands vigorously. 'He'll be watching on T.V.'

T.V. There was always the fair chance that one of the people I knew at Fenland might be watching television, though none that I'd heard of was interested in racing. I turned my back on the cameras, as usual.

'Just don't disgrace me,' said Mr. Thackery happily. 'Don't disgrace me, that's all I ask.'

'You could have got a professional,' I pointed out.

'Oh, eh, I could. But frankly, it hasn't done me any harm, here and there, for folks to know you're riding my horses.'

'A mutually satisfactory arrangement, then,' I said dryly.

'Yes,' said Mr. Thackery contentedly. 'That's about it.'

I swung up on his horse, walked out in the parade, and cantered down to the start. Clobber, an eight year old thoroughbred chestnut hunter, had only once won (thanks to being low in the handicap) in the company he was taking on now at level weights, but he shone with condition and his step was bursting with good feeling. Like so many horses, he responded well to spring air and sun on his back and my own spirits lifted with his. It was not, after all, going to be a fiasco.

We lined up and the tapes went up, and Clobber set off to the first fence pulling like a train. As he hadn't a snowball's hope in hell of winning, I thought Mr. Thackery might as well enjoy a few moments in the limelight, and I let Clobber surge his way to the front. Once he got there he settled down and stopped trying to run away with me and we stayed there, surprisingly leading the distinguished field for over two and a half of the three and a quarter miles.

Clobber had never been run in front before, according to the form book, but from his willingness it was evidently to his liking. Holding him up against his inclination, I thought, probably accounted for his inconsistency: he must have lost interest on many occasions when thwarted, and simply packed up trying.

The others came up to him fast and hard going into the second last fence, and three went ahead before the last: but Clobber jumped it cleanly and attacked the hill with his ears still pricked good temperedly, and he finished fourth out of eight with some good ones still behind him. I was pleased with the result myself, having thoroughly enjoyed the whole race, and so it appeared was Mr. Thackery.

'By damn,' he said, beaming, 'that's the best he's ever run.'

'He likes it in front.'

'So it seems, yes. We've not tried that before, I must say.'

A large bunch of congratulating females advanced on him and I rolled the girths round my saddle and escaped to the weighing room to change for the next race. The colours were those of Old Strawberry Leaves, who had commented sourly that it was disgraceful of me to ride in public only three weeks after my father's death, but had luckily agreed not to remove me from his horse. The truth was that he begrudged paying professionals when he could bully the sons of his friends and acquaintances for nothing. Boathook was his best horse, and for the pleasure of winning on him I could easily put up with the insults I got from losing on the others. On that day, however, there was one too good for him from Ireland, and for being beaten by half a length I got the customary bawling out. Not a good loser by any means, Old Strawberry Leaves.

All in all I'd had a good Cheltenham, I thought, as I changed into street clothes: a winner, a second, an also ran, one harmless fall, and fourth in the Gold Cup. I wouldn't improve on it very easily.

Patrick and the other two were waiting for me outside, and after we'd watched the last race together, I drove them down to the station to catch the last train to London. They had all made a mint out of the engineer's tips and were in a fine collective state of euphoria.

'I can see why you like it,' Patrick said on the way. 'It's a magnificent sport. I'll come again.'

'Good,' I said, stopping at the station to let them out. 'I'll see you tomorrow, then.'

He grinned. 'Milan first stop.'

'Arabia again for us,' said Kyle resignedly, shutting the door.

They waved their thanks and began to walk away into the station. An elderly man tottered slowly across in front of my car, and as I was waiting for him to pass the engineer's voice floated back to me, clear and unmistakable.

'It's f . . . funny,' he said, 'you qu . . . quite forget he's a L . . . Lord.'

I turned my head round to them, startled. Patrick looked over his shoulder and saw that I had heard, and laughed. I grinned sardonically in return, and drove off reflecting that I was much in favour of people like him who could let me forget it too.

Chapter Ten

Fire can't burn without air. Deprived of an oxygen supply in a sealed space, it goes out. There existed a state of affairs like a smouldering room which had been shuttered and left to cool down in safety. Nothing much would have happened if I hadn't been trying to find Simon: but when I finally came on a trace of him, it was like throwing wide the door. Fresh air poured in and the whole thing banged into flames.

The fine Cheltenham weather was still in operation on the Friday, the day after the Gold Cup. The met reports in the charter company's office showed clear skies right across Europe, with an extended high pressure area almost stationary over France. No break up of the system was expected for at least twenty-four hours. Someone tapped me on the shoulder and I half turned to find Patrick reading over my shoulder.

'Trouble free trip,' he commented with satisfaction. 'Piece of cake.'

'We've got that old D.C.4 again, I see,' I said, looking out of the window across to where it stood on the tarmac.

'Nice reliable old bus.'

'Bloody uncomfortable old bus.'

Patrick grinned. 'You'll be joining a union next.'

'Workers unite,' I agreed.

He looked me up and down. 'Some worker. You remind me of Fanny Cradock.'

'Of *who?*' I said.

'That woman on television who cooks in a ball gown without marking it.'

'Oh.' I looked down at my neat charcoal worsted, my black tie, and the fraction of white showing at the cuffs. Beside me, in the small overnight bag I now carried everywhere, was the high necked black jersey I worked in, and a hanger for my jacket. Tidiness was addictive: one couldn't kick it, even when it was inappropriate.

'You're no slouch yourself,' I pointed out defensively. He wore his navy gold-braided uniform with the air of authority, his handsome good natured face radiating confidence. A wonderful bedside manner for nervous passengers, I thought. An inborn conviction that one only had to keep to the rules for everything to be all right. Fatal.

'Eight each way, today?' he said.

'Eight out, four back. All brood mares.'

'Ready to drop?'

'Let's hope not too ready.'

'Let's indeed.' He grinned and turned away to check over his flight plan with one of the office staff. 'I suppose,' he said over his shoulder, 'you'd like me to organise an overnight delay at Milan?'

'You suppose correctly.'

'You could do it yourself.'

'How?'

'Load up all the horses and then "lose" the papers for a front one. Like John Kyle said, by the time they'd unloaded and reloaded, it was too late to take off.'

I laughed. 'An absolutely brilliant idea. I shall act on it immediately.'

'That'll be the day.' He smiled over his papers, checking the lists.

The door opened briskly and Yardman came in, letting a blast of cold six-thirty air slip past him.

'All set?' he said, impressing on us his early hour alertness.

'The horses haven't arrived yet,' I said mildly. 'They're late again.'

'Oh.' He shut the door behind him and came in, putting down his briefcase and rubbing his thin hands together for warmth. 'They were due at six.' He frowned and looked at Patrick. 'Are you the pilot?'

'That's right.'

'What sort of trip are we going to have?'

'Easy,' said Patrick. 'The weather's perfect.'

Yardman nodded in satisfaction. 'Good, good.' He pulled out a chair and sat down, lifting and opening his brief case. He had brought all the brood mares' papers with him, and as he seemed content to check them with the airline people himself I leaned lazily against the office wall and thought about Gabriella. The office work went steadily on, regardless of the hour. No nine-to-five about an airline. As usual, some of the flying staff were lying there fast asleep, one on a canvas bed under the counter Patrick was leaning on, another underneath the big table where Yardman sat, and a third on my right, stretched along the top of a row of cupboards. They were all wrapped in blankets, heads and all, and were so motionless that one didn't notice them at first. They managed to sleep solidly through the comings and goings and telephoning and typing, and even when Yardman inadvertently kicked the one under the table he didn't stir.

The first of the horseboxes rolled past the window and drove across to the waiting plane. I peeled myself off the wall, temporarily banished Gabriella, and touched Yardman's arm.

'They're here,' I said.

He looked round and glanced through the window. 'Ah, yes. Well here you are, my dear boy, here's the list. You can load the first six, they are all checked. There's just one more to do . . . it seems there's some query of insurance on this one . . .' He bent back to his work, riffling through his brief case for more papers.

I took the list and walked across to the plane. I had expected Timmie and Conker to arrive in a horsebox as they lived near the stud one lot of horses had come from, but when I got over there I found it was to be Billy and Alf again. They had come with Yardman, and were already sitting on the stacked box sides in the plane, eating sandwiches. With them sat a third man in jodhpurs and a grubby tweed jacket a size too small. He was wearing an old greenish cap and he didn't bother to look up.

'The horses are here,' I said.

Billy turned his wide insolent glare full on and didn't answer. I bent down and touched Alf's knee, and pointed out of the oval window. He saw the horseboxes, nodded philosophically, and began to wrap up his remaining sandwiches. I left them and went down the ramp again, knowing very well that Billy would never obey an instruction of mine if I waited over him to see he did it.

The horsebox drivers said they'd had to make a detour because of roadworks. A detour into a transport café, more like.

Two grooms who had travelled with the mares gave a hand with the loading, which made it easy. The man who had come with Billy and Alf, whose name was John, was more abstracted than skilful, but with six of us it was the quickest job I had done when Billy was along. I imagined that it was because he knew Yardman was within complaining distance that he left me alone.

Yardman came across with the all clear for the other two mares, and we stowed them on board. Then as always we trooped along to the Immigration Office in the main passenger building where a bored official collected our dog-eared passports, flipped through them, and handed them back. Mine still had Mr. on it, because I'd originally applied for it that way, and I intended to put off changing it as long as possible.

'Four grooms and you,' he said to Yardman. 'That's the lot?'

'That's the lot.' Yardman stifled a yawn. Early starts disagreed with him.

A party of bleary-eyed passengers from a cut rate night flight shuffled past in an untidy crocodile.

'O.K. then.' The passport man flicked the tourists a supercilious glance and retired into his office. Not everyone was at his best before breakfast.

Yardman walked back to the plane beside me.

'I've arranged to meet our opposite numbers for lunch,' he said. 'You know what business lunches are, my dear boy. I'm afraid it may drag on a little, and that you'll be kicking your heels about the airport for a few hours. Don't let any of them get . . . er . . . the worse for wear.'

'No,' I agreed insincerely. The longer his lunch, the better I'd be pleased. Billy drunk couldn't be worse than Billy sober, and I didn't intend to waste my hours at Malpensa supervising his intake.

Patrick and his crew were ready out by the plane, and had done their checks. The mobile battery truck stood by the nose cone with its power lead plugged into the aircraft: Patrick liked always to start his engines from the truck, so that he took off with the plane's own batteries fully charged.

Yardman and I followed Billy, Alf and John up the ramp at the rear, and Patrick with his co-pilot Bob, and the engineer, Mike, climbed the forward stairs into the nose. The airport staff wheeled away the stairs and unfastened and removed the two long sections of ramp. The inner port propeller began to grind slowly round as I swung shut the double doors, then sparked into life with a roar, and the plane came alive with vibration. The moment of the first engine firing gave me its usual lift of the spirits and I went along the cabin checking the horses with a smile in my mind.

Patrick moved down the taxi track and turned on to the apron set aside for power checks, the airframe quivering against the brakes as he pushed the throttles open. Holding two of the horses by their head collars I automatically followed him in imagination through the last series of checks before he closed the throttles, released the brakes and rolled round to Gatwick's large single runway. The engine's note deepened and the plane began to move, horses and men leaning against the thrust as the speed built up to a hundred over the tarmac. We unstuck as per schedule and climbed away in a great wheeling turn, heading towards the channel on course to the radio beacon at Dieppe. The heavy mares took the whole thing philosophically, and having checked round the lot of them I went forward into the galley, bending under the luggage racks and stepping over the guy chains as always in the cramped D.C.4.

Mike, the engineer, was already writing names on disposable cups with a red-felt pen.

'All O.K.?' he asked, the eyebrow going up and down like a yo-yo.

'All fine,' I said.

He wrote 'Patrick' and 'Bob' and 'Henry' and asked me the names of the others. 'Mr. Y', 'Billy', 'Alf' and 'John' joined the roll. He filled the crew's cups and mine, and I took Patrick's and Bob's forward while he went back to ask the others if they were thirsty. The rising sun blazed into the cockpit, dazzling after the comparative gloom of the cabin. Both pilots were wearing dark glasses, and Patrick already had his jacket off, and had started on the first of his attendant bunch of bananas. The chart lay handy, the usual unlikely mass of half-inch circles denoting radio stations connected by broad pale blue areas of authorised airlines, with the normal shape of the land beneath only faintly drawn in and difficult to distinguish. Bob pulled a tuft of cotton wool off a shaving cut, made it bleed again, and swore, his exact words inaudible against the racket of the engines. Both of them were wearing head-sets, earphones combined with a microphone mounted on a metal band which curved round in front of the mouth. They spoke to each other by means of a transmitting switch set into the wheel on the control column, since normal speech in that noise was impossible. Giving me a grin and a thumbs up sign for the coffee, they went on with their endless attention to the job in hand. I watched for a bit, then strolled back through the galley, picking up 'Henry' en route, and relaxed on a hay bale to drink, looking down out of the oval window and seeing the coast of France tilt underneath as we passed the Dieppe beacon and set course for Paris.

A day like any other day, a flight like any other flight. And Gabriella waiting at the other end of it. Every half hour or so I checked round the mares, but they were a docile lot and travelled like veterans. Mostly horses didn't eat much in the air, but one or two were picking at their haynets, and a chestnut in the rearmost box was fairly guzzling. I began to untie her depleted net to fill it again for her from one of the bales when a voice said in my ear, 'I'll do that.'

I looked round sharply and found Billy's face two feet from my own.

'You?' The surprise and sarcasm got drowned by the engine noise.

He nodded, elbowed me out of the way, and finished untying the haynet. I watched with astonishment as he carried it away into the narrow starboard gangway and began to stuff it full again. He came back pulling the drawstring tight round the neck, slung it over to hang inside the box, and re-tied its rope on to the cleat. Wordlessly he treated me to a wide sneering glare from the searchlight eyes, pushing past, and flung himself with what suddenly looked like pent-up fury into one of the seats at the back.

In the pair of seats immediately behind him Yardman and John sat side by side. Yardman was frowning crossly at Billy, though to my mind he should have been giving him a pat on the head and a medal for self control.

Yardman turned his head from Billy to me and gave me his graveyard smile. 'What time do we arrive?' he shouted.

'About half an hour.'

He nodded and looked away through the window. I glanced at John and saw that he was dozing, with his grubby cap pushed back on his head and his hands lying limp on his lap. He opened his eyes while I was looking at him, and his relaxed facial muscles sharply contracted so that suddenly he seemed familiar to me, though I was certain I hadn't met him before. It puzzled me for only a second because Billy, getting up again, managed to kick my ankle just out of Yardman's sight. I turned away from him, lashed backwards with my heel, and felt a satisfactory clunking jar as it landed full on his shin. One day, I thought, smiling to myself as I squeezed forward along the plane, one day he'll get tired of it.

We joined the circuit at Malpensa four hours from Gatwick; a smooth, easy trip. Holding the mares' heads I saw the familiar red and white chequered huts near the edge of the airfield grow bigger and bigger as we descended, when they were suddenly behind us at eye level as Patrick levelled out twenty feet from the ground at about a hundred and ten miles an hour. The bump from the tricycle undercarriage as we touched down will full flaps at a fraction above stalling speed wasn't enough to rock the mares on their feet. Top of the class, I thought.

The customs man with his two helpers came on board, and Yardman produced the mares' papers from his briefcase. The checking went on without a hitch, brisk but thorough. The customs man handed the papers back to Yardman with a small bow and signed that the unloading could begin.

Yardman ducked out of any danger of giving a hand with that by saying that he'd better see if the opposite numbers were waiting for him inside the airport. As it was barely half past eleven, it seemed doubtful, but all the same he marched purposefully down the ramp and away across the tarmac, a gaunt black figure with sunshine flashing on his glasses.

The crew got off at the sharp end and followed him, a navy blue trio in peaked caps. A large yellow Shell tanker pulled up in front of the aircraft, and three men in white overalls began the job of refuelling.

We unloaded into the waiting horseboxes in record time, Billy seemingly being as anxious as me to get it done quickly, and within half an hour of landing I had changed my jersey for my jacket and was pushing open the glass doors of the airport. I stood just inside, watching Gabriella. She was selling a native doll, fluffing up the rich dark skirt to show the petticoats underneath, her face solemn and absorbed. The heavy dark club-cut hair swung forward as she leaned across the counter, and her eyes were cool and quiet as she shook her head gently at her customer, the engineer Mike. My chest constricted at the sight of her, and I wondered how I was possibly going to bear leaving again in three hours time. She looked up suddenly as if she felt my gaze, and she saw me and smiled, her soft mouth curving sweet and wide.

Mike looked quite startled at the transformation and turned to see the reason.

'Henry,' said Gabriella, with welcome and gaiety shimmering in her voice. 'Hullo, darling.'

'Darling?' exclaimed Mike, the eyebrow doing its stuff.

Gabriella said in French, 'I've doubled my English vocabulary, as you see. I know two words now.'

'Essential ones, I'm glad to say.'

'Hey,' said Mike. 'If you can talk to her, Henry, ask her about this doll. It's my elder girl's birthday tomorrow, and she's started collecting these things, but I'm damned if I know whether she'll like this one.'

'How old is she?'

'Twelve.'

I explained the situation to Gabriella, who promptly produced a different doll, much prettier and more colourful, which she wrapped up for him while he sorted out some lire. Like Patrick's his wallet was stuffed with several different currencies, and he scattered a day's pay in deutschmarks over the merchandise before finding what he wanted. Collecting his cash in an untidy handful he thanked her cheerfully in basic French, picked up his parcel and walked off upstairs into the restaurant. There were always lunches provided for us on the planes, tourist class lunches packed in boxes, but both Mike and Bob preferred eating on the ground, copiously and in comfort.

I turned back to Gabriella and tried to satisfy my own sort of hunger by looking at her and touching her hand. And I could see in her face that to her too this was like a bowl of rice to the famine of India.

'When do you go?' she said.

'The horses arrive at two thirty. I have to go then to load them. I might get back for a few minutes afterwards, if my boss dallies over his coffee.'

She sighed, looking at the clock. It was ten past noon. 'I have an hour off in twenty minutes. I'll make it two hours . . .' She turned away into swift chatter with the girl along on the duty free shop, and came back smiling. 'I'm doing her last hour today, and she'll do the gift shop in her lunch hour.'

I bowed my thanks to the girl and she laughed back with a flash of teeth, very white against the gloom of her bottle shop.

'Do you want to have lunch up there?' I suggested to Gabriella pointing where Mike and Bob had gone.

She shook her head. 'Too public. Everyone knows me so well. We've time to go to Milan, if you can do that?'

'If the horses get here early, they can wait.'

'Serve them right.' She nodded approvingly her lips twitching.

A crowd of outgoing passengers erupted into the hall and swarmed round the gift counter. I retired to the snack bar at the far end to wait out the twenty minutes, and found Yardman sitting alone at one of the small tables. He waved me to join him, which I would just as soon not have done, and told me to order myself a double gin and tonic, like his.

'I'd really rather have coffee.'

He waved a limp hand permissively. 'Have whatever you like, my dear boy.'

I looked casually round the big airy place, at the glass, the polished wood, the terrazza. Along one side, next to a stall of sweets and chocolates, stretched the serving counter with coffee and beer rubbing shoulders with milk and gin. And down at the far end, close-grouped round another little table and clutching pint glasses, sat Alf and Billy, and with his back to us, John. Two and a half hours of that, I thought wryly, and we'd have a riotous trip home.

'Haven't your people turned up?' I asked Yardman.

'Delayed,' he said resignedly. 'They'll be here about one, though.'

'Good,' I said, but not for his sake. 'You won't forget to ask them about Simon?'

'Simon?'

'Searle.'

'Searle . . . oh yes. Yes, all right, I'll remember.'

Patrick walked through the hall from the office department, exchanged a greeting with Gabriella over the heads of her customers and came on to join us.

'Drink?' suggested Yardman, indicating his glass. He only meant to be hospitable, but Patrick was shocked.

'Of course not.'

'Eh?'

'Well . . . I thought you'd know. One isn't allowed to fly within eight hours of drinking alcohol.'

'Eight hours,' repeated Yardman in astonishment.

'That's right. Twenty-four hours after a heavy party, and better not for forty-eight if you get paralytic.'

'I didn't know,' said Yardman weakly.

'Air Ministry regulations,' Patrick explained. 'I'd like some coffee, though.'

A waitress brought him some, and he unwrapped four sugars and stirred them in. 'I enjoyed yesterday,' he said, smiling at me with his yellow eyes. 'I'll go again. When do you race next?'

'Tomorrow.'

'That's out for a start. When else?'

I glanced at Yardman. 'It depends on the schedules.'

Patrick turned to him in his usual friendly way. 'I went to Cheltenham yesterday and saw our Henry here come forth in the Gold Cup. Very interesting.'

'You know each other well, then?' Yardman asked. His deep set eyes were invisible behind the glasses, and the slanting sunlight showed up every blemish in his sallow skin. I still had no feeling for him either way, not liking, nor disliking. He was easy to work for. He was friendly enough. He was still an enigma.

'We know each other,' Patrick agreed. 'We've been on trips together before.'

'I see.'

Gabriella came down towards us, wearing a supple brown suede coat over her black working dress. She had flat black round-toed patent leather shoes and swung a handbag with the same shine. A neat, composed, self-reliant, nearly beautiful girl who took work for granted and a lover for fun.

I stood up as she came near, trying to stifle a ridiculous feeling of pride, and introduced her to Yardman. He smiled politely and spoke to her in slow Italian, which surprised me a little, and Patrick translated for me into one ear.

'He's telling her he was in Italy during the war. Rather tactless of him, considering her grandfather was killed fighting off the invasion of Sicily.'

'Before she was born,' I protested.

'True.' He grinned. 'She's pro-British enough now, anyway.'

'Miss Barzini tells me you are taking her to lunch in Milan,' Yardman said.

'Yes,' I agreed. 'If that's all right with you? I'll be back by two-thirty when the return mares come.'

'I can't see any objection,' he said mildly. 'Where do you have in mind?'

'Trattoria Romana,' I said promptly. It was where Gabriella, Patrick and I had eaten on our first evening together.

Gabriella put her hand in mine. 'Good. I'm very hungry.' She shook hands with Yardman and waggled her fingers at Patrick. 'Arrivederci.'

We walked away up the hall, the voltage tingling gently through our joined palms. I looked back once, briefly, and saw Yardman and Patrick watching us go. They were both smiling.

Chapter Eleven

Neither of us had much appetite, when it came to the point. We ate half our lasagne and drank coffee, and needed nothing else but proximity. We didn't talk a great deal, but at one point, clairvoyantly reading my disreputable thoughts, she said out of the blue that we cduldn't go to her sister's flat as her sister would be in, complete with two or three kids.

'I was afraid of that,' I said wryly.

'It will have to be next time.'

'Yes.' We both sighed deeply in unison, and laughed.

A little later, sipping her hot coffee, she said, 'How many pills were there in the bottle you sent with Simon Searle?'

'I don't know. Dozens. I didn't count them. The bottle was over three-quarters full.'

'I thought so.' She sighed. 'The baker's wife rang up last night to ask me whether I could let her have some more. She said the bottom of the bottle was all filled up with paper, but if you ask me she's given half of them away to a friend, or something, and now regrets it.'

'There wasn't any paper in the bottle. Only cotton wool on top.'

'I thought so.' She frowned, wrinkling her nose in sorrow. 'I wish she'd told me the truth.'

I stood up abruptly. 'Come on,' I said. 'Leave the coffee.'

'Why?' She began to put on her coat.

'I want to see that bottle.'

She was puzzled. 'She'll have thrown it away.'

'I hope to God she hasn't,' I said urgently, paying the bill. 'If there's paper in the bottle, Simon put it there.'

'You mean . . . it could matter?'

'He thought I was giving the pills to you. He didn't know they'd go to someone else. And I forgot to tell him you didn't speak English. Perhaps he thought when you'd finished the pills you'd read the paper and tell me what it said. Heaven knows. Anyway, we must find it. It's the first and only trace of him we've had.'

We hurried out of the restaurant, caught a taxi, and sped to the bakery. The baker's wife was fat and motherly and looked fifty, though she was probably only thirty-five. Her warm smile for Gabriella slowly turned anxious as she listened, and she shook her head and spread her hands wide.

'It's in the dustbin,' Gabriella said. 'She threw it away this morning.'

'We'll have to look. Ask her if I can look for it.'

The two women consulted.

'She says you'll dirty your fine suit.'

'Gabriella . . .'

'She says the English are mad, but you can look.'

There were three dustbins in the backyard, two luckily empty and one full. We turned this one out and I raked through the stinking contents with a broom handle. The little brown bottle was there, camouflaged by wet coffee grounds and half a dozen noodles. Gabriella took it and wiped it clean on a piece of newspaper while I shovelled the muck back into the dustbin and swept the yard.

'The paper won't come out,' she said. She had the cap off and was poking down the neck of the bottle with her finger. 'It's quite right. There is some in there.' She held it out to me.

I looked and nodded, wrapped the bottle in newspaper, put it on the ground, and smashed it with the shovel. She squatted beside me as I unfolded the paper and watched me pick out from the winking fragments of brown glass the things which had been inside.

I stood up slowly, holding them. A strip torn off the top of a piece of Yardman's stationery. A bank note of a currency I did not recognise, and some pieces of hay. The scrap of writing paper and the money were pinned together, and the hay had been folded up inside them.

'They are nonsense,' said Gabriella slowly.

'Do you have any idea where this comes from?' I touched the note. She flicked it over to see both sides.

'Yugoslavia. One hundred dinars.'

'Is that a lot?'

'About five thousand one hundred lire.'

Three pounds. Wisps of hay. A strip of paper. In a bottle.

Gabriella took the money and paper out of my hands and removed the pin which joined them.

'What do they mean?' she asked.

'I don't know.'

A message in a bottle.

'There are some holes in the paper.'

'Where he put the pin.'

'No. More holes than that. Look.' She held it up to the sky. 'You can see the light through.'

The printed heading said in thick red letters 'Yardman Transport Ltd., Carriers.' The strip of paper was about six inches across and two inches deep from the top smooth edge to the jagged one where it had been torn off the page. I held it up to the light.

Simon had pinpricked four letters. S.M.E.N. I felt the first distant tremor of cold apprehension.

'What is it?' she asked. 'What does it say?'

'Yardman Transport.' I showed her. 'See where he has added to it. If you read it with the pin hole letters tacked on, it says. "Yardman Transports MEN".'

She looked frightened by the bleakness in my voice, as if she could feel the inner coldness growing. 'What does it mean?'

'It means he didn't have a pencil,' I said grimly, evading the final implication. 'Only pins in his coat.'

A message in a bottle, washed ashore.

'I've got to think it out,' I said. 'I've got to remember.'

We perched on a pile of empty boxes stacked in one corner of the baker's yard, and I stared sightlessly at the whitewashed wall opposite and at the single bush in a tub standing in one corner.

'Tell me,' Gabriella said. 'Tell me. You look so . . . so terrible.'

'Billy,' I said. 'Billy put up a smoke screen, after all.'

'Who is Billy?'

'A groom. At least, he works as one. Men . . . Every time Billy has been on a trip, there has been a man who didn't come back.'

'Simon?' she said incredulously.

'No, I don't mean Simon, though he went with Billy . . . No. Someone who went as a groom, but wasn't a groom at all. And didn't come back. I can't remember any of their faces, not to be sure, because I never talked to any of them much. Billy saw to that.'

'How?'

'Oh, by insults and . . .' I stopped, concentrating back. 'The first time I went with Billy, there was a very fat man called John. At least, that was what I was told he was called. He was absolutely useless. Didn't know how to handle horses at all. We did two trips to France that day, and I think he wanted to vanish after the first. I saw him arguing furiously with Billy just before we came back the first time. But Billy made him do the double journey . . . and when he told me John had gone to Paris instead of coming back with us, he poured beer over my foot, so that I'd think about that, and not about John. And he made sure of it by picking a fight on the plane coming back . . .'

'But who was this John?'

I shook my head. 'I've no idea.'

'And were there others?'

'Yes . . . we went to New York next, he and I. There was a groom travelling with a half-bred Norwegian horse. He hardly talked at all, said he didn't speak English much. I understood he was staying in the States for a fortnight; but who knows if he came back? And on that trip Billy smashed a bar across my fingers so that they hurt all the way across, and I thought about them, not the Norwegian groom.'

'Are you sure?' She was frowning.

'Oh yes, I'm sure. I thought once before that Billy had done it for a purpose. I just got the purpose wrong.' I pondered. 'There was a day we took a man with a large bushy moustache to France, and a fortnight later we brought a man with a large bushy moustache back again. I never looked beyond the moustache . . . I think it could have been two different men.'

'What did Billy do, those times?'

'On the way over he poured syrupy coffee on my head, and I spent nearly all the time in the washroom getting it out. And on the way back he hit me with a chain, and I went up into the galley all the way with the engineer to avoid any more.'

She looked at me very gravely. 'Is that . . . is that the lot?'

I shook my head. 'We went to New York last week. I told Yardman if Billy didn't leave me alone I'd quit. The journey out went quite all right, but coming back ... there was a man who was plainly not a horseman. He wasn't even comfortable in the riding clothes he had on. I thought at the time he was the owner's nephew or something, cadging a free ride, but again I didn't talk to him much. I slept all the way back. All ten hours ... I don't usually get tired like that, but I thought it was only because it was my fourth Atlantic crossing in six days ...'

'A sleeping pill?' she said slowly.

'It might have been. Alf brought some coffee back for me soon after we left. There was a restive colt in the aft box and I was trying to soothe him ... It could have been in that.'

'Alf?'

'An old deaf man, who always goes with Billy.'

'Do you think it *was* a sleeping pill?'

'It could ... I was still tired long after I got home. I even went to sleep in the bath.'

'It's serious,' she said.

'Today,' I said. 'There's a stranger with us today. His name is John too. I've never met him before, but there's something about him ... I was looking at him on the plane and wondering what it was, and Billy kicked me on the ankle. I kicked him back, but I went away, and stopped thinking about that man.'

'Can you think now?'

'Well ... his hands are wrong for one thing. Stablemen's hands are rough and chafed from being wet so often in cold weather, with washing tack and so on, but his are smooth, with well shaped nails.'

She picked up one of my hands and looked at it, running the tips of her fingers over the roughnesses which had developed since I left my desk job.

'They are not like yours, then.'

'Not like mine. But it's expression really. I watched him wake up. It was what came into his face with consciousness ...' I could remember that moment vividly, in spite of Billy's kick. I knew that expression very well ... so what was it? 'Oh,' I exclaimed in enlightenment, half laughing at my own stupidity, 'I know what it is ... he went to the same school as I did.'

'You do know him then, I mean, you've seen him before, if you were at school together.'

'Not together. He's older. He must have left about five years before I went. No, I've never seen him before, but the look he has is typical of some of the boys there. Not the nicest ones ... only the ones who think they are God's gift to mankind and everyone else is a bit inferior. He's one of those. Definitely *not* a groom. He looked as if wearing the grubby riding clothes he's got on was a kick in the dignity.'

'But you don't wear riding clothes,' she pointed out. 'It isn't necessary for him if he doesn't like them.'

'It is though. Alf wears jodhpurs, Billy wears jeans. The two grooms who travel turn about with these two, Timmie and Conker, they both wear breeches to work in. It's a sort of badge of office ... No one would think twice about a man arriving on a horse transport dressed in breeches or jodhpurs.'

'No, I see that.'

'No one bothers much about our passports,' I said. 'Look how simply I came out into Milan today, through the airport staff door. Hardly any airports, especially the very small ones, take much notice of you, if you work on aeroplanes. It's dead easy just to walk off most airfields round at the loading bays without ever being challenged. The Americans are strictest, but even they are used to our comings and goings.'

'But people do look at your passports sometimes, surely,' she protested.

I produced mine, battered and dogeared in the last three months after several years of dark blue stiffness. 'Look at it. It gets like that from always being in my pocket, but it doesn't get stamped much.' I turned through the pages. 'American visa, certainly. But look, the only stamp from Milan is the time I came on a scheduled flight and went through immigration with the other passengers. Hardly a mark for France, and I've been over there several times . . . of course it gets looked at, but never very thoroughly. It must be easy to fake one in this condition, and even travelling without one wouldn't be impossible. A pilot told me he'd done it for three weeks once, all over the world.'

'People who work on aircraft would go mad if everyone started checking their passports thoroughly every time they walked in or out.'

'Well . . . normally there's no need for it. It isn't all that easy to get on a single one way flight as a worker. Impossible, if you haven't a strong pull somewhere or other. Just any odd person who fancies a quiet trip to foreign parts wouldn't have a hope of getting himself into a horse transport. But if the transport agency itself, or someone working for it, is ready to export people illegally along with the horses, then it's easy.'

'But . . . what people?'

'What indeed! Billy can hardly advertise his service in the daily press. But he has no shortage of customers.'

'Crooks, do you think?' Gabriella asked frowning.

I fingered the bank-note and twisted the small pieces of hay.

'Hay,' I said. 'Why hay?'

Gabriella shrugged. 'Perhaps he found the money in some hay.'

'Of course!' I exclaimed. 'You're dead right. Haynets. Carried openly on and off the planes and never searched by customs officers. Perhaps they're transporting currency as well as men.' I told her about Billy refilling the net for me on the trip over, and how astonished I had been.

'But Henry darling, what I really do not understand is why you were not astonished all along at the unpleasant things Billy has been doing to you. I would have thought it utterly extraordinary, and I would have made a very big fuss about it.' She looked solemn and doubtful.

'Oh, I thought it was simply because I . . .' I stopped.

'Because you what?'

I smiled slightly. 'Because I belong to a sort of people he thinks should be exterminated.'

'Henry!' Her mouth lost its severity. 'What sort of people?'

'Well . . . you have counts and countesses still in Italy . . .'

'But you're not . . . you're not, are you . . . a count?'

'Sort of. Yes.'

She looked at me doubtfully, halfway to laughing, not sure that I was not teasing her.

'I don't believe you.'

'The reason I wasn't astonished at Billy knocking me about was that I knew he hated my guts for having a title.'

'That makes sense, I suppose.' She managed to frown and smile at the same time, which looked adorable. 'But if you have a title, Henry, why are you working in a horse transport?'

'You tell me why,' I said.

She looked at me searchingly for a moment, then she put her arms round my neck and her cheek on mine, with her mouth against my ear.

'It isn't enough for you to have a title,' she said. 'It isn't enough for anyone. It is necessary to show also that you are . . .' She fished around in her French vocabulary, and came up with a word: '. . . véritable. Real.'

I took a deep breath of relief and overspilling love, and kissed her neck where the dark hair swung below her ear.

'My wife will be a countess,' I said. 'Would you mind that?'

'I could perhaps bear it.'

'And me? Could you bear me? For always?'

'I love you,' she said in my ear. 'Yes. For always. Only, Henry . . .'

'Only what?'

'You won't stop being real?'

'No,' I said sadly.

She pulled away from me, shaking her head.

'I'm stupid. I'm sorry. But if even I can doubt you . . . and so quickly . . . you must always be having to prove . . .'

'Always,' I agreed.

'Still, you don't have to go quite so far.'

My heart sank.

'It's not everyone,' she said, 'who gets proposed to in a baker's backyard surrounded by dustbins.' Her mouth trembled and melted into the heart-wrenching smile.

'You wretch, my love.'

'Henry,' she said, 'I'm so happy I could burst.'

I kissed her and felt the same, and lived another half minute of oblivion before I thought again of Simon.

'What is it?' she said, feeling me straighten.

'The time . . .'

'Oh.'

'And Simon . . .'

'I fear for him,' she said, half under her breath.

'I too.'

She took the piece of paper out of my hand and looked at it again.

'We've been trying to avoid realising what this means.'

'Yes,' I said softly.

'Say it, then.'

'This was the only message he had a chance of sending. The only way he could send it.' I paused, looking into her serious dark eyes. After ten seconds I finished it. 'He is dead.'

She said in distress, 'Perhaps he is a prisoner.'

I shook my head. 'He's the third man who's disappeared. There was a man called Ballard who used to arrange trips from this end, and the man who used to have my own job, a man called Peters. They both vanished, Ballard over a year ago, and no one's heard of them since.'

'This Billy . . .' she said slowly, her eyes anxious.

'This Billy,' I said, 'is young and heartless, and carries a loaded revolver under his left arm.'

'Please . . . don't go back with him.'

'It will be quite safe as long as I keep quiet about this.' I took the hurried, desperate, pinpricked message back, folded it up with the banknote and the hay, and put them all in my wallet. 'When I get back to England, I'll find out who I have to tell.'

'The police,' she said, nodding.

'I'm not sure . . .' I thought about the Yugoslav currency and remembered Gabriella saying on our first evening 'Communists begin at Trieste.' I felt like someone who had trodden through a surface into a mole run underneath, and had suddenly realised that it was part of a whole dark invisible network. I thought it very unlikely that the men I'd flow with were ordinary crooks. They were couriers, agents . . . heaven knew what. It seemed fantastic to me to have brushed so closely with people I had known must exist but never expected to see; but I supposed the suburban people who had lived next door to Peter and Helen Kroger in Cranley Drive, Ruislip, had been pretty astonished too.

'Billy must have unloaded whatever he brought over in the haynet today,' I said. 'But going back . . .'.

'No,' Gabriella said vehemently. 'Don't look. That's what Simon must have done. Found the money. And Billy saw him.'

It might have been like that. And there had been two extra grooms on that trip, men I'd never seen before. Somehow, on the way, Simon had come across something I'd been blind to: perhaps because there was one more man than he'd arranged for; perhaps because Billy couldn't distract his attention by the methods he'd used on me; perhaps because of other happenings in the past which I didn't know about. In any case. Simon had found Billy out, and had let Billy know it. I thought drearily of Simon suddenly realising towards the end of that flight that Ballard and Peters had never come back, and that he wouldn't get a chance to put Billy in gaol. Billy the young thug, with his ready gun. A few minutes in the lavatory, that was all the time he'd had. No pencil. Only his pins, and the little bottle I'd given him in the privacy of the airline office; the bottle Billy didn't know existed, with Gabriella's name on it. Pills into loo. Banknote and paper with its inadequate message into bottle. Simon into eternity.

'Please don't search the haynets,' Gabriella said again.

'No,' I agreed. 'Someone official had better do it, next time Billy goes on a trip.'

She relaxed with relief. 'I'd hate you to disappear.'

I smiled. 'I won't do that. I'll go back most of the way up front with the crew, with Patrick and the man who bought the doll. And when I get to England I'll telephone you to let you know I arrived safely. How's that?'

'It would be wonderful. I could stop worrying.'

'Don't start,' I said confidently. 'Nothing will go wrong.'

How the local gods must have laughed their Roman heads off.

Chapter Twelve

We went through the baker's shop and out into the street I looked somewhat anxiously at my watch and calculated a dead heat with the brood mares.

'We need a taxi,' I said.

Gabriella shook her head. 'Very unlikely to find one in this quarter. We'd better catch a tram back to the centre, and take one on from there.'

'All right,' I agreed. 'Tram or taxi, whichever comes first.'

The trams ran along the busy street at the end of the quiet empty road where the baker lived, and we began to walk towards them with some dispatch.

'I didn't realise how late it is,' Gabriella said, catching sight of a clock with the hands together pointing north-east.

'And that one's slow. It's a quarter past.'

'Oh dear.'

One of the long green and cream single decker trams rolled across the end of the road, not far ahead.

'Run,' Gabriella said. 'The stop's just round the corner. We must catch it.'

We ran, holding hands. It couldn't have been more than ten strides to the corner. Not more.

Gabriella cried out suddenly and stumbled, whirling against me as I pulled her hand. There was a sharp scaring stab in my side and we fell down on the pavement, Gabriella's weight pulling me over as I tried to save her from hurting herself.

Two or three passers by stopped to help her up, but she didn't move. She was lying face down, crumpled. Without belief, I stared at the small round hole near the centre of the back of her coat. Numbly, kneeling beside her, I put my left hand inside my jacket against my scorching right side, and when I brought it out it was covered in blood.

'Oh no,' I said in English. 'Oh dear God, no.'

I bent over her and rolled her up and on to her back in my arms. Her eyes were open. They focused on my face. She was alive. It wasn't much.

'Henry,' her voice was a whisper. 'I can't . . . breathe.'

The three passers by had grown to a small crowd. I looked up desperately into their enquiring faces.

'Doctor,' I said. 'Medico.' That was Spanish. 'Doctor.'

'Si si,' said a small boy at my elbow. 'Un dottore, si.'

There was a stir in the crowd and a great deal of speculation of which I understood only one word. 'Inglese,' they said, and I nodded. 'Inglese.'

I opened gently the front of Gabriella's brown suede coat. There was a jagged tear in the right side, nearest me, and the edges of it were dark. Underneath, the black dress was soaking. I waved my arm wildly round at the people to get them to stand back a bit, and they did take one pace away. A motherly looking women produced a pair of scissors from her handbag and knelt down on Gabriella's other side. She pointed at me to open the coat again, and when I'd tucked it back between Gabriella's body and my own she began to cut away the dress. Gentle as she was, Gabriella moved in my arms and gave a small gasping cry.

'Hush,' I said, 'my love, it's all right.'

'Henry . . .' She shut her eyes.

I held her in anguish while the woman with the scissors carefully cut and peeled away a large piece of dress. When she saw what lay underneath her big face filled with overwhelming compassion, and she began to shake her head. 'Signor,' she said to me, 'mi dispiace molto. Molto.'

I took the clean white handkerchief out of my top pocket, folded it inside out, and put it over the terrible wound. The bullet had smashed a rib on its way out. There were splinters of it showing in the bleeding area just below her breast. The bottom edge of her white bra had a new scarlet border. I gently untucked the coat and put it over her again to keep her warm and I thought in utter agony that she would die before the doctor came.

A carabiniere in glossy boots and greenish khaki breeches appeared beside us, but I doubt if I could have spoken to him even if he'd known the same language. The crowd chattered to him in subdued voices and he left me alone.

Gabriella opened her eyes. Her face was grey and wet with the sweat of appalling pain.

'Henry . . .'.

'I'm here.'

'I can't . . . breathe.'

I raised her a little more so that she was half sitting, supported by my arm and my bent knee. The movement was almost too much for her. Her pallor became pronounced. The short difficult breaths passed audibly through her slackly open mouth.

'Don't . . . leave me.'

'No,' I said. 'Hush, my dearest love.'

'What . . . happened?'

'You were shot,' I said.

'Shot . . .'. She showed no surprise. 'Was it . . . Billy?'

'I don't know. I didn't see. Don't talk, my sweet love, don't talk. The doctor will be here soon.'

'Henry . . .'. She was exhausted, her skin the colour of death. 'Henry . . . I love you.'

Her eyes flickered shut again, but she was still conscious, her left hand moved spasmodically and restlessly on the ground beside her and the lines of suffering deepening in her face.

I would have given anything, anything on earth, to have had her whole again, to have taken that pain away.

The doctor, when at last he came, was young enough to have been newly qualified. He had thick black curly hair and thin clever hands: this was what I most saw of him as he bent over Gabriella, and all I remembered. He looked briefly under my white handkerchief and turned to speak to the policeman.

I heard the words 'auto ambulanza' and 'pallota,' and eager information from the crowd.

The young doctor went down on one knee and felt Gabriella's pulse. She opened her eyes, but only a fraction.

'Henry . . .'.

'I'm here. Don't talk.'

'Mm . . .'.

The young doctor said something soothing to her in Italian, and she said faintly 'Si.' He opened his case beside him on the ground and with quick skilful fingers prepared an injection, made a hole in her stocking, swabbed her skin with surgical spirit, and pushed the needle firmly into her thigh. Again he spoke to her gently, and again felt her pulse. I could read nothing but reassurance in his manner, and the reassurance was for her, not me.

After a while she opened her eyes wider and looked at me, and a smile struggled on to her damp face.

'That's better,' she said. Her voice was so weak as to be scarcely audible, and she was growing visibly more breathless. Nothing was better, except the pain.

I smiled back. 'Good. You'll be all right soon, when they get you to hospital.'

She nodded a fraction. The doctor continued to hold her pulse, checking it on his watch.

Two vehicles drove up and stopped with a screech of tyres. A Citroen police car and an ambulance like a large estate car. Two carabinieri of obvious seniority emerged from one, and stretcher bearers from the other. These last, and the doctor, lifted Gabriella gently out of my arms and on to the stretcher. They piled blankets behind her to support her, and I saw the doctor take a look at what he could see of the small hole in her back. He didn't try to take off her coat.

One of the policeman said, 'I understand you speak French.'

'Yes,' I said, standing up. I hadn't felt the hardness of the pavement until that moment. The leg I'd been kneeling on was numb.

'What are the young lady's name and address?'

I told him. He wrote them down.

'And your own?'

I told him.

'What happened?' he said, indicating the whole scene with a flickering wave of the hand.

'We were running to catch the tram. Someone shot at us from back there.' I pointed down the empty street towards the baker's.

'Who?'

'I didn't see.' They were lifting Gabriella into the ambulance. 'I must go with her,' I said.

The policeman shook his head. 'You can see her later. You must come with us, and tell us exactly what happened.'

'I said I wouldn't leave her . . .' I couldn't bear to leave her. I took a quick stride and caught the doctor by the arm. 'Look,' I said, pulling open my jacket.

He looked. He tugged my bloodstained shirt out of my trousers to inspect the damage more closely. A ridged furrow five inches long along my lowest rib. Not very deep. It felt like a burn. The doctor told the policeman who also looked.

'All right,' said the one who spoke French, 'I suppose you'd better go and have it dressed.' He wrote an address on a page of his notebook, tore it off and gave it to me. 'Come here, afterwards.'

'Yes.'

'Have you your passport with you?'

I took it out of my pocket and gave it to him, and put the address he'd given me in my wallet. The doctor jerked his head towards the ambulance to get in, and I did.

'Wait,' said the policeman as they were shutting the door. 'Did the bullet go through the girl into you?'

'No,' I said. 'Two bullets. She was hit first, me after.'

'We will look for them,' he said.

Gabriella was still alive when we reached the hospital. Still alive when they lifted her, stretcher and all, on to a trolley. Still alive while one of the ambulance men explained rapidly to a doctor what had happened, and while that doctor and another took in her general condition, left my handkerchief undisturbed, and whisked her away at high speed.

'Inglese.' I shook my head. 'Non parlo italiano.'

'Sit down,' he said in English. His accent was thick, his vocabulary tiny, but it was a relief to be able to talk to him at all. He led me into a small white cubicle containing a hard, high narrow bed and a chair. He pointed to the chair and I sat on it. He went away and returned with a nurse carrying some papers.

'The name of the miss?'

I told him. The nurse wrote it down, name, address and age, gave me a comforting smile, took the papers away and came back with a trolley of equipment and a message.

She told it to the doctor, and he translated, as it was for me.

'Telephone from carabinieri. Please go to see them before four.'

I looked at my watch, blank to the time. It was still less than an hour since Gabriella and I had run for the tram. I had lived several ages.

'I understand,' I said.

'Please now, remove the coat,' the doctor said.

I stood up, took off my jacket and slid my right arm out of my shirt. He put two dressings over the bullet mark, an impregnated gauze one and a slightly padded one with adhesive tape. He pressed the tapes firmly into my skin and stood back. I put my arm back into my shirt sleeve.

'Don't you feel it?' he said. He seemed surprised.

'No.'

His rugged face softened. 'E sua moglie?'

I didn't understand.

'I am sorry . . . is she your wife?'

'I love her,' I said. The prospect of losing her was past bearing. There were tears suddenly in my eyes and on my cheeks. 'I love her.'

'Yes.' He nodded, sympathetic and unembarrassed, one of a nation who saw no value in stiff upper lips. 'Wait here. We will tell you . . .' He left the sentence unfinished and went away, and I didn't know whether it was because he didn't want to tell me she was dying or because he simply didn't know enough English to say what he meant.

I waited an hour I couldn't endure again. At the end of it another doctor came, a tall grey haired man with a fine boned face.

'You wish to know about Signora Barzini?' His English was perfect, his voice quiet and very precise.

I nodded, unable to ask.

'We have cleaned and dressed her wound. The bullet passed straight through her lung, breaking a rib on the way out. The lung was collapsed. The air from it, and also a good deal of blood, had passed into the chest cavity. It was necessary to remove the air and blood at once so that the lung would have room to inflate again, and we have done that.' He was coolly clinical.

'May I . . . may I see her?'

'Later,' he said, without considering it. 'She is unconscious from the anaesthetic and she is in the post-operative unit. You may see her later.'

'And . . . the future?'

He half smiled. 'There is always danger in such a case, but with good care she could certainly recover. The bullet itself hit nothing immediately fatal; none of the big blood vessels. If it had, she would have died soon, in the street. The longer she lived, the better were her chances.'

'She seemed to get worse,' I said, not daring to believe him.

'In some ways that was so,' he explained patiently. 'Her injury was very painful, she was bleeding internally, and she was suffering from the onset of shock, which as you may know is a physical condition often as dangerous as the original damage.'

I nodded, swallowing.

'We are dealing with all those things. She is young and healthy, which is good, but there will be more pain and there may be difficulties. I can give you no assurances. It is too soon for that. But hope, yes definitely, there is considerable hope.'

'Thank you,' I said dully, 'for being so honest.'

He gave his small smile again. 'Your name is Henry?'

I nodded.

'You have a brave girl,' he said.

If I couldn't see her yet I thought, I would have to go and talk to the police. They had said to be with them by four and it was already twenty past; not that that mattered a jot.

I was so unused to thinking in the terms of the strange half world into which I had stumbled that I failed to take the most elementary precautions. Distraught about Gabriella, it didn't even cross my mind that if I had been found and shot at in a distant back street I was equally vulnerable outside the hospital.

There was a taxi standing in the forecourt, the driver reading a newspaper. I waved an arm at him, and he folded the paper, started the engine and drove over. I gave him the paper with the address the policeman had written out for me, and he looked at it in a bored sort of way and nodded. I opened the cab door and got in. He waited politely till I was settled, his head half turned, and then drove smoothly out of the hospital gates. Fifty yards away he turned right down a tree-lined secondary road beside the hospital, and fifty yards down there he stopped. From a tree one yard from the curb a lithe figure peeled itself, wrenched open the nearest door, and stepped inside.

He was grinning fiercely, unable to contain his triumph. The gun with the silencer grew in his hand as if born there. I had walked right into his ambush.

Billy the Kid.

'You took your bloody time, you stinking bastard,' he said.

I looked at him blankly, trying to keep the shattering dismay from showing. He sat down beside me and shoved his gun into my ribs, just above the line it had already drawn there.

'Get cracking Vittorio,' he said. 'His effing Lordship is late.'

The taxi rolled smoothly away and gathered speed.

'Four o'clock we said,' said Billy, grinning widely. 'Didn't you get the message?'

'The police . . .' I said weakly.

'Hear that, Vittorio?' Billy laughed. 'The hospital thought you were the police. Fancy that. How extraordinary.'

I looked away from him, out of the window on my left.

'You just try it,' Billy said. 'You'll have a bullet through you before you get the door open.'

I looked back at him.

'Yeah,' he grinned. 'Takes a bit of swallowing, don't it, for you to have to do what I say. Sweet, I call it. And believe me, matey, you've hardly bloody started.'

I didn't answer. It didn't worry him. He sat sideways, the gloating grin fixed like a rictus.

'How's the bird . . . Miss what's her name?' He flicked his fingers. 'The girl friend.'

I did some belated thinking.

I said stonily, 'She's dead.'

'Well, well,' said Billy gleefully. 'How terribly sad. Do you hear that, Vittorio? His Lordship's bit of skirt has passed on.'

Vittorio's head nodded. He concentrated on his driving, mostly down side streets, avoiding heavy traffic. I stared numbly at the greasy back of his neck and wondered what chance I had of grabbing Billy's gun before he pulled the trigger. The answer to that, I decided, feeling its steady pressure against my side, was none.

'Come on now, come on,' said Billy. 'Don't you think I'm clever.'

I didn't answer. Out of the corner of my eye I sensed the grin change from triumph to vindictiveness.

'I'll wipe that bloody superior look off your face,' he said. 'You sodding blue-arsed—'

I said nothing. He jerked the gun hard into my ribs.

'You just wait, your high and mighty Lordship, you just bloody well wait.'

There didn't in fact seem to be much else I could do. The taxi bowled steadily on, leaving the city centre behind.

'Hurry it up, Vittorio,' said Billy 'We're late.'

Vittorio put his foot down and we drove on away from the town and out into an area of scrubland. The road twisted twice and then ran straight, and I stared in astonishment and disbelief at what lay ahead at the end of it. It was the broad open sweep of Malpensa Airport. We had approached it from the side road leading away from the loading bay, the road the horseboxes sometimes took.

The D.C.4 stood there on the tarmac less than a hundred yards away, still waiting to take four mares back to England. Vittorio stopped the taxi fifty yards from the loading area. 'Now,' said Billy to me, enjoying himself again. 'You listen and do as you are told, otherwise I'll put a hole in you. And it'll be in the breadbasket, not the heart. That's a promise.' I didn't doubt him. 'Walk down the road, straight across to the plane, up the ramp and into the toilet. Get it? I'll be two steps behind you, all the way.'

I was puzzled, but greatly relieved. I had hardly expected such a mild end to the ride. Without a word I opened the door and climbed out. Billy wriggled agilely across and stood up beside me, the triumphant sneer reasserting itself on his babyish mouth.

'Go on,' he said.

There was no one about at that side of the airfield. Four hundred yards ahead there were people moving round the main building, but four hundred yards across open tarmac looked a very long way. Behind lay scrubland and the taxi. Mentally shrugging, I followed Billy's instructions: walked down the short stretch of road, across to the plane, and up the ramp. Billy stalked a steady two paces behind me, too far to touch, too near to miss.

At the top of the ramp stood Yardman. He was frowning heavily, though his eyes were as usual inscrutable behind the glasses, and he was tapping his watch.

'You've cut it very fine,' he said in annoyance. 'Another quarter of an hour and we'd have been in trouble.'

My chief feeling was still of astonishment and unreality. Billy broke the bubble, speaking over my shoulder.

'Yeah, he was dead late coming out of the hospital. Another five minutes, and we'd have had to go in for him.'

My skin rose in goose pimples. The ride had after all led straight to the heart of things. The pit yawned before me.

'Get in then,' Yardman said. 'I'll go and tell the pilot our wandering boy has at last returned from lunch and we can start back for England.' He went past us and down the ramp, hurrying.

Billy sniggered. 'Move, your effing Lordship,' he said. 'Open the toilet door and go in. The one on the left.' The pistol jabbed against the bottom of my spine. 'Do as you're told.'

I walked the three necessary steps, opened the left hand door, and went in.

'Put your hands on the wall,' said Billy. 'Right there in front of you, so that I can see them.'

I did as he said. He swung the door shut behind him and leaned against it. We waited in silence. He sniggered complacently from time to time, and I considered my blind stupidity.

Yardman. Yardman transports men. Simon had fought through to a conclusion, where I had only gone halfway. Billy's smoke screen had filled my eyes. I hadn't seen beyond it to Yardman. And instead of grasping from Simon's message and my own memory that it had to be Yardman too, I had kissed Gabriella and lost the thread of it. And five minutes later she had been bleeding on the pavement . . .

I shut my eyes and rested my forehead momentarily against the wall. Whatever the future held it meant nothing to me if Gabriella didn't live.

After a while Yardman returned. He rapped on the door and Billy moved over to give him room to come in.

'They're all coming across, now,' he said. 'We'll be away shortly. But before we go . . . how about the girl?'

'Croaked,' said Billy laconically.

'Good,' Yardman said. 'One less job for Vittorio.'

My head jerked.

'My dear boy,' said Yardman. 'Such a pity. Such a nice girl too.' In quite a different voice he said to Billy, 'Your shooting was feeble. You are expected to do better than that.'

'Hey,' there was a suspicion of a whine in Billy's reply. 'They started running.'

'You should have been closer.'

'I *was* close. Close enough. Ten yards at the most. I was waiting in a doorway, ready to pump it into them just after they'd passed me. And then they just suddenly started running. I got the girl all right, though, didn't I? I mean, I got her, even if she lingered a bit, like. As for him, well, granted I did miss him, but she sort of swung round and knocked him over just as I pulled the trigger.'

'If Vittorio hadn't been with you,' Yardman began coldly.

'Well, he was with me, then, wasn't he?' Billy defended himself. 'After all, it was me that told him to worm into that crowd round the girl and keep his ears flapping. Granted it was Vittorio who heard the police telling this creep to go and see them straight from the hospital, but it was me that thought of ringing up the hospital and winkling him out. And anyway, when I rang you up the second time, didn't you say it was just as well, you could do with him back here alive as you'd got a use for him?'

'All right,' said Yardman. 'It's worked out all right, but it was still very poor shooting.'

He opened the door, letting in a brief murmur of people moving the ramp away, and closed it behind him. Billy sullenly delivered a long string of obscenity, exclusively concerned with the lower part of the body. Not one to take criticism sweetly.

The aircraft trembled as the engines started one after the other. I glanced at my watch, on a level with my eyes. If it had been much later, Patrick would have refused to take off that day. As it was, there was little enough margin for him to get back to Gatwick within fifteen hours of going on duty that morning. It was the total time which mattered, not just flying hours, with enquiries and fines to face for the merest minutes over.

'Kneel down.' Billy said, jabbing me in the spine. 'Keep your hands on the wall. And don't try lurching into me accidental like when we take off. It wouldn't do you an effing bit of good.'

I didn't move.

'You'll do as you're ruddy well told, matey,' said Billy, viciously kicking the back of one of my knees. 'Get down.'

I knelt down on the floor. Billy said 'There's a good little earl,' with a pleased sneer in his voice, and rubbed the snout of his pistol up and down the back of my neck.

The plane began to taxi, stopped at the perimeter for power checks, rolled forward on to the runway, and gathered speed. Inside the windowless lavatory compartment it was impossible to tell the exact moment of unstick, but the subsequent climb held me close anyway against the wall, as I faced the tail, and Billy stopped himself from overbalancing on to me by putting his gun between my shoulder blades and leaning on it. I hoped remotely that Patrick wouldn't strike an air pocket.

Up in the cockpit, as far away in the plane as one could get and no doubt furious with me for coming back so late, he would be drinking his first coffee, and peeling his first banana, a mile from imagining I could need his help. He completed a long climbing turn and after a while levelled off and reduced power. We were well on the first leg south to the Mediterranean.

The Mediterranean. A tremor as nasty as the one I'd had on finding Yardman at the heart of things fluttered through my chest. The D.C.4 was unpressurised. The cabin doors could be opened in flight. Perhaps Billy had simply opened the door and pushed Simon out.

The traceless exit. Ten thousand feet down to the jewel blue sea.

Chapter Thirteen

Yardman came back, edging round the door.

'It's time,' he said.

Billy sniggered. 'Can't be too soon.'

'Stand up, stand up, my dear boy,' Yardman said. 'You look most undignified down there. Face the wall all the time.'

As I stood up he reached out, grasped my jacket by the collar, and pulled it backwards and downwards. Two more jerks and it was off.

'I regret this, I do indeed,' he said. 'But I'm afraid we must ask you to put your hands together behind your back.'

I thought that if I did that I was as good as dead. I didn't move. Billy squeezed round into the small space between me and the washbasin and put the silencer against my neck.

Yardman's unhurried voice floated into my ear. 'I really must warn you, my dear boy, that your life hangs by the merest thread. If Billy hadn't clumsily missed you in the street, you would be in the Milan morgue by now. If you do not do as we ask, he will be pleased to rectify his mistake immediately.'

I put my hands behind my back.

'That's right,' Yardman said approvingly. He tied them together with a rough piece of rope.

'Now, my dear boy,' he went on. 'You are going to help us. We have a little job for you.'

'Billy's searchlight eyes were wide and bright, and I didn't like his smile.

'You don't ask what it is,' Yardman said. 'So I will tell you. You are going to persuade your friend the pilot to alter course.'

Alter course. Simple words. Premonition shook me to the roots. Patrick wasn't strong enough.

I said nothing. After a moment Yardman continued conversationally, 'We were going to use the engineer originally, but as I find you and the pilot are goods friends I am sure he will do as you ask.'

I still said nothing.

'He doesn't understand,' Billy sneered.

I understood all right. Patrick would do what they told him. Yardman opened the washroom door. 'Turn round,' he said.

I turned. Yardman's eyes fell immediately to the dried bloodstains on my shirt. He reached out a long arm, pulled the once white poplin out of my trousers and saw the bandage underneath.

'You grazed him,' he said to Billy, still critical.

'Considering he was running and falling at the same time that isn't bad, not with a silencer.'

'Inefficient.' Yardman wasn't letting him off the hook.

'I'll make up for it,' Billy said viciously.

'Yes, you do that.'

Yardman turned his head back to me. 'Outside, dear boy.'

I followed him out of the washroom into the cabin, and stopped. It looked utterly normal. The four mares stood peacefully in the two middle boxes, installed, I presumed, by Yardman and Alf. The foremost and aft boxes were strapped down flat. There were the normal bales of hay dotted about. The noise was the normal noise, the air neither hotter nor colder than usual. All familiar. Normal. As normal as a coffin.

Yardman walked on.

'This way,' he said. He crossed the small area at the back of the plane, stepped up on to the shallow platform formed by the flattened rear box, walked across it, and finished down again on the plane's floor, against the nearest box containing mares. Billy prodded his gun into my back. I joined Yardman.

'So wise, my dear boy,' nodded my employer. 'Stand with your back to the box.'

I turned round to face the tail of the aircraft. Yardman took some time fastening my tied hands to the centre banding bar round the mare's box. Billy stood up on the flattened box and amused himself by pointing his gun at various parts of my anatomy. He wasn't going to fire it. I took no notice of his antics but looked beyond him, to the pair of seats at the back. There was a man sitting there, relaxed and interested. The man who had flown out with us, whose name was John. Milan hadn't been the end of his journey, I thought. Yardman wanted to land him somewhere else.

He stood up slowly, his pompous manner a complete contradiction to his grubby ill-fitting clothes.

'Is this sort of thing really necessary?' he asked, but with curiosity, not distress. His voice was loud against the beat of the engine.

'Yes,' said Yardman shortly. I turned my head to look at him. He was staring gravely at my face, the bones of his skull sharp under the stretched skin. 'We know our business.'

Billy got tired of waving his gun about to an unappreciative audience. He stepped off the low platform and began dragging a bale of hay into the narrow alleyway between the standing box and the flattened one, settling it firmly longways between the two. On top of that bale he put another, and on top of that another and another. Four bales high. Jammed against these, on top of the flattened box, he raised three more, using all the bales on the plane. Together, they formed a solid wall three feet away on my left. Yardman, John and I watched him in silence.

'Right,' Yardman said when he'd finished it. He checked the time and looked out of the window. 'Ready?'

Billy and John said they were. I refrained from saying that I wasn't, and never would be.

All three of them went away up the plane, crouching under the luggage racks and stumbling over the guy chains. I at once discovered by tugging that Yardman knew his stuff with a rope. I couldn't budge my hands.

Jerking them in vain, I suddenly discovered Alf watching me. He had come back from somewhere up front, and was standing on my right with his customary look of missing intelligence.

'Alf,' I shouted. 'Untie me.'

He didn't hear. He simply stood and looked at me without surprise. Without feeling. Then he slowly turned and went away. Genuinely deaf; but it paid him to be blind too, I thought bitterly. Whatever he saw he didn't tell. He had told me nothing about Simon.

I thought achingly of Gabriella hanging on to life in Milan. She must still be alive, I thought. She must. Difficulties, the doctor had said. There might be difficulties. Like infection. Like pneumonia. Nothing would matter if she died . . . but she wouldn't . . . she couldn't. Anxiety for her went so deep that it pretty well blotted out the hovering knowledge that I should spare some for myself. The odds on her survival were about even: I wouldn't have taken a hundred to one on my own.

After ten eternal minutes Yardman and Billy came back, with Patrick between them. Patrick stared at me, his face tight and stiff with disbelief. I knew exactly how he felt. Billy pushed him to the back with his gun, and Yardman pointed to the pair of seats at the back. He and Patrick sat down on them, side by side, fifteen feet away. A captive audience, I reflected sourly. Front row of the stalls.

Billy put his mouth close to my ear. 'He doesn't fancy a detour, your pilot friend. Ask him to change his mind.'

I didn't look at Billy, but at Patrick. Yardman was talking to him unhurriedly, but against the engine noise I couldn't hear what he said. Patrick's amber eyes looked dark in the gauntness of his face, and he shook his head slightly, staring at me beseechingly. Beseech all you like, I thought, but don't give in. I knew it was no good. He wasn't tough enough.

'Ask him,' Billy said.

'Patrick,' I shouted.

He could hear me. His head tilted to listen. It was difficult to get urgency and conviction across when one had to shout to be heard at all, but I did my best. 'Please . . . fly back to Milan.'

Nothing happened for three seconds. Then Patrick tried to stand up and Yardman pulled him back, saying something which killed the beginning of resolution is his shattered face. Patrick, for God's sake, I thought, have some sense. Get up and go.

Billy unscrewed the silencer from his gun and put in in his pocket. He carefully unbuttoned my shirt, pulled the collar back over my shoulders, and tucked the fronts round into the back of my trousers. I felt very naked and rather silly. Patrick's face grew, if anything, whiter.

Billy firmly cutched the dressing over the bullet mark and with one wrench pulled the whole thing off.

'Hey,' he shouted to Yardman, 'I don't call that a miss.'

Yardman's reply got lost on the way back.

'Want to know something?' Billy said, thrusting his sneering face close to mine. 'I'm enjoying this.'

I saved my breath.

He put the barrel of his revolver very carefully against my skin, laying it flat along a rib just above the existing cut. Then he pushed me round until I was half facing the wall he had made of the hay bales. 'Keep still,' he said. He drew the revolver four inches backwards with the barrel still touching me and pulled the trigger. At such close quarters, without the silencer, the shot was a crashing explosion. The bullet sliced through the skin over my ribs and embedded itself in the wall of hay. The spit of flame from the barrel scorched in its wake. In the box behind me, the startled mares began making a fuss. It would create a handy diversion, I thought, if they were frightened into dropping their foals.

Patrick was on his feet, aghast and swaying. I heard him shouting something unintelligible to Billy, and Billy shouting back, 'Only you can stop it, mate.'

'Patrick,' I yelled. 'Go to Milan.'

'That's bloody enough,' Billy said. He put his gun back on my side, as before. 'Keep still.'

Yardman couldn't afford me dead until Patrick had flown where they wanted. I was all for staying alive as long as possible, and jerking around in the circumstances could cut me off short. I did as Billy said, and kept still. He pulled the trigger.

The flash, the crash, the burn, as before.

I looked down at myself, but I couldn't see clearly because of the angle. There were three long furrows now, parallel and fiery. The top two were beginning to bleed.

Patrick sat down heavily as if his knees had given way and put his hands over his eyes. Yardman was talking to him, clearly urging him to save me any more. Billy wasn't for waiting. He put his gun in position, told me to keep still, and shot.

Whether he intended it or not, that one went deeper, closer to the bone. The force of it spun me round hard against the mares' box and wrenched my arms, and my feet stumbed as I tried to keep my balance. The mares whinnied and skittered around, but on the whole they were getting less agitated, not more. A pity.

I had shut my eyes, that time. I opened them slowly to see Patrick and Yardman much nearer, only eight feet away on the far side of the flattened box. Patrick was staring with unreassuring horror at Billy's straight lines. Too soft-hearted, I thought despairingly. The only chance we had was for him to leave Billy to get on with it and go and turn back to Milan. We weren't much more than half an hour out. In half an hour we could be back. Half an hour of this . . .

I swallowed and ran my tongue round my dry lips.

'If you go where they say,' I said urgently to Patrick, 'they will kill us all.'

He didn't believe it. It wasn't in his nature to believe it. He listened to Yardman instead.

'Don't be silly, my dear boy. Of course we won't kill you. You will land, we will disembark, and you can all fly off again, perfectly free.'

'Patrick,' I said desperately. 'Go to Milan.'

Billy put his gun along my ribs.

'How long do you think he can keep still?' he asked, as if with genuine interest. 'What'll you bet?'

I tried to say, 'They shot Gabriella,' but Billy was waiting for that. I got the first two words out but he pulled the trigger as I started her name, and the rest of it got lost in the explosion and my own gasping breath.

When I opened my eyes that time, Patrick and Yardman had gone.

For a little while I clung to a distant hope that Patrick would turn back, but Billy merely blew across the top of his hot revolver and laughed at me, and when the plane banked it was to the left, and not a one eighty degree turn. After he had straightened out I looked at the acute angle of the late afternoon sun as it sliced forwards in narrow slivers of brilliance through the row of oval windows on my right.

No surprise, I thought drearily.

We were going east.

Billy had a pocket full of bullets. He sat on the flattened box, feeding his gun. The revolving cylinder broke out sideways with its axis still in line with the barrel, and an ejector rod, pushed back towards the butt, had lifted the spent cartridges out into his hand. The empty cases now lay beside him in a cluster, rolling slightly on their rims. When all the chambers were full again he snapped the gun shut and fondled it. His eyes suddenly switched up to me, the wide stare full of malice.

'Stinking earl,' he said.

A la lanterne, I thought tiredly. And all that jazz.

He stood up suddenly and spoke fiercely, with some sort of inner rage.

'I'll make you,' he said.

'What?'

'Ask.'

'Ask what?'

'Something ... anything. I'll make you bloody well ask me for something.'

I said nothing.

'Ask,' he said savagely.

I stared past him as if he wasn't there. Fights, I thought with some chill, weren't always physical.

'All right,' he said abruptly. 'All right. You'll ask in the end. You bloody sodding well will.'

I didn't feel sure enough to say I bloody sodding well wouldn't. The taunting sneer reappeared on his face, without the same infallible confidence perhaps, but none the less dangerous for that. He nodded sharply, and went off along the alleyway towards the nose, where I hoped he'd stay.

I watched the chips of sunshine grow smaller and tried to concentrate on working out our course, more for distraction than from any hope of needing the information for a return journey. The bullets had hurt enough when Billy fired them, but the burns, as burns do, had hotted up afterwards. The force generated inside the barrel of a pistol was, if I remembered correctly, somewhere in the region of five tons. A bullet left a revolver at a rate of approximately seven hundred feet per second and if not stopped carried about five hundred yards. The explosion which drove the bullet spinning on its way also shot out flames, smoke, hot propulsive gases and burning particles of gunpowder, and at close quarters they made a very dirty mess. Knowing these charming facts was of no comfort at all. The whole ruddy area simply burnt and went on burning, as if someone had stood an electric iron on it and had forgotten to switch off.

After Billy went away it was about an hour before I saw anyone again, and then it was Alf. He shuffled into my sight round the corner of the box I was tied to, and stood looking at me with one of the disposable mugs in his hand. His lined old face was, as usual, without expression.

'Alf,' I shouted. 'Untie me.'

There wasn't anywhere to run to. I just wanted to sit down. But Alf either couldn't hear, or wouldn't. He looked unhurriedly at my ribs, a sight which as far as I could see produced no reaction in him at all. But something must have stirred somewhere, because he took a slow step forward, and being careful not to touch me, lifted his mug. It had 'Alf' in red where Mike had written it that morning, in that distant sane and safe lost world or normality.

'Want some?' he said.

I nodded, half afraid he'd pour it out on the floor, as Billy would have done; but he held it up to my mouth, and let me finish it all. Lukewarm, oversweet neo-coffee. The best drink I ever had.

'Thank you,' I said.

He nodded, produced the nearest he could do to a smile, and shuffled away again. Not an ally. A non-combatant, rather.

More time passed. I couldn't see my watch or trust my judgment, but I would have guessed it was getting on for two hours since we had turned. I had lost all sense of direction. The sun had gone, and we were travelling into dusk. Inside the cabin the air grew colder. I would have liked to have had my shirt on properly, not to mention a jersey, but the mares behind my back provided enough warmth to keep me from shivering. On a full load in that cramped plane eight horses generated a summer's day even with icing conditions outside, and we seldom needed the cabin heaters. It was far too much to hope in the circumstances that Patrick would think of switching them on.

Two hours flying. We must, I thought, have been down near Albenga when we turned, which meant that since then, if we were still going east and the winds were the same as in the morning, we could have been crossing Italy somewhere north of Florence. Ahead lay the Adriatic, beyond that, Yugoslavia, and beyond that, Roumania.

It didn't matter a damn where we went, the end would be the same

I shifted wearily, trying to find some ease, and worried for t' thousandth time whether Gabriella was winning, back in Milan. T police there, I supposed, wrenching my mind away from her, woul furious I hadn't turned up. They still had my passport. There mig' least be a decent investigation if I never went back for it, and Gab

knew enough to explain what I'd inadvertently got caught up in. If she
lived. If she lived . . .

The plane banked sharply in a steep turn to the left. I leant against
the roll and tried to gauge its extent. Ninety degrees turn, I thought. No;
more. It didn't seem to make much sense. But if – if – we had reached
the Adriatic I supposed it was possible we were now going up it, north
west, back towards Venice . . . and Trieste. I admitted gloomily to myself
that it was utter guesswork; that I was lost, and in more than one sense.

Ten minutes later the engine note changed and the volume of noise
decreased. We had started going down. My heart sank with the plane.
Not much time left. Oncoming night and a slow descent, the stuff of
death.

There were two rows of what looked like car headlights marking each
end of a runway. We circled once so steeply that I caught a glimpse of
them through the tipped window, and then we levelled out for the
approach and lost speed, and the plane bumped down on to a rough
surface. Grass, not tarmac. The plane taxied round a bit, and then
stopped. One by one the four engines died. The plane was quiet and
dark, and for three long deceptive minutes at my end of it there was
peace.

The cabin lights flashed on, bright overhead. The mares behind me
kicked the box. Further along, the other pair whinnied restlessly. There
was a clatter in the galley, and the noise of people coming back through
the plane, stumbling over the chains.

Patrick came first, with Billy after. Billy had screwed the silencer back
on his gun.

Patrick went past the flattened box into the small area in front of the
two washroom doors. He moved stiffly, as if he couldn't feel his feet on
the floor, as if he were sleep walking.

Billy had stopped near me, on my right.

'Turn round, pilot,' he said.

Patrick turned, his body first and his legs untwisting after. He staggered
slightly, and stood swaying. If his face had been white before, it was
leaden grey now. His eyes were stretched and glazed with shock, and his
good-natured mouth trembled.

He stared at me with terrible intensity.

'He . . . shot . . . them,' he said. 'Bob . . . and Mike. Bob and Mike.'
His voice broke on the horror of it.

Billy sniggered quietly.

'You said . . . they would kill us all.' A tremor shook him. 'I didn't
. . . believe it.'

His eyes went down to my side. 'I couldn't . . .' he said. 'They said
they'd go on and on . . .'

'Where are we?' I said sharply.

His eyes came back in a snap, as if I'd kicked his brain.

'Italy,' he began automatically. 'South west of . . .'   Billy raised his
, aiming high for the skull.

'No.' I yelled at him in rage and horror at the top of my voice. 'No.'
jumped slightly, but he didn't even pause. The gun coughed

through the silencer and the bullet hit its target. Patrick got both his hands half-way to his head before the blackness took him. He spun on his collapsing legs and crashed headlong, face down, his long body still and silent, the auburn hair brushing against the washroom door. The soles of his feet were turned mutely up, and one of his shoes needed mending.

Chapter Fourteen

Yardman and John edged round Billy and the flattened box and stood in the rear area, looking down at Patrick's body.

'Why did you do it back here?' John said.

Billy didn't answer. His gaze was fixed on me.

Yardman said mildly, 'Billy, Mr. Rous-Wheeler wants to know why you brought the pilot here to shoot him?'

Billy smiled and spoke to me. 'I wanted you to watch,' he said.

John – Rous-Wheeler – said faintly 'My God,' and I turned my head and found him staring at my ribs.

'Pretty good shooting,' said Billy complacently, following the direction of his eyes and taking his tone as a compliment. 'There's no fat on him and the skin over his ribs is thin. See where I've got every shot straight along a bone? Neat, that's what it is. A bit of craftsmanship I'd say. These lines are what I'm talking about,' he was anxious to make his point, 'not all that black and red around them. That's only dried blood and powder burn.'

Rous-Wheeler, to do him justice, looked faintly sick.

'All right, Billy,' Yardman said calmly. 'Finish him off.'

Billy lifted his gun. I had long accepted the inevitability of that moment, and I felt no emotion but regret.

'He's not afraid,' Billy said. He sounded disappointed.

'What of it?' Yardman asked.

'I want him to be afraid.'

Yardman shrugged. 'I can't see what difference it makes.'

To Billy it made all the difference in the world. 'Let me take a little time over him, huh? We've got hours to wait.'

Yardman sighed. 'All right, Billy, if that's what you want. Do all the other little jobs first, eh? Shut all the curtains on the plane first, we don't want to advertise ourselves. And then go down and tell Giuseppe to turn those landing lights off, the stupid fool's left them on. He'll have ladders and paint waiting for us. He and you and Alf can start straight away on painting out the airline's name and the plane's registration letters.'

'Yeah,' said Billy. 'O.K. And while I'm doing it I'll think of something.' He put his face close to mine, mocking. 'Something special for your effing Lordship.'

He put the gun in its holster and the silencer in his pocket, and drew all the curtains in the back part of the plane, before starting forward to do the rest.

Rous-Wheeler stepped over Patrick's body, sat down in one of the seats, and lit a cigarette. His hands were shaking.

'Why do you let him?' he said to Yardman. 'Why do you let him do what he likes?'

'He is invaluable,' Yardman sighed. 'A natural killer. They're not at all common, you know. That combination of callousness and enjoyment, it's unbeatable. I let him have his way if I can as a sort of reward, because he'll kill anyone I tell him to. I couldn't do what he does. He kills like stepping on a beetle.'

'He's so young,' Rous-Wheeler protested.

'They're only any good when they're young,' Yardman said. 'Billy is nineteen. In another seven or eight years, I wouldn't trust him as I do now. And there's a risk a killer will turn maudlin any time after thirty.'

'It sounds,' Rous-Wheeler cleared his throat, trying to speak as unconcernedly as Yardman, 'it sounds rather like keeping a pet tiger on a leash.'

He began to cross his legs and his shoes knocked against Patrick's body. With an expression of distaste he said, 'Can't we cover him up?'

Yardman nodded casually and went away up the plane. He came back with a grey blanket from the pile in the luggage bay, opened it out, and spread it over, covering head and all. I spent the short time that he was away watching Rous-Wheeler refuse to meet my eyes and wondering just who he was, and why he was so important that taking him beyond Milan was worth the lives of three totally uninvolved and innocent airmen.

An unremarkable looking man of about thirty-five, with incipient bags under his eyes, and a prim mouth. Unused to the violence surrounding him, and trying to wash his hands of it. A man with his fare paid in death and grief.

When Yardman had covered Patrick, he perched himself down on the edge of the flattened box. The overhead lights shone on the bald patch on his skull and the black spectacle frames made heavy bars of shadow on his eyes and cheeks.

'I regret this, my dear boy, believe me, I regret it sincerely,' he said, eyeing the result of Billy's target practice. Like Rous-Wheeler he took out a cigarette and lit it. 'He really has made a very nasty mess.'

But only skin deep, if one thought about it. I thought about it. Not much good.

'Do you understand what Billy wants?' Yardman said, shaking out his match.

I nodded.

He sighed. 'Then couldn't you ... er ... satisfy him, my dear boy? You will make it so hard for yourself, if you don't.'

I remembered the stupid boast I'd made to Billy the first day I'd met him, that I could be as tough as necessary. Now that I looked like having to prove it, I had the gravest doubts.

When I didn't answer Yardman shook his head sorrowfully. 'Foolish boy, whatever difference would it make, after you are dead?'

'Defeat . . .' I cleared my throat and tried again. 'Defeat on all levels.'

He frowned. 'What do you mean?'

'Communists are greedy,' I said.

'Greedy,' he echoed. 'You're wandering, my dear boy.'

'They like to . . . crumble . . . people, before they kill them. And that's . . . gluttony.'

'Nonsense,' said Rous-Wheeler in a vintage Establishment voice.

'You must have read newspaper accounts of trials in Russia,' I said, raising an eyebrow. 'All those "confessions".'

'The Russians,' he said stiffly, 'are a great warm-hearted simple people.'

'Oh, sure,' I agreed. 'And some are like Billy.'

'Billy is English.'

'So are you,' I said. 'And where are you going?'

He compressed his lips and didn't answer.

'I hope,' I said, looking at the blanket which covered Patrick, 'that your travel agents have confirmed your belief in the greatness, warm-heartedness and simplicity of the hemisphere you propose to join.'

'My dear boy,' interrupted Yardman smoothly, 'what eloquence!'

'Talking,' I explained, 'takes the mind off . . . this and that.'

A sort of recklessness seemed to be running in my blood, and my mind felt clear and sharp. To have even those two to talk to was suddenly a great deal more attractive than waiting for Billy on my own.

'The end justifies the means,' said Rous-Wheeler pompously, as if he'd heard it somewhere before.

'Crap,' I said inelegantly. 'You set yourself too high.'

'I am . . .' he began angrily, and stopped.

'Go on,' I said. 'You are what? Feel free to tell me. Moriturus, and all that.'

It upset him, which was pleasant. He said stiffly, 'I am a civil servant.'

'Were,' I pointed out.

'Er, yes.'

'Which ministry?'

'The Treasury,' he said, with the smugness of those accepted in the inner of inner sanctums.

The Treasury. It was a stopper, that one.

'What rank?' I asked.

'Principal.' There was a grudge in his voice. He hadn't risen.

'And why are you defecting?'

The forthcomingness vanished. 'It's none of your business.'

'Well it is rather,' I said in mock apology, 'since your change of allegiance looks like having fairly decisive effect on my future.'

He looked mulish and kept silent.

'I suppose,' I said with mild irony, 'you are going where you think your talents will be appreciated.'

For a second he looked almost as spiteful as Billy. A petty-minded man I thought, full of imagined slights, ducking the admission that he wasn't as brilliant as he thought he was. None of that lessened one jot the value of the information he carried in his head.

'And you,' I said to Yardman. 'Why do you do it? All this.'

He looked back gravely, the tight skin pulling over his shut mouth.

'Ideology?' I suggested.

He tapped ash off his cigarette, made a nibbling movement with his lip, and said briefly, 'Money.'

'The brand of goods doesn't trouble you, as long as the carriage is paid?'

'Correct,' he said.

'A mercenary soldier. Slaughter arranged. Allegiance always to the highest bidder?'

'That,' he said, inclining his head, 'is so.'

It wasn't so strange, I thought inconsequentially, that I'd never been able to understand him.

'But believe me, my dear boy,' he said earnestly, 'I never really intended you any harm. Not you.'

'Thanks,' I said dryly.

'When you asked me for a job I nearly refused you . . . but I didn't think you'd stay long, and your name gave my agency some useful respectability, so I agreed.' He sighed. 'I must admit, you surprised me. You were very good at that job, if it's of any comfort to you. Very good. Too good. I should have stopped it when your father died, when I had the chance, before you stumbled on anything . . . it was selfish of me. Selfish.'

'Simon Searle stumbled,' I reminded him. 'Not me.'

'I fear so,' he agreed without concern. 'A pity. He too was invaluable. An excellent accurate man. Very hard to replace.'

'Would you be so good as to untuck my shirt?' I said. 'I'm getting cold.'

Without a word he stood up, came round, tugged the bunched cloth out of the back of my trousers and pulled the collar and shoulders back to their right place. The shirt fronts fell together edge to edge, the light touch of the cloth on the burns being more than compensated by the amount of cool air shut out.

Yardman sat down again where he had been before and lit another cigarette from the stub of the first, without offering one to Rous-Wheeler.

'I didn't mean to bring you on this part of the trip,' he said. 'Believe me, my dear boy, when we set off from Gatwick I intended to organise some little delaying diversion for you in Milan, so that you wouldn't embark on the trip back.'

I said bleakly, 'Do you call sh . . . shooting my girl a little diversion.'

He looked distressed. 'Of course not. Of course not. I didn't know you had a girl until you introduced her. But then I thought it would be an excellent idea to tell you to stay with her for a day or two, that we could easily manage without you on the way back. 'He,' he nodded at Patrick's shrouded body, 'told me you were . . . er . . . crazy about her. Unfortunately for you, he also told me how assiduous you had been in searching for Searle. He told me all about that bottle of pills. Now, my dear boy, that was a risk we couldn't take.'

'Risk,' I said bitterly.

'Oh yes, my dear boy, of course. Risk is something we can't afford in this business. I always act on risk. Waiting for certain knowledge may be fatal. And I was quite right in this instance, isn't that so? You had told me yourself where you were going to lunch, so I instructed Billy to go and find you and follow you from there, and make sure it was all love's young dream and no excitement. But you went bursting out of the restaurant and off at high speed to an obscure little bakery. Billy followed you in Vittorio's cab and rang me up from near there.' He spread his hands. 'I told him to kill you both and search you under cover of helping, as soon as you came out.'

'Without waiting to find out if there was anything in the bottle except pills?'

'Risk,' he nodded. 'I told you. We can't afford it. And that reminds me; where is Searle's message?'

'No message,' I said wearily.

'Of course there was, my dear boy,' he chided. 'You've shown so little surprise, asked so few questions. It was clear to me at once that you knew far too much when Billy brought you back to the plane. I have experience in these things, you see.'

I shrugged a shoulder. 'In my wallet,' I said.

He drew on his cigarette, gave me an approving look, stepped over Patrick, and fetched my jacket from the washroom. He took everything out of the wallet and spread them beside him on the flattened box. When he picked out the hundred dinar note and unfolded it, the pieces of writing paper and hay fell out.

He fingered the note. 'It was plain carelessness on Billy's part,' he said. 'He didn't hide the canisters properly.'

'There was a lot of money, then, on the plane?'

'Wheels have to be oiled,' Yardman said reasonably, 'and it's no good paying Yugoslavs in sterling. All agents insist on being paid in the currency they can spend without arousing comment. I do, myself.'

I watched him turn the scrap of his stationery over and over, frowning. He saw the pin holes in the end, and held them up to the light. After a few seconds he put it down and looked from me to Rous-Wheeler.

'Men,' he said without inflection. 'And when you read that, my dear boy, you understood a great deal.' A statement, not a question.

Gabriella, I thought dumbly, for God's sake live. Live and tell. I shut my eyes and thought of her as she had been at lunch. Gay and sweet and vital. Gabriella my dearest love . . .

'Dear boy,' said Yardman in his dry unconcerned voice, 'are you feeling all right?'

I opened my eyes and shut Gabriella away out of reach of his frightening intuition.

'No,' I said with truth.

Yardman actually laughed. 'I like you, my dear boy, I really do. I shall miss you very much in the agency.'

'Miss . . .' I stared at him. 'You are going back?'

'Of course.' He seemed surprised, then smiled his bony smile. 'How could you know, I was forgetting. Oh yes, of course we're going back. My transport system . . . is . . . er . . . much needed, and much appreciated. Yes. Only the plane and Mr. Rous-Wheeler are going on.'

'And the horses?' I asked.

'Those too,' he nodded. 'They carry good blood lines, those mares. We expected to have to slaughter them, but we have heard they will be acceptable alive, on account of their foals. No, my dear boy, Billy and I go back by road, half way with Giuseppe, the second half with Vittorio.'

'Back to Milan?'

'Quite so. And tomorrow morning we learn the tragic news that the plane we missed by minutes this afternoon has disappeared and must be presumed lost with all souls, including yours, my dear boy, in the Mediterranean.'

'There would be a radar trace . . .' I began.

'My dear boy, we are professionals.'

'Oiled wheels?' I said ironically.

'So quick,' he said nodding. 'A pity I can't tempt you to join us.'

'Why can't you?' said Rous-Wheeler truculently.

Yardman answered with slightly exaggerated patience. 'What do I offer him?'

'His life,' Rous-Wheeler said with an air of triumph.

Yardman didn't even bother to explain why that wouldn't work. The Treasury, I thought dryly, really hadn't lost much.

Billy's voice suddenly spoke from the far end of the plane.

'Hey, Mr. Yardman,' he called. 'Can't you and Mr. Rous-flipping-Wheeler come and give us a hand? This ruddy aeroplane's bloody covered with names and letters. We're practically having to paint the whole sodding crate.'

Yardman stood up. 'Yes, all right,' he said.

Rous-Wheeler didn't want to paint. 'I don't feel . . .' he began importantly.

'And you don't want to be late,' Yardman said flatly.

He stood aside to let the deflated Rous-Wheeler pass, and they both made their way up past the two boxes, through the galley, and down the telescopic ladder from the forward door.

Desperation can move mountains. I'd never hoped to have another minute alone to put it to the test, but I'd thought of a way of detaching myself from the mare's box, if I had enough strength. Yardman had had difficulty squeezing the rope down between the banding bar and the wooden box side when he'd tied me there: he'd had to push it through with the blade of his penknife. It wouldn't have gone through at all I thought, if either the box side wasn't a fraction warped or the bar a shade bent. Most of the bars lay flat and tight along the boxes, with no space at all between them.

I was standing less than two feet from the corner of the box: and along at the corner the bar was fastened by a lynch pin.

I got splinters in my wrists, and after I'd moved along six inches I thought I'd never manage it. The bar and the box seemed to come closer together the further I went, and jerking the rope along between them grew harder and harder, until at last it was impossible. I shook my head in bitter frustration. Then I thought of getting my feet to help, and bending my knee put my foot flat on the box as high behind me as I could get leverage. Thrusting back with my foot, pulling forward on the bar with my arms, and jerking my wrists sideways at the same time, I moved along a good inch. It worked. I kept at it grimly and finally arrived at the last three inches. From there, twisting, I could reach the lynch pin with my fingers. Slowly, agonisingly slowly, I pushed it up from the bottom, transferred my weak grip to the rounded top, slid it fraction by fraction up in my palm, and with an enormous sense of triumph felt it come free. The iron bands parted at the corner, and it required the smallest of jerks to tug the rope out through the gap.

Call that nothing, I said to myself with the beginnings of a grin. All that remained was to free my hands from each other.

Yardman had left my jacket lying on the flattened box, and in my jacket pocket was a small sharp penknife. I sat down on the side of the shallow platform, trying to pretend to myself that it wasn't because my legs were buckling at the knees but only the quickest way to reach the jacket. The knife was there, slim and familiar. I clicked open the blade, gripped it firmly, and sawed away blindly at some unseen point between my wrists. The friction of dragging the rope along had frayed it helpfully, and before I'd begun to hope for it I felt the strands stretch and give, and in two more seconds my hands were free. With stiff shoulders I brought them round in front of me Yardman had no personal brutality and hadn't tied tight enough to stop the blood. I flexed my fingers and they were fine.

Scooping up wallet and jacket I began the bent walk forward under the luggage rack and over the guy chains, stepping with care so as not to make a noise and fetch the five outdoor decorators in at the double. I reached the galley safely and went through it. In the space behind the cockpit I stopped dead for a moment. The body of Mike the engineer lay tumbled in a heap against the left hand wall.

Tearing both mind and eyes away from him I edged towards the way out. On my immediate right I came first to the luggage bay, and beyond that lay the door. The sight of my overnight bag in the bay made me remember the black jersey inside it. Better than my jacket, I thought. It had a high neck, was easier to move in, and wouldn't be so heavy on my raw skin. In a few seconds I had it on, and had transferred my wallet to my trousers.

Five of them round the plane, I thought. The exit door was ajar, but when I opened it the light would spill out, and for the time it took to get on to the ladder they would be able to see me clearly. Unless by some miracle they were all over on the port side, painting the tail. Well, I thought coldly, I would just be unlucky if the nearest to me happened to be Billy with his gun.

It wasn't Billy, it was the man I didn't know, Giuseppe. He was standing at the root of the starboard wing painting out the airline's name

on the fuselage, and he saw me as soon as I opened the door not far
below him. I pulled the door shut behind me and started down the ladder,
hearing Giuseppe shouting and warning all the others. They had ladders
to get down too, I thought. I could still make it.

Giuseppe was of the hard core, a practising militant communist. He
was also young and extremely agile. Without attempting to reach a ladder
he ran along the wing to its tip, put his hands down, swung over the
edge, and dropped ten feet to the ground. Seeing his running form
outlined on the wing against the stars I veered away to the left as soon
as I had slid down the ladder, and struck out forwards, more or less on
the same axis as the plane.

My eyes weren't accustomed to the light as theirs were. I couldn't see
where I was going. I heard Giuseppe shouting in Italian, and Yardman
answering. Billy tried a shot which missed by a mile. I scrambled on,
holding my arms up defensively and hoping I wouldn't run into anything
too hard. All I had to do, I told myself, was to keep going. I was difficult
to see in black and moved silently over the grass of the field. If I got far
enough from the plane they wouldn't be able to find me, not five of them
with Alf no better than a snail. Keep going and get lost. After that I'd
have all night to search out a bit of civilisation and someone who could
speak English.

The field seemed endless. Endless. And running hurt. What the hell
did that matter, I thought dispassionately, with Billy behind me. I had
also to refrain from making a noise about it in case they should hear me,
and with every rib-stretching breath that got more difficult. In the end
I stopped, went down on my knees, and tried to get air in shallow silent
gulps. I could hear nothing behind but a faint breeze, see nothing above
but the stars, nothing ahead but the dark. After a few moments I stood
up again and went on, but more slowly. Only in nightmares did fields
go on for ever. Even airfields.

At the exact second that I first thought I'd got away with it, bright
white lights blazed out and held me squarely in their beams. A distant
row of four in front, a nearer row of four behind, and I a black figure
in the flarepath. Sick devastating understanding flooded through me. I
had been trying to escape down the runway.

Sharply, almost without missing a step, I wheeled left and sprinted;
but Giuseppe wasn't very far behind after all. I didn't see or hear him
until the last moment when he closed in from almost in front. I swerved
to avoid him, and he threw out his leg at a low angle and tripped me up.

Even though I didn't fall very heavily, it was enough. Giuseppe very
slickly put one of his feet on each side of my head and closed them tight
on my ears. Grass pressed into my eyes, nose and mouth, and I couldn't
move in the vice.

Billy came up shouting as if with intoxication, the relief showing with
the triumph.

'What you got there then, my friend? A bleeding aristocrat, then?
Biting the dust, too, ain't that a gas?'

I guessed with a split second to spare what he would do, and caught
his swinging shoe on my elbow instead of my ribs.

Yardman arrived at a smart military double.

'Stop it,' he said. 'Let him get up.'

Giuseppe stepped away from my head and when I put my hands up by my shoulders and began to push myself up, Billy delivered the kick I had avoided before. I rolled half over, trying not to care. The beams from the runway lights shone through my shut eyelids, and the world seemed a molten river of fire, scarlet and gold.

Without, I hoped, taking too long about it I again started to get up. No one spoke. I completed the incredibly long journey to my feet and stood there, quiet and calm. We were still on the runway between the distant lights, Yardman close in front of me, Giuseppe and Billy behind, with Rous-Wheeler struggling breathlessly up from the plane. Yardman's eyes, level with mine, were lit into an incandescent greenness by the glow. I had never clearly seen his eyes before. It was like drawing back curtains and looking into a soul.

A soldier without patriotism. Strategy, striking power and transport were skills he hired out, like any other craftsman. His pride was to exercise his skill to the most perfect possible degree. His pride overrode all else.

I think he probably meant it when he said he liked me. In a curious way, though I couldn't forgive him Gabriella, I felt respect for him, not hatred. Battle against him wasn't personal or emotional, as with Billy. But I understood that in spite of any unexpected warmth he might feel, he would be too prudent to extend foolish mercy to the enemy.

We eyed each other in a long moment of cool appraisal. Then his gaze slid past me, over my shoulder, and he paid me what was from his point of view a compliment.

'You won't crack him, Billy. Kill him now. One shot, nice and clean.'

Chapter Fifteen

I owed my life to Billy's greed. He was still hungry, still unsatisfied, and he shook his head to Yardman's request. Seeing the way Yardman delicately deferred to Billy's wishes it struck me that Rous-Wheeler's simile of a tiger on a leash might not be too far off the mark. In any case for the first time I was definitely glad of Billy's lust to spill my blue blood ounce by ounce, as I really was most averse to being shot down on the spot; and I acknowledged that I already had him to thank that I was still breathing at all. If I'd been anyone but who I was I would have died with the crew.

We walked back up the runway, I in front, the other four behind. I could hear Rous-Wheeler puffing, the only one not physically fit. Fit ... It was only yesterday, I thought incredulously, that I rode in the Gold Cup.

The plane was a faintly lit shape to the left of the end of the runway. A hundred yards short of it Yardman said, 'Turn left, dear boy. That's it. Walk straight on. You will see a building. Go in.'

There was, in fact, a building. A large one. It resembled an outsize prefabricated garage, made of asbestos sheets on a metal frame. The door was ajar and rimmed by light. I pushed it open, and with Billy's gun touching my back, walked in.

The right hand two-thirds of the concrete floor space was occupied by a small four-seater single-engined aeroplane, a new looking high winged Cessna with an Italian registration. On its left stood a dusty black Citroen, its bonnet towards me. Behind the car and the plane the whole far wall consisted of sliding doors. No windows anywhere. Three metal girders rose from floor to ceiling on the left of the car, supporting the flat roof and dividing the left hand part of the hangar into a kind of bay. In that section stood Alf.

'Right,' said Yardman briskly. 'Well done, Alf, turn them off now.' His voice echoed hollowly in space.

Alf stared at him without hearing.

Yardman went up to him and shouted in his ear. 'Turn the runway lights off.'

Alf nodded, walked up to the wall on the left of the door I had come in by, and pushed up a heavy switch beside a black fuse box. A second similar box worked, I suppose, the fluorescent strips across the ceilings and the low-powered radiant heaters mounted high on both side walls. Beside the switches stood a mechanic's bench with various tools and a vice, and further along two sturdy brackets held up a rack of gardening implements; spades, fork, rake, hoe and shears. Filling all the back of the bay was a giant motor mower with a seat for the driver, and dotted about there were some five gallon petrol cans, funnels, tins of paint, an assortment of overalls and several greasy looking metal chairs.

That Cessna, I thought briefly; I could fly it like riding a bicycle. And the car . . . if only I had known they were there.

Yardman searched among the clutter on the bench and produced a length of chain and two padlocks, one large, one small. Billy had shut the door and was standing with his back to it, the gun pointing steadily in my direction. Alf, Rous-Wheeler and Giuseppe had prudently removed themselves from his line of fire.

Yardman said, 'Go over to that first girder, my dear boy, and sit down on the floor.'

To say I was reluctant to be tied again is to put it mildly. It wasn't only that it was the end of any hope of escape, but I had a strong physical repugnance to being attached to things, the result of having been roped to a fir in a Scottish forest one late afternoon in a childhood game by some cousins I was staying with: they had run away to frighten me and got lost themselves, and it had been morning before the subsequent search had found me.

When I didn't obey at once, Yardman, Giuseppe and Billy all took a step forward as if moved by the same mind. There was no percentage in having them jump on me: I was sore enough already. I walked over to the girder and sat down facing them, leaning back idly against the flat metal surface.

'That's better,' Yardman said. He came round and knelt down on the ground at my back. 'Hands behind, my dear boy.'

He twined the chain round my wrists and clicked on both padlocks. Tossing the keys on his palm he stood up and came round in front of me. All five of them stared down with varying degrees of ill-feeling and I stared glassily back.

'Right,' said Yardman after a pause. 'We'd better get out and finish the painting. But this time we must leave someone with him, just in case.' He reviewed his available troops, and alighted on Rous-Wheeler. 'You sit here,' he said to him, picking up a chair and taking it over beside the switches, 'and if he does anything you aren't sure about, switch on the runway lights and we'll come at once. Clear?'

Rous-Wheeler was delighted to avoid any more painting and accepted his new task with enthusiasm.

'Good.' Yardman looked at his watch. 'Go on then, Billy.' Billy, Alf and Giuseppe filed out and Yardman stopped as he followed them to say to Rous-Wheeler, 'The cargo will be arriving soon. Don't be alarmed.'

'Cargo?' said Rous-Wheeler in surprise.

'That's right,' Yardman said. 'Cargo. The reason for this . . . um . . . operation.'

'But I thought I . . .' began Rous-Wheeler.

'My dear Rous-Wheeler, no,' said Yardman. 'Had it been just you, I could have sent you down the usual discreet pipeline from Milan. Your journey would have been just as secret as it is now. No, we needed the plane for a rather special cargo, and as you know, my dear boy,' he swung round to speak directly to me with a small ironic smile, 'I do hate wasting space on flights. I always try to make up a full load, so as not to neglect an opportunity.'

'What is this cargo, then?' asked Rous-Wheeler with a damaged sense of self-importance.

'Mm?' said Yardman, putting the padlock keys down on the bench. 'Well now, it's the brain child of a brilliant little research establishment near Brescia. A sort of machine. An interesting little development, one might say. Broadly speaking, it's a device for emitting ultrasonic rays on the natural frequency of any chosen mineral substance.'

'Ultrasonics have been extensively researched,' Rous-Wheeler said testily.

Yardman smiled tightly. 'Take it from me, dear fellow, this particular development has great possibilities. Our friends have been trying to arrange photographs of the drawings and specifications, but these have been too well guarded. It proved easier in the end to . . . er . . . remove some vital parts of the device itself. But that of course presented a transport problem, a difficult transport problem, requiring my own personal supervision.' He was talking for my benefit as much as Rous-Wheeler's: letting me know how expert he was at his job. 'Once we were committed to the plane, of course it was the easiest way to take you too.

No opportunity wasted. But he hadn't originally intended to take me as well: to give him his due.

Yardman went out of the hangar. Rous-Wheeler sat on his hard chair and I on the hard concrete and again my presence and/or predicament embarrassed him.

'Played any good wall games lately?' I said at length.

A hit, a palpable hit. He hadn't expected any needling school chums on his little trip. He looked offended.

'Have you been to ... er ... wherever you're going ... before?' I asked.

'No,' he said shortly. He wouldn't look at me.

'And do you speak the language?'

He said stiffly, 'I am learning.'

'What are they offering you?'

Some heavy smugness crept into his manner. 'I am to have a flat and a car, and a better salary. I will of course be in an important advisory position.'

'Of course,' I said dryly.

He flicked me his first glance. Disapproving.

'I am to be a consultant interpreter of the British way of life ... I pride myself that in my own small way I shall be promoting better understanding between two great peoples and making a positive contribution to the establishment of fruitful relations.'

He spoke as if he really meant it; and if he were as self-satisfied as that, he wouldn't consider turning round and going back. But Yardman had left the padlock keys on the bench ...

'Your actions may be misunderstood, back home,' I said.

'At first. That has been explained to me. But in time ...'

'You're wrong,' I said roughly. 'They'll call you a traitor. A plain stinking common or garden traitor.'

'No,' he said uneasily.

'What you need is someone to put your views forward, to explain what you are doing, so that your former colleagues admire you, and wish they had made more use of your undoubted abilities while they had the chance ...' I thought I'd laid it on too thick, but not so. He was looking seriously pensive.

'You mean ... you? You would represent me?' He pursed his lips.

'I don't always look so dirty,' I said earnestly. 'I could pull a certain amount of weight with my father's friends, and ... er ... I have an uncle who more or less lives in the Reform Club.'

He was nodding, taking it all in.

'A word in the right ear,' he said judiciously.

'Recognition,' I put in gently.

He looked modest. 'That's too much to hope for.'

'In time,' I insinuated.

'Do you really think so?'

'Well, of course.' I paused. 'I would be happy to clear up any ... er ... bad feelings which your ... move ... may have left.'

'Uncommonly kind of you,' he said pompously.

'At the moment, however, I don't look like being able to.'

He looked disappointed. 'I suppose not.' He frowned. 'You could have done me an excellent . . . as I see it now, an essential . . . service.'

I said casually, 'A great pity, yes. Of course . . . the keys are just beside you . . . if you felt like it.'

He looked at the keys and at me. He stood up. He took the keys into his hand. I could feel my heart thudding as I tried to look unconcerned. He took a step in my direction. Then, looking uneasily round, his glance fell on the runway lights switch. He stared at it, transfixed.

'Yardman said to put the light on, if you tried anything.' There was consternation in his voice. He turned and put the keys back on the bench as if they were suddenly hot. 'Yardman considers it essential for you to remain here. It would not be an auspicious start for me with my new friends if the first thing I did was so exactly contrary to their wishes.'

'Yardman's wishes.'

He used a modicum of brain. 'If I let you go back to England, Yardman wouldn't be able to. His invaluable transport service would have come to an end . . .' He looked horrified at the abyss he had almost stepped into. 'I would have been most unpopular.'

I didn't say anything. Down the snakes and back to square one. I tried again without success to do a Houdini on Yardman's chain job, and Rous-Wheeler sat down again and watched me with a mixture of anxiety and annoyance.

'What branch of the Treasury?' I said, giving it up.

'Initial finance,' he replied stiffly.

'What does that mean?'

'Grants.'

'You mean, your department settles who gets grants of public money, and how much?'

'That is so.'

'Development, research, defence, and so on?'

'Precisely.'

'So that you personally would know what projects are in hand . . . or contemplated?'

'Yes.'

They wouldn't have bothered with him, I supposed, for any less.

After a pause, I said, 'What about this ultrasonic transmitter?'

'What about it? It isn't a British project, if that's what you mean.'

'Did I get it right . . . that it will emit waves on the natural frequency of any mineral substance?'

'I believe that's what Yardman said,' he agreed stiffly.

'It would break things . . . like sound breaks glass?'

'I am not a scientist. I've no idea.' And from the tone of his voice he didn't care.

I stared gloomily at the floor and wondered what made a man change his allegiance. Rous-Wheeler might have been self-important and disappointed and have refused to face his own limitations, but thousands of men were like that, and thousands of men didn't give away a slice of their nation's future in return for a flat, a car, and a pat on the back

There had to be more to it. Deep obsessive murky convoluted motives I couldn't guess at, pushing him irresistibly over. But he would be the same man wherever he went: in five years or less, again disgruntled and passed over. A useless dispensable piece of flotsam.

He, it appeared, took as pessimistic a view of my future as I of his.

'Do you think,' he cleared his throat. 'Do you think Billy will really kill you?'

'Be your age,' I said. 'You saw what he did to the crew.'

'He keeps putting it off,' he said.

'Saving the icing till last.'

'How can you be so frivolous?' he exclaimed. 'Your position is very serious.'

'So is yours,' I said. 'And I wouldn't swop.'

He gave me a small pitying smile of contemptuous disbelief, but it was true enough. Everyone dies sometime, as Simon had once said, and one was probably as little eager at eighty as at twenty-six. And there really were, I reflected with a smile for Victorian melodramas, fates worse than death.

A heavy van or lorry of some sort pulled up with a squeak of brakes somewhere near the door and after a few moments its driver came into the hangar. He was like Giuseppe, young, hard, cold-eyed and quick. He looked at me without apparent surprise and spoke to Rous-Wheeler in rapid Italian, of which the only intelligible word as far as I was concerned was Brescia.

Rous-Wheeler held up a hand, palm towards the driver. 'I don't understand you, my good fellow. Wait until I fetch Yardman.'

This proved unnecessary as my ex-employer had already seen the lorry's arrival. Followed by his entourage carrying ladders, paint pots, brushes and overalls, Yardman came forward into the hangar and exchanged some careful salutations with the driver.

'Right,' Yardman said in English to Billy. 'There should be several small light cases and one large heavy one. It will be easiest to load the light cases up through the forward door and stow them in the luggage bay. Then we will open the back doors, haul the heavy case in on the block and tackle, and stand it in the peat tray of the last box, the one that's now flattened. Clear?'

Billy nodded.

I opened my mouth to speak, and shut it again.

Yardman noticed. 'What is it?' he said sharply.

'Nothing.' I spoke listlessly.

He came over to me and looked down. Then he squatted on his haunches to peer on a level with my face.

'Oh yes, my dear boy, there is something. Now what, what?'

He stared at me as if he could read my thoughts while the calculations ticked over in his own. 'You were going to tell me something, and decided not to. And I feel I really should know what it is. I feel it must be to my disadvantage, something definitely to my disadvantage, as things stand between us.'

'I'll shoot it out of him,' Billy offered.

'It'll be quicker if I guess it ... Now, what is wrong with stowing the cases the way I suggested? Ah yes, my dear boy, you know all about loading aeroplanes, don't you? You know what I said was wrong ...' He snapped his fingers and stood up. 'The heavy case at the back is wrong. Billy, move the mares forward so that they occupy the two front boxes, and put the heavy case in the second to back box, and leave the rear one as it is.'

'Move the mares?' Billy complained.

'Yes, certainly. The centre of gravity is all-important, isn't that right, my dear boy?' He was pleased with himself, smiling. Quick as lightning. If I gave him even a thousandth of a second of suspicion that Gabriella was still alive ...

Billy came over and stood looking down at me with a revoltingly self-satisfied smile.

'Not long now,' he promised.

'Load the plane first,' Yardman said. 'The van has to go back as soon as possible. You can ... er ... have your fun when I go to fetch the pilot. And be sure he's dead by the time I get back.'

'O.K.' Billy agreed. He went away with Alf, Giuseppe and the driver, and the van ground away on the short stretch to the D.C.4.

'What pilot?' Rous-Wheeler asked.

'My dear Rous-Wheeler,' Yardman explained with a touch of weary contempt. 'How do you think the plane is going on?'

'Oh ... Well, why did you kill the other one? He would have flown on to wherever you said.'

Yardman sighed. 'He would have done no such thing without Billy at hand to shoot pieces off our young friend here. And frankly, my dear fellow, quite apart from the problem of Billy's and my return journey, it would have been embarrassing for us to kill the crew in your new country. Much better here. Much more discreet, don't you think?'

'Where exactly ... where are we?' asked Rous-Wheeler. A good question if ever there was one.

'A private landing field,' Yardman said. 'An elderly respected nobleman lets us use it from time to time.'

Elderly and respected: Yardman's voice held some heavy irony.

'The usual sort of blackmail?' I asked. 'Filmed in a bed he had no right in?'

Yardman said 'No,' unconvincingly.

'What's he talking about?' Rous-Wheeler asked testily.

'I'm talking about the methods employed by your new friends,' I said. 'If they can't get help and information by bamboozling and subverting people like you, they do it by any form of blackmail or intimidation that comes to hand.'

Rous-Wheeler was offended. 'I haven't been bamboozled.'

'Nuts,' I said. 'You're a proper sucker.'

Yardman took three threatening steps towards me with the first anger he had shown. 'That's enough.'

'Nothing's enough,' I said mildly. 'What the hell do you think I have to lose?'

Yardman's glasses flashed in the light, and Rous-Wheeler said self-righteously, 'He tried to get me to free him, while you were painting the plane. He asked me to unlock him. I didn't, of course.'

'You nearly did,' I said. 'Anyone can reach you; your overgrown self-esteem makes you permanently gullible.'

Yardman looked from me to him with a taut mouth. 'I have to go over to the plane, Mr. Rous-Wheeler, and I think it would be best if you came with me.'

'But I wouldn't let him go,' he said, like a scolded schoolboy.

'All the same . . .' Yardman came behind me and bent down to check that his chains were still effective, which unfortunately they were. 'You look so gentle, dear boy,' he said into my ear. 'So misleading, isn't it?'

They went away and left me alone. I had another go at the chains, tantalised by the Cessna standing so close behind me: but this time Yardman had been more careful. The girder was rooted in concrete, the chain wouldn't fray like rope, and try as I might I couldn't slide my hands out.

Little time to go, I thought. And no questions left. There wasn't much profit in knowing the answers, since in a very short while I would know nothing at all. I thought about that too. I didn't believe in any form of after life. To die was to finish. I'd been knocked out several times in racing falls, and death was just a knockout from which one didn't awake. I couldn't honestly say that I much feared it. I never had. Undoubtedly on my part a defect of the imagination, a lack of sensitivity. All I felt was a strong reluctance to leave the party so soon when there was so much I would have liked to do. But there was the messy business of Billy to be got through first . . . and I admitted gloomily to myself that I would have avoided that if I could have dredged up the smallest excuse.

Alf shuffed into the hangar, went across to the rack of gardening tools and took down a spade. I shouted to him, but he showed no sign of having heard, and disappeared as purposefully as he'd come.

More minutes passed. I spent them thinking about Gabriella. Gabriella alive and loving, her solemnity a crust over depths of warmth and strength. A girl for always. For what was left of always.

The lorry came back, halted briefly outside, and rumbled away into the distance. Yardman and all his crew except Alf trooped into the hangar. Giuseppe walked past me across to the sliding doors at the back and opened a space behind the Citroen. A cool draught blew in and sent the dust round in little squirls on the concrete floor, and outside the sky was an intense velvety black.

Yardman said, 'Right Billy. If the new crew are on time, we'll be back with them in a little over an hour. I want you ready to go then, immediately the plane has taken off. All jobs done. Understood?'

'O.K.' Billy nodded. 'Relax.'

Yardman walked over and paused in front of me, looking down with a mixture of regret and satisfaction.

'Good-bye, my dear boy.'

'Good-bye,' I answered politely.

His taut mouth twisted. He looked across at Billy. 'Take no chances,

Billy, do you understand? You underestimate this man. He's not one of your fancy nitwits, however much you may want him to be. You ought to know that by now. And Billy, I'm warning you, I'm warning you my dear Billy, that if you should let him escape at this stage, knowing everything that he does, you may as well put one of your little bullets through your own brain, because otherwise, rest assured, my dear Billy, I will do it for you.'

Even Billy was slightly impressed by the cold menace in Yardman's usually uninflected voice. 'Yeah,' he said uneasily. 'Well he won't bloody escape, not a chance.'

'Make sure of it.' Yardman nodded, turned, and went and sat in the front passenger seat of the Citroen. Giuseppe beside him started the engine, reversed the car out of the hangar, and drove smoothly away, Yardman facing forwards and not looking back. Billy slid the door shut again behind them and came slowly across the concrete, putting his feet down carefully and silently like a stalker. He stopped four paces away, and the silence slowly thickened.

Rous-Wheeler cleared his throat nervously, and it sounded loud.

Billy flicked him a glance. 'Go for a walk,' he said.

'A . . . walk?'

'Yeah, a walk. One foot in front of the other.' He was offensive. 'Down the runway and back should just about do it.'

Rous-Wheeler understood. He wouldn't meet my eyes and he hadn't even enough humanity to plead for me. He turned his back on the situation and made for the exit. So much for the old school tie.

'Now,' said Billy. 'Just the two of us.'

Chapter Sixteen

He walked cat-footed round the hangar in his quiet shoes, looking for things. Eventually he came back towards me carrying an old supple broken bicycle chain and a full flat five gallon tin of petrol. I looked at these objects with what I hoped was fair impassiveness and refrained from asking what he intended to do with them. I supposed I would find out soon enough.

He squatted on his haunches and grinned at me, his face level with mine, the bicycle chain in one hand and the petrol can on the floor in the other. His gun was far away, on the bench.

'Ask me nicely,' he said. 'And I'll make it easy.'

I didn't believe him anyway. He waited through my silence and sniggered.

'You will,' he said. 'You'll ask all right, your sodding lordship.'

He brought forward the bicycle chain, but instead of hitting me wi' it as I'd expected he slid it round my ankle and tied it there into two h hitches. He had difficulty doing this but once the knots were tied links looked like holding for ever. The free end he led through the handle of the petrol can and again bent it back on itself into knots. When he had finished there was a stalk of about six inches between the knots on my ankle and those on the can. Billy picked up the can and jerked it. My leg duly followed, firmly attached. Billy smiled, well satisfied. He unscrewed the cap of the can and let some of the petrol run out over my feet and make a small pool on the floor. He screwed the cap back on, but looser.

Then he went round behind the girder and unlocked both the padlocks on my wrists. The chain fell off, but owing to a mixture of surprise and stiffened shoulders I could do nothing towards getting my hands down to undo the bicycle chain before Billy was across the bay for his gun and turning with it at the ready.

'Stand up,' he said. 'Nice and easy. If you don't, I'll throw this in the petrol.' This, in his left hand, was a cigarette lighter: a gas lighter with a top which stayed open until one snapped it shut. The flame burned bright as he flicked his thumb.

I stood up stiffly, using the girder for support, the sick and certain knowledge of what Billy intended growing like a lump of ice in my abdomen. So much for not being afraid of death. I had changed my mind about it. Some forms were worse than others.

Billy's mouth curled. 'Ask, then,' he said.

I didn't. He waved his pistol slowly towards the floor. 'Outside, matey. I've a little job for you to do. Careful now, we don't want a bleeding explosion in here if we can help it.' His face was alight with greedy enjoyment. He'd never had such fun in his life. I found it definitely irritating.

The can was heavy as I dragged it along with slow steps to the door and through on to the grass outside. Petrol slopped continuously in small amounts through the loosened cap, leaving a highly inflammable trail in my wake. The night air was sweet and the stars were very bright. There was no moon. A gentle wind. A beautiful night for flying.

'Turn right,' Billy said behind me. 'That's Alf along there where the light is. Go there, and don't take too bloody long about it, we haven't got all night.' He sniggered at his feeble joke.

Alf wasn't more than a tennis court away, but I was fed up with the petrol can before I got there. He had been digging, I found. A six or seven foot square of grass had been cut out, the turf lying along one edge in a tidy heap, and about a foot of earth had been excavated into a crumbling mound. A large torch standing on the pile of turf shone on Alf's old face as he stood in the shallow hole. He held the spade loosely and looked at Billy enquiringly.

'Go for a walk,' Billy said loudly. Alf interpreted the meaning if not the words, nodded briefly, leaned the spade against the turf, stepped up on to the grass and shuffled away into the engulfing dark.

'O.K., then,' said Billy. 'Get in there and start digging. Any time you want to stop, you've only got to ask. Just ask.'

'And if I do?'

The light shone aslant on Billy's wide bright eyes and his jeering delighted mouth. He lifted the pistol a fraction. 'In the head,' he said. 'And I'll have bloody well beaten you, your effing bloody lordship. And it's a pity I haven't got the whole lot like you here as well.'

'We don't do any harm,' I said, and wryly knew that history gave me the lie. There'd been trampling enough done in the past, and resentment could persist for centuries.

'Keep both hands on the spade,' he said. 'You try and untie the bicycle chain, and you've had it.'

He watched me dig, standing safely out of reach of any slash I might make with the spade and snapping his lighter on and off. The smell of petrol rose sharply into my nostrils as it oozed drop by drop through the leaking cap and soaked into the ground I stood on. The earth was soft and loamy, not too heavy to move, but Billy hadn't chosen this task without careful malice aforethought. Try as I might, I found I could scarcely shift a single spadeful without in some way knocking or rubbing my arm against my side. Jersey and shirt were inadequate buffers, and every scoop took its toll. The soreness increased like a geometrical progression.

Billy watched and waited. The hole grew slowly deeper. I told myself severely that a lot of other people had had to face far worse than this, that others before me had dug what they knew to be their own graves, that others had gone up in flames for a principle . . . that it was possible, even if not jolly.

Billy began to get impatient. 'Ask,' he said. I threw a spadeful of earth at him in reply and very nearly ended things there and then. The gun barrel jerked up fiercely at my head, and then slowly subsided. 'You'll be lucky,' he said angrily. 'You'll have to go down on your bloody knees.'

When I was sure my feet must be below his line of sight I tugged my foot as far away from the petrol can as the chain would allow, and jammed the spade down hard on the six inches of links between the knots. It made less noise than I'd feared on the soft earth. I did it again and again with every spadeful, which apart from being slightly rough on my ankle produced no noticeable results.

'Hurry up,' Billy said crossly. He flicked the lighter. 'Hurry it up.'

Excellent advice. Time was fast running out and Yardman would be back. I jammed the spade fiercely down and with a surge of long dead hope felt the battered links begin to split. It wasn't enough. Even if I got free of the petrol can I was still waist deep in a hole, and Billy still had his revolver: but even a little hope was better than none at all. The next slice of the spade split the chain further. The one after that severed it: but I had hit it with such force that when it broke I fell over, sprawing on hands and knees.

'Stand up,' Billy said sharply. 'Or I'll . . .'

I wasn't listening to him. I was acknowledging with speechless horror that the grave which was big enough for Patrick and Mike and Bob as well as myself was already occupied. My right hand had closed on a piece of cloth which flapped up through the soil. I ran my fingers along it, burrowing, and stabbed them into something sharp. I felt, and knew A row of pins.

I stood up slowly and stared at Billy. He advanced nearly to the edge of the hole, looked briefly down, and back to me.

'Simon,' I said lifelessly. 'It's . . . Simon.'

Billy smiled. A cold, terrible, satisfied smile.

There were no more time. Time was only the distance from his gun to my head, from his gas lighter to my petrol-soaked shoes and the leaking can at my feet. He'd only been waiting for me to find Simon. His hunger was almost assuaged.

'Well,' he said, his eyes wide. 'Ask. It's your last chance.'

I said nothing.

'Ask,' he repeated furiously. 'You must.'

I shook my head. A fool, I thought. I'm a bloody fool. I must be mad.

'All right,' he said, raging. 'If I had more time you'd ask. But if you won't . . .' His voice died, and he seemed suddenly almost as afraid as I was at what he was going to do. He hesitated, half lifting the gun instead: but the moment passed and his nerve came back, renewed and pitiless.

He flicked the lighter. The flame shot up, sharp and blazing against the night sky. He poised it just for a second so as to be sure to toss it where I couldn't catch it on the way: and in that second I bent down, picked up the petrol can, and flung it at him. The loose cap unexpectedly came right off on the way up, and the petrol splayed out in a great glittering volatile stream, curving round to meet the flame.

A split second for evasion before the world caught fire.

The flying petrol burnt in the air with a great rushing noise and fell like a fountain over both the spots where Billy and I had just been standing. The can exploded with a gust of heat. The grave was a square blazing pit and flames flickered over the mound of dug out soil like brandy on an outsize plum pudding. Five gallons made dandy pyrotechnics.

I rolled out on my back over the lip of the grave with nothing to spare before it became a crematorium, and by some blessed miracle my feet escaped becoming part of the general holocaust. More than I had hoped.

Billy was running away screaming with his coat on fire along the left shoulder and down his arm. He was making frantic efforts to get it off but he was still clinging to his gun and this made it impossible. I had to have the gun and would have fought for it, but as I went after him I saw him drop it and stagger on, tearing at his jacket buttons in panic and agony: and my spine and scalp shuddered at the terror I had escaped.

With weak knees I half stumbled, half ran for the place where the revolver had fallen. The light of the flames glinted on it in the grass, and I bent and took it into my hand, the bulbous silencer heavy on the barrel and the butt a good fit in my palm.

Billy had finally wrenched his jacket off and it lay on the ground ahead in a deserted smouldering heap. Billy himself was still on his feet and making for the hangar, running and staggering and yelling for Alf.

I went after him.

Alf wasn't in the hangar. When I reached it Billy was standing with his back to me in the place where the car had been, rocking on his feet and still yelling. I stepped through the door and shut it behind me.

Billy swung round. The left sleeve of his shirt had burned into ribbons and his skin was red and glistening underneath. He stared unbelievingly at me and then at his gun in my hand. His mouth shut with a snap; and even then he could still raise a sneer.

'You won't do it,' he said, panting.

'Earls' sons,' I said, 'learn to shoot.'

'Only birds.' He was contemptuous. 'You haven't the guts.'

'You're wrong, Billy. You've been wrong about me from the start.'

I watched the doubt creep in and grow. I watched his eyes and then his head move from side to side as he looked for escape. I watched his muscles bunch to run for it. And when I saw that he finally realised in a moment of stark astonishment that I was going to, I shot him.

Chapter Seventeen

The Cessna had full tanks. Hurriedly I pressed the master switch in the cockpit and watched the needles swing round the fuel gauges. All the instruments looked all right, the radio worked, and the latest date on the maintenance card was only three days old. As far as I could tell from a cursory check, the little aircraft was ready to fly. All the same . . .

Alf and Rous-Wheeler came bursting in together through the door, both of them startled and wild looking and out of breath. Back from their little walks and alarmed by the bonfire. Alf gave an inarticulate cry and hurried over to Billy's quiet body. Rous-Wheeler followed more slowly, not liking it.

'It's Billy,' he said, as if stupefied. 'Billy.'

Alf gave no sign of hearing. They stood looking down at Billy as he lay on his back. There was a small scarlet star just left of his breastbone, and he had died with his eyes wide open, staring sightlessly up to the roof. Alf and Rous-Wheeler looked lost and bewildered.

I climbed quickly and quietly out of the Cessna and walked round its tail. They turned after a moment or two and saw me standing there not six paces away, holding the gun. I wore black. I imagine my face was grim. I frightened them.

Alf backed away two steps, and Rous-Wheeler three. He pointed a shaking arm at Billy.

'You . . . you killed him.'

'Yes.' My tone gave him no comfort. 'And you too, if you don't do exactly as I say.'

He had less difficulty in believing it than Billy. He made little protesting movements with his hands, and when I said, 'Go outside. Take Alf,' he complied without hesitation.

Just outside the door I touched Alf's arm, pointed back at Billy and then down to where the grave was. The flames had burnt out.

'Bury Billy,' I shouted in his ear.

He heard me, and looked searchingly into my face. He too found no reassurance: and he was used to doing what I said. Accepting the situation with only a shade more dumb resignation than usual he went slowly back across the concrete. I watched him shut the glazing eyes with rough humane fingers, and remembered the cup of coffee he'd given me when I badly needed it. He had nothing to fear from me as long as he stayed down by the grave. He picked Billy up, swung him over his shoulder in a fireman's lift, and carried him out and away across the grass, a sturdy old horseman who should never have got caught up in this sort of thing. Any more than I should.

I stretched an arm back into the hangar and pulled down the lever which controlled the runway lights. At each end of the long strip the four powerful beams sprang out, and in that glow Alf could see where he was going and what he was going to do.

That Cessna, I thought, glancing at it, probably had a range of about six or seven hundred miles . . .

'You,' I said abruptly to Rous-Wheeler. 'Go and get into the plane we came in. Go up the forward steps, back through the galley, right back through the cabin, and sit down on those seats. Understand?'

'What . . .?' He began nervously.

'Hurry up.'

He gave me another frightened glance and set off to the plane, a lumbering grey shape behind the runway lights. I walked three steps behind him and unsympathetically watched him stumble in his fear.

'Hurry.' I said again, and he stumbled faster. The thought of the Citroen returning was like a devil on my tail. I was just not going to be taken again. There was five bullets left in the gun. The first for Rous-Wheeler, the next for Yardman, and after that . . . he would have Giuseppe with him, and at least two others. Not nice.

'Faster.' I said.

Rous-Wheeler reached the ladder and stumbled up it, tripping over half the steps. He went awkwardly back through the plane just as I had said and flopped down panting on one of the seats. I followed him. Someone, Alf I supposed, had given the mares some hay, and one of the bales from Billy's now dismantled wall had been clipped open and split. The binding wire from it lay handy on the flattened aft box. I picked it up to use on Rous-Wheeler, but there was nothing on the comfortable upholstered double seat I could tie him to.

He made no fuss when I bound his wrists together. His obvious fear made him flabby and malleable, and his eyes looked as if he could feel shock waves from the violence and urgency which were flowing through me.

'Kneel down,' I said, pointing to the floor in front of the seats. He didn't like that. Too undignified.

'Kneel,' I said. 'I haven't time to bother about your comfort.'

With a pained expression that at any other time would have been funny he lowered himself on to his knees. I slid the ends of the wire through one of the holes in the seat anchorages on the floor, and fastened him there securely by the wrists.

'I ss . . . say,' he protested.

'You're bloody lucky to be alive at all, so shut up.'

He shut up. His hands were tied only a couple of feet away from the blanket which covered Patrick. He stared at the quiet mound and he didn't like that either. Serve him right, I thought callously.

'What . . . what are you going to do?' he said.

'I didn't answer. I went back up the cabin, looking at the way they'd re-stored the cargo. Aft box still flat. The walls of the next one, dismantled, had been stacked in the starboard alley. On the peat tray now stood a giant packing case six feet long, four feet wide, and nearly five feet tall. Chains ran over it in both directions, fastening it down to the anchorages. It had rope handles all the way round, and Yardman had said something about using a block and tackle, but all the same manoeuvring it into its present position must have been a tricky sweaty business. However, for the sake of forwarding the passage of this uninformative crate Yardman had also been prepared to steal a plane and kill three airmen. Those who had no right to it wanted it very badly.

I went up further. The four mares were unconcernedly munching at full haynets and paid me scant attention. Through the galley and into the space behind the cockpit, where Mike's body still lay. Burial had been the last of the jobs. Uncompleted.

The luggage compartment held four more crates, the size of tea chests. They all had rope handles and no markings.

Beyond them was the open door. It represented to me a last chance of not going through with what I had in mind. Yardman hadn't yet come back, and the Cessna was ready. If I took it, with its radio and full tanks, I would undoubtedly be safe, and Yardman's transport business would be busted. But he'd still have the D.C.4 and the packing cases . . .

Abruptly I pulled up the telescopic ladder and shut the door with a clang. Too much trouble, I told myself, to change my mind now. I'd have to take Rous-Wheeler all the way back to the Cessna or shoot him, and neither course appealed. But the situation I found in the cockpit nearly defeated me before I began.

Billy had shot Bob as he sat, through the back of the head. The upper part of him had fallen forward over the wheel, the rest held firmly in the seat by the still fastened safety strap across his thighs. In the ordinary way even stepping into the co-pilot's seat in the cramped space was awkward enough, and lifting a dead man out of it bodily was beyond me. Blacking my mind to the sapping thought that this was a man I had known, and considering him solely as an object which spelled disaster to me if I didn't move it I undid the seat belt, heaved the pathetic jack-knifed figure round far enough to clear his feet and head from the controls, and fastened the belt tight across him again in his new position, his back half towards me.

With the same icy concentration I sat in Patrick's place and set about starting the plane. Switches. Dozens of switches everywhere: On the control panel, on the roof, in the left side wall and in the bank of throttles on my right. Each labelled in small metal letters, and too many having to be set correctly before the plane would fly.

Patrick had shown me how. Quite different from doing it. I pared the pre-starting checks down to the barest minimum; fuel supply on, mixture rich, propeller revs maximum, throttle just open, brakes on, trimmer central, direction indicator synchronised with the compass.

My boats were burned with the first ignition switch, because it worked. The three bladed propeller swung and ground and the inner port engine roared into action with an earsplitting clatter. Throttle too far open. Gently I pulled the long lever with its black knob down until the engine fell back to warming up speed, and after that in quick succession and with increasing urgency I started the other three. Last, I switched on the headlights: Alf might not have heard the engines, but he would certainly see the lights. It couldn't be helped. I had to be able to see where I was going. With luck he wouldn't know what do do, and do nothing.

I throttled back a bit and took the brakes off and the plane began to roll. Too fast. Too fast. I was heading straight for the runway lights and could smash them, and I needed them alight. I pulled the two starboard throttles back for a second and the plane slewed round in a sort of skid and missed the lights and rolled forward on to the runway.

The wind was behind me, which meant taxi-ing to the far end and turning back to take off. No one ever taxied a D.C.4 faster. And at the far end I skipped all the power checks and everything else I'd been taught and swung the plane round facing the way I'd come and without a pause pushed forward all the four throttles wide open.

The great heavy plane roared and vibrated and began to gather speed with what seemed to me agonising slowness. The runway looked too short. Grass was slower than tarmac, the strip was designed for light aircraft, and heaven alone knew the weight of that packing case . . . For short runways, lower flaps. The answer came automatically from the subconscious, not as a clear coherent thought. I put my hand on the lever and lowered the trailing edges of the wings. Twenty degrees. Just under half-way. Full slaps were brakes . . .

Yardman came back.

Unlike Alf, he knew exactly what to do, and wasted no time doing it. Towards the far end the Citroen was driven straight out on to the centre line of the runway, and my headlights shone on distant black figures scrambling out and running towards the hangar. Swerve wide enough to miss the car, I thought, and I'll get unbalanced on rough ground and pile up. Go straight up the runway and not be able to lift off in time, and I'll hit it either with the wheels or the propellers . . .

Yardman did what Alf hadn't. He switched off the runway lights. Darkness clamped down like a sack over the head. Then I saw that the plane's bright headlights raised a gleam on the car now frighteningly close ahead and at least gave me the direction to head for. I was going far too fast to stop, even if I'd felt like it. Past the point of no return, and still on the ground. I eased gently back on the control column, but she wouldn't come. The throttles were wide; no power anywhere in reserve. I ground my teeth and with the car coming back to me now at a hundred miles an hour hung on for precious moments I couldn't spare, until it was then or never. No point in never. I hauled back on the control column and at the same time slammed up the lever which retracted the under-carriage. Belly flop or car crash; I wasn't going to be around to have second thoughts. But the D.C.4 flew. Unbelievably there was no explosive finale, just a smooth roaring upward glide. The plane's headlights slanted skywards, the car vanished beneath, the friction of the grass fell away. Airborne was the sweetest word in the dictionary.

Sweat was running down my face; part exertion, part fear. The D.C.4 was heavy, like driving a fully loaded pantechnicon after passing a test on empty minis, and the sheer muscle power needed to hold it straight on the ground and get it into the air was in the circumstances exhausting. But it was up, and climbing steadily at a reasonable angle, and the hands were circling reassuringly round the clock face of the altimeter. Two thousand, three thousand, four thousand feet. I levelled out at that and closed the throttles a little as the airspeed increased to two twenty knots. A slow old plane, built in nineteen-forty-five. Two twenty was the most it could manage.

The little modern Cessna I'd left behind was just about as fast. Yardman had brought a pilot. If he too took off without checks, he could be only scant minutes behind.

Get lost, I thought, I'd the whole sky to get lost in. The headlights were out, but from habit I'd switched on the navigation lights on the wing tips and tail and also the revolving beacon over the cockpit. The circling red beam from it washed the wings alternately with pale pink light. I switched it out, and the navigation lights too. Just one more broken law in a trail of others.

The runway had been laid out from due east to west. I had taken off to the west and flown straight on, urgent to get out, regardless of where. Too easy for them. I banked tentatively to the left and felt the plane respond cumbrously, heavy on my arms. South-west, into the wind. I straightened up and flew on, an invisible shell in the darkness, and after five minutes knew they wouldn't find me. Not with the Cessna, anyway.

The tight-strung tension of my nerves relaxed a little: with most uncomfortable results. I was suddenly far too aware of the wicked square of burn over my ribs, and realised that I hadn't really felt it since the moment I found Simon. Under the pressure of events its insistent message hadn't got through. Now it proceeded to rectify that with enthusiasm.

Weakness seeped down my limbs. I shivered, although I was still sweating from exertion. My hands started trembling on the wheel, and I began to realise the extent to which I was unfit to fly anything, let alone take a first try at an airliner way out of my normal class. But far worse than the physical stress was the mental let-down which accom-panied it. It was pride which had got me into that plane and up into the air. Nothing but pride. I was still trying to prove something to Billy, even though he was dead. I hadn't chosen the D.C.4 because of any passionate conviction that the ultrasonic gadget needed saving at all costs, but simply to show them, Yardman and Billy's ghost, that there wasn't much I couldn't do. Childish, vainglorious, stupid, ridiculous: I was the lot.

And now I was stuck with it. Up in the air in thundering tons of metal, going I didn't know where.

I wiped the sleeve of my jersey over my face and tried to think. Direction and height were vital if I were ever to get down again. Four thousand feet, I thought, looking at the altimeter; at that height I could fly straight into a mountain . . . if there were any. South west steady: but south west from where? I hunted round the cockpit for a map of any sort, but there wasn't one to be found.

Patrick had said we were in Italy, and Giuseppe was Italian, and so was the registration on the Cessna, and the ultrasonic device had been driven straight from Brescia. Conclusive, I thought. Northern Italy, probably somewhere near the east cost. Impossible to get closer than that. If I continued south-west, in the end I'd be over the Mediteranean. And before that . . . new sweat broke out on my forehead. Between the northern plain and the Mediterranean lay the Apennines, and I couldn't remember at all how high they were. But four thousand was much too low . . . and for all I knew they were only a mile ahead . . .

I put the nose up and opened the throttles and slowly gained height. Five thousand, six thousand, seven thousand, eight. That ought to be enough . . . The Alps only reached above twelve thousand at the peaks, and the Apennines were a good deal lower. I was guessing. They might be higher than I thought. I went up again to ten thousand.

At that height I was flying where I had no business to be, and at some point I'd be crossing the airways to Rome. Crossing a main road in the dark, without lights. I switched the navigation lights on again, and the revolving beacon too. They wouldn't give much warning to a jetliner on a collision course, but possibly better than none.

The thunderous noise of the engines was tiring in itself. I stretched out a hand for Patrick's headset and put it on, the padded earphones reducing the din to a more manageable level. I had taken it for granted from the beginning that Yardman would have put the radio out of order before ever asking Patrick to change course, and some short tuning with the knobs confirmed it. Not a peep or crackle from the air. There had been just a chance that he wouldn't have disconnected the V.O.R. – Very high frequency Omni-range – by which one navigated from one radio beacon to the next: it worked independently of two-way ground to air communication, and he might have needed to use it to find the airfield we had landed on. But that too was dead.

Time, I thought. If I didn't keep track of the time I'd be more lost than ever. I looked at my watch. Half-past eleven. I stared at the hands blankly. If they'd said half nine or half one it would have felt the same. The sort of time one measured in minutes and hours had ceased to exist in a quite street in Milan. I shook myself. Half past eleven. From now on it was important. Essential. Without maps or radio, time and the compass were going to decide my fate. Like all modern pilots I had been taught to stick meticulously to using all the aids and keeping all the regulations. The 'seat of the pants' stuff of the pioneers was held to be unscientific and no longer necessary. This was a fine time to have to learn it from scratch.

If I'd been up for a quarter of an hour, I thought, and if I'd started from the northern plain, and if I could only remember within a hundred miles how broad Italy was, then I might have some idea of when I'd be over the sea. Not yet, anyway. There were pinpricks of lights below me, and several small clusters of towns. No conveniently lit airports with welcoming runways.

If I'd taken the Cessna, I thought wretchedly, it would have been easy. Somewhere, by twiddling the knobs, I'd have raised radio contact with the ground. The international air language was English. A piece of cake. They'd have told me my position, what course to set, how to get down, everything. But if I'd taken the Cessna, I would have had to leave the D.C.4 intact, because of the mares. I'd thought at first of piling a couple more five gallon cans under the big plane and putting a match to it, and then remembered the living half of the cargo. Yardman might be cold-bloodedly prepared to kill airmen, but I baulked at roasting alive four horses. And I couldn't get them out, because the plane carried no ramp. With time I could have put the engines out of action ... and with time they could have mended them again. But I hadn't had time. If I'd done that, I couldn't have got the Cessna out and away before Yardman's return.

I could have taken Rous-Wheeler in the Cessna and landed safely and put Yardman Transport out of business. But I was as greedy as Billy: half wasn't enough. It had to be all. I could choke on all, as Billy had.

The useless thoughts squirrelled round and round, achieving nothing. I wiped my face again on the sleeve of my jersey and understood why Patrick had nearly always flown in shirt sleeves, even though it was winter.

Italy couldn't be much wider than England. If as wide. A hundred and twenty, a hundred and forty nautical miles. Perhaps more. I hadn't looked at the time when I took off. I should have done. It was routine. I hadn't a hope if I couldn't concentrate better than that. A hundred and forty miles of two twenty knots ... say a hundred and sixty miles to be sure ... it would take somewhere between forty and forty-five minutes. If I'd had the sense to look at my watch earlier I would have known how far I'd gone.

The lights below grew scarcer and went out. It was probably too soon to be the sea ... it had to be mountains. I flew on for some time, and then checked my watch. Midnight. And still no lights underneath. The Apennines couldn't be so broad ... but if I went down too soon, I'd hit them. I gave it another five minutes and spent them wishing Billy's burns would let up again. They were a five star nuisance.

Still no lights. I couldn't understand it. I couldn't possibly still be over the narrow Apennines. It was no good. I'd have to go down for a closer look. I throttled back, let the nose go down, and watched the altimeter hands go anti-clockwise through seven, six, five, four. At four thousand feet I levelled out again, and the night was as black as ever. I'd certainly hit no mountains, but for all I could see I was a lost soul in Limbo. It wasn't a safe feeling, not at all.

When at last I saw lights ahead I was much more uneasy than reassured. It was twelve fifteen by my watch, which meant I had come nearly two hundred miles already, and Italy couldn't be as wide as that. Or at least I wouldn't have thought so.

The lights ahead resolved themselves into little clusters strung out in a horizontal line. I knew the formation too well to mistake it. I was approaching a coastline. Incredulity swamped me. I was approaching *from the sea.*

Nightmares weren't in it. I felt a great sense of unreality, as if the world had spun and rearranged its face, and nothing was ever going to be familiar again. I must be somewhere, I thought, taking a fierce grip on my escaping imagination. But where on earth, where literally on earth, was I?

I couldn't go on flying blindly south-west for ever. The coast line must have a shape. About three miles short of it I banked to the right, wheeling northwards, guided by nothing more rational than instinct, and flew along parallel with the few and scattered lights on the shore. The sea beneath was black but the land was blacker. The line where they met was like ebony against coal, a shadowy change of texture, a barely perceptible rub of one mass against another.

I couldn't, I thought, bullying my mind into some sort of order, I couldn't possibly have flown straight across the Gulf of Genoa and now be following the Italian coast northwards from Alassio. There weren't enough lights, even for that time of night. And I knew that coastline well. This one, I didn't. Moreover, it ran due north for far too long. I had already been following it for fifteen minutes: fifty-five miles.

It had to be faced that I'd been wrong about where I started from. Or else the directional gyro was jammed. It couldn't be . . . I'd checked it twice against the remote reading compass, which worked independently. I checked again: they matched. They couldn't both be wrong. But I *must* have started in Italy. I went right back in my mind to the flight out, when Patrick had first turned east. It had been east. I was still sure of that: and that was all.

There was a flashing light up aheal, on the edge of the sea. A lighthouse. Very useful if I'd had a nautical chart, which I hadn't. I swept on past the lighthouse and stopped dead in my mental tracks. There was no land beyond.

I banked the plane round to the left and went back. The light-house stood at the end of a long narrow finger of land pointing due north. I flew southwards along the western side of it for about twenty miles until the sporadic lights spread wider and my direction swung again to the south-west. A fist pointing north.

Supposing I'd been right about starting from Italy, but wrong about being so far east. Then I would have been over the sea when I thought I was over the mountains. Supposing I'd been going for longer than a quarter of an hour when I first looked at my watch: then I would have gone further than I guessed. All the same, there simply wasn't any land this shape in the northern Mediterranean, not even an island.

An island of this size . . .

Corsica.

It couldn't be, I thought. I couldn't be so far south. I wheeled the plane round again and went back to the lighthouse. If it was Corsica and I flew north-west I'd reach the south of France and be back on the map. If it was Corsica I'd started from right down on the southern edge of the northern plain, not near Trieste or Venice as I'd imagined. It wasn't impossible. It made sense. The world began to fall back into place. I flew north-west over the black invisible sea. Twenty-seven minutes. About a hundred miles.

The strings and patterns of lights along the French coast looked like lace sewn with diamonds, and were just as precious. I turned and followed them westwards, looking for Nice airport. It was easy to spot by day: the runways seemed to be almost on the beach, as the airfield had been built on an outward curve of the shoreline. But either I was further west than I thought, or the airport had closed for the night, because I missed it. The first place I was sure of was Cannes with its bay of embracing arms, and that was so close to Nice that if the runway had been lit I must have seen it.

A wave of tiredness washed through me, along with a numb feeling of futility. Even if I could find one, which was doubtful, I couldn't fly into a major airport without radio, and all the minor ones had gone to bed. I couldn't land anywhere in the dark. All I looked like being able to do was fly around in circles until it got light again and land at Nice . . . and the fuel would very likely give out before then.

It was at that depressing point that I first thought about trying to go all the way to England. The homing instinct in time of trouble. Primitive. I couldn't think of a thing against it except that I was likely to go to sleep from tiredness on the way, and I could do that even more easily going round in circles outside Cannes.

Committed from the moment I'd thought of it, I followed the coast until it turned slightly north again and the widespread lights of Marseilles lay beneath. The well-known way home from there lay up the Rhone Valley over the beacons at Montélimar and Lyons, with a left wheel at Dijon to Paris. But though the radio landmarks were unmistakable the geographical ones weren't, and I couldn't blindly stumble into the busy Paris complex without endangering every other plane in the area. North of Paris was just as bad, with the airlanes to Germany and the East. South, then. A straight line across France south of Paris. It would be unutterably handy to have known where Paris lay; what precise bearing. I had to guess again . . . and my first guesses hadn't exactly been a riotous triumph.

Three-twenty degrees, I thought. I'd try that. Allow ten degrees for wind drift from the south-west. Three ten. And climb a bit . . . the centre of France was occupied by the Massif Central and it would be fairly inefficient to crash into it. I increased the power and went back up to ten thousand feet. That left fuel, the worst problem of all.

I'd taken off on the main tanks and the gauges now stood in half full. I switched over to the auxiliaries and they also were half full. And half empty, too. The plane had been refuelled at Milan that morning, ten centuries ago. It carried ... I thought searchingly back to Patrick's casually thrown out snippets of information the first day I flew with him ... it carried twelve hundred United States gallons, giving a range of approximately eighteen hundred miles in normal conditions with a normal load. The load, though unconventional, was normal enough in weight. The condition of the weather was perfect, even if the condition of the pilot wasn't. Nine hundred miles from Marseilles would see me well over England, but it wouldn't take much more than four hours at the present speed until the tanks ran dry and it would still be too dark ...

There was just one thing to be done about that. I put my hand on the throttle levers and closed them considerably. The airspeed fell back from two-twenty, back through two hundred, one-eighty, steadied on one-fifty. I didn't dare go any slower than that because one thing Patrick hadn't told me was the stalling speed, and a stall I could do without. The nose wanted to go down heavily with the decreased airspeed and I was holding it up by brute strength, the wheel of the control column lodged against my whole left forearm. I stretched my right hand up to the trimmer handle in the roof and gave it four complete turns, and cursed as a piece of shirt which was sticking to the furrows and burns unhelpfully unstuck itself. The nose of the plane steadied; ten thousand feet at one-fifty knots; and blood oozed warmly through my jersey.

A hundred and fifty knots should reduce the petrol consumption enough for me to stay in the air until long enough after dawn to find an airfield. I hoped. It also meant not four hours ahead, but more than five: and I'd had enough already. Still, now that I knew roughly where I was going, the plane could fly itself. I made small adjustments to the trimmer until the needle on the instrument which showed whether she was climbing or descending pointed unwaveringly to level, and then switched in the automatic pilot. I took my hands off the wheel and learned back. The D.C.4 flew straight on. Very restful.

Nothing happened for several minutes except that I developed a thirst and remembered Rous-Wheeler for the first time since takeoff. Still on his knees, I supposed, and extremely uncomfortable. His bad luck.

There was water in the galley only five or six steps behind me, cold and too tempting. Gingerly I edged out of my seat. The plane took no notice. I took two steps backwards. The instruments didn't quiver. I went into the galley and drew a quick cup of water, and went back towards the cockpit drinking it. Clearly the plane was doing splendidly without me. I returned to the galley for a refill of the cold delicious liquid, and when I'd got it, nearly dropped it.

Even above the noise of the engines I could hear Rous-Wheeler's scream. Something about the raw terror in it raised the hair on my neck. That wasn't pain, I thought, not the sort he'd get from cramp anyway. It was fear.

He screamed again, twice.

One of the horses, I thought immediately. If Billy hadn't boxed them properly ... My newly irrigated mouth went dry again. A loose horse was just too much.

I went back to the cockpit, hurrying. Nothing had moved on the instrument panel. I'd have to risk it.

The plane had never seemed longer, the chains and racks more obstructing. And none of the mares was loose. They weren't even fretting, but simply eating hay. Half relieved, half furious. I went on past the packing case. Rous-Wheeler was still there, still kneeling. His eyes protruded whitely and his face was wet. The last of his screams hung like an echo in the air.

'What the hell's the matter?' I shouted o him angrily.

'He ...' his voice shrieked uncontrollably. 'He ... moved.'

'Who moved?'

'Him.' His eyes were staring fixedly at the blanket covering Patrick.

He couldn't have moved. Poor, poor Patrick. I went across and pulled the rug off and stood looking down at him, the tall silent body, the tumbled hair, the big pool of blood under his downturned face.

Pool of blood.

It was impossible. He hadn't had time to bleed as much as that. I knelt down beside him and rolled him over, and he opened his yellow eyes.

Chapter Eighteen

He'd been out cold for six hours and he was still unconscious. Nothing moved in his eyes, and after a few seconds they fell slowly shut again.

My fingers were clumsy on his wrist and for anxious moments I could feel nothing; but his pulse was there. Slow and faint, but regular. He was on his way up from the depths. I was so glad that he wasn't dead that had Rous-Wheeler not been there I would undoubtedly have wept. As it was, I fought against the flooding back of the grief I'd suppressed when Billy shot him. Odd that I should be tumbled into such intense emotion only because the reason for it was gone.

Rous-Wheeler stuttered 'What ... what is it?' with a face the colour and texture of putty, and I glanced at him with dislike.

'He's alive,' I said tersely.

'He can't be.'

'Shut up.'

Billy's bullet had hit Patrick high, above the hairline and at a rising angle, and instead of penetrating his skull had slid along outside it. The long, swollen and clotted wound looked dreadful, but was altogether beautiful in comparison with a neat round hole. I stood up and spread the blanket over him again, to keep him warm. Then, disregarding Rous-Wheeler's protest, I went away up the plane.

In the cockpit nothing had changed. The plane roared steadily on its three ten heading and all the instruments were like rocks. I touched the back of the co-pilot, awake again to his presence. The silence in him was eternal: he wouldn't feel my sympathy, but he had it.

Turning back a pace or two, I knelt down beside Mike. He too had been shot in the head, and about him too there was no question. The agile eyebrow was finished. I straightened him out from his crumpled position and laid him flat on his back. It wouldn't help any, but it seemed to give him more dignity. That was all you could give the dead, it seemed; and all you could take away.

The four packing cases in the luggage bay were heavy and had been thrust in with more force than finesse, pushing aside and crushing most of the things already there. Shifting the first case a few inches I stretched a long arm past it and tugged out a blanket, which I laid over Mike. Armed with a second one I went back into the galley. Sometime in the past I'd seen the first-aid box in one of the cupboards under the counter, and to my relief it was still in the same place.

Lying on top of it was a gay parcel wrapped in the stripped paper of Malpensa Airport. The doll for Mike's daughter. I felt the jolt physically. Nothing could soften the facts. I was taking her a dead father for her birthday.

And Gabriella . . . anxiety for her still hovered in my mind like a low cloud ceiling, thick, threatening and unchanged. I picked up the parcel she had wrapped and put it on the counter beside the plastic cups and the bag of sugar. People often did recover from bullets in the lungs: I knew they did. But the precise Italian doctor had only offered hope, and hope had tearing claws. I was flying home to nothing if she didn't live.

Taking the blanket and the first aid kid I went back to Patrick. In the lavatory compartment I washed my filthy hands and afterwards soaked a chunk of cotton wool with clean water to wipe his blood-streaked face. Dabbing dry with more cotton wool I found a large hard lump on his forehead where it had hit the floor: two heavy concussing shocks within seconds, his brain had received. His eyelids hadn't flickered while I cleaned him, and with a new burst of worry I reached for his pulse: but it was still there, faint but persevering.

Sighing with relief I broke open the wrapping of a large sterile wound dressing, laid it gently over the deep gash in his scalp, and tied it on with the tape. Under his head I slid the second blanket, folded flat, to shield him a little from the vibration in the aircraft's metal skin. I loosened his tie and undid the top button of his shirt and also the waistband of his trousers: and beyond that there was no help I could give him. I stood up slowly with the first aid kit and turned to go.

With anxiety bordering on hysteria Rous-Wheeler shouted, 'You aren't going to leave me like this again, are you?'

I looked back to him. He was half sitting, half kneeling, with his hands still fastened to the floor in front of him. He'd been there for nearly three hours, and his flabby muscles must have been cracking. It was probably too cruel to leave him like that for the rest of the trip. I put the first aid kid down on the flattened box, pulled a bale of hay along on the starboard side and lodged it against the untrasonic packing case. Then with Alf's cutter I clipped through the wire round his wrists and pointed to the bale.

'Sit there.'

He got up slowly and stiffly, crying out. Shuffling, half-falling, he sat where I said. I picked up another piece of wire and in spite of his protests bound his wrists together again and fastened them to one of the chains anchoring the crate. I didn't want him bumbling all over the plane and breathing down my neck.

'Where are we going?' he said, the pomposity reawakening now that he'd got something from me.

I didn't answer.

'And who is flying the plane?'

'George,' I said, finishing his wrists with a twirl he'd never undo. 'Naturally.'

'George who?'

'A good question,' I said, nodding casually.

He was beautifully disconcerted. I left him to stew in it, picked up the first aid kit, checked again that Patrick's pulse was plodding quietly along, and made my way back to the galley.

There were a number of dressings in the first aid box, including several especially for burns, and I wasn't keen on my shirt sticking and tearing away again. Gingerly I pulled my jersey up under my arms and tucked the side of the shirt away under it. No one except Billy would have found the view entertaining, and the air at once started everything going again at full blast. I opened one of the largest of the burn dressings and laid it in place with that exquisite kind of gentleness you only give to yourself. Even so, it was quite enough. After a moment I fastened it on and pulled my shirt and jersey down on top. It felt so bad for a bit that I really wished I hadn't bothered.

I drank another cup of water, which failed to put out the fire. The first aid kit, on further inspection, offered a three-way choice in pain killers: a bottle each of aspirin and codeine tablets, and six ampoules of morphine. I shook out two of the codeines, and swallowed these. Then I packed everything back into the box, shut the lid, and left it on the counter.

Slowly I went up to the cockpit and stood looking at the instruments. All working fine. I fetched a third blanket from the luggage bay and tucked it over and round the body of Bob. He became immediately less of a harsh reality, and I wondered if that was why people always covered the faces of the dead.

I checked the time. An hour from Marseilles. Only a hundred and fifty miles, and a daunting way still to go. I learned against the metal wall and shut my eyes. It was no good feeling the way I did with so much still to do. Parts of Air Ministry regulations drifted ironically into my mind . . . 'Many flying accidents have occurred as a result of pilots flying while medically unfit . . . and the more exacting the flying task the more likely are minor indispositions to be serious . . . so don't go up at all if you are ill enough to need drugs . . . and if coffee isn't enough to keep you awake you are not fit to fly.'

Good old Air Ministry I thought: they'd hit the nail on the head. Where they would have me be was down on the solid earth, and I wholeheartedly agreed.

The radio, I thought inconsequentially. Out of order. I opened my eyes, pushed myself off the wall, and set about finding out why. I hadn't far to look. Yardman had removed all the circuit breakers, and the result was like an electric light system with no fuses in the fuse box. Every plane carried spares, however. I located the place where the spares should have been, and there weren't any. The whole lot in Yardman's pockets, no doubt.

Fetching a fresh cup of water, I climbed again into Patrick's seat and put on the headset to reduce the noise. I leaned back in the comfortable leather upholstery and rested my elbows on the stubby arms, and after a while the codeine and the bandage turned in a reasonable job.

Outside the sky was still black and dotted with brilliant stars, and the revolving anti-collision beacon still skimmed pinkly over the great wide span of the wings, but there was also a new misty greyish quality in the light. Not dawn. The moon coming up. Very helpful of it, I thought appreciatively. Although it was well on the wane I would probably be able to see what I was doing the next time I flew out over the coastline. I began to work out what time I would get there. More guesses. North-west across France coast to coast had to be all of five hundred miles. It had been one-forty when I left Marseilles; was three-ten now. E.T.A. English Channel, somewhere about five.

Patrick's being alive made a lot of difference to everything. I was now thankful without reservation that I had taken the D.C.4 however stupid my motive at the time, for if I'd left it, and Yardman had found him alive, they would simply have pumped another bullet into him, or even buried him as he was. The tiring mental merry-go-round of whether I should have taken the Cessna troubled me no more.

I yawned. Not good. Of all things I couldn't afford to go to sleep. I shouldn't have taken those pills, I thought: there was nothing like the odd spot of agony for keeping you awake. I rubbed my hand over my face and it felt as if it belonged to someone else.

I murdered Billy, I thought.

I could have shot him in the leg and left him to Yardman, and I'd chosen to kill him myself. Choice and those cold-blooded seconds of revenge . . . they made it murder. An interesting technical point, where self-defence went over the edge into something else. Well . . . no one would ever find out; and my conscience didn't stir.

I yawned again more deeply, and thought about eating one of Patrick's bananas. A depleted bunch of them lay on the edge by the windscreen, with four blackening stalks showing where he had fended off starvation on the morning trip. But I imagined the sweet pappiness of them in my mouth, and left them alone. I wasn't hungry enough. The last thing I'd eaten had been the lasagne with Gabriella.

Gabriella . . .

After a while I got up and went through the plane to look at Patrick. He lay relaxed and unmoving, but his eyes were open again. I knelt beside him and felt his pulse. Unchanged.

'Patrick,' I said. 'Can you hear?'

There was no response of any sort.

I stood up slowly and looked at Rous-Wheeler sitting on the bale of hay. He seemed to have shrunk slightly as if the gas had leaked out, and there was a defeated sag to his whole body which showed that he realised his future was unlikely to be rosy. I left him without speaking and went back to the cockpit.

Four o'clock. France had never seemed so large. I checked the fuel gauges for the hundredth time and saw that the needles on the auxiliary tanks were knocking uncomfortably near zero. The plane's four engines used a hundred and fifty gallons an hour at normal speed and even with the power reduced they seemed to be drinking the stuff. Fuel didn't flow automatically from the main tanks when the auxiliaries were empty: one had to switch over by hand. And I simply couldn't afford to use every drop in the auxiliaries, because the engines would stop without warning the second the juice dried up. My fingers hovered on the switch until I hadn't the nerve to wait any longer, and then flipped it over to the mains.

Time passed, and the sleeping country slipped by underneath. When I got to the coast, I thought wearily, I was going to have the same old problem. I wouldn't know within two hundred miles where I was, and the sky was ruthless to the lost. One couldn't stop to ask the way. One couldn't stop at all. A hundred and fifty an hour might be slow in terms of jetliners, but it was much too fast in the wrong direction.

In Patrick's briefcase there would be not only a thick book of radio charts but also some topographical ground maps: they weren't needed for ordinary aerial navigation, but they had to be carried in case of radio failure. The briefcase was almost certainly somewhere under or behind the four packing cases in the luggage bay. I went to have a look, but I already knew. The heavy cases were jammed in tight, and even if there had been room to pull them all out into the small area behind the cockpit I hadn't enough strength to do it.

At about half past four I went back for another check on Patrick, and found things very different. He had thrown off the blanket covering him and was plucking with lax uncoordinated hands at the bandage on his head. His eyes were open but unfocused still, and his breath came out in short regular groans.

'He's dying,' Rous-Wheeler shouted unhelpfully.

Far from dying, he was up close to the threshold of consciousness, and his head was letting him know it. Without answering Rous-Wheeler I went back along the alley and fetched the morphine from the first aid kit.

There were six glass ampoules in a flat box, each with its own built-in hypodermic needle enclosed in a glass cap. I read the instruction leaflet carefully and Rous-Wheeler shouted his unasked opinion that I had no right to give an injection, I wasn't a doctor, I should leave it for someone who knew how.

'Do you?' I said.

'Er, no.'

'Then shut up.'

He couldn't. 'Ask the pilot, then.'

I glanced at him. 'I'm the pilot.'

That did shut him up. His jaw dropped to allow a clear view of his tonsils and he didn't say another word.

While I was rolling up his sleeve Patrick stopped groaning. I looked quickly at his face and his eyes moved slowly round to meet mine.

'Henry,' he said. His voice didn't reach me, but the lip movement was clear.

I bent down and said, 'Yes, Patrick. You're O.K. Just relax.'

His mouth moved. I put my ear to his lips, and he said 'My bloody head hurts.'

I nodded, smiling. 'Not for long.'

He watched me snap the glass to uncover the needle and didn't stir when I pushed it into his arm, though I'd never been on the delivering end of an injection before and I must have been clumsy. When I'd finished he was talking again. I put my head down to hear.

'Where . . . are . . . we?'

'On your way to a doctor. Go to sleep.'

He lay looking vaguely at the roof for a few minutes and then gradually shut his eyes. His pulse was stronger and not so slow. I put the blanket over him again and tucked it under his legs and arms and with barely a glance for Rous-Wheeler went back to the cockpit.

A quarter to five. Time to go down. I checked all the gauges, found I was still carrying the box of ampoules, and put it up on the ledge beside the bananas and the cup of water. I switched out the cockpit lights so that I could see better outside, leaving the round dial faces illuminated only by rims of red, and finally unlocked the automatic pilot.

It was when I'd put the nose down and felt again the great weight of the plane that I really doubted that I could ever land it, even if I found an airfield. I wasn't a mile off exhaustion and my muscles were packing up, and not far beyond this point I knew the brain started missing on a cylinder or two, and haze took the place of thought. If I couldn't think in crystalline terms and at reflex speed I was going to make an irretrievable mistake, and for Patrick's sake, quite apart from my own, I couldn't afford it.

Four thousand feet. I levelled out and flew on, looking down through the moonlit blackness, searching for the sea. Tiredness was insidious and crept up like a tide, I thought, until it drowned you. I shouldn't have taken that codeine, it was probably making me sleepy . . . though I'd had some at other times after racing injuries, and never noticed it. But that was on the ground, and nothing to do but recover.

There. There was the sea. A charcoal change from black, the moonlight just reflecting enough to make it certain. I flew out a little way, banked the plane to the right and began to follow the shore. Compass heading, east-south-east. This seemed extra-ordinary, but it certainly had to be the north-east coast of France somewhere, and I wasn't going to lose myself again. There were lighthouses, flashing their signals. No charts to interpret them. The biggest port along that coast, I thought, was Le Havre. I couldn't miss that. There would be a lot of lights even at five in the morning. If I turned roughly north from there I couldn't help but reach England. Roughly was just the trouble. The map in my head couldn't be trusted. Roughly north could find me barging straight into the London Control Zone, which would be even worse than Paris.

It wouldn't be light until six at the earliest. Sunrise had been about a quarter to seven, the day before.

The lights of Le Havre were ahead and then below me before I'd decided a thing. Too slow, I thought numbly, I was already too slow. I'd never get down.

The coast swung northwards, and I followed. Five twenty a.m. The fuel gauges looked reasonable with dawn not far ahead. But I'd got to decide where I was going. I'd got to.

If I simply went on for a bit I'd reach Calais. It still wouldn't be light. Somewhere over in Kent were Lympne, Lydd and Manston airports. Somewhere. My mind felt paralysed.

I went on and on along the French coast like an automaton until at last I knew I'd gone too far. I hadn't watched the compass heading closely enough and it had crept round from north to nearly east. That light I'd passed a while back, I thought vaguely, the light flashing at five second intervals, that must have been Gris Nez. I'd gone past Calais. I was nearly round to Belgium. I'd simply got to decide . . .

The sky was definitely lighter. With surprise I realised that for several minutes the coastline had been easier to see, the water beneath lightening to a flat dark grey. Soon I could look for an airport: but not in Belgium. The explanations would be too complicated. Back to Kent, perhaps . . .

In a way, the solution when it came was simple. I would go to the place I knew best. To Fenland. In daylight I could find my way unerringly there from any direction, which meant no anxious circling around, and familiarity would cancel out a good deal of the tiredness. The flying club used grass runways which were nothing like long enough for a D.C.4, but its buildings had once been part of an old Air Force base, and the concrete runways the bombers had used were still there. Grass grew through the cracks in them and they weren't maintained, but they were marked at the ends with a white cross over a white bar, air traffic signal for a safe enough landing in an emergency.

My mental fog lifted. I banked left and set off North Seawards, and only after five decisive minutes remembered the fuel.

The burns were hurting again and my spirits fell to zero. Would I never get it right? I was an amateur, I thought despairingly. Still an amateur. The jockey business all over again. I had never achieved anything worthwhile and I certainly hadn't built the solid life I wanted. Simon had been quite right, I couldn't have gone on carting racehorses all my life; and now that Yardman Transport no longer existed I wouldn't look for the same job again.

It was a measure of my exhausted state that having once decided to go to Fenland I hadn't the will to plunge back into uncertainty. The fuel margin was far too small for it to be prudent to go so far. Prudence in the air was what kept one alive. If I went to Fenland I'd be landing on a thimbleful, and if the engines stopped five miles away it would be too late to wish I hadn't.

Streaks of faint red crept into the sky and the sea turned to grey pearl. The sky wasn't so clear any more: there were layers of hazy cloud on the horizon, shading from dark grey-blue to a wisp of silver. The moment before dawn had always seemed to me as restoring as sleep, but that time when I really needed it, it had no effect. My eyes felt gritty and my limbs trembled under every strain. And the codeine had worn off.

The coast of East Anglia lay like a great grey blur ahead on my left. I would follow it round, I thought, and go in over the Wash . . .

A swift dark shape flashed across in front of the D.C.4 and my heart jumped at least two beats. A fighter, I thought incredulously. It had been a jet fighter. Another came over the top of me ridiculously close and screamed away ahead leaving me bumping horribly in the turbulence he left in his wake. They both turned a long way ahead and roared back towards me, flying level together with their wing tips, almost touching. Expert formation pilots: and unfriendly. They closed at something like the speed of sound and swept over the D.C.4 with less than a hundred feet between. To them I must have seemed to be standing still. To me, the trail they left me was very nearly the clincher.

Yardman couldn't have found me, I thought desperately. Not after the wavering roundabout route I'd taken. They couldn't have followed me and wouldn't have guessed I'd go up the North Sea . . . it couldn't be Yardman's doing. So who?

I looked out at East Anglia away on my left, and didn't know whether to laugh or die of fear. Americans. East Anglia was stiff with American air bases. They would have picked me up on their radar, an unidentified plane flying in at dawn and not answering to radio. Superb watchdogs, they would send someone to investigate . . . and they'd found a plane without registration numbers of markings of any sort. A plane like that couldn't be up to any good . . . had to be hostile. One could almost hear them think it.

They wouldn't start shooting, not without making sure . . . not yet. If I just went straight on and could deal with the buffeting, what would they do? I wouldn't let them force me down . . . I had only to plod straight on . . . They swept past on each side and threw the D.C.4 about like a cockleshell.

I couldn't do it, I thought, not this on top of everything else. My hands were slipping on the wheel with sweat. If the fighters went on much longer the sturdy old plane would shake to bits. They came past twice more and proved me wrong. They also reduced me to a dripping wreck. But after that they vanished somewhere above me, and when I looked up I saw them still circling overhead like angry bees. They were welcome to accompany me home, I thought weakly, if that was only where they'd stay.

I could see the lightship off Cromer still flashing its group of four every fifteen seconds. The first real sign of home. Only sixty miles to go. Fifteen minutes to the lightship in the Wash, and the sun rose as I went over it. I turned the plane on to the last leg to Fenland, and up above the escorts came with me.

The fuel gauges looked horrible. I drove what was left of my mind into doing some vital checks. Pitch fully fine, brakes off, mixture rich, fuel pumps on. There must have been a list somewhere, but heaven knew where. I had no business to be flying the plane at all, I didn't know its drill . . . The Air Ministry could take away my licence altogether and I was liable for a prison sentence as well. Except, I thought suddenly with a flicker of amusement, that Patrick was qualified to fly it, and he might be said to be technically in charge. Resident, anyway.

I throttled back and began to go down. If I managed it, I thought, I would be a professional. The decision was suddenly standing there full-blown like a certainty that had been a long time growing. This time it wasn't too late. I would take Tom Wells' job and make him stick to it when he inevitably found out my name. I would fly his car firm executives around and earn the sort of life I wanted, and if it meant giving up racing . . . I'd do that too.

The airspeed indicator stood at a hundred and thirty knots on the slow descent, and I could see the airfield ahead. The fighters were there already, circling high. The place would be crawling with investigators before my wheels stopped rolling. Questions, when I could do with sleep.

The distant orange wind sock blew out lazily, still from the south west. There wasn't enough fuel for frills like circuits, the gauges registered empty. I'd have to go straight in, and get down first time . . . get down. If I could.

I was close now. The club building developed windows, and there was Tom's bungalow . . .

A wide banking turn to line up with the old concrete runway . . . It looked so narrow, but the bombers had used it. Six hundred feet. My arms were shaking. I pushed down the lever of the undercarriage and the light went green as it locked. Five hundred . . . I put on full flap, maximum drag . . . retrimmed . . . felt the plane get slower and heavier, soft on the controls . . . I could stall and fall out of the sky . . . a shade more power . . . still some fuel left . . . the end of the runway ahead with its white cross coming up to meet me, rushing up . . . two hundred feet . . . I was doing a hundred and twenty . . . I'd never landed a plane with a cockpit so high off the ground . . . allow for that . . . One hundred . . . lower . . . I seemed to be holding the whole plane up . . . I closed the throttles completely and levelled out as the white cross and the bar slid underneath, and waited an agonised few seconds while the air speed fell down and down until there was too little lift to the wings and the whole mass began to sink . . .

The wheels touched and bounced, touched and stayed down, squeaking and screeching on the rough surface. With muscles like jelly, with only tendons, I fought to keep her straight. I couldn't crash now . . . I wouldn't. The big plane rocketted along the bumpy concrete . . . I'd never handled anything so powerful . . . I'd misjudged the speed and landed too fast and she'd never stop . . .

A touch of brake . . . agonising to be gentle with them and fatal if I wasn't . . . They gripped and tugged and the plane stayed straight . . . more brake, heavier . . . it was making an impression . . . she wouldn't flip over on to her back, she had a tricycle undercarriage with a nose wheel . . . I'd have to risk it . . . I pulled the brakes on hard and the plane shuddered with the strain, but the tyres didn't burst and I hadn't dipped and smashed a wing or bent the propellers and there wasn't going to be a scratch on the blessed old bus . . . She slowed to taxi-ing speed with a hundred yards to spare before the runway tapered off into barbed wire and gorse bushes. Anything would have been enough. A hundred yards was a whole future.

Trembling, feeling sick, I wheeled round in a circle and rolled slowly back up the runway to where it ran closest to the airport buildings. There I put the brakes full on and stretched out a hand which no longer seemed part of me, and stopped the engines. The roar died to a whisper, and to nothing. I slowly pulled off the headset and listened to the cracking noises of the hot metal cooling.

It was done. And so was I. I couldn't move from my seat. I felt disembodied. Burnt out. Yet in a sort of exhausted peace I found myself believing that as against all probability I had survived the night, so had Gabriella . . . that away back in Milan she would be breathing safely through her damaged lung. I had to believe it. Nothing else would do.

Through the window I saw Tom Wells come out of his bungalow, staring first up at the circling fighters and then down at the D.C.4. He shrugged his arms into his old sheepskin jacket and began to run towards me over the grass.